Karen Rose was introduced to suspense and horror at the tender age of eight when she accidentally read Poe's *The Pit and The Pendulum* and was afraid to go to sleep for years. She now enjoys writing books that make other people afraid to go to sleep.

Karen lives in Florida with her husband of twenty years and their children. When she's not writing, she enjoys travelling, karate and, though not a popular Florida pastime, skiing.

KAREN ROSE

SILENT SCREAM

headline

This edition is published by arrangement with Grand Central Publishing,
a division of Hachette Book Group, USA, Inc., New York, USA.
All rights reserved.

First published in 2010 by
HEADLINE PUBLISHING GROUP

First published in paperback in 2010 by
HEADLINE PUBLISHING GROUP

1

Cataloguing in Publication Data is available from the British Library

ISBN 978 0 7553 4658 5 (B-format)
ISBN 978 0 7553 7696 4 (A-format)

Typeset in Palatino by Avon DataSet Ltd,
Bidford-on-Avon, Warwickshire

Printed and bound in Great Britain by
Clays Ltd, St Ives plc

Headline's policy is to use papers that are natural, renewable and
recyclable products and made from wood grown in sustainable forests.
The logging and manufacturing processes are expected to conform
to the environmental regulations of the country of origin.

HEADLINE PUBLISHING GROUP
An Hachette UK Company
338 Euston Road
London NW1 3BH

www.headline.co.uk
www.hachette.co.uk

To Martin, my heart.

To Lt. Kate Czaja and firefighters everywhere.
Thank you for your courage and sacrifice.

To Karen Kosztolnyik. Thank you.

Acknowledgements

Lt. Kate Czaja and Fire Station 2, Charlotte County Fire and EMS, for allowing me to visit your firehouse and for answering my firefighter questions. You guys rock.

Katrina Gibson, for her help on firefighting in cold climates.

Ginny Czaja, for putting in a good word for me with her delightful daughter Kate.

Julia Roper, for assistance with Latin phrases. *Gratias tibi ago*.

Beth Miller and Rita Grindle, for their insight into the Jewish faith.

Sonie Lasker, for her help with the fight scenes.

Marc Conterato, for all things medical.

Danny Agan, for answering all my law enforcement protocol questions.

Robin Rue, for everything.

Kay Conterato, Terri Bolyard, and Jean Mason for all your support.

Cheryl Wilson and Betina Krahn for your insight and patience as I plotted this book.

As always, all mistakes are my own.

Prologue

Minneapolis, Minnesota, Monday, September 20, 12:00 A.M.

They'd shown up. He had to admit he was surprised. He didn't think they'd had the cojones, especially the girl. Of all of them, he hadn't thought she'd follow through.

Four college kids, all dressed in black. Four college kids with way too much time. Two of them with way too much of their daddy's money. If all went according to plan, a great deal of their daddy's money would soon belong to him.

It was rule number one of his world – if people didn't want to be blackmailed, they shouldn't do bad things. Rule number two – if they did bad things, they should be smart enough not to get caught. The four college kids weren't very smart.

From the cover of the trees the condo developer had taken such pains to preserve, he watched the four approach, while he filmed every step they took. Their faces were plainly visible in the moonlight, and although he'd bet their daddy's money they believed they were being stealthy, they moved with enough noise to wake the dead.

'Wait.' One of the four stopped. His name was Joel, and of the three young men, he had been the most enthusiastic proponent of their plan. 'Let's think this through.'

Interesting. Conflict always added a little excitement. Unseen, he kept filming.

'No waiting,' the girl said. Her name was Mary, and she was a bitch. 'We agreed. All of us, Joel. This condo has got to go. We have to send a message.'

'She's right.' This from Eric, the so-called brains of the group. As if. 'This is our one chance to make a difference to these wetlands. If we do nothing, this whole lake will be nothing but condos.' He turned to the large brute standing behind him. 'The guard will be doing his outside sweep in two minutes. He'll exit the building from the service door in the back. You know what to do. Come on, people. Let's roll.'

The brute was Albert, pronounced without the *t*. French Canadian, he was at the university on a hockey scholarship. Right wing. Hell of a checker. Albert set off around the building, obediently. His research had revealed that Albert had been quite the juvenile delinquent, back in the day. He was quite certain Albert would know exactly what to do.

The show was about to begin. *Hurry*, he told himself, taking his second camera from his pack. This was his stationary camera and was attached to a small tripod which he stuck into the soft ground, positioning the lens just in time to capture Mary, Eric, and Joel entering a stairwell door on the east side of the condo.

The door had been propped open with a rock, probably by a construction worker who'd wanted to save a little time and effort. The best security system in the world could be neutralized by lazy workers. Apparently the College Four had done their homework and knew exactly which door would be open. Kudos to them.

Leaving his stationary camera running, he moved the

way Albert had gone, arriving just as the guard exited, right on schedule. Five seconds later the guard lay unconscious on the ground. A satisfied Albert slid a small club back into his pocket.

All caught on my tape. Albert's family was dirt poor, so there was no money now, but there was a good chance that Albert would someday have an NHL salary ending in lots of zeroes. *I can wait.* Eric and Joel both had daddies rich enough to fill his bank accounts for now. As for Mary's daddy . . . some paybacks didn't require a dollar sign.

Some paybacks are personal.

Within another minute, Mary emerged from the side entrance and joined Albert. Both stared up at the windows, waiting.

He waited with them, from a safe distance away. He saw the first wisps of smoke rise in the upper floors. Mary threw her fist in the air with a whispered, *'Yes.'*

Minutes later there was lots of smoke, on every floor. But the side door had not opened again. Mary took a step forward, the triumph on her face turned to concern, but Albert stopped her, his beefy hand closing around her arm.

'They're still inside,' she said, yanking at her arm. 'Let me go.'

Albert shook his head. 'Give them another minute.'

And then the door burst open, both Eric and Joel gasping for breath. Mary and Albert ran to the wheezing boys, pulling them away from the building.

'Goddamn idiot,' Eric snarled, jerking in huge breaths. 'You nearly got us killed.'

Joel fell to his knees, spasms of coughing shaking his body. He looked up, his eyes terrified, desperate. 'She'll die.'

Mary and Albert shared shocked looks. 'Who will die?' Albert asked carefully.

Joel scrambled to his feet. 'A girl. She's trapped. We have to get her out.' He started to run. 'Dammit,' he cried when Eric and Albert dragged him back. 'Let me go.'

Mary grabbed Joel's face. 'There's somebody in there?' She flashed a panicked glare at Eric. 'You said nobody would be in there. You said it was safe.'

'Nobody's supposed to be in there,' Eric gritted through clenched teeth. 'Joel didn't see anything. Let's go before somebody sees the smoke and calls 911.'

'She's in there,' Joel insisted, hysterical now. 'I saw her. Look!'

As a group they looked up and he followed suit, pointing his lens upward as a collective gasp rose from the group. In that moment, he saw her, too. A girl, her fists banging on the window that had been designed to provide a view of the lake, not an escape. She was young, a teenager maybe, her mouth opened on a terrified cry they could not hear. Her fists pounded weakly now, her face pressed to the glass. Then her hands flattened against the window as she slid from their sight.

Joel gave a final, desperate yank. 'She's going to die. Don't you care? Nobody was supposed to get hurt. Let me go. I've got to get her out.'

Mary grabbed his hair. 'Stop it. You go back in there and you'll both be dead.'

Joel was sobbing now. 'Then call 911. Please. Dammit, please.'

'Listen to me,' Mary said, her voice low and urgent. 'If we call 911, we all go to prison. Prison, Joel. That's not going to happen. Stop this, right now.'

But Joel wasn't listening. He thrashed, trying to escape

their grip like a man possessed. Behind his head, Eric gave Albert a grim nod. Albert pulled the club from his pocket and a second later Joel collapsed, just as the guard had done.

'Let's go,' Eric said tersely and he and Albert picked Joel up and carried him through the woods to where their car was parked.

Mary gave a final look back, up at the now-empty window. 'Shit,' she hissed, then turned and ran, passing the struggling boys to pull at the chain-link fence they'd cut on their way in. 'Hurry. Shove him through.'

Well. He lowered his camera, watching as the taillights from their car disappeared. That had been a lot more exciting than he'd thought it would be. A simple arson would have been good for years of blackmailing fun. But murder trumped arson and just about anything else. He had several clients who would agree to that.

He quickly packed his two cameras and the tripod. Smoke was billowing into the sky and he heard the pop of glass as windows began to burst. The authorities would soon be here. *And I will be long gone.* Hefting his backpack, he jogged around the building to the lakeside where he'd left his boat tied to the dock.

'You there. Stop.' It was a thin, ragged cry, but he heard it. Spinning around, he found himself face-to-face with the security guard, who staggered forward, dazed. Blood oozed from the open wound on his head. Albert hadn't hit him hard enough. The man held his radio in one bloody hand, a gun in the other. 'Stop or I'll shoot. I will.'

Not today, Pops. Calmly he drew his own gun and fired. The guard's mouth fell open in shock. He dropped to his knees, then collapsed for the second time that night.

'Shoulda stayed down, Pops,' he muttered. He ran to

5

his boat and dropped his pack inside. With a quiet roar, the motor engaged. Quickly he pulled off the ski mask he wore. If anyone saw him now he could claim he'd seen the smoke and was coming to help, versus trying to flee. But nobody saw him. Nobody ever did.

Which made listening to their whispered secrets so much easier. He patted the cameras in his pack. Which made taking their money so much easier still. *I love my job.*

Oh my God oh my God oh my God. From behind the tree where he'd hidden, Austin Dent watched the small boat speed away, his hands pressed to his mouth. The guard was dead. That man had shot him. *Dead.*

They'll say I did it. Run. I have to run. He took a few unsteady steps backward, lifting his eyes to the burning building once again.

Tracey. She'd been behind him as they'd run from the building. But when he got out, she wasn't behind him anymore. And when he'd turned back . . . All he could see was smoke. A sob of anguish rose up in his chest. *Tracey.*

In the distance he could see the lights flashing. They were coming. The cops were coming. *They'll take me away. Put me in a cage. No. Not again. I can't do that again.* He stumbled back a few more steps, then turned and started to run.

Chapter One

'Higher, Zell,' David Hunter said into his radio, his voice muffled by the mask covering his face. He turned his shoulder into the wind that blew the acrid smoke into the night sky. Suspended four stories up, the bucket in which he stood held firm. The belt anchored him to the apparatus, but his legs still clenched as he held his position.

'Going up.' Jeff Zoellner, his partner, operated the lift from the base of the ladder.

David adjusted the angle of the nozzle mounted on the bucket as he rose, aiming at the flames that had consumed the lower two floors of the structure before they'd arrived. None of them had gone in. Too dangerous. Their only hope was to control this fire so that it didn't spread to the trees surrounding what had been a six-story luxury condo.

Thank God this place isn't finished. In a few weeks there would have been people inside. *There may be one.* The guard was missing. If he'd been on one of the lower floors, he was dead. If he'd made it a little higher, there was still a chance of saving him.

Arson. David's jaw clenched as the platform rose. Had to be. He'd seen it before, up close and way too personally.

The wind shifted again and he flinched when the flames lurched his way. For a split second he lost his footing. *Focus, boy. Stay alive.*

'David?' Jeff's voice was urgent amid the crackling. 'You okay?'

'Yeah.' The platform rose a few more feet, lifting him alongside a large picture window. Every condo on the upper floors had them. He saw no flames, but smoke billowed from the smaller windows which had already burst from the heat.

But all the picture windows were intact. Made of impact-resistant glass, they didn't burst. They also didn't open. They were for the view of the lake. Not for escape.

And then he saw them. His heart began to race faster.

'Stop.' He leaned over the edge of the bucket in which he stood, so he could get closer to the window. It couldn't be. *Nobody's supposed to be inside.* But it was.

'What is it?' The platform lurched as Jeff hit the brakes.

Handprints. The faint outline of small handprints that somehow . . . shimmered in the light from his spotlight. *What the hell?* 'Handprints.' And streaks, made from fingers clawing at the window, trying to escape. 'Somebody's in there. We have to go in.'

'Hunter?' Captain Tyson Casey's voice cut through the static. 'Do you see a body?'

Using the controls mounted in the bucket, David edged closer until the platform bumped the wall. Straining to see through the smoke, his racing heart sank. 'I see arms.' Thin, bare arms and a slim back. Long blond hair. Not the missing guard, a man in his fifties. 'It's a woman. Appears unconscious. Window is impact-resistant.'

'Hold your position,' Casey told him. 'Sheridan, cut the nozzle. Zell's on his way up with the saw.'

David felt the pressure in the line lessen as firefighter Gabe Sheridan closed off the valve from the ground. He looked down to see Jeff steadily climbing the ladder. *Hurry*, he wanted to hiss, but knew Jeff was doing it right. Doing it safe. For a moment he considered taking his own ax to the window, but knew the power saw would do the job on the impact-resistant glass a lot faster than he could, so he conserved his energy.

He glanced back through the window at the woman inside. She hadn't moved.

She was probably dead. *Don't be dead.* He peered through the glass, wondering if anyone else was in the room. Wondering if she could have set the fire.

Jeff climbed into the bucket, power saw in hand. David pointed to the far edge of the glass, away from the victim and her handprints, blocking out the mental picture of how terrified she must have been as she pounded and clawed, trying to escape. She might have set this fire. They needed to preserve her prints on the glass for the cops.

His air can was almost empty so he switched it while Jeff forced the saw through the nearly impenetrable glass until the hole was big enough for David to push through.

Jeff grabbed his shoulder. 'She could have done this,' he shouted. 'Be careful.'

'I will,' he shouted back. He climbed through, landing as close to the wall as possible in case the floor was weak. He crouched low and searched the room for anyone else.

But there was no one. *Go. Get her out and go.* She was light, her weight barely registering when he hefted her over his shoulder. He handed her to Jeff, then climbed back through the window and radioed Gabe Sheridan to take them down.

The platform backed away from the building, away

from the flames that were still licking at the second floor. The paramedic was waiting on the ground to take the victim.

David pulled off his mask the moment his feet hit the dirt, Jeff doing the same. For a moment David closed his eyes, letting the air cool his face. The night air that would have been otherwise brisk was still hot all around them, but compared to wearing that damn mask it was like stepping into A/C. Medic Scotty Schooner looked up, grim.

David knew. 'She's dead?'

Scotty nodded. 'Yeah.'

Jeff's hand clasped his shoulder. 'Sorry, buddy.'

'Me too.' David remembered the handprints on the window. 'Check her hands.'

Scotty knelt next to the gurney holding the body of a girl David could now see was no more than a teenager wearing ratty jeans and a thin T-shirt. *What a waste*.

Scotty was frowning at the girl's hands. 'They're covered in some kind of gel.'

David's captain and two uniformed cops joined them, the three of them bending over the gurney to see her hands.

'What is this shit on her hands?' one of the cops asked.

'I don't know, but whatever it is, it reflects light. I saw her handprints on the window,' David told him. 'My light hit the glass and the prints shone. Fire investigator's going to want to sample it. If she set this fire, she got stuck up there and panicked. There were lots of fist-sized prints, like she pounded, trying to get out.'

'If she didn't do this fire, it's murder,' the other cop said. 'I'll make the call.'

'Tell them it's a double,' a female voice said behind

them. Carrie Jackson stood behind them. Her engine team had been spraying the west side of the structure, next to the lake. 'I was laying line and nearly tripped over the guard. He was shot in the chest.'

Scotty stood up. 'I'll go check him out.'

Carrie shrugged. 'Go ahead. But he's definitely dead. Has been for a while.'

'I believe you,' Scotty said. 'But it's regs. Show me where he is.' Together, Scotty and Carrie set off around the building with the first cop.

The second cop straightened with a sigh. 'I'll get Homicide, the ME, and CSU out here. They'll want to talk to all of you. Especially Hunter, since he brought her out.'

Homicide. David's throat closed as the word left the cop's mouth and for a moment another thought scrambled to the top of his mind. There were lots of detectives in Homicide. Odds were it wouldn't be her. And if it was? *I'll cross that bridge when I get there.* He cleared his throat harshly and nodded. 'Of course. Whatever they need.'

'As soon as we're done,' Captain Casey added. 'We've got to get the second floor under control. Hunter, you and Zell go back in. Search the upper floors. Find out if anyone else was where they shouldn't have been, and make sure we got no fire in the walls.'

'Will do,' Jeff said.

David pushed homicide detectives from his mind and took a last look at the girl on the gurney. What the hell was she doing in there? *Why wasn't someone taking care of you?* But he knew all too well that life wasn't nearly that idyllic. 'I'll check where I found her, see if I can find some ID. She's just a kid. She's got to belong to somebody.'

'Don't touch anything,' the cop said and David fought

the urge to roll his eyes. Cops treated them like damn kindergartners sometimes. 'Got it?'

'Don't worry. I got it.'

Monday, September 20, 1:15 A.M.

Homicide detective Olivia Sutherland flashed her badge at the uniform guarding the condo's construction entrance and drove through the gate, past the news vans and cameramen, acutely aware of all the flashing bulbs at her back. By the questions the press were shouting, they'd already correctly concluded it was arson.

Her churning gut tightened further. Just by being here she'd stirred up their recent collective memory. Amid their shouted arson questions were targeted references to her last big case. It was inevitable, she knew. Didn't mean she had to like it.

'How've you been, Detective?' A reporter she knew and at one time hadn't despised ran alongside her car until the uniform stopped him cold. 'Are you over the body pit yet?' the reporter shouted at her back. 'Still seeing the department shrink?'

Olivia gritted her teeth. She'd been to the shrink three department-mandated times and this guy made it sound like she had a standing appointment with a couch.

With a cold glare Olivia raised her window, not slowing down until she reached the bank of parked official vehicles and rolled to a stop next to her partner's Ford. A piece of her settled. Kane was here. *He'll know what to do.*

The thought startled her. 'And so do I,' she said aloud. Firmly. 'Get a grip.' But she was afraid she couldn't. Because her breathing was changing, hitching up in her lungs and her heart was racing. Because the three department-mandated visits to the shrink hadn't helped. She still wasn't over the body pit, the mass burial pit they'd discovered in the basement of a serial killer seven months before.

In four years on the homicide squad she'd seen a lot of bodies, but nothing could compare to the serial killer they'd chased last February. Dubbed the 'Red Dress Killer' by the press for the way he'd dressed his final victims, he'd been quietly murdering for thirty years and burying his victims in a lime pit in his basement. It wasn't until he'd stepped up his pace that he'd made mistakes and they'd caught him, discovering his grisly secret.

And it had fallen to Olivia and her partner, Kane, to process the dead. There had been blocks of days when she hadn't slept, hadn't eaten, hadn't done anything but process the dead, inform their families, and return to the pit for more. Lime was not kind to human flesh. She didn't need nightmares. The reality was plenty bad enough.

The press could call him what they wished. In her mind he was 'Pit-Guy,' because it was the pit that ruled her dreams – dark, bottomless, and filled with the dead.

She kneaded her steering wheel, taking deep breaths, trying to will the panic away. Because seven months and dozens of bodies later, she froze every time she knew a new victim waited. *A wee bit of a problem for a homicide detective*, she thought bitterly.

'Get out of the car,' she muttered. 'Do your job.' Clenching her jaw, she pushed her door open and forced her feet to move, her lungs to take one more breath. Then forced her face to look like she didn't harbor a thought that didn't have to do with this scene. This night. These two victims. A middle-aged guard and a teenaged girl.

Think about them. Think about justice for them. Do your damn job.

She drew another breath, grimacing at the stench of smoke. It had been a bad fire. Two companies had responded to the scene – two pumpers, an aerial tower truck, and the two rescue squads they wouldn't be needing after all.

Only the morgue rig would be transporting tonight.

As her feet moved, she found herself searching the fire trucks for station numbers, another habit she'd picked up in the last seven months, one she found nearly as distasteful as her new fear of dead bodies. That she even knew which truck was his was completely humiliating. Like she should care if he was here or not. But of course she did. *How pathetic am I? Pretty damn.*

She winced when she saw the L21 painted on the side of the tower truck with its aerial platform. He was here. Or his firehouse was, at least. *Don't let him be on duty tonight. Just find Kane. Do your job.*

She easily found Kane in the crowd. Her partner was a big man, even compared to the firefighters and cops, standing head and shoulders above everyone else. He was also the only one in the crowd wearing a black fedora. It was his fire fedora, she knew, the one he always wore when he knew he'd be going to an arson. It smelled like stale smoke, and his wife Jennie made him keep it in their garage.

All of his other fedoras were kept with care on Styrofoam heads in their guest room. Every man in the homicide division wore fedoras on the job, a nice tradition someone had started long before her time. It was a symbol, a connection to detectives past, and now it was part of local lore. Homicide was known around town as the 'Hat Squad.'

New detectives, on solving their first homicide, were presented with their first fedora by the squad, their peers. Kane had presented Olivia's to her, but she'd felt a little silly wearing it. Her hat sat on her desk back at the office, adorning the head of a Grecian goddess bust she'd found at a yard sale.

But Kane, he liked his hats. He must have had a dozen. Kane liked to look good.

At the moment, Kane looked perplexed. Olivia made her way up the hill to where he stood over a gurney, a uniformed cop at his side. The ME crouched next to the body, bagging the victim's hands, and Olivia's heart started to pound, her stomach lurching dangerously. *Not again. Not again.*

Look at her, she told herself harshly. *She'll be . . . whole.* Olivia drew a steadying breath, forced her eyes down, then let the breath out as relief washed over her. The victim was indeed intact. Flesh covered her bones. All of her bones.

The worst was over. *Now I can do my job.* The girl looked about sixteen. Her waxen face and long blond hair were streaked with soot and grime, as was the faded, thin T-shirt she wore. Her jeans were tattered, by design versus genuine wear. Her feet were bare, her soles burned badly. Her toenails were painted bright orange.

Fighting the shakes that always seemed to follow the relief, Olivia waited until she could trust her voice not to tremble. 'What do we have?'

'Caucasian female,' the uniform said. 'No ID. Was found on the fourth floor. She was already dead when the firefighter got to her.'

'Cause?' she asked.

Isaac Londo, the ME tech, looked up from bagging the

victim's hands. 'Probably smoke inhalation. I didn't see any recent injuries. She's got older ones, though.'

'Where and what?' Kane asked.

'Finger appears to be fractured, and there's a twist burn on the right forearm.'

Olivia's eyes narrowed. The last vestiges of her panic were receding, replaced by cold fury. *Runaway*, her instincts told her. She'd made working with runaways a personal mission over the last few years, since meeting her two half sisters. Mia was a decorated cop, but Kelsey was a convict, having been a runaway first. The signs were crystal clear. 'Someone put their hands on her.'

'That's my guess.' Londo sat back on his heels. 'Your other guy? Different story. The guard took a blow to the head with a blunt instrument, then a slug to the chest.'

'Where is he?' Olivia asked.

'On the other side of the building, by the lake. Dale and Mick are over there now.'

Dale was Londo's partner and Micki Ridgewell was the CSU leader. 'And that guy?' She pointed to a fortyish man in a jogging suit who paced behind the crime scene tape looking very worried.

'Sammy Sothberg,' the uniform said. 'He's the construction manager. Sothberg said the guard's name was Henry Weems, age fifty-seven. He's local.'

'You talk to him yet?' she asked Kane.

'Yeah,' Kane said. 'Briefly. He's shaken. Has an alibi. We'll have to check it out. He gave us Henry Weems's personnel info. We'll need to inform Mrs Weems.'

And what fun that always is. Olivia looked way up and saw a large hole with jagged edges in one of the picture windows on the fourth floor. 'She came from up there?'

'Yeah.' This answer came from Micah Barlow, the police

department's arson investigator, who'd walked up to join them. Immediately Olivia's hackles rose and she had to choke back what would have been a hiss.

'Hell,' Kane muttered, loud enough for Barlow to hear. 'Not him.'

'Kane,' Olivia rebuked under her breath and was rewarded by Kane's long-suffering sigh. She and Micah Barlow had gone through the academy together. They'd been friends once. Now, not so much. Because Barlow was a meddling, arrogant bastard.

Barlow looked from Olivia to Kane, then shook his head with exaggerated patience. 'Let's just get this done, okay? The firefighters saw her handprints on the glass. It's impact-resistant, so they had to cut their way in. The guy that brought her out made sure they cut the far side of the window. He wanted to leave her prints intact for you.'

'Forward-thinking of him,' Olivia said mildly. 'We'll want to talk to him.'

'He's still inside. I'll bring him to you when he comes out.'

'Fine,' Olivia said, shrugging off the annoyance she felt every time she was subjected to Barlow's presence. 'How did the arsonist set the fire?'

'From what we can see, they opened several cans of carpet-padding adhesive, spread them on the first and second floors. Sprinklers were rendered inoperable. Somebody cut the chain on the OS and Y and closed the valve.'

The OS&Y was the outside screw and yoke valve on the line that brought city water to the sprinklers, Olivia knew. 'Are any bolt cutters missing from the toolshed?'

'Don't seem to be. We'll get a full inventory, but it looks like they brought their own.'

'They came prepared then. Incendiary devices?' Kane asked.

'Nothing yet, but we haven't really been able to start looking. I don't think they used a simple match. After dumping an entire can of adhesive, the fumes would have already been hanging in the air. If they'd dropped a match, they wouldn't have made it to the door. That stuff is incredibly flammable.'

'Had the carpet been laid?' Olivia asked.

'No, the construction manager said that was going to be done tomorrow. Well, today, now. The carpet, padding, and cans of adhesive had been staged on the first three floors. Floors four through six have mostly hardwood floors and were finished.'

'Somebody knew those materials were there,' Kane mused. 'Surveillance tapes?'

Barlow frowned. 'Cameras were rendered inoperable five minutes before midnight. The guard would have come outside on his normal beat at five after twelve.'

'Inside job,' Olivia said. 'Or at least inside information.'

Barlow nodded. 'We're getting the personnel list.'

'Where's the control room?' Kane asked.

Barlow pointed to the closer of two construction trailers. 'Up until last month, they had a man in the trailer, monitoring the camera feeds. Budget overruns cut staff. They were down to one guard per shift. The trailer was always the night guy's first stop.'

'You're sending the used adhesive cans to the lab for prints?' Olivia asked.

'Already gave them to CSU,' Barlow answered. 'The manager seems pretty ripped up. Weems was his friend, and he was working two jobs to send his kid to college.'

Olivia sighed. 'We'll check his financials anyway.

Somebody profits from the insurance. Maybe nobody was supposed to get hurt.' She looked down at the gurney, at the girl's lifeless body. 'I guess something went wrong.'

'Check out her hands, Liv,' Kane said. 'Some kind of gel.'

ME tech Londo held up the victim's left hand and Olivia could see that whatever covered the girl's palms had already smeared the plastic bag. 'Accelerant?' she asked.

'No,' Barlow said. 'We ran a sniffer over her. The gel didn't register. Nothing on her clothes either, so if she was involved in spreading the carpet-pad adhesive, she was careful enough not to splash any on herself.'

The sniffer measured the hydrocarbons in accelerants, so Barlow was most likely right. 'Did the firefighters find anything with her?'

'Nothing yet. They just finished knocking the fire down a half hour ago. They're up there now, checking for any other vics. We'll give you and CSU the go-ahead as soon as we know it's safe.' And he would. Obnoxious as he was on a personal level, Micah Barlow did his job. *As do we. So do yours. Look at her, Liv. Really look.*

'Thanks,' she said to Barlow, then crouched next to the gurney, studying the hand Londo had bagged. The polish was the same bright orange as the girl had used on her toenails. 'You done with her, Londo?' When he nodded, she hesitated only a moment before taking the victim's hand and lifting it to the light. 'Look at the decals on her nails. She's not from around here.'

'G-A-T-O-R,' Kane read, then checked the right hand. 'S-R-U-L-E. Gators Rule.'

'It's an unfortunate truth,' Londo muttered. 'I lost a bundle on last week's game.'

'University of Florida Gators,' Olivia mused. 'She

doesn't look old enough to be in college. Maybe she lived in Florida.'

'Maybe she was just a fan,' Kane cautioned and Olivia shrugged.

'Gotta start someplace. We'll run her prints. If she's got a record, hopefully it's not sealed. If she's missing, somebody may have filed an Amber Alert or reported her to the Center for Missing and Exploited Children.'

'If she ran away, chances are good they haven't reported her missing,' Kane said.

'I know. But her jeans are pretty new, and they're not cheap. She hasn't been on the run long. We'll get her photo out there and maybe we'll get lucky.' Olivia placed the girl's hand carefully at her side, then rose and looked down at the girl's face, pity stirring. *So young.* 'Do we have any idea what she was doing up there?'

Barlow shook his head. 'So far we haven't found any evidence that there was anyone with her. As soon as the firefighters come out, I'll send them over to you.'

'If you're done, I'll take her to the morgue,' Londo said, and Kane nodded.

'Liv, let's check out the guard.' He waited until they'd broken away from the group before murmuring, 'You okay, kid? You looked a little green getting out of your car.'

Olivia's cheeks heated. 'Yes,' she said curtly, embarrassed she'd let it show, even in front of Kane. 'Let's just get this done.' Except it was never done. There would always be another kid in the wrong place at the wrong time. Another kid with bruises. Another runaway. Another guy with a bullet whose wife they had to inform. It stuck in her throat, choking her. 'Come on. We've got one more body to process tonight.'

Monday, September 20, 1:20 A.M.

'Anything?' Jeff asked. They'd strapped their masks on and changed air tanks. The fumes generated by building materials were often toxic, and David knew too many veteran firefighters with lung damage. He hated the mask, but he liked his lungs.

'No.' David swept the thermal camera over the central wall. Behind it was the ventilating shaft, a prime spot for hidden fire. But there was nothing. They'd come up through the stairwell, searching the top three floors. They were now back on the fourth, where he'd found the girl. So far, no fire and no more victims. *Thank you.*

David turned to the window they'd cut through. Now that the smoke had dissipated, he could clearly see the palm prints she'd left behind. He shone his flashlight along the floor, hoping to find a purse, a backpack, something to tell them who she was.

And then he blinked as his light was abruptly reflected back at him. 'Zell, look,' he said, pointing the beam at a ball that glistened as her handprints had. It was about four inches across and lay about two feet from where he'd found her. He'd taken a few steps closer when he felt the wood floor go spongy.

He took a large step back, holding his breath until the floor felt solid again.

'David?' Zell had also frozen in place.

'I'm okay.' His heart raced from the adrenaline surge. Ignoring it, he once again shone his light on the glistening ball. 'Do you see that?'

'Yeah. What is it?'

'Don't know, but it's covered in gel.'

'Like her hands. I say leave it for the cops.'

'Agree.' He turned to the stairwell – then all he felt was air as the floor collapsed. '*Zell.*' On reflex, David spread his arms wide, hooking his elbows on the edges of the floor that remained. His body wedged in the hole, his feet dangling. Below him, he saw only blackness. The third-floor fire had burned through the ceiling. If he let go, he might land on solid floor, but chances were better that he'd crash through the third floor, too.

Jeff dropped to his stomach, the handle of his ax outstretched. 'On three.'

David grabbed the ax handle with his left hand, keeping his right elbow anchored for leverage. On 'three,' he threw his hips up and over and a few seconds later lay on his stomach on solid floor, breathing hard, his eyes squeezed shut. More of the floor had broken away when he'd pushed against it, widening the hole. Most of the condo's living-room floor was now gone. Too close. That had been too damn close.

He rolled to his side, opening his eyes just as the slimy ball began to slide down one of the broken planks of the hardwood floor, down into the hole. Again, sheer reflex had him stretching his arm out over the hole, and the ball plopped into his glove.

'Safe,' he muttered and behind him Jeff laughed, a wheezing sound.

'That ball better be worth it, pal.'

David looked into the palm of his glove, then into the dark hole, trying not to let himself dwell on how close he'd come. 'Shit. Now what do I do with it?'

'Put it back where you found it. Cops'll shit a ring if you take evidence.'

'I can't put it where I found it. Where I found it is nothing but air.'

'Then take it with you. But the cops'll still shit a ring.' Jeff tapped his radio. 'Fourth floor has collapsed. Hunter and I are unhurt. We're coming back down via the stairwell.'

'Acknowledged,' came the crackled reply from their captain.

David pushed to his knees, the ball clutched in his glove. They crawled to the stairwell, not breathing easily until they stood on solid earth. He ripped off his mask with his free hand, sucking in air. His knees were weak, but he'd never let anyone see that.

'Hunter?'

MPD's arson guy had arrived. David considered him a straight shooter. 'Barlow.'

'I hear the floor collapsed. You two okay?'

'Yeah.' He held out his gloved hand, the ball still tucked in his palm. 'I found this near where the girl died.'

Barlow's brows shot up. 'You disturbed the scene?'

'There is no more scene,' David said dryly. 'The floor where I found her is completely gone. The ball was headed for the hole and I grabbed it. Reflex.'

'It was a hell of a save,' Jeff put in. 'Bottom of the ninth, bases loaded, then *pow*. Hunter pulls it out. Then I pulled him out,' he added wryly. 'Now he owes me big-time.'

David rolled his eyes. 'Barlow, you want the damn ball or not?'

Barlow shook his head. 'Come with me. You can give it to Homicide yourself. She's not going to be happy that you disturbed the scene.'

For the second time that night David had the sensation of free-fall. *She*. He only knew of one female homicide detective. He started walking. *Thank you*.

Monday, September 20, 1:25 A.M.

Eric lifted his head from his hands, looking up as Mary came into the room, toweling her hair. She frowned over at his sofa, where Joel lay motionless, eyes closed.

'He's still out cold? Damn, Albert, you hit him too hard.'

Albert grunted from his chair. 'He came to while you were using all the hot water.'

She shot Albert a hostile look. 'Fuck off. My roommates would ask questions if I came home smelling like a goddamn forest fire.' Gently, she sat on the sofa, hip to hip with Joel. 'Come on, baby,' she said quietly. 'You gotta snap out of this.'

Joel's swallow was audible. 'We killed her.'

Mary lifted a shoulder. 'Yes, we did. And we'll have to live with that. But we're not telling anyone. We have to act like everything's normal, or we all go to jail.'

Joel nodded, miserably. 'I see her face. Pressed up against the glass.'

As did Eric. Every time he closed his eyes, all he could see was her mouth, open. Screaming. They hadn't seen her when they were pouring out the glue. She must have been hiding somewhere. Squatting. 'She was in that building illegally.'

Joel's laugh bordered on hysterical. 'You can actually use the word *illegally*? So it's not our fault? Is that what you're saying? Do you honestly believe that shit?'

'That's exactly what I'm saying,' Eric said firmly. They had to face facts, and the fact was, he wasn't going to prison. 'We stand together, Joel.'

'But we killed her,' Joel whispered, his voice breaking. 'We killed her.'

'Be a man, Fischer,' Albert snarled. 'Yeah, we fucking killed her. Get over it.'

Mary's eyes narrowed. 'Leave him alone. He's in shock and in pain. You didn't have to hit him so hard.'

Albert's face was darkly ominous. 'I should have hit him harder. Then I wouldn't have to listen to him whine. *We killed her,*' he mimicked cruelly. 'So goddamn fucking what? We can't change it, so tell your pussy boyfriend just to shut the hell up about it or I'll shut him up myself.'

White-faced with fury, Mary opened her mouth to deliver what would surely have been a diatribe every neighbor on Eric's floor would hear.

'Settle down,' Eric snapped. 'We set out to make a statement. We wanted to send a message to the developers – keep away from our wetlands. We sent that message.'

Joel sat up, gingerly pressing his fingertips to the knot on the back of his head left by Albert's club. 'Don't kid yourself. Nobody's going to hear our message. All anyone will remember is that girl *died*. Because of *us*, she is no longer alive.'

'A regrettable loss,' Mary said, smoothing Joel's hair. 'You said that this is war.'

Joel closed his eyes. 'I know what I said. That was before. We killed a human being, Mary. The cops aren't going to ignore this. They're going to hunt us down.'

'They wouldn't have had to hunt far if we'd let you call 911,' Albert muttered.

'Albert,' Mary hissed. 'Shut. Up.'

Eric felt a childish yearning for a redo button. But there were no redos here. They'd done what they'd done. Now they had to stay under the radar.

'All of you, just be quiet. We need to be calm or we'll all end up in prison.' He turned on the TV and started changing channels. Then flinched when the fire scene filled his fifty-inch screen. 'Let's see what the press is saying. Then we'll figure out what, if anything, we need to do next.'

Chapter Two

Monday, September 20, 1:30 A.M.

'Liv. Wait.'

Olivia had been walking at a near jog around the burned-out building but stilled at the sound of Kane's steady voice behind her. She'd been curt with him when he'd only been trying to help. 'I'm sorry,' she said quietly. 'I shouldn't have bitten your head off.'

'I'm used to it,' he said in the singsong tone that always reminded her of Eeyore and made her smile. He smiled back. 'There we go. I knew your mouth could bend. It doesn't do that so much lately. Look . . . I didn't mean to make it worse.'

Olivia's shoulders sagged. 'I'm doing my job, Kane.'

'I know you are,' he said, his voice soothing without being patronizing. 'The department shrink isn't helping?'

'I don't need any damn shrink.' Her voice sounded childish to her own ears and she sighed. 'Dammit, Kane. I just need some time.'

'Then take some time. But promise me something. If it's not any easier by the new year, tell me. I know a shrink who might be able to help. One I bet you'll like.'

She knew why he'd picked that date. New Year's Eve

was his last official day on the job. Kane was retiring after nearly thirty years on the force. Olivia didn't want to think about it. Didn't want to think about breaking in a new partner. But she knew he worried about her, so she nodded. 'Okay. Now can we get to the dead guard?'

They turned the corner and immediately saw the body of security guard Henry Weems illuminated by the CSU spotlights. He was lying on his stomach, one arm beneath him, the other outstretched. His pistol lay a few inches from his fingertips. The back of his uniform was dark with blood, the exit wound bigger than Kane's fist.

Next to his body was a gurney with an unzipped body bag. Londo's partner, ME tech Dale Eastman, waited patiently as CSU's Micki Ridgewell snapped pictures.

'Hollow-point bullet?' Olivia asked.

'Likely,' Micki said. 'We're still looking for the slug. As soon as we're done with the body, we're going to run a metal detector. But with so much construction crap, it could take a while. We found blood on the ground near the back door, the one that exits lakeside, so that's probably where he was hit on the head. By the amount of blood on the ground, I think he lay there for several minutes, at least. Let's roll him.'

Kane and Dale did so. The front of the guard's uniform was completely blood-soaked, but a small entry wound was visible, right at his heart.

'Shot to kill,' Kane remarked. 'How long has he been dead?'

'A couple of hours, tops,' Dale said. 'Doc'll get you a tighter time window.'

Olivia picked up the guard's gun and sniffed. 'Hasn't been fired, but he was ready. Safety's off. If he was knocked out, maybe he came to and surprised the arsonist?'

'Who was standing between him and the lake when the shot was fired.' Kane pointed to the lake. 'There are two ways to get out of here fast – through the front gate then getaway by car or via the lake by boat. Let's check the fence for cuts, Mick.'

'Already did. We found three. One there by the dock, one off to the side' – she pointed away from the building – 'and one on the same side as the girl was found. We'll test the wire for oxidation to determine when each cut in the fence was made.'

Olivia looked way up. A security camera was mounted on the corner pole of the fence. 'You heard about the cameras?'

'Yeah.' Micki looked very unhappy. 'Frickin' inside job.'

'We're getting the personnel records,' Kane said. 'How hard would it have been to turn off the cameras?'

'Don't know yet. I'll get Sugar to check out their system and let you know.' Sugar was Micki's electronics guru.

'Detectives? You wanted to talk to the firefighter who pulled the girl out?'

Micah Barlow was rounding the building, a firefighter at his side, and any hope she'd held when she'd seen fire truck L21 fizzled away. Her heart squeezed so hard that she sucked in a sharp, involuntary breath. Few men walked like he did. No man looked like that as he did so. No man had the right to look like that.

He was big, the firefighter – at least three inches taller than Barlow who was at least six feet tall himself. The bright CSU spotlights shone on a face grimy and streaked with sweat, but no amount of dirt could change the fact that he was the most beautiful man she'd ever seen. Or could ever hope to see again. *Goddamn him for that alone.*

Of course he'd been on duty tonight. Of course he'd been the firefighter to find the victim, to try to save her, to be smart enough to keep key evidence intact.

Of course he was the one man she hadn't wanted to see, tonight or any other night. Because he'd gone to great lengths to keep from seeing her. *Seven months*. He'd moved to Minneapolis seven months ago, but there hadn't been a single phone call or e-mail. For months she'd wondered why he'd come here. Now she didn't care.

She steeled her spine. Summoning a tone she hoped to hell sounded casually friendly, she stepped forward. 'David Hunter. Long time, no see. How are you?'

For a moment, David's smooth gait seemed to hitch, but when he spoke he sounded only mildly surprised. 'Olivia. Good to see you.'

Barlow's brows lifted and Olivia didn't even need to look at Kane to know his had done the same. 'You know each other?' Barlow asked.

'We have mutual friends,' Olivia said with a calmness that was a complete façade. Her heart was pounding so hard it was all she could hear, just as it had every other time she'd seen him. None of which had obviously meant anything to him. None of which mattered right now. 'Kane, you remember Mr Hunter? He's Eve's friend.'

And Eve was Olivia's friend. It was Eve who'd told her that David had decided to move to the Twin Cities. Eve who'd told her David got a job with the fire department. And Eve who had ceased giving updates because it was obvious Olivia no longer cared.

'Of course I remember,' Kane said, cautiously, Olivia thought. 'How's the arm?'

The arm that had fractured seven months before when Pit-Guy forced David off the road, thinking it was Eve driving the car. He'd been in the hospital, one of the last times Olivia had seen him. David raised his arm, rotating it a few times. 'Good as new. Thanks.'

Enough of this. 'Sergeant Barlow said you found the girl,' she said, more curtly than she'd intended.

David flinched, his throat working as he swallowed hard. 'We were too late. She was already dead.'

And that hurt him, it was easy to see. Against her better judgment, Olivia met his gray eyes and saw the raw misery there, and her pounding heart hurt for him. She saw death every day. Luckily, he did not. 'There wasn't anything you could do, David,' she murmured. 'She wasn't supposed to be in there. Nobody was, right?'

For just a moment, there was a connection. The connection. The same one she'd felt that one night he'd made her forget . . . nearly everything. For a moment he wasn't David Hunter, tall, dark, Greek god who made women everywhere melt into puddles of goo. He was the man who'd had a truly beautiful soul and who, for a few short hours, *showed it to me*. But as she watched, his eyes shuttered, pushing her away once again.

'That's right,' he said quietly. 'But she was in there, for whatever reason. I looked for an ID, a purse, a backpack, but didn't see anything. It's pretty dark, though. You might find something on one of the other floors come daybreak.'

Barlow was looking back and forth between the two of them avidly and to her consternation, Olivia realized she'd been staring up into David's face like a love-struck teenager. But then, every woman stared at David Hunter's face like a love-struck teenager, so nobody would think her any different. *Because I wasn't.*

'When can we go up to check the scene?' she asked, a chill in her voice.

'You can't tonight,' Barlow said. 'Part of the fourth floor collapsed. It's not safe. You'll need to wait until the structure can be reinforced before going up to where they found her. But they did bring something out you'll want to see. David?'

'It was on the floor next to where I found her.' He held out his gloved right hand. On it rested a glass ball, about the size of Olivia's clenched fist. It was covered in something shiny and gelatinous.

Olivia frowned. 'You disturbed the scene?' she asked sharply.

'Hunter was on the floor when it collapsed,' Barlow said quietly and her eyes involuntarily flickered up to David's in alarm. 'That you have this evidence at all is due to his quick thinking.'

'We were fine,' David said. 'The ball was about to slide into the hole in the floor. My adrenaline was pumping and I grabbed it by reflex but then couldn't put it back where I found it. The area doesn't exist anymore.'

She forced her muscles to relax. The thought of him crashing through a fourth-story floor had her own adrenaline pumping. 'Is this the gel we found on the girl's hands?'

'Likely,' Barlow said. 'The lab will confirm it.'

Kane leaned over her shoulder to study the glass globe. 'Why the gel?'

'I guess that's for you to find out,' David said.

Olivia turned to find Micki, startled when she found the CSU leader standing inches behind her. 'Can you bag it, Mick?'

Micki's gaze shifted from the globe to Olivia's face knowingly. 'Absolutely.'

'Take his glove, too, just in case we need to check for

residue. Do you have another glove?' she asked David, this time schooling her glance to remain impersonal.

'I've got extras on the truck. If you're done with me, I've still got work to do.'

If you're done with me . . . No, she didn't think she ever would have been. Not that it mattered one iota. He'd been done with her after one night. *What an idiot I was.*

Olivia made herself look at him, made her smile as impersonal as her glance had been. 'Thank you. We'll be in touch if we have more questions. Kane, we need to inform Mr Weems's widow before she sees it on the news. Anything else we need here?'

Kane shook his head. 'Not until we can get inside. You have our cells, Barlow?'

Barlow nodded. 'I do. I'll call you as soon as it's safe.'

Micki bagged the glass globe and now tugged at the glove on David's hand. 'I'll get this back to you as soon as I can,' she said, dropping the glove in a paper sack.

'Not a problem,' David said and without another word, turned and was around the building and gone from sight when Olivia realized she'd been holding her breath.

Hell. 'Micki, can you run the dead girl's prints? Watch for anything that pops from Florida. She's got Gator nail art. Call us when you get a match on the gel. Thanks.'

'As the man said, not a problem,' Micki responded evenly, but Olivia knew that look in her friend's eyes. She'd expect an explanation.

As if I have one. 'Abbott's going to want us in his office at oh-eight in the morning,' Olivia said, changing the subject. Her captain was big on meetings starting at oh-eight.

'Looking forward to it,' was all Micki said. 'I'll try to run the girl's prints before then. Afterward, we can grab a coffee. Catch up.'

'You bet,' Olivia said flatly, then turned to Micah Barlow who was watching her too closely and she felt a flare of temper. That she'd even considered David Hunter for a nanosecond was partially Barlow's fault, goddamn meddling bastard. 'He'll want you there, too,' she said coolly. 'You know where to find Abbott's office?'

'I've worked with your captain before,' Barlow said. 'I'll be there.'

She jerked a nod, then headed to her car, Kane at her side. He didn't say a word until she'd unlocked her car door.

Leaning against her hood, he folded his arms across his chest. 'And that was . . . ?'

She jerked open her door. 'I have no idea what you're talking about.'

Kane pushed her door closed with the palm of his hand. 'Olivia.'

She sighed. 'One mammoth mistake, okay? One I don't care to repeat or discuss.'

He looked disappointed. Kane did like his gossip. 'Oh, all right,' he grumbled. 'Here's Weems's home address. You want me to lead?'

'No, you did it last time. It's my turn to break the news.' Unlike other detective teams, they never flipped a coin. They split the nasty duties fifty-fifty. It had always been that way, even when she was totally green and he was her mentor. 'I'll meet you there.'

She opened her door when Kane walked away, then stopped, suddenly uneasy. Looking over her shoulder, she saw David standing next to his truck, watching her, and a shudder rippled across her skin. For a moment their eyes locked, then his chin tilted as if issuing a challenge. He pulled a new glove on his hand, then turned back to his work.

Trembling, Olivia got in her car. *I don't need this. Not now.*

He's had seven months. Seven fucking months to say something. Do something. She'd waited, patiently at first. Then the hurt started to rise, higher, deeper with each passing day. Each passing week. Until she'd given up. *I've given him enough time.* It had been two and a half years since the night they'd met at her sister's wedding in Chicago. Since the night they'd . . . *Dammit.* Remembering wasn't supposed to make her want it again. But it did. Which made her pathetic. He's had two and a half years to do something.

Maybe he's waiting for you to make the first move.

And maybe you're the biggest idiot on earth. She knew for whom David waited. *And it sure as hell's not me.* Cursing herself for even entertaining the notion someone like him could be waiting for her, she followed Kane, ignoring the reporters' questions. There would be a press conference soon enough. She was about to inform Mrs Henry Weems that she'd become a widow, that her life had been irrevocably changed.

As she drove, she rehearsed the words that four years in Homicide had not made any easier to say.

David could hear nothing over the low roar of the truck beside him as he pulled a pike pole from its compartment, but he knew when her car pulled away. Turning, he watched her taillights disappear through the construction gate.

She'd been tired tonight. Worried. *And not happy to see me.* Irritation had filled those round blue eyes of hers. But there had been more. Compassion, concern. And then shame. The shame scraped at him as he knew he'd put it there.

35

KAREN ROSE

But most of all, he'd seen the bone-weariness that weighed so heavily on her slender shoulders. He'd been watching her closely enough over the last seven months to know it wasn't getting any better. If anything, it was getting worse.

The call had pulled her from sleep. The mental picture was a distracting one. She'd forgone her usual neat French braid, instead pulling her blond hair into a ponytail so severely tight that he'd gotten a headache just looking at it. When she wasn't working, she let her hair fall loosely around her shoulders and he had a vague recollection of how it felt between his fingers.

He swallowed hard. He had a vague recollection about a lot of things, none of which he had any business thinking about right now.

How many times in the last seven months had he almost knocked on her door? Too many. He'd about given up waiting for her to come to him. And then tonight, here she was. She'd felt it, whatever it was between them. He'd seen it in her eyes. So he'd wait a little bit longer.

How much longer? How much longer before you either fish or cut bait?

'So?' said a voice behind him.

David whipped around and Micah Barlow jumped backward, his eyes focused on the pike pole David clutched in his hand. 'Don't sneak up on me like that, Barlow,' he gritted between clenched teeth, then made himself relax. 'What do you need?'

Micah's gaze flicked from the pole to the gate the uniformed guard had just pulled closed behind Olivia's car, then back to his face. 'She really doesn't like you. Why?'

David felt his face heat. 'That's none of your business.'

Micah frowned. 'Yeah, it kind of is. But we'll deal with that later. For now, I want you to walk me through exactly what happened tonight, from the minute you got here until the minute you walked out of the building with that damn jelly ball in your hand.'

Annoyance spurted and with it the desire to tell Micah to stay the hell away from Olivia Sutherland. *But it's not my business either.* Not yet anyway. If he had his way, that would change, very soon. For now, he'd do his job.

'It wasn't a jelly ball,' he said. 'The ball was solid glass. It was just covered in gel.'

'That's a start. So take me through it, step by step.'

Monday, September 20, 2:00 A.M.

He flipped on the tube and sat back in his easy chair, nursing the beer he allowed himself after snagging a new 'client.' Tonight he'd earned the whole six-pack, but he never allowed himself more than one. Drunk men made stupid mistakes. He should know. The stupid mistakes of drunk men accounted for a good portion of his business.

Remote in hand, he viewed the DVD he'd burned, smiling as smoke filled the screen. Every word the quartet had spoken was discernible. Some parts were louder than others, but the audio was crisp because his equipment was top-of-the-line. Skimping on equipment was bad economy in the long run.

And I plan for the long run. He looked around his small apartment. It was stark, utilitarian. But eventually his bank accounts would be plump enough for him to buy an island villa staffed with discreet servants. He already knew which villa he'd choose. It was currently owned by a wealthy politician with a very nasty proclivity toward underage youths. The politician actually believed he'd be free when he'd finished depositing his blackmail payments into an offshore account in small, monthly installments.

His marks always believed they'd be free. *That I'll be satisfied and go away.* But he never went away. He just quietly raised the price, and his marks always paid.

Because he chose his marks wisely, just as he'd done tonight. These four had parents who'd be willing to sacrifice a great deal to keep their darlings from going to prison. And prison was exactly where they'd go. They'd been very naughty, setting a bad fire. Two people were dead. Of course the guard belonged to him, but he was quite willing to give the College Four the credit. They'd walked away from a screaming teen, left her to die. The cops would have no trouble believing they'd shoot a guard, too.

Eyes on his TV screen, he watched, wincing when the burly Albert smacked the whiny Joel with his club. *Ouch.* He bet Joel had a hell of a headache right now.

He wondered if they'd started to turn on each other yet. They would, eventually, when the reality of what they'd done permeated the shock. There was art in the timing of his initial contact. He wanted to let them stew long enough to be terrified of capture, but not so long that they did anything stupid. Like confess. Especially Joel the Whiny.

Of course if he became too big a liability, Joel could be taken care of.

He rewound back to the point where Eric the Brain gave Albert the Muscle the order to smack Joel upside the head. There was a coolness to Eric, a willingness to do what was necessary that could become quite an asset.

Because I've been thinking. His investments had taken a beating in the stock market collapse. At the rate he was going, he'd hit forty before he rebuilt his portfolio enough to support the lifestyle he'd been planning. He didn't plan to wait anywhere near that long. He wanted to be young enough to enjoy his ill-gotten gains.

For a long time he'd been thinking of hiring on. Expanding. But who to trust?

He'd been in the business long enough to know that a man was only as trustworthy as the length of rope tied around his neck. This was equally true for women. Hell, especially for women. The rope had to be kept short, the knot too strong to slither from. He watched Albert and Eric carry the unconscious Joel away, Mary trailing behind. Arson, murder . . . It made for a damn tight knot and a very short length of rope.

He lifted his beer bottle in a toast. 'To my new employees. May you make me lots of money.' He ejected the DVD from the player and slid it into a paper jacket. Through the beauty of streaming video, Eric the Brain would soon know his dick was in a sling.

He smacked a kiss on the disk. 'All of you,' he murmured, 'are mine.'

Monday, September 20, 2:15 A.M.

Eric opened his living-room window and let the breeze cool his overheated skin. It would be dawn soon. But he doubted the morning light would produce any new options. He stared at the fire he'd lit in his fireplace. The dancing flames sickened him.

Mocked him. *Murderer. Murderer. Murderer.*

Twenty-four hours ago everything had been golden. He'd been poised to do something great. Something that would evoke conversation. For once *he* was going to make a difference, like Joel was always doing. *I was going to change people's lives.*

He laughed bitterly. That he had done. His life, the lives of the others . . . They'd never be the same.

What had she been doing there? He gritted his teeth. *Stop asking.* The answer was the same as it was the first hundred times he'd asked. Wrong place, wrong time.

What the hell was I thinking? I shouldn't have listened to Joel. I shouldn't have cared about his damn wetlands. He's going to talk. He'll ruin everything.

He's going to ruin my life. I never should have let him leave.

But he had. They'd all showered, washing the scent of the fire from their skin as best they could. Then the others had left. *Maintain your normal routine*, he'd told them. *Go home. Act naturally. Go to class today like nothing happened.* So they'd gone and now his apartment was empty, silent save the crackling of the flames.

He'd started the fire in the fireplace to mask the smell they'd brought back from the condo. Now he could say the odor of stale smoke was from his fireplace, should anyone notice or think to ask.

You mean, if we get caught. Which, Eric thought firmly, was unlikely. Nobody had seen them. He'd cut the camera feed himself. Hacking into the construction company's computer-controlled surveillance system had been child's play. Rankin and Sons had automated everything so they could cut back on manpower. Mistake number one.

Mistake two – uploading the security guard's route to their server. And mistake three, not hiring a five-year-old to try to hack in. They'd left the door into their system wide open. It had almost been insulting. *We took every precaution. Nobody saw us.*

Except the girl and she was dead. He could see her face, every time he closed his eyes. Screaming, her hands sliding down the window.

Eric narrowed his eyes. The guard was inept – he should have known the girl was there. *It's not our fault*. She wasn't supposed to be there to start with.

'It's not our fault,' he said out loud, and thought maybe if he said it another million times he might actually start to believe it. *We killed her*. It was the truth. The ugly truth.

But no one knows. Unless Joel tells them. Eric thought about Albert's whispered words as he'd left the apartment. *I should have hit him harder. I still can.*

Eric had told him no, in no uncertain terms. But if Joel didn't pull himself together, then what? His stomach churning, he sank into the chair next to the television.

What a mess. What a goddamned mess. All because of some stupid waterfowl.

'To hell with the birds,' he muttered, turning the television on. The anchorwoman stared into the camera and Eric bet she secretly got a charge from the excitement.

'Firefighters are in cleanup mode at this time. Damage to the condo is estimated to exceed fifty million dollars. But the true loss is in the two victims.'

Eric snapped to attention. *Two? What the hell?*

'Sources tell us that one of the victims was a female who was discovered on the fourth floor.' The screen switched to show the picture window where the girl had stood, screaming. A large jagged hole had been cut on the far end. 'The second victim is a male in his midfifties. Police are withholding his name pending notification of his family. But our source tells us the man was shot to death.'

For a moment Eric was too stunned to do anything but

stare. Shot to death? No. Albert hit him. Just hit him. None of them had guns. What the fuck was this?

He jumped when his cell phone buzzed on the table next to him. He stared at it, waiting. For what? Hell if he knew. But his heart was pounding, hard, slow and his hand moved as if through molasses. He flipped the phone open and his pounding heart stopped as his lungs froze at the text that popped up.

i know what you did.

Eric continued to stare and the phone vibrated again as a new text popped up.

need proof?

There was a link and, dread mounting, Eric clicked it. It was a video. He saw himself and the others staring up at the burning condo. Then the camera panned up to the girl in the window, her mouth open on that silent scream that still filled his mind. Then it was back on them and he was nodding at Albert as they held the struggling Joel. Albert struck Joel and they dragged him away. The video lasted only thirty seconds.

But it was enough. They'd been seen. They were fucked.

Hands shaking, Eric's thumbs somehow hit the right keys. *Who are you?*

your master.

His whole body shook now, violent trembles. *What do you want?*

don't worry. will tell you soon enough. will text address when im ready. be waiting. tell no one. yes or no?

He couldn't think. Couldn't breathe. Could only stare.

A minute later another text popped up. *im losing patience. you think prison will be fun? ur awful cute. dont drop the soap. yes or no?*

Eric took several deep breaths, nausea mounting with each one. There was only one answer. *Yes*, he typed, then closed the phone. He stood, carefully placing the phone back on the table. Then he ran to the bathroom and threw up.

He sat back in his easy chair, the grin nearly splitting his face when Eric's reply popped up. *Yes*. Of course he'd say yes. 'Take that, rich boy. Your ass belongs to me.'

Monday, September 20, 3:30 A.M.

Austin Dent froze, one leg over his windowsill, the beam of a flashlight blinding him. His hand sliced through the air. 'Stop.'

Austin climbed through the window, closing it behind him. He was in no mood for his roommate's stupid questions, but it didn't look like Kenny was going to let it go.

Kenny's finger wagged, side to side. 'Where were you?'

Austin climbed into bed, ignoring him, but Kenny wouldn't leave him alone, sniffing. 'What is that? Smoke? Fire?'

'Shut up.' Austin buried his face in his pillow. He could smell the smoke on his skin. The dorm staff would smell it tomorrow. They would know. Everyone would know.

It didn't matter. Tracey was dead.

Oh God. A sob built in his chest and he fought it back, but it burst out and his shoulders shook. *She's dead. Oh God. I promised I'd take care of her and she's dead.*

The bed shifted as Kenny slid down to the floor, patting

his shoulder. Austin lifted his face and stared his friend in the eye. Kenny looked scared. 'What did you do?'

Austin rolled over so that his hands were free. 'You can't tell anyone.'

'Tell them what?'

'That I wasn't here. That I came in through the window. That I smell like smoke.'

Kenny looked more scared now. 'What the hell did you do?'

Austin shook his head hard. 'You're my friend. You have to help me.'

Kenny stared a minute, then pushed the window open. 'Get rid of the smell.'

'They'll smell it tomorrow.' Panic grabbed Austin's chest. 'What do I do?'

Kenny lifted his mattress and pulled out a flattened pack of cigarettes. 'Is what you did worse than getting caught smoking?'

Austin thought of Tracey, trapped. He thought of the dead guard and the man who'd shot him. Miserably, he nodded and in the darkness saw Kenny flinch.

'Smoke one,' Kenny said. 'Breathe out the window or it'll set off the sprinklers. Tomorrow morning, smoke another. They'll think the smell comes from these. You'll get busted for cigarettes and nobody will know.' Kenny produced the matches he'd hidden. 'Give me a cigarette, I'll light it for you. Your hands are shaking. You'll drop the match and burn the place down.' Kenny's brows crunched. 'It's okay. It'll be okay.'

No, Austin thought numbly, flinching as the flame flared. *It'll never be okay again*.

Chapter Three

Olivia pummeled the bag with a barrage of short jabs that left her knuckles aching, but pain was easier to deal with than the howl she'd kept restrained since walking away from Mrs Henry Weems's heartbreaking sobs. *I'm sorry for your loss, ma'am.*

The grunting bodybuilder next to her paid her no attention as he did his reps, which was why she came to the gym this time of the morning. People who were here at this hour came to work out, not to be seen. There was a certain anonymity in that.

There were days she craved anonymity, especially from herself. Especially after telling another grieving family she was sorry for their loss. She'd done that a lot in the past months, walked away from a lot of sobbing parents, brothers, sisters.

We found your daughter's remains in a bone pit. No, you can't identify her. I'm sorry for your loss. Such inadequate bullshit. And it never ended. *Your husband is dead. He was shot to death by an arsonist. I'm sorry for your loss.*

Frustration surged and Olivia tore into the bag again,

then collapsed against it. 'I'm sorry for your goddamn loss,' she muttered, spent.

'Easy, tiger.'

Olivia shuddered at the calm voice. 'What are you doing here?' she asked wearily. Paige Holden wasn't on duty till eight. Which was precisely why Olivia had come now.

'Making sure you leave some of Jasper for everyone else,' Paige said dryly.

Olivia pushed away from the bag that took the name of Paige's old boyfriend after each breakup. 'He's Jasper now?' Olivia had lost count of all the names Paige's punching bags had borne in the fifteen years they'd been friends. 'What did Jasper do?'

'Left me with the check as he ran off to a client for the very last time.'

Olivia once again marveled at how smart women could be so stupid when it came to men. *Present company totally not excluded.* 'Filet and a hundred-dollar bottle of wine?'

Paige shrugged. 'Close enough. Speaking of dinner, when did you eat, Emo-girl?'

Olivia shot her a dirty look. 'Dinner.'

'Which was?' Paige pressed.

Olivia closed her eyes, digging deep for patience. 'Salad.'

Paige pulled a PowerBar from her pocket. 'You need protein, even if it's not meat.'

Olivia took the bar, knowing it would taste like cardboard. All food tasted like cardboard since the Pit. Meat was especially hard to stomach. Just thinking about it brought the memories back. Flesh falling off the bone. She shook her head to clear it.

'What are you doing here?' Olivia asked again.

'A little bird told me you were here, knocking the stuffing out of Jasper.'

Olivia looked over her shoulder to the man behind the counter who had muscles on his muscles. Caught watching them, Rudy suddenly developed an interest in the sign-in sheet. 'Son of a gun,' Olivia muttered. 'Freaking little weasel.'

'I prefer to think of him as my confidential informant,' Paige said archly, then sniffed. 'You smell like an old fireplace. What happened tonight?'

'Fire. Two dead,' Olivia said briefly, sharing no more than the reporters knew.

But Paige had known her a long time. 'You had to inform the families.'

'Just one. So far anyway.'

Paige winced. 'The other's a John Doe?'

'Jane.' Olivia swallowed hard, remembering the girl's ashen face. 'Just a kid.'

Paige squeezed her arm. 'I'm sorry, honey.'

'Me too.' She cleared her throat. 'I'm not going to have time to work out later, so I stopped by on my way home for just a few minutes. I was going to call you.'

'You'll call me. Famous last words of Jasper.' Paige pointed at the Nautilus equipment. 'You're warmed up already, so let's get started.'

Olivia hesitated. 'That's okay. You don't have to stay.'

'I know. But if I don't, you'll keep avoiding me like you have for the past few months. So get to the leg press, Detective.'

Sulking, Olivia obeyed, giving Rudy a dirty look as she passed him. 'Traitor.'

'Leave him alone,' Paige murmured. 'He's worried about you. So am I.'

Olivia flopped onto the first machine. 'Let's get this over with.'

Paige said no more of a personal nature, simply counting reps. They moved through the rotation as they had a hundred times before, Olivia mindlessly going through the motions. It wasn't until they were near the end that the wall crumbled.

'She was expecting us.' Olivia was lying on her back, staring at the tiled ceiling.

Paige was sitting on her heels, next to the bench. 'Who?' she asked, unsurprised.

'The widow.' Olivia never gave names and Paige knew not to ask. 'The daughter saw the fire on the news, knew it was dad's shift. She went to sit with mom and wait for us, the bringers of great joy to all people.' Her words were bitter. 'He'd been a cop.'

'Oh no. Liv.'

'Yeah. Did his twenty-five years and retired. Never took a bullet. Tonight he did. And all I had to say was "I'm sorry for your loss."'

'What else could you say?' Paige asked logically.

'I don't know. All I know is I'm damn tired of saying it.'

'You're just damn tired. Your boss offered you a vacation. Why don't you take it?'

A vacation. *Right.* 'I tried,' Olivia spat. 'It was too quiet. All I could see was . . .'

'The bodies in the pit,' Paige finished for her.

Olivia sat up, glared at Paige through narrowed eyes. 'And then *he* shows up.' Which was what she'd wanted to say all along and been afraid to, all at once.

Paige's black brows went up, surprised now. 'Who?'

'That guy. From Mia's wedding.'

Paige blinked. She was the only one who knew the story which had been pried from Olivia's margarita-numbed lips. 'You mean your sister's wedding? No way. That was two years ago, in Chicago. He just showed up, after all this time? What a jerk.'

Olivia flicked her gaze back up to the ceiling. Paige hadn't been updated recently. 'Two and a half years, and actually, he lives here now. Moved here seven months ago.'

'Lots of stuff happened seven months ago,' Paige observed quietly. 'Why did he move here?'

'His friend lives here. You met her. Eve.'

'The one you saved from Pit-Guy. Rest over. Another set. Go.'

Olivia winced as she pumped. 'Pit-Guy' had killed dozens of people, most of them women. Eve had come within a hair of being his thirty-sixth victim. 'Another cop saved Eve, not me. I got there after all the killing was done, just in time to clean out the pit.'

Paige sighed. 'Two more. One, and you're done. So what about Wedding-Guy?'

'Came to visit Eve, ended up buying a place. She told me. He hasn't said a word.'

Paige winced. 'Not a word? So, does Wedding-Guy have a name?'

Olivia's throat closed and she swallowed harshly. 'David.'

'And what does David the wedding-guy do?'

'He's a goddamn firefighter.' And from the corner of her eye she watched Paige's black eyes flicker. 'What?'

'Just that he was at the fire tonight and you got the homicide. Helluva coincidence. So he's been here, in Minneapolis, all this time? And he didn't, like, call or anything?'

'Not once.' And that hurt. A lot.

'Pig.'

'I know, right? Except . . .' Olivia closed her eyes. *Be truthful, at least to yourself.* 'Except he's a nice guy. He likes cartoons and dogs and loves his mother. He cooks and fixes cars. We'd read the same books, liked the same music, dreamed of traveling to all the same places. He volunteered in shelters for women and teen runaways, fixing plumbing and roofs and whatever got broken. He did karate, too. Like you.'

'Oh? Really?'

Olivia nodded. 'He was a brown belt, practicing for his black-belt test. He also taught a class at the Y in Chicago, to kids. For free. I'd have thought he was lying, that nobody could be so perfect, but Mia had already told me he was a nice guy.'

'Wow.' Paige looked stunned. 'I thought you'd only met him that one night.'

'Two, actually. We met at Mia's rehearsal dinner. It was spring, and I guess I was wide open for getting swept off my feet. A weekend fling. How cliché.'

Paige frowned at her disparaging tone. 'Liv. You'd gotten dumped by your ass of a fiancé just a few weeks before the wedding. I'd still like to use him for a punching bag for what he did to you. Going back to his old fiancée. Who was a ho.'

'I remember,' Olivia said dryly. 'I was there.' Paige's punching bag had been named Doug for quite some time after that.

'Then, not a week later, finding out the father you'd never known was dead? Then finding out you had two half sisters?'

'The cop and the con,' Olivia said affectionately. 'Meeting Mia and Kelsey was the only good thing to come out of all that.'

Paige's scowl relaxed a little. 'I'm just saying that you'd been through a lot that winter. To fall under the spell of a sexy, nice Mr Perfect could happen to any of us. He took advantage of you.'

Olivia shrugged. 'Probably. The day of the rehearsal dinner, I was kind of a mess. I was late. I'd just come back from meeting Kelsey for the first time.'

'At the prison,' Paige murmured.

Where Olivia's half sister was serving eight to twenty-five for armed robbery. 'Yeah. The prison's about an hour away from Chicago, and I hadn't been able to get out there before then. I was kind of shaken up, meeting my sister that way, behind the glass. I got to the church late for the rehearsal and was running up to the steps on these stupid high heels, and then I saw him sitting there.'

'This David guy.'

'Yeah.' Olivia closed her eyes. 'It was like getting kicked in the gut. I was mesmerized. His face . . . just, wow. He's got this face, Paige. And the shoulders. And the rest of him . . . You can't forget him. I was staring at his face when my heel hit a rock and I tripped. Flew right into his lap. I was too star struck to even be embarrassed.'

'I don't think I've ever known you to be star struck,' Paige said quietly.

'I never was before. Not with Doug, not with anyone. I'd skinned my knee and he patched me up.' Her lips curved bitterly. 'He had me at hello. It's a wonder I got through the rehearsal and the dinner. All the women looked like they wanted to gouge my eyes out because he stayed with me. And we talked. We talked all night.'

'Did he know about Doug?'

'God, no. I didn't want to look pathetic. I didn't tell any of them. Mia didn't even know. And frankly, sitting there with David, Doug was the last thing on my mind. He never took his eyes off my face. I felt . . . important. Sounds stupid now.'

Paige's brow creased in sympathy. 'It sounds normal to me.'

'I guess I really wanted to feel important to somebody, you know?'

Paige squeezed her hand. 'Yeah, babe. I know.'

Olivia's eyes stung and she willed back what would have been mortifying tears. 'It wasn't all bad, though. I told him about Kelsey. He'd known Mia for a long time, knew about our father. About the abuse. I was so sad to see Kelsey there, in prison like that, even if she did do the crime. David suggested volunteering with teen runaways, to help give them a chance. To help them not turn out like my sister.'

'And you do. It's good work, Liv. You make a difference in those kids' lives.'

'Thanks. So like I said, it wasn't all bad. The rehearsal dinner was wonderful. It was the night after the wedding that went wrong.'

'After it went really well,' Paige said, brows lifted meaningfully and Olivia sighed.

'I wish I'd never met him, because I can't imagine it ever being that good again.'

'But you didn't . . .'

'Not all the way.' She sighed again. 'But based on what did happen, I think all the way would have freaking killed me.'

Paige was quiet a moment. 'Maybe he just lied about doing all that nice stuff. Maybe he's really a colossal jerk.'

'I wish. Since he's been here, he donates his time to charity. Habitat for Humanity, fixing stuff at the local shelters. Eve tells me about him all the time. She thinks David hung the moon. He really is a nice guy. He just . . . doesn't want me.'

There. She'd said it out loud. *I should be feeling better now.* But she wasn't.

'Liv, did it occur to you that maybe he's waiting for you to make the first move?'

Olivia scoffed. 'In my fantasies, sure.'

'Liv?' Paige waited until Olivia looked at her. 'If I were a guy and we'd parted ways under the circumstances you described?'

'Only after you got me drunk,' Olivia interjected, frowning.

'Like you would have ever told me otherwise? Duh. Of course I got you drunk. But as I was saying, if I were Wedding-Guy, I'd be waiting for you to make the first move.'

Olivia remembered the tilt of David Hunter's perfect chin before she'd driven away. It had felt like a challenge. But she also remembered that one night vividly. She remembered the one word, that one name he'd said, even more vividly. 'No.'

'Why not?' Paige asked, exasperated. 'What's the worst that could happen?'

'The same thing that happened the last time,' Olivia said darkly, and her body throbbed in places that had nothing to do with her workout.

'And that would be a bad thing, how? You haven't had anyone since. You're under so much stress that you're about to crack wide open. What's the harm in a fling? So he used you. Use him back. What's the worst that can happen?'

Olivia sat up and swiped at her neck with a towel. *I*

become like you, she thought, *with so many boyfriends I need a spreadsheet to keep track of them all.* But of course she said nothing of the kind. Paige was her oldest friend. 'I'll think about it,' was what she said instead. 'Let's stretch. I have to catch a little sleep before morning meeting.'

Monday, September 20, 7:10 A.M.

'Whoa.' Jeff Zoellner stood on the condo's first floor, staring up through the room-sized hole that went all the way up to the fourth floor. 'You woulda felt that for sure.'

Grimly, David followed his gaze up, then looked down into the basement. The first floor had also been burned through. 'Yeah. I guess I owe you one.'

'Don't worry, I'll think of something.' Jeff started walking again, tapping the handle of his ax on the floor as he sounded for weak spots. David did the same with the end of his Halligan, and together they moved toward the back of the condo. Each of the six floors had six units, but the units on this side of the building had sustained the worst damage. 'I think we're solid from here on out,' Jeff said. 'We can let Barlow in now.'

Micah waited in the doorway. He wore a hard hat and boots, but was otherwise dressed like a detective. The end of his yellow tie poked up from the pocket of his suit. He held a video camera in one hand and a light bar in the other, and had worked alongside them diligently but intelligently, treading in areas they'd declared safe.

And he hadn't said another word about Olivia and for that David was grateful. There were too many dangers here to be thinking about anything else but the job.

Which is what David had told himself every time he

caught himself thinking about her, wondering why Micah Barlow felt she was his business, wondering if the two of them had history, not wanting that picture in his head. David grimaced. Except now that he'd thought it, the picture existed, if only in his imagination. Taunting him.

If Micah and Olivia had a past, at least they had no present. David had kept a close enough eye on her that he'd have known. But if she did have someone? *I'll walk away.*

And if she doesn't have anyone but just doesn't want you? Given the facts, that was the more likely outcome. *I'll cross that bridge when I get there.*

'Where can I step?' Micah called from the doorway.

'Floor's solid where you're standing,' David said, forcing himself to focus yet again, 'but it gets spongy about two feet from the edge of the hole.'

Micah looked up, then down, just as David had. 'Goddamn. You're a lucky bastard.'

'Yeah, I got that part,' David said. 'Over here was what we wanted you to see. They poured the carpet-padding glue along this line.' David pointed to the pour patterns zigzagging from the front door of the unit to the hole, continuing through to the back bedrooms. 'It's the same pour pattern we found on the second floor. I think they poured a line from the door and from the back of the unit, meeting here.'

'Makes sense,' Micah said, filming. 'They probably dumped what was left in the cans where the floor failed. Fire would have been hotter there. The manager said rolls of carpet were stored here, same place on each floor. Water-logged, that would have been enough weight to crash through the second and third floors. When the first floor collapsed, all three carpet rolls fell into the basement.'

For a minute David thought Micah would venture to the edge of the hole to get video straight down, but he stopped while still in the safe zone. From the corner of his eye, David could see Jeff's mouth snap shut, discarding the warning he'd been about to bark. It hadn't taken more than a few runs with Jeff to know cops made him real edgy.

'After they poured the glue, they tossed the cans to the side.' David pointed with the end of his Halligan, and Micah kept filming. 'Two cans there, and two more upstairs, roughly in the same spot. Together with the one we found at the entrance, they poured out five. One can on each floor would have been too much. These were amateurs.'

'I think you're right.' Micah lowered the camera. 'Anything else you see?'

'We're working our way outward,' Jeff said, tapping his way as he went.

David did the same, then stopped when his Halligan hit something soft and he heard the crackle of charred paper. 'Look at that.'

Jeff sighed. 'Last time you said that I had to pull your ass out of the abyss.'

But David was already kneeling, shining his light on what he'd found. 'It's a backpack, or it was anyway.'

'We'll get it to the lab,' Micah said. 'Maybe they can find something left.'

Jeff gently nudged the corner of the bag with his ax handle and part of the side crumbled away. 'Good luck with that. What the hell are you looking at, David?'

David had bent low, shining his light on a lump of black that stuck up from the debris. 'I don't know. Some kind of a case, warped open. Whatever it held is melted to the bottom of it.' A bit of pink plastic peeked from the charred lump.

'I'll get some stills to show Homicide.' Micah sighed impatiently. 'Damn. I'm late for their morning meeting.' He snapped a few pictures with his digital camera. 'CSU will bag it. We'll figure out what it is at the lab. I'll be back later. Don't touch anything.'

'We're not stupid,' Jeff muttered when Micah was gone.

'Neither is he,' David said absently, still staring at the case's melted contents.

'He's a cop,' Jeff stated flatly, 'and they all want to be firefighters. Idiots. They'd burn up if it weren't for us, charging in without gear, with the wrong kind of extinguisher. Ready to save the damn day before they even know what kind of fire they got.'

David let him rant, knowing he'd say the same thing regardless of any response David made. There was a story there, he figured, and one day Jeff would tell it.

Story. David stared at the mangled case, his mind pulling a long-forgotten memory. He'd been a small boy, sitting on his grandmother's lap. He'd always been more fascinated with gadgets than the story she'd tell, especially the gadget that sat behind her ear. He'd reach for it, only to have his small hands gently pushed away. *No, David*, she'd say, *don't touch. That's not a toy.*

'We should have told Barlow to bring us food,' Jeff finished with a sigh. 'I'm starving. Let's take a break and see what's left on the truck. Hey. Dave. Come on.'

'I know what this pink plastic thing is,' David said.

'Don't tell me. I want to guess,' Jeff said. 'Okay, give me a hint.'

It was a game they sometimes played that helped them deal when they had to poke around the ashes of people's lives. 'It whistles as it works.' David straightened, hoping he could catch Micah before he left, but through the broken window he could see the cop's taillights going through the gate.

Behind him, he heard Jeff's heavy sigh and knew he'd figured it out. 'Dammit, David. The girl never had a chance, did she?'

'Doesn't look like it. I'm going outside to call Micah's cell. He'll want to tell Olivia.'

'Olivia?' Jeff asked, new curiosity in his voice. 'You mean Detective Sutherland? She was pretty hot. And she was watching you.'

'Leave it alone,' David said flatly. 'And don't ask. I mean it.'

For all his teasing, Jeff knew when to quit. 'Chill, man. I'm going out with you. I need to get some food.'

Monday, September 20, 8:00 A.M.

'Happy Monday.' Captain Bruce Abbott dropped a plastic bowl of cookies on the round table in his office. 'Compliments of Lorna.'

Olivia eyed the bowl skeptically. 'Lorna's cooking again?'

Abbott settled into the chair behind his desk. 'Her guidance counselor said if she retook the class and got a better grade, it would cancel last year's D.'

Micki popped the lid off the bowl. 'How bad can they be?'

'Some people ought not bake,' Kane said sourly.

'Got it.' Micki shot a wicked look at Olivia. 'Let Barlow test them. If they're awful, it'll serve him right.' She glanced at Abbott. 'No offense.'

Abbott's lips were twitching beneath his mustache. 'None taken.' He looked at the empty chairs meaningfully. 'Speaking of which, where are Barlow and Gilles?'

'Ian's not coming,' Olivia said. 'He was almost ready to start the girl's autopsy when I stopped by the morgue.'

Kane studied her face. 'When did you stop by the morgue?' he asked, when *Why didn't you go home to sleep like I told you to?* was what he really wanted to know.

'On my way in. I wanted a photo of the girl.' Which wasn't entirely untrue. After her workout she'd gone home but couldn't sleep, so she'd done what she always did – worked. 'I don't know where Barlow is. I told him oh-eight.'

'I'm here, I'm here.' Barlow barreled through Abbott's doorway and dropped into a chair. Instantly, everyone leaned away from him. 'Sorry,' he muttered. 'I came straight from the scene. Didn't have a chance to shower.'

'We can tell,' Micki said, then smiled kindly. 'Here, have a cookie.'

Beside Olivia, Kane coughed to cover what would have been a chuckle.

'Thanks. I didn't have time for breakfast.' Barlow grabbed a handful and Olivia felt the prick of conscience.

'I'd take a little bite first,' she said and he narrowed his eyes.

'You made these?' he asked suspiciously. 'You trying to poison me now?'

Olivia rolled her eyes. *Let him suffer.* 'Since we're all here, we can get started.' She started to close Abbott's door, but Abbott lifted his hand.

'Leave it open,' he said. 'Dr Donahue will be joining us.'

Olivia's shoulders went rigid. Donahue was the

department shrink. The one who wasn't helping after three mandated visits. She sat back down. *Great.*

'I want a profile of this arsonist,' Abbott went on and Olivia could feel his eyes on her. To be accurate, everyone's eyes were on her, even Barlow's. Meddling bastard. 'Donahue's got time and experience with arsonists. And here she is.'

The psychiatrist came through the door, dressed in a trim blue suit that looked like it had been tailored just for her. 'Good morning,' she said. 'I'm sorry to keep you waiting.'

'Dr Donahue,' Abbott said as she took her seat. 'Do you know everyone?'

'Everyone but you.' She smiled at Barlow. 'I'm Jessie Donahue.'

'Micah Barlow, arson investigator. Don't eat the cookies,' Barlow added dryly.

The confusion on Donahue's face under other circumstances would have made Olivia smile, but the very presence of the woman had her on edge. She shook off the discomfort. 'Let's get this done, okay? What do we know, Mick? Any ID on the girl?'

'Nothing so far. The girl's prints aren't in AFIS, so no criminal record, at least one that isn't sealed. No response yet from the Missing Children database, but I'm expecting an answer any hour now. No Amber Alerts, so as of this minute, no ID.'

'I sent her morgue photo to the Florida Highway Patrol,' Olivia said. 'I hope the Gator nail decals pan out, even if she's not in the databases. What about the gel?'

'I won't get those results till after lunch,' Micki said, 'but I do have something on the ball. We wanted to preserve it, just the way the firefighter found it until we knew what the gel was. So we did an image of what was underneath all that gel. This came through just as I was leaving to come up here.' She put a photograph on the table.

The ball was a glass globe of the world. Etched onto the glass were the continents.

'It looks like a paperweight,' Olivia said cautiously, although her mind was already stringing *globe*, *world*, and *arson* together, creating a very bad feeling.

Beside her, Micah Barlow swore softly and grabbed the photograph, staring at it in consternation. 'No, it's a signature. One that hasn't been seen for ten years.'

'Twelve,' Micki said. 'I cross-referenced *glass globe*s with *arson*.'

Barlow rubbed his hands over his eyes in a tired gesture. 'And you came up with SPOT – *Societus Patronus Orbis Terra*. Shit.'

'Fellowship of the protectors of the earth,' Dr Donahue murmured.

Olivia sat back, frowning. The bad feeling just got worse. 'Ecoterrorists? Hell.'

'With bad Latin grammar,' Donahue said, almost to herself, then looked up at the group. 'It's an interesting addition to the profile.'

'Grammar aside,' Abbott said, 'what are we dealing with?'

'A group of environmental activists we believed had disbanded,' Barlow said. 'They were at their most active in the early nineties. SPOT operated on the leaderless resistance model – small cells that allegedly have no lateral connection to one another or vertical connection to a "boss." They targeted commercial development of wildlife habitats, like the wetlands bordered by last night's condo.'

Abbott had leaned forward, chin on his folded hands. 'M.O.?'

'Usually smart,' Barlow said. 'They used electronic timers to start their fires and always left behind a glass globe paperweight, but not covered in any gel. They'd wrap it in fire-resistant fabrics, usually pieces of firefighters' protective gear, coats, et cetera.'

'They wanted it found,' Olivia murmured. 'Intact.'

'Absolutely,' Barlow said, brows crunched. 'But they always, *always* contacted the local news minutes after the firefighters were called to the scene.'

'They didn't this time,' Kane said. 'Why?'

Barlow shook his head. 'I don't know. They also never used guns.'

'Was this a smart fire?' Olivia asked.

'Aspects were. Like shutting down the camera systems and shutting off the water to the sprinklers. That took planning. They also had access to the guard's schedule and they knew to open all the fire doors. If the girl tried to get out via the stairwell, she would have been stopped by the smoke and the heat. But in other ways they were stupid. They used the carpet adhesive, which is incredibly flammable. The fire would have spread quickly. It's a wonder they made it out alive. Their M.O. last night wasn't consistent with their M.O. before.'

'What are you saying?' Olivia asked. 'They've reopened under new management?'

Barlow lifted a shoulder. 'Maybe. Or maybe it's a front. If someone knew about SPOT and wanted to deflect attention from their real motive, they could leave the globe behind and have us chasing our tails.'

'Or that could be wishful thinking and they really are ecoterrorists,' Kane said.

'Meaning, we call in the Feds,' Abbott said flatly.

Olivia's jaw tightened. 'I had to tell Henry Weems's widow that he wasn't ever coming home again. Weems was MPD, one of ours. So whoever shot him is ours, too.'

'I agree,' Abbott said grimly. 'For now, we call the Feds, just to check on anything new they might have on this group. If these are eco-nuts, I don't want my ass on the line for sitting on information. But if these SPOT assholes claim responsibility, we will bring the Feds in. No arguments.'

He was right, Olivia knew, just as she knew she was being emotional. 'No arguments. Besides, the differences far outweigh the similarities.'

Barlow was frowning. 'Maybe not. There is one other similarity. In their last arson twelve years ago, a woman died. Nobody was supposed to be in the building, but this woman was working late and had fallen asleep at her desk. After that, the group went dormant. It was assumed they'd gone their separate ways.'

'*That* was SPOT?' Abbott asked. 'I remember that fire now.'

'That's a disturbing coincidence,' Jess Donahue said. 'If they knew this girl was in the condo last night and set the fire anyway . . . that's a whole different ball game.'

'Find them first, then find out what they knew and when,' Abbott said, then turned to Barlow. 'Leaderless resistance groups often have a symbolic leader. Did SPOT?'

'Yeah, but I think I'm too tired to think of his name now.'

'Preston Moss,' Micki supplied. 'I pulled a few articles from Google. Moss grew up here, in the Twin Cities, but during the nineties was a professor in some private college in Oregon. He authored a few books on preserving forest habitats. His first few books were more mainstream, but he

got more radical. He's believed to have founded SPOT –
with appropriate Latin grammar, Dr Donahue. His
followers bastardized the name as they formed their own
cells across the northwest and east into Wisconsin. Later he
came back to teach in Minnesota. The wetlands were one
of his causes, and Moss was believed to have been directly
involved in that last fire. He dropped out of sight after the
woman's death and hasn't been seen again.'

Barlow smiled, but wearily. 'You did your homework.
Anything else I forgot?'

'No, you covered it,' Micki said kindly. 'You have a
good memory.'

'How *did* you remember this, Sergeant?' Donahue
asked. 'This SPOT group was active before you joined the
force.'

Olivia shot a quick look at the shrink, impressed and
wary at the same time. That Donahue had known Barlow
was on the case and had already checked his personnel file
seemed to have floated over the man's head, because he
replied without a blink.

'During one of my training classes, we had speakers
from the FBI and ATF. One of the FBI guys had been chasing
Preston Moss for years. Kind of his great white whale, if
you know what I mean. Seemed a little too intense for my
liking, but he may have more information that isn't in the
files. His name is Special Agent Angus Crawford, and then
he was with the Minneapolis field office.'

'I'll give him a call,' Abbott said. 'Barlow, do you have
enough resources? Should we call the Feds in for support?'

'I'm good for now. We've got MFD fire investigators on
the scene, and I got some help from one of the firefighters.'
Barlow slid a look at Olivia. 'The one who found the girl
– David Hunter. He's got a good eye.'

Olivia felt her cheeks heat. *David's eyes weren't the only things that were good*, she thought as Paige's words came back to taunt her. *Focus*. She looked Barlow in the eye. 'What did you find?' she asked, relieved her voice was professionally brisk.

'Hunter and Zell found a backpack in the debris on the first floor, just before I left to come here,' Barlow said. 'The backpack was mostly burned. It may have been on the fourth floor when it collapsed and fell through, landing on the first floor before the fire was completely out. Some of the contents had fallen out and melted.' He produced a camera, turned it on, and passed it to Olivia so that she could view the digital display. 'Haven't had time to print my photos. We found this a few feet away.'

In the screen was a black case that looked like it should have held eyeglasses, but it didn't. What it did hold, she couldn't tell, as the contents were misshapen. 'What is it?'

'A hearing aid,' Barlow said. 'Hunter ID'd it. That pink part is the earpiece. I'm assuming it belonged to the girl.'

'If it does, it narrows the search for her a good bit.' Olivia put the photo of the dead girl on the table. 'She had gel on her hands, and Hunter said he found the ball near where he found her. She'd held the ball. Maybe she planted it there. Maybe she was with the arsonists and the fire got out of their control and she got trapped.'

'We can't ignore the possibility,' Abbott said. 'And if she was part of their cell, identifying her could lead us to them.'

'Or she could have been forced to be one of them.' Kane pointed to the girl's arm. 'Her injuries were real. She'd been slapped around by somebody.'

'Or she could have been an innocent bystander who

found the ball and picked it up,' Olivia finished. 'In which case, we're back to square one.'

'Did you find any ID in the backpack?' Micki asked.

Barlow shook his head. 'No. The contents were too burned. I told your CSU tech to bag it. We got some charred papers, books. The paper took a lot of water damage, but the lab might be able to piece together the scraps for a name or a lead.'

'Can we get in the building now?' Kane asked, but Barlow shook his head.

'Not yet. We're still checking the fifth and sixth floors, but the damage that made the fourth floor collapse under Hunter goes all the way down. If he hadn't caught himself, he would have gone all the way down to the basement. The tower truck's still at the scene, though. Captain Casey said Hunter or Zell could take you up in the bucket, let you look through the windows. I also shot video as we went through the debris. I'll transfer the files to my PC and e-mail them to you when we're finished here.'

Olivia couldn't stifle the icy shiver that cut through her at the thought of David plunging four stories. She did, however, manage to stifle the mixed dread and anticipation at sharing the close quarters of a bucket with him. She'd do her job, as would he. 'We'll take the videos if that's all we can get right now, but I want to see the scene. I guess going up in the bucket is our best option at the moment. We should get out there before they leave. They've been there for about eight hours now.'

'They've probably got another two hours ahead of them,' Barlow said, 'so you don't have to rush.' He pulled a sooty envelope from his front pocket and handed it to Kane. 'You asked for the Rankin and Sons personnel list. I had them run an extra copy for you.'

'Thanks. We'll start background checks. Anyone we should be looking at?'

'As in anyone who'd have access to the guard's schedule and their camera feeds?' Micki asked sarcastically. 'Try anyone on that list and just about any entry-level hacker.'

Olivia winced. 'You snuck into the system that easily, huh?'

Micki rolled her eyes. 'We didn't have to sneak. Rankin's IT guy left their server wide open. I'd check the IT guy. If he's not on the take, he's the most inept we've ever come across.'

'So anyone could have cut the camera feed,' Kane said glumly.

'Sorry,' Micki said. 'I wish I could give you better news. We are trying to trace where the command to disable the cameras came from. That'll take a little while. Like Barlow said, that aspect of this job was done very well.'

Dr Donahue sat back in her chair. 'Sergeant Barlow, could this fire have been set by one individual?'

Barlow hesitated. 'Maybe. But if this really was SPOT, then they probably were a cell of two to four people. If it was arson for hire or some other reason, it could have been one. The job itself could have been accomplished solo, with adequate planning.'

'So we have one to four people, educated in computer networks but who didn't do their homework on actually setting the fire,' Donahue said. 'At least one of them was capable of shooting a guard in cold blood. They brought at least one gun with them, so they were prepared for violence of some nature – even if it was to protect themselves. Were any warning shots fired that you could see?'

'No,' Micki said. 'We found the slug that killed Weems. Hollow-point, .38. We didn't see evidence of other shots fired. We'll keep looking now that it's daylight.'

Donahue nodded. 'So for now we'll assume they did not fire warning shots, just the one shot that hit Mr Weems . . . where?'

'Right through the heart,' Kane said grimly and Donahue's brows rose.

'Interesting. A more surefire target would have been his head. I mean, Weems could have been wearing a vest. Through the heart is very personal.'

'Weems represented authority, even if they didn't know he'd been a cop,' Olivia said. 'Most of these groups are anarchists. That they'd despise Weems isn't unusual.'

'But apparently to shoot him, is.' Donahue scribbled in a small notebook. 'I'll do some research on SPOT. See if anyone developed profiles back in the nineties.'

'We'll keep on the girl's ID,' Olivia said. 'Ian's supposed to call when he's done with the girl's autopsy. For now we'll start checking into Rankin's personnel.'

'And I'll call Special Agent Crawford at the Bureau's field office,' Abbott said. 'We keep the details of the glass globe from the press for as long as we can. Can this firefighter be trusted not to talk to reporters?'

'Yes,' Olivia said quickly. Too quickly, she thought when everyone looked at her. She shrugged. 'He's an old family friend with no love for reporters. He won't talk.'

Abbott nodded. 'Good. Barlow, let me know if you need support. I have a few detectives I can pull in from other cases if we need them. Everyone back here at five.'

Chapter Four

Monday, September 20, 8:55 A.M.

Eric could recite the thirty-minute newscast from memory. *What am I going to do?*

You're going to sit here and wait, just like he told you to. Just as he had for the past five hours. The news wasn't new since disclosing the second victim had died of gunshot wounds. So he'd sat, listening to the same report again and again and watching his cell phone. Waiting for it to buzz, waiting for the next text from his 'master.' *Sonofabitch.*

And if he makes me wait days? Eventually he'd have to leave his apartment, go to class. Maybe even eat. Although the very thought of food made him want to gag.

We killed that girl. But they had not shot that guard. Which meant somebody else did. The only other person was the damn blackmailer. He did it. He shot the guard.

But who would believe them? The texter had them on video. Video, goddamn it.

How could we have been so stupid? How did he know we'd even be there? He'd racked his brain all night, trying to think of where, when they'd been together, discussing their plan. But so far he'd come up blank. Unless one of them had told.

He closed his eyes. It was top of the hour. Time for another identical report on the condo arson, word for word. He started to murmur the words along with the anchor, then bolted upright in his chair when the mouth on the tube said, 'This just in.'

The television screen had split. The anchor was on the right, but on the left was a picture of the guard. In a cop's uniform. Eric's mouth went bone dry and he stared at the man's badge as the talking head on the right began to speak.

'Minneapolis police have confirmed the identity of the guard killed in last night's arson. The victim is Henry Weems, who retired last year after a twenty-five-year career with the Minneapolis police. His daughter, Brenda Weems, gave this statement.'

The screen switched to Brenda Weems who stood on the steps of a modest house in a modest suburb, arms tightly crossed over her chest, her face tearstained.

'My father was a good cop, a good husband and father. He was murdered last night, along with another victim. I know the police will not rest until his killer is brought to justice – not because my father was a cop, but because he was a member of this community. My mother and I ask for privacy so that we may grieve. Thank you.'

The screen switched back to the anchor and Eric felt numb.

A cop was dead. *So are w*e. The police wouldn't rest until they'd hunted them down.

Joel had said as much last night, when they'd still thought their worst problem was the dead girl. Eric stood abruptly. He had to get to Joel before he found out about this. There was no telling how Joel would respond. He might break, crack, tell everyone.

And we all go to prison. Not going to happen.

He'd turned to wash up when his phone buzzed on the table. For a moment he just looked at it, then carefully picked it up, as if it were poisonous. His shoulders sagged. Not a text. It was an incoming call from Albert.

'Did you see the news? I didn't kill him. I only hit him. Somebody shot him. *Who*?'

'I . . . I don't know,' Eric said numbly.

'He was a cop. If that pussy Joel tells, we're dead.'

He thought of the video. The texts. *You have no idea how dead we are.* 'I know.' Eric made a decision. 'We have to stop Joel from talking.' And he had to keep the texter from showing the video that would damn them all. 'Just don't hurt him, okay?'

Albert said, very quietly, 'We will not speak of this again.'

Eric drew a breath, knowing he was sentencing Joel to death. 'No, we will not.' He closed his phone, completely unsurprised when a text popped up immediately.

go to 11th and nicollet. sit on bench at bus stop. find envelope taped to seat. come alone. tell no one. yes or no?

Suddenly, coolly calm, Eric texted back, *yes*. He went to his bedroom and grabbed the plastic bag in which he'd stuffed his smoky-smelling clothes. He couldn't let the maid find them. He'd throw them in a dumpster.

Then he slid his hand behind the stacks of video games on his closet shelf, finding his gun. He checked the magazine, found it full. He smacked it back into place with the heel of his hand. Just in case the texter actually showed his face, he'd be ready.

He chuckled on the inside as he closed the disposable phone. Then lifted his gaze to the television mounted on

71

the wall, his pose appropriately somber. The report was ending with old news, but the first few minutes had made his day.

The guard had been a fucking cop. It just got better. Or worse if you were Eric and the gang. A murdered guard was one thing, but a murdered retired *cop*? Pure gold.

He wondered if Eric had told the others. Wondered what Eric's attempt at countering him would be. It didn't matter. *I hold all the cards. I always do.*

'Excuse me.'

He dropped his eyes from the television to the slightly impatient face of the next customer. 'I'm sorry,' he said soberly. 'It's just the fire. Those poor people. That officer.'

The customer sighed, her impatience gone. 'I know. It's so disturbing. You take your life in your hands every time you leave your house these days.'

'Ain't that the truth?' he said sympathetically. 'So, how can I help you today?'

Monday, September 20, 9:20 A.M.

Olivia tidily folded the paper wrapper as she swallowed the last bit of her breakfast sandwich. Not saying a word, Kane took his hand off the steering wheel long enough to hand her the large coffee in the cup holder between them.

'Thanks,' she said. 'You know I could have driven. It was my day.'

He slanted her his 'bullshit' look. 'I slept. You didn't.'

'I tried,' she said quietly. 'I really did. I went and worked my ass off at the gym so that I'd be tired. Took my dog for a run, took a hot shower, even drank some of that herbal tea you're so keen on, which is totally nasty, by the way.

Nothing worked. So I dropped Mojo off at Brie's and came in. And you would have done the same.'

'Well, maybe,' he said grudgingly. 'All except taking my dog to doggy day care.'

Olivia's friend, Brie Franconi, ran a canine training kennel but had begun letting cops drop off their dogs when they knew they'd be working a long shift. Olivia didn't care what Brie called the service, she was just grateful for it.

'Mojo gets to play with the other dogs while I'm working, and I don't feel so guilty. He keeps me company,' she added a little wistfully. She'd gotten the dog shortly after her fiancé, Doug, left her. 'The house gets too quiet sometimes.'

Kane shot her a look. 'Seeing Barlow can't be easy for you.'

She shrugged. Seeing David was somehow a hell of a lot worse. 'Micah made his choice a long time ago, but I suppose his siding with Doug was for the best. If Doug didn't want me, I guess it's better I found out before I tied the knot.' She sipped at her coffee, glad it was strong. 'I've been thinking about the girl. If she was in business with the arsonists, her purpose for being in the building is straightforward.'

'I agree. But if she wasn't,' Kane said, 'and if her being there was just very bad timing, we have to wonder what drove her there. To that building.'

'If she's not local, how would she know about it? You can't see it from the road.'

'But you can see it from different points around the lake,' Kane said.

'Right again.' She took a sheet of paper from the briefcase at her feet. 'I printed a map of the lake, which is primarily residential. Small houses, a lot of vacation cabins.'

'Good. We can take her photo around, see if anyone's seen her and ask if anyone noticed any unusual activity last night. It would have been hard to see through the fence, but we might get lucky. We can't ignore the possibility that it was an inside job.'

'I did a search on Rankin and Sons this morning. I was hoping to find they were on the verge of bankruptcy or something that would make the motive for the arson clear.'

'But Rankin's solid?'

'Well, they were before last night. A good percentage of the shoreline property has been bought up by a company named KRB, which planned to build six condos in total. It's supposed to be a planned community and Rankin was hired to build phase one, which were the luxury condos. Phase two will be two more buildings, targeted to upper-middle-class families. Construction is scheduled to begin in the spring.' She studied the map. 'A lot of these cabins will be leveled.'

'Homeowners might be angry about that,' Kane said.

'Angry enough to set a fire, though?'

'Maybe. We should see if any of the homeowners have protested the construction project. Is Rankin the builder of the next phase?' Kane asked.

'Maybe, maybe not,' Olivia replied. 'The newspaper article I read said that KRB would evaluate Rankin after phase one, to see how well they managed budget.'

'Barlow said they'd fired a security guard because they were running over budget.'

'Yeah, he did. So Rankin may have been in a spot. Depending on how badly they were screwing up, arson may have seemed a good idea to somebody at the time.

74

Anyway, phase three would be two buildings for retirees and an assisted-living facility. Future plans show shopping, a medical center, an entire planned community. Last night's fire took out the first building, so I'm betting the whole schedule is up in the air.'

'Who owns this KRB company?'

'I was just getting into that when the morgue called. I forwarded what I had so far to Faye and asked her to finish the search.' Abbott's clerk was a research whiz. 'I did run the construction manager through the system. Squeaky clean.'

'Does the construction manager own a gun?'

'He doesn't have a permit. Micki did a residue test on his hands last night. He didn't fire a gun, or if he did, he was smart enough to wear gloves.'

'We'll need to check his finances and those of KRB. When we're done here, we should start warrants.'

'Unless SPOT claims responsibility and then we have to bring in the Feds.'

Kane shrugged. 'I've worked task forces with the Feds before. It's not so bad, so stop worrying. You'll give yourself wrinkles.'

'I've already got wrinkles,' Olivia muttered. Thirty-one and she was falling apart.

He stuck out his hand. 'Give me another sandwich.'

Frowning, she dug into the bag on the seat between them. 'You're not leaving any for the firefighters.' She slapped one into his hand. 'No more for you after this.'

They'd hit the Deli on their way out of the city, the coffee/sandwich shop that catered to cops, students, and professors, and anyone else who liked a good meal. It had been her turn to get breakfast, so she'd ordered Kane's favorite – egg and pastrami on rye – then on impulse, added a dozen breakfast sandwiches for the firefighters, who wouldn't have any trouble wolfing them down. When the Deli's manager had found out who the food was for, he'd thrown in a thermos of coffee for free.

'There are still ten left,' Kane said. 'How many can one pretty-boy firefighter eat?'

Olivia's face flushed hot. 'Kane,' she said warningly.

He looked unapologetic. 'We're almost there. You should do something with those bags under your eyes. Powder or something.'

She drew a breath. 'Kane,' she said, the warning gone ominous.

They'd stopped at a red light, so he leaned over and pulled her purse from the glove box and dropped it in her lap. 'Little lipstick wouldn't hurt either.'

The light turned green and he started through the intersection without another word. Fuming, she flipped the visor down and checked the mirror. And winced. 'Ye gods.'

'Indeed,' Kane said gravely.

She gave him a dirty look. 'At least my hair's okay.'

Kane shrugged. 'If it makes you feel better to think that.'

Her long hair was pulled back in a tidy bun at the base of her neck. Which made her tired eyes look even more haggard. She sighed. 'I really hate you sometimes.'

'No, you don't.' He glanced over at her. 'Any more than you hate him. You didn't see your face, Liv,' he added when she opened her mouth to protest. 'When Barlow said Hunter had nearly fallen four stories, you went white as a ghost.'

'I'm always white as a ghost. I never tan.' But she snapped her compact open and powdered her face with hurried strokes. Worse than driving up to the scene all haggard would be driving up while doing her face. She did have some pride, after all.

Kane handed her his comb. 'Lose the bun, girlfriend. Braid it if you have to, but lose the bun. It makes you look' – he gave a mock shudder – 'like a librarian.'

She laughed as he'd wanted her to and he grinned. Kane's wife was a retired librarian and Olivia knew he loved her dearly. 'Jennie would kick your ass for that.'

'Not if she knew it made you laugh. Hurry, now. We're almost there.'

Monday, September 20, 9:45 A.M.

Eric found the bench and the padded envelope taped underneath. He leaned forward as if to tie his shoe and grabbed the envelope, slipping it inside his jacket, his fingertips brushing the cold steel of his gun as he did so. Heart pounding, he sat back, sure everyone on the street was watching him, sure they all knew he had the gun.

But no one glanced his way. Everyone was busy going about their own lives while he sat on a bench in plain sight, a fucking gun tucked into the waistband of his jeans and picking up packages like he was some James Bond wannabe.

I am an engineering student. I'm on the dean's list. I'm one of the good guys. This cannot be happening. But it was. He walked the six blocks back to his car and got in.

He stared at the envelope, then ripped it open and shook out a cell phone and an MP3 player with a two-inch video screen and earbuds. A brittle laugh broke free. Soon that guy from *Mission Impossible* would be telling him the tape would self-destruct.

But it wasn't funny. This was a nightmare. Whoever this guy was, he had video that could bury them all. Eric found the texter had painted a '1' on the back of the MP3 player and a '2' on the back of the cell phone with red nail polish.

Feeling like a fool, he put the buds in his ears and turned the MP3 player on. He hit play and instantly the *Mission Impossible* theme blared in his ears. He gritted his teeth, then felt his stomach lurch when the video of the fire began to play on the tiny screen. Fury boiled up within him and he wanted to throw the MP3 player out the window. But he didn't, and seconds later the music quieted and a computer-altered voice began to speak. It was impossible to tell if it was a man or a woman.

'You followed my directions. Very good. It is now time for your first test. If you pass, you remain in my good favor. If you refuse or if you fail, this video will be released to the police and the media and you will live the rest of your life in a very small jail cell surrounded by ape-sized men who will find you most entertaining.'

A prison filled the screen, followed by a photo of a man being sodomized. A pain shot up Eric's neck and he realized he'd clenched his teeth almost to the breaking point.

'This is your target.' The photo changed and Eric let out a breath, swallowing the bile that had risen in his throat. The new picture appeared to be a factory. 'The address has been sent to your phone as a text. You are to take your three pals and set fire to his place of business tonight. Make sure not a timber is left standing.'

And then Eric understood. The texter's price was not money. It was far worse. Numbly he continued to watch the screen, but no new photos appeared.

'The proprietor has a guard dog,' the voice continued.

'Deal with it, however you wish. If you wish to tell your compatriots the truth, feel free. If you fear they will not comply with your direction, tell them anything you choose, but know if even one of you chooses not to participate, the video will be distributed and all of you will go to prison.'

The voice had not faltered once, had not shown a hint of emotion.

'If anyone stands in your way, kill them. If for any reason your target appears to have been warned, or if any inventory in his place of business is removed unexpectedly, your video will be revealed. When you are finished, use the camera in the cell phone to document your activity and text the photos to the number provided. More directions will be provided at that time. Good luck, Eric, and if you should be caught' – now the voice laughed, a cruel, brutal, smug sound – 'the world will know what you've done.'

The factory faded, replaced by a single frame from the video of last night. The very image that haunted him. The girl, her hands on the glass, her mouth yawning open in that horrible scream that, even in his mind, had no sound at all.

The file ended and the tiny screen went black. Eric opened the cell phone, clicked on the single text message it held. It was, as expected, an address. He wondered what the 'proprietor' of this business had done to earn the wrath of the texter.

And he wondered what the hell he was going to do.

For now, he'd go to his ten a.m. calculus class. Maintain his normal schedule. And he'd think. Hard. There had to be a way out of this. There had to be.

He started his car and had put it in gear when the disposable cell chirped, startling him. He took a second to gather his thoughts. And his courage.

He flipped the phone open. Another text. *yes or no?*

Wildly Eric looked around, wondering if the texter had followed him, was watching him. His eyes searched windows and cars and people standing idly on street corners. It could be anyone. Panic clawed up, grabbed his throat. It could be anyone.

who r u? he typed.

the invisible man.

A few seconds passed and the phone chirped again. *yes or no?* Next to the words was a link and before Eric even clicked on it he knew what he would see. The face in the window. His chest was so tight he could barely breathe. *Yes*, he typed back. 'You sonofabitch,' he muttered. Again the phone chirped.

wise choice. i look forward to seeing your pictures tonight.

Eric closed the phone and stared at it. How had the SOB known he'd listened to the MP3 file and read the text? Either he was standing nearby, watching, or he had the cell phone rigged. Eric looked around the interior of his car. *Or he's wired my car and is watching me on a PC somewhere.*

There had to be a way to track this guy. *And if I can't? Or if I can't before tonight?*

Then you'll have to do what he says. 'No,' Eric said firmly.

But when he pulled onto the street, his mind was already working the logistics of a factory arson. Just in case.

Monday, September 20, 9:55 A.M.

She's here. David's hands stilled on the line he was reeling in. He watched Kane's Ford pull through the construction gate, his heart pounding and stomach jumping like he was thirteen and just about to ask a girl to his first school dance.

A pang of regret pushed through his sudden nerves. *And we all know how well that ended*, he thought bitterly. Nearly twenty years of service hadn't been enough to atone. He was pretty sure a lifetime wouldn't be enough. He could only do what he could do. And make sure this time, with this woman, it ended differently.

'She's here,' Jeff said, dragging the last few feet of line to the truck. They'd spent the last hour walking the five-inch line, squeezing every drop of water from the hose. Every few minutes David had glanced toward the front gate, waiting. Now she was here.

Jeff's grin told him that any attempt at nonchalance would be folly. 'I see her,' he said, half expecting his voice to crack as it would have at thirteen. Gratefully it did not.

He watched as Olivia got out of the passenger side, the morning sun making her hair gleam gold. Then she bent over to get something from the front seat, giving him a perfect view of her very round rear end and he couldn't control the sudden breath that hissed between his teeth. Vague recollections taunted him once again and he jerked his eyes away, staring instead at his hands.

He knew how she felt. How those smooth round curves fit in his hands. Perfectly. He shouldn't know, but he did. And he needed to know again. Quelling a shudder, he exhaled, willing the need away. As if.

'I have to agree,' Jeff murmured in approval. 'Very nice.'

David gritted his teeth against the urge to tell Jeff to keep his damn eyes to his damn self, making his voice deceptively mild. 'Kayla would gouge your eyes out.'

Jeff's grin broadened. 'She can't say anything. I've caught her eyeing your ass.'

David rolled his eyes. 'Barlow called to say they wanted to see the fourth floor,' he made himself say reasonably. 'Give me a hand with this line so we can leave.'

But Jeff continued to stare at the detectives' car. 'Hey, your lady brought food. From the Deli. That's the good stuff. Take a break, Dave. You know you want to.'

Jeff walked off and David slowly stood, watching her kick the car door closed with her foot. *Your lady*. She wasn't, of course. She might have been, if things had gone differently. *If I hadn't done . . . whatever*. But she was here. *Because it's her job, idiot*.

But she'd brought food, so that was a good sign. *This is the opportunity you've waited for. Don't blow it like you blew it the last time*.

Which he obviously had, but that recollection was more vague than the others. Squaring his shoulders, he started to walk, knowing the exact instant she saw him coming. She went still, gripping a bag in one hand and a thermos in the other, and she looked right at him. He didn't breathe for the space of three hard beats of his heart.

And then she looked away when Jeff reached her first, taking the bag from her hands. 'There's coffee in the thermos,' he heard her say when he got close.

Jeff was already stuffing his face. 'Bacon, egg, and cheese,' he mumbled. 'God, I thought I was going to drop. Thank you. There's plenty, Dave. Have some.'

'There is plenty,' she said quietly, her eyes flickering everywhere but at his face, and David felt the frustration of being an adult trapped at a junior high party.

'Any news on the girl?' he asked and she finally met his eyes. Hers were round, blue as the sky, and very serious.

'Not yet. The hearing aid should help us narrow it down, so thank you.'

'Barlow said you wanted to see the fourth floor. I can take you up from the outside, but getting around on the inside still isn't safe, especially without boots.'

She nodded. 'Got it. Is there room for both Kane and me in the bucket?'

Kane walked up, a small black bag in one hand. 'Me, go up in the bucket? I don't think so. You go up. Here's the camera. And my field glasses.'

She took the items he shoved into her hands. 'You're not going? Why the hell not?'

Kane's expression was one of mild embarrassment. 'Heights and me . . . a big no.'

She gave her partner a dirty look. 'Wuss,' she muttered, then looked back up at David resolutely. 'Then let's go up. You want to eat something first?'

He didn't think he could. 'No, thanks. Zell, let's go. I need you to man the truck.'

'I could go up with her. Or not,' Jeff added when David's eyes narrowed. With a jovial grin, Jeff wiped his hands on the bandana he kept in his pocket and passed the bag of sandwiches to the captain, who'd just joined them. 'Save me one.'

Casey smiled at Olivia. 'Thanks, Detective. This was really nice of you,' he said.

'Our pleasure. I figured you'd all be hungry, staying here all night. We won't keep you here any longer than we have to.' She looked around. 'Where is Sergeant Barlow?'

'He said he had some reports to write,' Casey said, 'and he'd be back after noon. Two guys from Arson are in there now, gridding off each floor so they can search.'

They'd search carefully, David knew, sifting the ash,

looking for anything that could lead them to the arsonist. 'Barlow said we should show you what we showed him. You can see the first floor through that window.'

David led Olivia and Kane to the first-floor window. 'This window was regular glass and probably blew out in the first minutes of the fire. We found the backpack and the hearing aid on the other side of that hole.' Standing behind her, he leaned so that his cheek was inches from her temple and pointed. 'There, where CSU left the markers.'

'I see,' she murmured. Her shoulders stiffened, but she didn't shrink away and he took that as a good sign. 'CSU took the items already?'

'About an hour ago.' He should move. He really should. He knew he reeked from smoke and sweat. But her hair smelled like honeysuckle, just as he remembered, and he took another second to fill his head with her scent before backing away.

Kane had leaned around her other side to stick his head through the window and whistled softly. 'That is one hell of a hole, Hunter.'

'Tell me about it,' David said grimly.

Olivia's brows crunched as she strained to see around the interior walls that remained. 'The gel that covered the ball,' she said. 'Did you find any down here?'

'No,' David said. 'And I looked. But this area is a mess. If there was any gel, it'd be mixed with ash by now. The water pushes everything together. If it's there, the arson guys will find it while they're sifting. It's thicker than kindergarten paste.'

She glanced up at him then. 'We need you to keep the gel and the ball to yourself. It's important. Who else knows about it?'

'Just me and Zell,' he said. 'And Barlow. And the captain.'

'And Carrie and Gabe,' Jeff added from behind them, then shrugged when Olivia turned a mild glare on him. 'I didn't know, and Dave's catch was too good not to tell.'

'Carrie and Gabe are on our team,' David told her when she turned the mild glare from Jeff to him. 'They can keep a secret.'

'So can I,' Jeff said, aggrieved. 'When I know I have to.'

'Can we talk to Carrie and Gabe?' Kane asked. 'We need to keep it under wraps.'

'Certainly,' Casey said. 'They're walking line. I'll call them back to the truck.'

'I'll talk to the other firefighters,' Kane told Olivia, 'while you go up. Have fun.'

The glare she flashed Kane was a lot less mild, David thought. She was clearly annoyed and once again seemed none too happy to see him. That did not bode well.

David climbed to where the platform rested on the front end of the truck and lowered the bucket until it was two feet from the ground where she waited. There was no expression on her face, but her foot tapped impatiently. He extended his hand and after the briefest hesitation she grabbed it, not looking at him.

He hauled her up and held on until she'd steadied herself. 'You have to belt in,' he said. Silently she raised her arms and he looped the ladder belt around her slim waist, trying hard not to fumble the hooks. Or lift his eyes to stare at her breasts which were throwing a shadow on his hands. He tugged to test the connection, then rose, keeping his eyes to himself, very aware of Jeff's smirk and Kane's watchful gaze. 'You're good.'

'Okay,' she said, her voice slightly breathless. 'Take me up.'

Oh, I will, he thought. He wasn't sure when it would be or how he would manage it, but those recollections of his were just clear enough that he knew he had to have her again. 'Are you bothered by heights?'

'No.' Her attention was on the condo wall as he toggled switches, lifting them in the air. After rising ten feet, she looked up at him, surprised. 'I thought it would be jumpy.'

'No, it's pretty smooth.' They were alone now, the two of them rising in a three-by-four space. He briefly fantasized standing behind her, grabbing the rails on either side of her, caging her in. Pressing against her. Feeling her against him. But of course he couldn't do that, so he stood at her side, contenting himself with breathing honeysuckle.

There were so many things he wanted to ask. *What's between you and Barlow? Is there someone else?* And the million-dollar question – *why did you leave my bed?*

But this wasn't the time for any of that, so he asked the one question in his mind that wasn't personal. 'What's the significance of the ball I found?'

For a moment he thought she wouldn't answer. Then she sighed. 'You'll probably just Google it when you get home.'

'Before I get home,' he said. 'Left my laptop back at the firehouse.'

'You can't speak of this, not even to your partner.'

'Zell?' David found his lips curving. 'He's a good guy, but he does have trouble keeping a secret. I won't tell him. Cross my heart.' And he did.

Her eyes had dropped to his bare hand and lingered a beat too long before lifting again to his face. Her cheeks were a shade pinker than they had been. 'Environmental arson,' she said, throwing cold water on his thoughts. 'It's a glass globe. A radical activist group left similar etched glass globes at their fires more than ten years ago.'

'Shit,' he breathed quietly. 'But they shot that guard. Right in the heart. Those groups don't normally target people.'

'Not normally, although this group had an accidental death, twelve years ago.'

He thought of the girl, her waxen face. Her fight to escape. 'Like last night.'

'Maybe. The girl held the ball. For now we have to include her with the suspects.'

He shook his head. 'She wasn't dressed for arson. She wasn't even wearing shoes. Barlow ran the sniffer over her. Nothing. No hydrocarbons on her hands.'

She assessed him. 'True. But she had the ball. We have to find out how and why.'

'Has this radical group claimed credit?'

'Not yet, and they always did twelve years ago.'

'Maybe because they killed two people,' David said harshly and her eyes softened.

'Maybe. We're probably going to have to bring in the Feds at some point. They'll want to talk to you. Just a heads-up.'

'Thanks.' They'd risen to the fourth floor and he stopped their ascent. 'This is where I found her.'

She leaned forward, squinting. 'I don't see any handprints.'

David switched on the spotlight and aimed it at the window. 'Now?'

She stared a minute, then shook her head. 'No.'

Thank you, he whispered in his mind, then stepped

behind her, taking her shoulders in both hands. Lowering his head until his chin brushed her hair, he adjusted their angle until he could see the shimmer. 'There,' he murmured. 'See it now?'

She'd stiffened in his hands and it was when she drew a shaky breath that he realized she hadn't been breathing before. Which did bode well.

'You saw *that*?' she asked, her voice gone husky, and a thrill raced across his skin. She cleared her throat and when she spoke again, it was briskly. Still, he'd heard the awareness in her voice. It was enough. It was what he'd been waiting for. 'Barlow's right,' she said matter-of-factly. 'You do have good eyes.'

A faint buzz of pride layered over the thrill. 'It was easier to see in the dark.'

She leaned forward and he let her go, stepping back to her side. 'Can you get us closer?' she asked, pointing. 'To that smear?'

He maneuvered until the rail was an inch from where she pointed. 'Close enough?'

She looked up at him, a wry smile on her lips. 'Now you're just showing off.' Before he could think of an answer, she pulled the camera from the bag around her neck. 'We need to get this window to the lab,' she said, snapping a picture.

It was his turn to lean closer until he saw what she'd pointed to – a small dent in the impact-resistant glass, with barely discernible lines spidering outward. 'You saw *that*?'

'I've got good eyes, too,' she said lightly. 'I also knew what I was looking for.'

'What?'

'I thought about her not wearing shoes. If she'd been

one of the arsonists, she would have worn shoes she could get away quickly in. Boots. Sneakers at the very least. But she didn't wear shoes *and* she held the ball. Why? She was about five-four, same as me.' Clutching the camera in one hand, she held it up, pretending to bang it against the window. 'Dent's right where it should be.'

He understood. 'She tried to use the glass ball to break the window. There was no furniture yet, no chairs, nothing she could use to break the glass. God. Poor kid.'

'I know,' she said. 'Barlow said the arsonists poured the carpet adhesive on the first and second floors.'

'True. I could show you the pour patterns if you want.'

'On the way down.' She crossed her arms, dangling the camera from her wrist as she frowned at the window. 'If the arsonists only hit the first two floors and she was up here on four, and she wasn't with them, how did she get the damn ball?'

'We think they poured on two floors, but started the fire on the first floor. That way they could get out. If they lit both floors, it could have spread before they were out.'

'Do we know how they got in and out?'

'Not that I know of. You'd have to ask Barlow.' He considered the night before. 'We got here about five minutes after we got the call. We had to smash through the gate, so it delayed us another two minutes. The first two floors were fully engaged at the time, and it wasn't safe to go in through any of the doors. We were fighting it from outside. That's what I was doing in the bucket in the first place.'

She still faced the window, but her frown had become thoughtful. 'Okay. And?'

'The fire doors on one and two were open. The smoke would have filled the stairwell. If she'd been squatting on one of the lower levels . . .' He thought about the hearing aid. 'And if she wasn't able to hear them coming . . .'

'She may have been asleep. Woke up from the smoke, tried to go down the stairs, found herself trapped.' She glanced up at him. 'Would she have been able to get out of the stairwell and into the hallway?'

'Possibly. But the heat would have been intense.'

'Hot enough to blister her feet?'

He remembered the soles of the girl's feet. 'Yeah.'

She nodded, and he could almost see the wheels turning in her mind. 'She would have been panicking,' she murmured. 'Not thinking clearly. Smoke choking her. Maybe she drops to her knees, below the smoke. And somehow she finds the ball.'

'She wouldn't have been able to see anything,' David said, his stomach turning at the thought of how terrified the girl must have been. 'The smoke would have filled the first floors and the stairwell in minutes. If she stumbled on the ball, found it somehow . . .'

Her blond brows lifted. 'Or if they used it to block open one of the fire doors?'

He'd admired her mind the first time they'd met. That much he clearly remembered. 'Possible. So she picks it up, but can't go farther, because it's too hot. The smoke is too thick. She backs up, to the stairwell.'

'Back to the fourth floor. No fire yet on four. She still has the ball. People hold on to weird things when they're scared. She gets to the window, tries to break it.'

'She could have hit it with that ball till kingdom come and that window wouldn't have broken,' David said. 'But I doubt she got more than a few hits in. Her lungs would have already been damaged by the smoke from the stairwell, if that's where she'd gone.'

'Where did you say you found the ball?'

'About two feet from where her fingertips had been. She was lying on her stomach, her arms extended.'

'Her body's angle to the wall?'

'Thirty, forty degrees, maybe.'

'So she tossed the ball, then pounded on the glass with her hands. She was desperate by then.' She studied the prints on the glass. 'She smacked the glass with her palms and pounded with her fists.'

'Probably in the reverse order,' he said quietly. 'Her hands were flattened on the glass when she collapsed to the floor. You can't see them well, but there are streaks from her fingers.'

'Poor kid.' She was silent for a moment while he studied her profile. It had been a long time since he'd been this close to her – two and a half years if he didn't count the minutes she'd sat next to his bed in the hospital after he'd rolled down an embankment in Evie's old Mazda last February. And he didn't count that time as his eye had been too swollen to see clearly. She'd been little more than a hazy image, but he'd known it was her by his bedside as soon as he'd smelled the honeysuckle.

Abruptly she lifted her eyes to his, blue and intense. 'That is one hell of a hole,' she said. 'I'm . . . I'm glad you're okay.'

A fist squeezed his heart and he struggled for what to say. But before he could find the words, she'd turned her gaze toward the lake. 'How high does this bucket go?'

He cleared his throat. 'Hundred feet. We're at about fifty feet now.'

'Can you take me all the way up?'

Sweet God. He sure wanted to try. *Focus, Hunter. Do not blow this again.* 'Yes.' The word came out gruffly, but she didn't seem to notice. 'Why?'

'We were wondering how the girl knew about this place. We don't think she's from around here. You can't see the condo from the road, but you can see it from the lake.'

He lifted the bucket past the roof. 'What are you looking for?'

'Don't know.' She held the camera to her face, searching and snapping photos with the zoom. 'A path through the trees, a hidden boat, something that shows us how she found this place. We should probably get someone on the ground, checking for a path through the woods.'

'You could try dogs.'

She lowered the camera, looking up at him. 'To track her?' A new light filled her eyes. 'It might work.' She jumped a little. 'Cell phone. Can you hold these?' She handed him the black bag with the binoculars and grabbed for her cell. 'Sutherland.'

Her little smile disappeared as she listened. 'We'll be there in thirty minutes.'

'Problem?' he asked when she hung up.

'ME. He has something on the girl. Can you take us down?'

'Sure.' He started their descent, debating his next words, filling his senses with honeysuckle while he could. 'Olivia.'

She stiffened and he realized it was the first time he'd said her name that morning. 'Yes?' she asked, her gaze focused on the lake.

Look at me. Give me something. Please.

Then he watched her draw a deep breath and let it out. Only her head turned, her eyes meeting his. 'Yes?' she asked again.

'I . . .' *Say it*. But years of fruitless waiting for the wrong woman had dulled his skills when it came to the woman who just might be the right one. 'I need to talk to you,' he blurted. 'But not here, where everyone can hear.'

She stared at him, then after what seemed like an eternity, nodded, just once. 'I'll call you when I get a break later. When are you off shift?'

Relief swamped him. At least she hadn't said no. So whatever he'd done, it couldn't have been that bad . . . right? 'About two hours ago. I'm on OT now.'

The bucket reached the ground and she unhooked the belt herself, looking for Kane who stood next to the captain ten feet from the truck. 'Kane, Ian called. He wants us at the morgue. I told him thirty.' She hopped down from the bucket gracefully. Her knees bent and for a moment she hung there, then straightened like a gymnast sticking a landing. 'Thanks for the view. I'll be in touch,' she said briskly.

Still in the bucket, David watched as she strode to her car, Kane ambling behind her. She didn't look back, not once. It wasn't until Kane's car had disappeared through the front gate that he realized she'd never reclaimed her binoculars.

He pocketed them. That had gone far better than he'd expected.

Chapter Five

'A question, Mr Marsh?'

Eric looked up, stunned to see that the classroom had cleared and his professor stood staring at him. 'No, sir. I'm sorry.'

'Mr Marsh, when you sleep, you snore. When you are awake, you participate. You did neither today, and you arrived fifteen minutes late. Is anything wrong?'

'A girl,' he said, feigning embarrassment. 'I'll have to get the notes from someone.'

'Fine. Just be on time for Wednesday's lecture.'

'I will.' Eric made his escape, then slumped against a wall outside. If anyone got suspicious, the prof would say, *He looked upset, preoccupied*. 'Terrific,' he muttered.

He had to tell the others. This impacted them all. Would they burn another building? Would he tell them about the video? Joel would freak. No telling what the idiot would do.

Albert, he thought, would not be surprised. Albert knew someone else was there, that someone else had murdered the guard. Because they had not.

Like anyone would believe that. 'We are so dead,' he

whispered, then, still slumped against the wall, pulled out his own cell phone. The texter's phone was in his pants pocket, set to vibrate. Couldn't have that bastard chirping at him during lecture.

Meet me outside the library at noon, he typed, then addressed the text to Albert, Joel, and Mary. Before he could hit SEND, his cell vibrated. It was Mary. 'What?'

'Oh God.' Her voice was unsteady, hollow. Scared. 'Did you hear about Joel?'

His dread intensified. *Had Joel told? Damn him.* 'Hear what?'

She sniffled and he realized she was crying. 'He didn't show up for class.'

Eric breathed a sigh of relief. *Is that all?* Mary was overreacting, as usual. Eric hadn't wanted to include her from the beginning, but Joel had insisted. Being around Mary always left Eric feeling hyped up and edgy. He'd never understood why Joel was so stuck on her. The sex must be good. 'He's probably holed up in his room.'

'No. He's dead.' Her voice broke. 'Joel is dead.'

Eric felt the air leave his lungs. *Wow. Albert worked fast.* 'How?' he asked.

'He was in his car, on his way to school.' She was sobbing now. 'He ran off the road, hit a tree. He went through the windshield. He bled to death.'

'Hell.' He'd told Albert to make it so that it wasn't painful. That sounded pretty damn painful. But it was done. And they'd have to live with that, too.

Better a guilty conscience than life behind bars.

But now Joel wouldn't be available tonight. All of them had to participate or the video would be leaked. *I should have told Albert*, he thought grimly. *We needed Joel.*

Maybe the texter would accept a note. *Please excuse Joel*

95

from any extortion-related arsons, as he is dead. Eric closed his eyes. Frickin' unbelievable.

'Who told you?' he asked.

'His sister called me. His . . . his parents didn't know about us. Joel said they wouldn't have approved. But his sister knew about me and knew I needed to know. But don't say anything to the Fischers. I don't want to get his sister in trouble.'

Joel's parents were Orthodox Jews. Mary was Irish Catholic. That they wouldn't approve was expected. That Joel hid his and Mary's relationship . . . well, Eric had known Joel since kindergarten, and that wasn't surprising either. *I should be crying, too*, he thought. *I should feel something*. But all he felt was weary dread. This whole mess was Joel's idea. So in a way, it was kind of his fault.

'We need to meet. The three of us. Library. Noon.'

'I can't,' she said numbly. 'I've got class.'

'Skip it,' he snapped. 'This is important.' He hung up. He had choices to make. Hard ones. To torch a stranger's warehouse or risk prison? To tell the others or not?

They could flee. Leave the country. They could be in Canada in less than three hours. From there . . . wherever people go who are fleeing the cops. *To whatever country doesn't have an extradition treaty with the United States*. He needed money. He needed new ID. He needed to buy some more time. But he had only thirteen hours.

Maybe the texter wouldn't follow through. Why wouldn't he? He had nothing to lose. *And I have everything to lose*.

Eric dug into his pants pocket and flipped open the disposable cell, checking the warehouse address again, even though he remembered it perfectly.

Who owned it? Were they good or bad? Maybe the owner had done something horrible. So horrible that taking out his warehouse might be doing a public service.

And I am lying to myself. I need to buy some time. Torching the stranger's warehouse would buy him that time. As long as no more people got hurt, it was just stuff. Stuff could be replaced. That's what insurance was for.

Hadn't he said that himself just yesterday? Yesterday when they were still environmental avengers? God. How had things gone so wrong?

He couldn't think about that. Now he needed information about the stranger whose warehouse would be ashes by midnight tonight. He needed to find a way to convince Albert and Mary that they were doing the right thing. He needed to buy some time.

Monday, September 20, 10:55 A.M.

Olivia was steady by the time she and Kane walked into the morgue, but David's voice still filled her head. *I need to talk to you.* About what? Why he'd been hiding for seven months? Or would he go for the tried-and-true *It's not you, Olivia, it's me*?

She'd kept it together in that bucket. Having him that close was a dream and a nightmare, all rolled into one. But she hadn't turned to goo, even when he'd put his hands on her shoulders and whispered in her ear. Even when he'd said her name, all husky and sexy. The man exuded sex. So considering, she'd done okay. Held her own.

'Liv?' Kane was regarding her with an amused, if pained, expression. 'Either put him out of your mind or go home and take a cold shower. You're making me think about going home for a very long lunch break with my wife.'

Her cheeks heated. 'Sorry.'

He patted her shoulder. 'Have Ian take you into the freezer. That'll cool your jets.'

'Who needs to go in the freezer?' ME Ian Gilles came out of his office.

'Nobody,' Olivia said firmly. 'So, what do you have?'

'Gold,' Ian said. 'Come on, have a look.' He led them to the light board, where an X-ray was mounted. 'The girl's skull.'

Olivia's heart started to beat faster as a puzzle piece fell into place. There was a distinctive dark, tombstone-shaped patch about the size of a half-dollar, just behind the girl's ear. 'Is that what I think it is?'

Ian looked a little disappointed. 'Depends on what you think it is.'

She looked up at Kane. 'David Hunter and his partner didn't find a hearing aid. Not exactly anyway. Our girl had a cochlear implant. What he saw was the processor.'

'What's a processor?' Kane asked.

'It's a . . . device . . .' Olivia groped for the words. 'It converts sounds . . . Explain, Ian.'

Ian perked up, his disappointment dissipating. 'The processor is worn behind the ear and converts sound into electrical signals. The signals are passed to the implant, here.' He tapped the bone behind his ear. 'The implant bypasses the normal auditory systems, stimulating the aural nerves. It's pretty cool. How do you know about it, Liv?'

'My friend has one. You know her, Kane. Brie Franconi. We just talked about her.'

'The lady who runs the doggy day care?' Kane asked.

'She used to be a cop, but lost her hearing. Ended up having to quit the force, start another career. She got the implant about two years ago.' She turned to Ian. 'So there will be a serial number on the implant part, right? Because the processor was so melted, it was almost unidentifiable.'

'Here it is.' Ian handed her a sticky note with the name of a manufacturer and the serial number written on it. 'I had this big buildup planned. Gee, thanks.'

Olivia patted his arm. 'I'm sorry. But this is really great. Thank you.'

'You're welcome. Don't run off,' he said when they started to. 'There's more.'

They followed him into the autopsy suite. The bodies here didn't bother her like they did in the field. By the time they got here, she'd gone through the panic.

The girl lay on the table, a sheet covering her from neck to knees. The soot had been washed from her hair and her face was ghastly white under the glaring lights.

'So young,' Kane murmured.

'Probably sixteen,' Ian said. 'Cause of death was smoke inhalation. Londo said he pointed out what appeared to be recent abuse trauma. Her X-rays showed fractures to her right arm and some damage to her left hand. She'd also been drinking last night. Her blood alcohol was point-oh-nine. She'd eaten tacos very shortly before the fire.'

'If she got food locally,' Olivia said, 'we might track her last hours.'

'Or her partner's,' Ian said. 'She'd had sex very shortly before death. Within an hour, quite probably less.'

Olivia frowned. 'Somebody was in there with her?' she said. 'Having sex?'

'I take it you haven't found another body,' Ian said.

'Not yet, but the first two floors are still a mess,' Kane said. Then he winced. 'What about the guard?'

Ian shook his head and both Olivia and Kane breathed fast sighs of relief. 'Wrong blood type. Plus, Henry Weems had a vasectomy ten years ago. Came through on his chart. The girl didn't use a condom, and her partner had a very high sperm count.'

'Oh, good,' Olivia said. 'I'd hate to have to break that to Mrs Weems.'

'On the other hand,' Kane said, 'we're either looking for another body or . . .'

'Or her partner got away.' Olivia's pulse kicked up. 'If he got out, we could have an eyewitness out there.'

'When she fell, she hit her knees.' Ian pulled the sheet back, revealing bruises on the girl's knees. 'She also has a slightly sprained ankle. She could have fallen and gotten separated from this other person.'

'David said the smoke would have been so thick she couldn't see, and she couldn't hear her partner, as she didn't have her processor on. Getting separated makes sense.'

'Is it possible the guy she had sex with is the arsonist?' Kane asked. 'That maybe he held her there against her will and set the fire with her there on purpose?'

Ian shrugged. 'Anything is possible, but the victim had no vaginal bruising or tearing, so it doesn't appear the sex was forced. The initial urine screen didn't show any of the typical drugs, and her BA wasn't high enough to incapacitate her. Of course, the blood tox may come back with something. I'll have that tomorrow morning.'

'What about the guy she had sex with?' Kane asked.

'Caucasian, dark hair. He left behind some pubic hair. Also, if they were together when the fire started, he may have some lung impairment from the smoke. It may be mild or severe, depending on how long he was exposed. You should check anyone admitted to hospitals for fluid in the lungs. It can sneak up after smoke exposure.'

'At a minimum, he could be very shaken up,' Olivia said.

'If he's still alive,' Kane countered. 'If he got caught in those flames, the firefighters could have walked right through his remains and not known.'

'What about the guard?' Olivia asked. 'Please tell me he was sober.'

'As a judge. Blood alcohol was zero, urine was clean. I'll do his exam after lunch.'

'Is that him?' Olivia asked, pointing at another sheet-covered body on a gurney parked off to the side of the room.

'No, that's a car accident victim, brought in this morning. Kid wasn't wearing a seat belt. Not much left of his face after going through the windshield. Don't worry. Your guy comes first,' Ian said when Olivia started to ask. 'I'll call you when I know anything.'

Olivia held up the sticky note with the implant's serial number. 'Thank you. Really. Now we can get an ID.'

Monday, September 20, 11:30 A.M.

David knew he should be tired, but he was not. A fine energy sizzled over his skin, one that had nothing to do with the rush of walking into a fire and coming out unscathed. No, this was an awareness that he stood on the verge of something important.

Something vital. If he played his cards right, he might end up with something he'd never found, but always craved. Something he probably still didn't deserve.

My own home. My own family. A wife, kids . . . all the things his family and friends had found, one at a time. As the years rolled by, he'd become the odd man out. The only one still single. The only one still alone.

He'd stayed in Chicago too long, watching while the woman he'd dreamed about for years got married and started a family with someone else. He'd tried to find someone to take her place. But there had been no one who came close.

Until one April night, two and a half years ago, when Olivia tumbled into his arms at her sister's rehearsal dinner. *And you had to go and blow it.* Well, tonight he had the opportunity to fix whatever it was that had made her run. He wouldn't fuck it up again.

He unlocked the front door to his apartment house. The walls in the entryway would be next on the paint list, he thought, looking around as he did every time he entered. But each time he entered, the place looked a little better. All it had needed was some 'sprucing,' as his mother would say.

He'd bought the old building on something of a whim seven months before. His old friend Evie had lived here before finding her own happy ending, which she so richly deserved. Seven months ago, she'd asked him for help with her leaky roof. He'd fixed the leaks, then decided to stay, for a lot of reasons. The biggest of which was the way his chest had gone tight when Olivia had walked into his hospital room after the car he'd been driving had been forced from the road by a psycho killer. That day in the hospital, it had been two years since he'd seen her. He'd almost convinced himself he'd dreamed her and the night they'd had together.

But the moment he'd smelled honeysuckle, he'd known it was real.

So he'd decided to stay, to start over. To build something that was his own. In the last seven months he'd more than 'spruced' this old building, gradually turning his ten apartments into showpieces urban professionals would jump to own – which had been his plan. Fix it, flip it, go on to the next. He looked at the names neatly stenciled on the row of antique oak mailboxes and had to smile.

It hadn't worked out exactly as he'd planned, but he found he liked the way it had ended up a lot better. He jogged up the three flights of stairs to his loft apartment, thinking about the kitchen tiling project he'd left half done. He could put a big dent in it while he waited for Olivia to call. He needed to keep busy, or he'd lose his mind.

'David?' It was a small voice, sounding more like a child than the mother of one. Unfortunately, Lacey was both.

He looked over the rail to the second-floor landing to where the young woman stood, a baby in her arms. 'Hey, Lace. What's up?'

'It's the refrigerator. It's not cold. I know you're just getting off shift, and I wouldn't have said anything, but Mrs Edwards said you needed to know. Sorry.'

'No, it's okay.' He walked down one flight of stairs and into the apartment he hadn't quite finished rehabbing, although it was livable. Toys littered the floor, and cases of baby formula were stacked against one wall. But the place was clean, even though at the moment it smelled faintly of baby puke. Mrs Edwards ran a tight ship on which each of her young mothers was responsible for the chores, but even Mrs Edwards couldn't keep babies from spitting up.

David opened the refrigerator and sighed. It was broken. 'Your groceries will spoil.'

Lacey ducked her head. 'Can you fix it?'

'No. This fridge has been ready for the junkyard. I've got a new one ready to put in, but I wanted to do the tile on the floor first. I can get the new fridge here by tomorrow, but we're going to need to move your stuff upstairs until then. Where is Mrs Edwards?'

'Elly had a doctor's appointment and Tiffany doesn't have her license yet, so Mrs E had to drive them.' Lacey sighed dramatically. 'Tiffany failed the drivers' test again.'

David winced. 'Again? What's wrong with Elly?'

'Nothing, just a well-baby exam. And shots.'

'Good.' He put out his hands and without hesitation, she placed her baby in them. Lacey's little boy was precious. 'Did you get the job at Martino's?'

Lacey smiled. 'Yeah. I have to work nights, but the tips are good and I can still do my GED classes during the day. Thanks for the good word you put in for me. It helped.'

As if picking up on his mother's sudden mood change, the baby giggled, making David grin. The kid had an infectious laugh, making him miss his own nieces and nephews. He kissed the baby's chubby cheek and handed him back to Lacey.

'Anytime.' Martino's was an Italian place run by the family of one of the firefighters on B shift at the firehouse. 'They'll treat you right there. I'll get your perishables up to my fridge. Mrs Edwards has a key if I have to leave.' *If Olivia calls, I am out of here.*

A few minutes later he was standing at his front door, juggling grocery bags while trying to get his key in his lock. He leaned against his door, stumbling when it opened, revealing a woman sitting at his dining-room table, a coffee cup in one hand. For a moment he stared, then he felt the smile crack his face.

'Ma?'

She set the cup down with a clatter and was across the room, opening her arms. 'I missed you,' she whispered, hugging him fiercely.

'I missed you, too,' he said and she backed away, dabbing at her eyes.

'Let me look at you,' she said, so he dropped the grocery bags on the table and obligingly held out his arms. She looked him up and down and nodded, satisfied.

'What are you doing here, Ma?' he asked. 'I'm glad to see you, but I wasn't expecting you for two weeks. I'm not ready for decorating yet. I was going to call you when I got all the floors done.'

His mother had an eye for color and she'd been itching to help with his building rehab. He'd promised she could pick out carpet and drapes and furniture and all the knickknacks that made the house he'd grown up in a real home.

'Grace started preschool,' she said. 'My last grandbaby is in school and I didn't have anything to do with my mornings. So I came to see you.'

'You should have called. I'd have left you a key or met you at the airport.'

She frowned mildly. 'I drove myself from Chicago. I'm not as old as you think.'

'That she is not,' a voice boomed from the kitchen and David turned, surprised. He'd heard the voice of his first-floor tenant but saw no body to go with it.

'Glenn? What the hell are you doing in my apartment?'

'David,' his mother admonished. 'Mr Redman had a key. He let me in.'

'I'm not mad he's here. I'm mad he's down there.' David went around the counter and looked down to where Glenn

105

Redman sat on the floor, meticulously lining up tiles, the light from the bare bulb reflecting off his shiny bald head. 'Are you all right?'

Redman gave him a sour glare. 'I'm fine. I know what I can do.'

'Famous last words,' David said, just as sourly. Then he looked at the tile the old man had arranged in a precise geometric design. 'Not bad.'

'It's damn good, boy,' Redman huffed. 'Better than you were doing. Admit it.'

'Okay. I admit it. Thank you.'

'Was that so hard?' Redman held out a hand and David pulled him to his feet, holding on until the older man was steady. He was on the tail end of what had been a long series of chemo, and his prognosis was good, but he still didn't have the energy he'd had when David first met him at the firehouse, seven months ago. That was just weeks before the doctors discovered Glenn's tumor and just a month before he became David's first paying tenant. Of course, payment was a relative thing.

David's apartment house was ideally located near the hospital, while Redman's retirement cabin was too far for him to easily get to his chemo treatments. So they'd made a trade. While Redman lived here, David got use of the cabin and its lake full of walleye. Both were happy with the arrangement.

'Nope, wasn't hard to admit at all. I hate tile work,' David said then looked at his mom. 'Don't believe anything he says, Ma. He's a consummate liar.'

She was looking through his grocery bags. 'Why do you have filled baby bottles?'

Redman held out his hand, looking satisfied. 'Ten.'

Narrowing his eyes, David pulled out his wallet and

smacked a ten-dollar bill into the old man's hand. 'Don't gloat. Glenn bet me that the refrigerator in 2A wouldn't last another week. I hoped it would last until I got the floor done.'

She pushed him gently out of the way and began putting the girls' groceries in his fridge. 'There are babies in 2A, I take it.'

'Damn revolving door,' Glenn grumbled. 'Mrs Edwards takes in unwed mothers.'

'He plays with the babies when he thinks nobody's looking,' David said.

'You've got yourself quite a full house,' his mother said. 'All those names on the mailboxes downstairs surprised me. I didn't think I'd find anyone living here yet.'

David shrugged. 'It wasn't my plan either. But people needed a place. I have room. It didn't seem right to say no.'

'Boy's a damn pushover,' Glenn grumbled.

His mother smiled. 'Where can I sleep, son? You don't have much furniture.'

Just a bed. Because he'd really, really hoped Olivia would call. 'I was waiting to let you pick everything out. You can have my bed. I've got an air mattress and—'

'David? David, are you here?' It was a new voice at his open front door, one that sounded abnormally upset. Moments later a tall, raven-haired beauty stood in his kitchen doorway, eyes narrowed. 'I need to talk to you. Now. Please.'

His mother looked at Glenn, who shrugged. 'Never seen this one,' Glenn said.

'Mom, this is Paige Holden. Paige, this is my mother and Glenn. Paige is from the dojo and is normally very polite.' David frowned at her. 'Why aren't you being polite?'

Paige drew a deep breath. 'It's a pleasure to meet you both. I'm sorry I barged in. I didn't know David had company.'

His mother looked fascinated. 'I'm always glad to meet my son's friends.'

'And that's all she is, Mom,' David inserted before his mother could get the wrong idea. 'Paige and I are friends and sparring partners. She kicks my ass every Tuesday and Thursday when I'm not on shift.'

'So you're a black belt, too?' his mother asked and Paige nodded.

'Yes, ma'am. David helps me with a self-defense class I teach. He's our *uke*.'

'The attacker,' David explained. 'Then her students get to kick my ass.'

Paige's brows lifted. 'One puts a great deal of *trust* in one's *uke*,' she said meaningfully. 'You trust him with your safety. You expect him to be *honest*.'

'I see,' his mother said. 'You obviously have something on your mind, so Glenn and I will put this food away, and the two of you can talk.'

'Thank you.' Puzzled, David led her back to his empty spare bedroom and closed the door. 'What the hell, Paige?' he asked, all pretense of politeness gone.

She jabbed her fists to her hips. 'You *used* me. You jerk.'

'How did I use you?'

'Olivia came into the gym this morning. Really early, so she could avoid me.'

David winced. 'It's been a while since she's been to the gym.'

'Which you know because you've been reading the sign-in sheets. Rudy told me. He also told me you'd asked

108

about Olivia and that he told you we were old friends.'

'Rudy's a weasel,' David muttered and her ruby lips twitched, but just once.

'That's what Olivia said this morning because Rudy told me she'd come in.' Her expression darkened. 'Goddammit, you *know* her. And I mean that in the *biblical* sense. You knew I knew her and you never said a word. Did you join my dojo just to use me to get to her?'

In the biblical sense. Based on his vague recollections, that was quite possibly the truth. 'It's not what you think.' He sighed. 'I met Olivia at a wedding.'

'I know. Her sister Mia's wedding two and a half years ago. After which the biblical knowing ensued.' Her voice rose. 'After which you never called her.'

'Quiet,' he hissed. 'My mother has ears like a damn bat. I met Olivia at the rehearsal dinner. I was sitting on the steps of the church, putting off going inside.'

Her eyes narrowed suspiciously. 'Why?'

'Because it was one more wedding I'd leave alone.'

Paige's look turned skeptical. 'Now you want me to believe you have trouble getting a woman. You? Mr Perfect, who's too nice to possibly be true? Please.'

His laugh was mirthless. 'Look at you. You're gorgeous. You're nice. Usually. Do *you* have a good man?'

Her shoulders sagged. 'Point taken, thank you very much. But *I'm* fucked up.'

'Well, honey, you're not the only one,' he said bitterly. 'We all have our issues.'

She considered this. 'Fair enough. So why did you glom onto me? Why me?'

'Evie took your self-defense class and she said you were good, so I came to the dojo to meet you. I liked it there, so I joined. I didn't know you knew Olivia, not at first.'

'Olivia recommended my class to Eve,' Paige said and he could see she believed him. 'So we're caught up in a circle of friends. But then you went all spy-guy. Why?'

'I saw Olivia's name on the sign-in sheet at the gym and was surprised, so I asked Rudy. He said she came in regularly, that the two of you are friends. So I let things go where they would. I kept an eye on the sign-in sheet and Rudy kept me filled in.'

Her brows lifted. 'He really is a weasel.'

'I prefer "confidential informant,"' he said and her lips twitched. 'What?'

'That's what I said to Liv. So you met her at a wedding, were obviously taken with her, you two did the horizontal shuffle, and then you don't *call*? That's not nice, David.'

'She left me,' David protested. 'I woke up and she was gone. No note, no nothing. And I did call, but the number I found in the online phone book had been changed.'

'She moved right about that time. You could have asked her sister for her number.'

David thought about Olivia's sister, Mia, who was one of the few who'd known how hopelessly he'd fallen for someone else. 'That was . . . complicated.'

'You slept with Mia, too?' she asked, her voice rising to a shriek.

'Goddammit,' he hissed. 'Be quiet. I did not sleep with Mia, too. I may not even have slept with Olivia. Whatever happened between Olivia and me is our business. I hoped she'd call and figured when she didn't that she regretted what happened.'

'Which she says she does.'

David lifted his brows. 'And does she?'

'You'll have to ask her. Why did you come to Minneapolis? I want the truth.'

He sighed. 'Evie needed help fixing her roof. I'd been looking for some kind of . . . I don't know, a sign or something. I get here and Evie gets attacked, then I get run off the road by that psycho and Olivia's the cop on the case.'

'Hell of a sign,' Paige said.

'Yeah. I should have left Chicago a long time ago. There was a woman named Dana . . .'

Her mouth drooped sadly. 'She died?'

'No. She met someone else.' And he'd thought he'd never live through it.

She sighed. 'Been there, done that. And?'

'And nothing. Dana was happy with this other guy. She never knew how I felt, and she never felt the same. I walked away. Just not far enough. Our families are all . . . connected. Birthdays, anniversaries, holidays. I had to see her all the time.'

'I know that name,' Paige said. 'Dana was in the wedding, too. I saw her picture.'

'She was Mia's matron of honor. I was glad I didn't know Mia's fiancé well enough to be asked to be the best man.'

'That would have sucked.'

Paige had a way with understatement. 'True,' he said. 'I'd been looking for a way out of Chicago for a while, but my job was there. My family. Evie gave me the shove I needed to make the move.' She'd dared him to stop hiding from the world, to stop watching other people be happy. And she'd been right.

'So after two years, you moved here. Why didn't you call Liv for seven months?'

'Because Olivia was digging bodies out of that psycho's lime pit, informing all those families. Evie would tell me how withdrawn Olivia was becoming, so I watched her for a few weeks. I wanted to see if she looked better, less stressed. I wanted to walk up to her front door and' – he drew a breath – 'take up where we left off. But she looked worse as the weeks passed, and there was never a good time. Look, Evie told her I'd bought this place. I figured if she didn't call, she didn't want to take up where we'd left off. So I waited. I could be patient.'

'Seven months?' Paige shook her head. 'Not even you're that patient. I want the *truth*.'

He closed his eyes. He wasn't certain he could handle the truth. 'The truth is, I don't remember much of that night.'

'Yeah, right. You remember everything you've ever seen or read. You have a photographic memory. How could you possibly not remember that night?'

'I had too much to drink at the reception. I never get drunk. Never.' A memory jabbed at him. He hadn't gotten drunk since that night nearly twenty years ago. A night that ruined so many lives. A night for which he'd done penance ever since, but all the good deeds in the world would never bring the dead back to life. 'I don't know why Olivia ran. *I don't know what I did*.'

'Can I give you some advice?' she said softly.

He opened his eyes, found hers warm again. 'Why not?'

'Olivia can take whatever demons you've got burning you from the inside out. Tell her the truth. Let her decide if you can take up where you left off. David, you can't take care of everyone. By trying to protect her, you did the exact opposite. You hurt her.'

'I never meant to. She said she'd talk to me.'

'Good. Don't fuck it up again.' She leaned up and kissed his cheek. 'Good luck, David. Trust yourself.'

He shook his head. 'I can't. It's too important.'

'You have to. I'll see you tomorrow at the dojo. And don't worry.' She made a locking motion across her lips. 'I won't tell. Gotta get back. My lunch break is over.'

Chapter Six

'You are batshit crazy,' Albert said, backing away, palms out. 'No fucking way.'

Mary sat on the grass in front of the library, her eyes red-rimmed. 'Eric, Joel's dead. How can you even suggest such a thing, now of all times?'

Joel's death had actually given him the argument he needed to convince the others to help him torch the texter's target. *Just this one*, he thought. *Tomorrow, we run.*

When do you tell them about the video so they know they need to run?

Tonight. After the job is done.

The warehouse belonged to a guy named Tomlinson who sold plumbing fixtures but who had to have done something bad to be a target of blackmail and arson.

'Albert, come over here and stop pacing like a tiger. People will notice.' Eric sat down next to Mary and patted her hand. 'Look, Tomlinson's warehouse was next on Joel's list.' Which was so totally not true, but fortunately Joel was not there to refute it.

'He sells plumbing fixtures. What does he have to do

114

with wetlands or habitat?' Mary asked. 'Joel never mentioned Tomlinson to me.'

'He mentioned him to me, lots of times,' Eric lied smoothly. 'Tomlinson's an investor in KRB, Inc. One of the bigger investors, in fact.' Of course he was not. But he didn't expect either Mary or Albert to know how to double-check him. 'If KRB goes forward with their project, it'll be with money this guy gives them.'

'You're batshit crazy,' Albert mumbled again. 'Doing another one, after last night?'

'It's the perfect time,' Eric said. 'Look at it this way. Who knows what Joel told his parents or what they may have suspected? He goes home upset. He's been going on about saving the wetlands and there's a fire. You all took showers, but his clothes still smelled like smoke. The Fischers aren't stupid. If we never do another, they'll think Joel did the condo fire. If we strike again, they'll know Joel had nothing to do with it.'

'They'll suspect you,' Albert said stonily. 'You were his friend.'

Hell of a friend. I gave the order to have him killed. 'No, they won't suspect me,' he said flatly. 'Mr Fischer used to say I had no imagination. No passion. Just a number cruncher. He'd laugh about it. Say I was the one safe person to have around Joel. That I kept him from running off half-cocked to do his causes.'

'How could this happen?' Mary lamented. 'Joel was upset when I dropped him off last night, but he wasn't . . . you know.'

'No, what?' Albert asked.

'Suicidal,' she said. 'The road was dry. It was daylight. I think he ran off the road deliberately. If I'd thought he'd hurt himself, I never would have left him.'

115

Eric didn't dare look at Albert. 'It was an accident, just like the girl. Nobody meant for the girl to get hurt. It was an accident.'

Mary covered her face with her hands. 'I can't watch the news. I couldn't stand knowing her name. I keep trying to forget her, but I see her there, screaming.'

A shiver slithered down Eric's spine. The image hadn't left his mind either. But at least Mary wasn't watching the news, so she hadn't heard about the guard yet.

'Mary, listen. Think about what had Joel so fired up. What had you fired up. Those wetlands. Our earth. We wanted to keep one corner of our earth . . . safe.' He oozed sincerity. He was choking on it. Yesterday he'd believed every word. Today he just wanted it to be over. 'We stopped them, but only temporarily. With Tomlinson's money, they'll rebuild. Bigger, maybe. That means all of our sacrifice was for nothing. Joel would have died in vain. You don't want that, do you?'

Mary shook her head. 'No,' she whispered.

'He would have wanted this,' Eric murmured. 'You know it. We owe it to him.'

She went very still. 'What do we do?' she whispered.

Eric wanted to blow out a relieved breath but kept it in. 'Meet in the parking lot, same place as before. Tomlinson has a guard dog. We'll need to bring some steak with some sleeping powder on it. Just to make him sleep, Mary,' he added when she flinched. 'I had some muscle relaxants, but they expired a long time ago.'

'I have some sleeping pills,' she murmured. 'Just to make him sleep.'

'Absolutely,' Eric assured her.

She squared her shoulders. 'Joel's burial is tomorrow.'

Eric's brows rose. 'Tomorrow? Oh yeah. That's some Orthodox rule, right?'

'Burial within twenty-four hours. I want to go, but if I go alone his parents will freak. You're going, right? You'll go with me?'

If I'm still in the country. 'Of course. Get some rest. Don't watch the news.'

He watched her go, then turned to Albert. 'You in?'

Albert looked straight ahead. 'What does he have?'

'What does who have?'

A muscle twitched in Albert's taut jaw. 'The guy who shot the guard. He saw us. He's making us do this stupid crime.' His accent became more pronounced, as it always did when he became emotional. Usually Eric found it a turn-on. Not today. 'That's the only explanation for this ridiculous charade. So what does he have on us?'

What was there to say? 'Video. The whole thing. Close-ups of our faces and of the girl's face in the window. You smacking Joel and us dragging him away.'

'So we are now his bitches?' Albert asked bitterly.

'Either that or we run.'

'Where would we run? The world is a very small place.'

Eric attempted a small smile that fell painfully flat. 'France? They don't extradite if there is a possibility of the death penalty. And you do speak the language.'

Albert did not smile. 'This is Minnesota. We'd just go to prison for life.' He turned only his head, spearing Eric with his eyes. 'When did you plan to tell me, *mon ami*?' What had once been an endearment was now a soft snarl.

'Tonight. After we were finished. I needed some time. If you refused, he'd show the video and I'd be trapped.'

'I, I, I,' murmured Albert. 'You took a lot on yourself. When did I get to choose?'

'What would you have done differently, Albert?'

For a moment Albert said nothing. When he spoke, his voice was cold. 'I wouldn't have kept it from you. I'm not going to run. This person, how does he contact you?'

Eric took the cell phone and MP3 player from his pocket. 'He texted me on my cell, then told me where to find these.'

'Tomlinson is not a KRB investor.'

'No.'

'That was not a question, Eric. Did you think I was too stupid to check on this myself? Before I agreed to this scheme of yours, I wanted to be sure you would remain unhurt. I checked the condo investors to be sure your father's company was not among them, that they would take no financial loss. That in your zeal you would not bite the hand that feeds you.'

'And that feeds you, too?' Eric asked bitterly.

Albert's expression remained unmoved. 'Did you not wonder why I went along with you?'

Eric shook his head, not sure he wanted to know. 'I thought you believed.'

'In saving a lake?' Albert scoffed. 'I believed in your future. I thought if you got this . . . obsession out of your system, you'd be able to go on. I wanted to be sure you'd be safe.' This was said stiffly, accusingly. 'So I did what needed to be done.'

'I'm sorry,' Eric said quietly. 'I didn't think.'

'No, you didn't. Now it's my turn to think. Tell me everything you know. Somehow we have to figure out who this blackmailer is.'

'And then?' Eric said.

Albert lifted a shoulder. 'We kill him. What's one more?'

Eric drew a breath, nodded. 'And then?'

'And then, I'm leaving. Find yourself another toy. I'm not interested anymore.'

Monday, September 20, 12:45 P.M.

Abbott leaned against Olivia's desk as she hung up the phone. 'Well?' he asked. 'You get anything from that serial number?'

'The girl's name is Tracey Mullen,' Olivia said, moving her goddess statue to one side so that Abbott didn't knock her fedora to the floor. 'Tracey was sixteen. Her father lives in Council Bluffs, Iowa, and her mother lives in Gainesville, Florida.'

'You were right about the Gators,' Abbott said, then pointed to Kane who was drumming his fingers impatiently, the phone crushed against his ear. 'What's with him?'

'He's talking with Tracey Mullen's father in Iowa, who is deaf. They're using a relay service. Kane speaks, the relay operator types into a TTY, Mr Mullen types back, and the operator reads to Kane. It's a slow process.'

'So what was Tracey Mullen doing in Minneapolis?' Abbott asked.

'We're still sorting it out. I spoke with the mother in Florida, who's hearing and who has custody, but who said Tracey begged to live with her father and go to the deaf school in Iowa. She put Tracey on a plane to dad two days before Labor Day. She thought Tracey was with dad. Dad thought she was with mom. It's not clear why Tracey ran away, but she hasn't been seen since Labor Day. She'd texted both of them, as recently as yesterday morning, indicating she was with the other parent.'

'Did either parent indicate the other was abusive?'

'Mom didn't, but they don't seem to communicate very frequently. Most of their communication went through Tracey. We haven't mentioned the bruises and arm fracture yet. We're going to talk with her teachers and area social workers in both Iowa and Florida to see if anyone noticed anything suspicious. This could take some time.'

'How did the mother sound?'

Olivia shrugged. 'Devastated. Stunned. Angry. She and her new husband are flying up here on the first flight they can get.'

Kane hung up and let out an exhausted breath. 'There has got to be a better way. Dad is on his way. He should be here after dinner. He seemed very upset, especially at his wife for "throwing Tracey out," but going through the operator, it's hard to say.'

'Mom said Tracey begged to live with dad,' Olivia remarked.

'Dad said Tracey hated Florida but never said she'd asked to live with him. It'll be interesting to have them all in the same room. I'll line up a sign-language interpreter.'

'What about the guy she had sex with?' Abbott asked.

'Mom said there was no boyfriend. Tracey was focused on her studies,' Olivia said. 'Whether that was true, mom wanted it to be, or mom was naïve remains to be seen.'

'Dad said Tracey didn't have a boyfriend because her mother forced her to go to hearing school in Gainesville and she was isolated,' Kane said.

Abbott sighed. 'I'll call Jess Donahue. I'm going to want a shrink's take on this family. I thought this girl had the implant, so she could hear.'

'Mom said they hadn't had a lot of success with the implant,' Olivia said. 'Tracey didn't get the surgery until she was ten, after Mrs Mullen got remarried. Her new husband paid for the surgery. Tracey didn't have good success. Not everyone does.'

Abbott smoothed his bushy mustache thoughtfully. 'I'm more concerned with the identity of the male she was with just before the fire started. Focus on him for now.'

'Let's go back out to the lake,' Olivia said, 'and see if anybody saw her there.'

'What's going on with the Feds?' Kane asked.

'I called Special Agent Crawford, but he wasn't in the office. Tried his boss, left a message.' Abbott got up to leave, but Micki breezed in from the elevator.

'I've been trying your phones for an hour.'

'We ID'd the girl,' Olivia said, 'and were talking to her family. What do you have?'

'I ID'd the gel.' Micki pulled up a chair and sank into it. 'Sodium polyacrylate.'

'And now we wait for English,' Kane said.

'Baby-diaper goo,' Micki said, chuckling when they stared. 'Commonly called super-absorbent polymer or SAP. The crystals in baby diapers that do all the absorbing.'

Olivia was starting to feel the tug of fatigue. 'Why?'

'Why coat the glass globe?' Micki asked. 'Turns out SAP is also a fire retardant.'

'Absorbs pee and puts out fires. Can it cure cancer?' Kane asked, tongue in cheek.

'Smart-ass,' Micki said. 'I couldn't find any record of arsonists coating a glass ball in diaper gel. The old SPOT group used ripped-up firefighter coats to keep the glass ball from becoming damaged from the heat.'

'So this isn't SPOT,' Kane said.

'Not necessarily,' Micki said. 'Ultrathin baby diapers were around in SPOT's heyday, but not the knowledge that the gel was fire retardant.'

'Can you track that particular kind of gel?' Olivia asked.

'No,' Micki said. 'That's what I wanted to tell you. This stuff is as accessible as a bag of baby diapers. Which is pretty damn accessible. There's no way to track it, and it's a lot easier to get and cheaper than firefighter coats.'

'Aren't you the bundle of joy?' Abbott asked sourly and she shrugged.

'Sorry. I'm going back to the site. We're processing the scene outside and assisting the arson guys inside.'

'We'll canvass the lake area with Tracey's picture,' Olivia said. 'Back at five.'

Monday, September 20, 1:00 P.M.

He checked his laptop, hidden under the counter. The phone he'd given Eric allowed him to track his movements all over town. Eric was on the move, but not on the run. He'd stopped at a butcher shop. He pictured Eric leaving with some thick steaks he could use to drug Tomlinson's guard dog.

That they hadn't been paranoid enough to have their conversation out of range of the bugged cell phone he'd provided disappointed him. He'd thought Eric smart enough to check for a bugged phone, but Eric was too scared to be smart right now.

That Joel was dead was a bit of a jolt. He wondered if Joel had really killed himself or if they'd already started to turn on one another. He'd put his money on Albert.

So . . . they're planning to kill me. He had to hand it to Albert. Hadn't given the big boy props for that many brains. His plan would never work, of course, but it was better than what Eric had proposed. Run to France. *Idiot.*

But they were obeying him on the Tomlinson warehouse, so at least they were smarter than Tomlinson.

Between customers, he quickly typed in a command and brought up Eric's bank account on his computer screen. Eric had withdrawn a thousand at the bank branch near the university. At least he was smart enough to withdraw from his normal bank and in an amount that wouldn't raise the brows of the teller. Eric routinely withdrew a thousand, and at first he'd been curious as to what the rich boy did with all that money.

Then he'd picked up on Albert and it made sense. Albert talked a good talk about walking away from his affair with Eric, but there was no way a poor kid like Albert was walking away from money like that.

He checked the cell phone he'd activated for Barney Tomlinson. His text to Tomlinson had been simple – *pay or else.*

Tomlinson had been one of the few marks he'd initially misread. He'd thought Barney a smart man, but after his demands had gone ignored, had changed his mind. Obviously Barney hadn't believed he'd follow through on his threats to expose the man's affairs to his wife. Barney Tomlinson had amassed a modest fortune in the last few years, and according to his sources, Mrs Tomlinson had not signed a prenup.

Tomlinson responded to his text this time. *My wife found out. She's divorcing me. What more can you do?*

He smiled. *Oh, a lot*, he thought. *I can do a helluva lot.*

He'd been invisible for so many years that he was used to being ignored in person. He used it to his full advantage, in fact. But to have been ignored in direct communication . . . Well, that was simply rude.

If Tomlinson had simply paid when he'd first asked, the man would have kept the bulk of his fortune, at least initially. Now, not only would Mrs Tomlinson get her share in the divorce, she'd get it all. Insurance would cover the loss of the warehouse. Plus the ten million Tomlinson had in life insurance would set his wife up for life.

I personally won't get a dime. And he was cool with that. What he would get was (a) the satisfaction of knowing Tomlinson would die, very scared indeed; (b) the satisfaction that Mrs Tomlinson would get the last laugh; (c) a visual aid for future marks who thought they could ignore him; and (d) more really great leverage on Eric, Albert, and, last but far from least, sweet Mary. And he was *very* cool with that.

Monday, September 20, 2:10 P.M.

Phoebe Hunter leaned in David's kitchen doorway, watching her son finish the tile medallion his neighbor had started. Finally admitting his fatigue, Glenn had gone back downstairs, leaving her alone with David, the child she worried about more than all of her other children put together. 'Not bad,' she said.

David looked up with a smile. 'Glenn did most of it.'

'He does good work,' she commented.

'That he does. I'm always trying to get him to rest, but he likes to keep busy.'

'I noticed that,' she said dryly. 'He sat at the table with

124

me for about a minute before he got up, grumbling about the big bare spot you'd left on your kitchen floor.'

'A whole minute? That's pretty good for him. I kept telling him I hadn't decided what I wanted for the medallion, and he kept going on about those "damn fancy tiles." He just wanted to do the design himself. Blowhard.' He said it affectionately.

'I noticed that, too. But he likes you.'

'I like him, too.' He refilled their coffee cups and they went to sit at the table. 'I met him at the firehouse my first day. He's one of the retired guys who can't stay away.'

'He told me. He talked more about that firehouse than anything else. But he also talked about you. He told me about all the tenants and how you take care of them. How you rock those babies in 2A to sleep in the night so that Mrs Edwards and the girls can rest. How you rescue the Gorski sisters' cat every time it climbs up a tree. How you make sure that he's taken care of every time he goes to chemo.'

David fidgeted in his chair. 'It's nothing, Ma. Just what anyone would do. So, what's going on at home?'

David always changed the subject when she wanted to talk about his charity work. Well, that's why she'd come to see him, so she wouldn't let him squirm away this time.

'Same old, same old adventures.' But she told him anyway, all the news of his siblings and nieces and nephews, no matter how mundane. As she talked, he studied her, much like he'd studied the floor. He was her hands-on son. Always loved his gadgets, taking things apart. Putting them back together, better than new. How often had she wished he'd do that with his own life? 'What are you looking at?' she asked. 'Do I have a new wrinkle?'

He smiled and she saw a glimmer of his father in his

eyes. Her husband had been a handsome devil, and their sons were, too. David, most of all. 'You look exactly the same,' he said. 'I was just thinking about you driving yourself all this way. That was pretty adventurous yourself, Ma.'

'You act like I'm old,' she sniffed.

'No, ma'am, just directionally challenged.'

That was a true fact, so she let it pass. 'Your place is coming together nicely. I'd hoped for a little more furniture, but I can see you've been busy.'

'Thanks. I put in windows, wood trim, and plumbing. I've got to do the floors on one and two, but you can start on color swatches and carpet styles now if you want.'

She nodded, sipping her coffee. 'Speaking of floors, I hear you had an adventure yourself this morning.' She said it calmly, even though her heart still hadn't returned to normal. 'But you appear to be all right.'

He rolled his eyes, but there was worry there. 'Who told Glenn about it?'

'Somebody named Raz, who heard it from somebody named Gabe, who heard it from somebody named Zell.'

'I'm sure the story was nowhere near the truth by the time it got to Glenn,' he said.

'Probably,' she agreed mildly. He was hiding something. She'd always been able to tell. Of all her children, David seemed the most straightforward, but he was the most complicated. And the most unhappy.

'So,' he said casually. 'What did Glenn tell you?'

'That you were searching for victims in that condo that's been on the news all morning, and the floor collapsed under your feet. You nearly plunged four stories.' She was still shaken. 'And you caught some kind of ball before it slid into the big dark hole.'

He frowned. 'I was hoping it would be a lot further from the truth.' He rubbed the back of his neck. 'The ball is supposed to be a secret. You can't tell anyone, okay?'

'I can keep a secret. It's your friends I'd be worried about.'

'Yeah, I got that. I need to call the detective.' On his cell phone, he dialed a number from memory, holding his breath as he waited for an answer.

She heard a woman answer before he pressed the phone to his ear. 'Sutherland.'

Dropping her eyes to her coffee, she eavesdropped shamelessly. Sutherland was a name she knew. She'd met Olivia at Mia's wedding. Mia's half sister seemed like a nice young woman. A little sad, but polite. And pretty. And apparently more involved with her youngest son than any of them had suspected. Paige's voice had carried.

'Hi. It's David Hunter. I just wanted to let you know that the news about the ball got out.' From beneath her lashes, Phoebe saw him wince. Mia's little sister wasn't happy.

He made a face. 'Even my mother knows,' he said wryly. 'She's visiting and heard it from a retired firefighter friend of mine who got it through the grapevine. What do you want me to do?' He listened a moment, then shot a concerned look across the table and turned away. 'You have an ETA?' he murmured.

Her head still down, Phoebe's brows went up. ETA? Olivia was coming here?

Abruptly David rose and left the apartment and Phoebe wondered if he knew the door hadn't shut behind him. 'My mother is staying here,' she heard him say. 'But I have a place we can meet. I'll text you the address.'

There was silence, then his surprised voice. 'You've

identified her? Already?' More silence, then he said quietly, 'Tell her father that we really tried. That I'm sorry.'

Phoebe sighed. Glenn told her that David had pulled a young girl from the fire, that she'd already been dead. David would worry over that. He'd go over it in his mind again and again, wondering if he could have done anything differently. If he could have fixed it. Saved the girl. Because that's what David did. He fixed things. Saved people.

It was time her son saved himself, and if he couldn't . . . *then I will.*

David disconnected, then reached for the doorknob, rolling his eyes when he found the door hadn't closed. *I need to fix that*, he thought. With it cracked open, sound carried. It was reasonable to assume his mother had heard every word.

She looked up when he came back in, brows raised. 'So how is Olivia?'

He swallowed his sigh. 'The condo victims were homicides. She caught the case.'

'So where will you be meeting her tonight?' She lifted her hand when he started to protest. 'I'm only asking because if you don't want me here, I can stay with Evie.'

He sank into the chair next to her. 'Ma.'

'I can keep secrets, son,' she said mildly. 'Even the ones you haven't told me.'

He didn't like the sound of that. 'What secrets haven't I told you?'

She sat back, tilted her head, crossed her arms and studied him. He knew the look. It was the same one she'd used every time he'd gotten into trouble as a kid, and he knew what would come next would not be comfortable.

'Well, for starters, that you fell in love with Dana Dupinsky at first sight.'

He looked away, his cheeks growing warm. 'You knew all along?' he asked quietly.

'Yes. I knew you loved her, but she thought of you as a brother. I knew you worked tirelessly to support her work with battered women, along with supporting a dozen other charities in town. And I knew that it broke your heart when she married someone else.'

He closed his eyes wearily. 'Who else knew about Dana?'

'The ones who figured it out for themselves. Max and Caroline.' David's older brother and his wife. Long ago, Dana had helped Caroline escape brutal domestic abuse. For that alone, Dana would forever be part of their family. 'The twins,' she added. Peter and Cathy were still 'the twins,' even though they were pushing forty-five.

He opened one eye. 'Elizabeth, too?' he asked.

'Yes. Your little sister picks up on more than we all give her credit for. We kept hoping you'd find someone else, that you'd be happy. But you didn't and we didn't know what to do, so we didn't say or do anything. Did we do wrong?'

He shook his head. 'No. There wasn't anything you could have done, Ma.'

'I know. Makes a mother feel helpless when her kids hurt and she can't do anything. When you told me you were moving, I wasn't surprised. I knew you'd have to get away. I was surprised you stayed as long as you did. When you told me Minneapolis, I figured you'd picked this town to be closer to Evie and Tom.'

David's old friend Evie had left Chicago to escape demons of her own, and his nephew, Caroline's son Tom, was a college basketball star here at the university. 'I did,' he said, and that was partly true. 'Though I don't see either of them much. They're both so busy at school, both with their own lives. And Noah watches out for Evie now.'

His mother smiled. 'Which is how it should be. Now, that you and Olivia had a biblical . . . *thing* after Mia's wedding? That I did not know until your friend Paige confronted you.' She lifted her brows. 'Because I have ears like a bat.'

He rolled his eyes, his face on fire. 'Ma.'

'David,' she returned, mimicking his tone. 'I have to eavesdrop. You never tell me anything. Thanks to Paige, I have a fuller picture of the puzzle that is my son.'

'I'm no puzzle. Anyway, you seem to have had it all figured out.'

She shook her head. 'Not really. There's a piece of you I've never been able to completely understand. I've admired it, loved it, bragged on it, but never understood it.'

He found himself lifting his chin defensively. 'And what's that?'

'What drives you to serve. You went from a headstrong, bullheaded, narcissistic teenager who cared for no one but himself to a man who serves more than anyone I know. Almost overnight.'

David controlled his flinch, knowing she was watching him. *God help me if you ever do understand*, he thought as the pictures from the past flooded his mind. Broken bodies. And so much blood. It had been eighteen years and his throat still closed when he thought of Megan, huddled over her brother's small body, protecting him with her last breath.

Because he'd been a headstrong, bullheaded narcissistic

fool who'd cared for no one but himself. Their blood was on his hands.

He realized he was staring at his hands and looked up. His mother watched him with worried eyes. He forced a smile. 'No real mystery. Dad died, and you and Max needed help with his therapy to walk again.' The car accident that had killed his father and paralyzed his brother had been another defining moment in his life. Helping his brother had become his salvation, the way to claw out of the abyss into which he'd fallen. After Megan. After that, service had become . . . necessary. 'I had to grow up.'

'And you did,' she said, her gaze piercing as she studied him. 'I know how much Max appreciates it. You dropped out of college after only one semester, gave up your own sports dream to get him through physical therapy, get him back on his feet again.'

He wanted to wince at the lie she'd always taken as truth, but didn't. He'd already dropped out of college before his father's accident, but his mother didn't know that. He'd been failing, unable to concentrate on his studies. Unable to sleep. Unable to make the pictures in his mind go away. Nursing his brother back to health all those years ago had been the excuse he'd needed to keep his family from finding out what a failure he really was.

'He needed me,' David managed. His throat was raw, his chest hurt. He'd never understood the people who became comfortable with a lie. Eighteen years and it still tore him up inside.

'Yes.' His mother still watched him and he fought the urge to squirm. 'But that still doesn't explain why you picked women's shelters and charities. Even before Dana's shelter, that's how you spent your time. Always working. Always helping.'

'It's a good cause.'

'Yes. When it's a cause. But for you, it's more than that.' She sighed. 'David, I was so devastated when your father died, events that happened around that time seemed to disappear. But the years passed and it began to occur to me that your focus on charity wasn't a passing fancy or even a healthy hobby. It was your life, at the exclusion of everything else adults normally seek. No girlfriends, nobody special. I looked back, tried to figure out when it started. I started thinking about that year. There was a tragedy in the neighborhood the spring before your dad died.'

A tragedy. Yes, it had been that. A tragedy that could have been completely avoided if he hadn't been so full of himself. He said nothing. He wasn't sure he could.

'Your friend died,' she said softly. 'Her name was Megan, wasn't it?'

He swallowed. Nodded.

'Her stepfather was a monster,' his mother murmured.

He swallowed again, the scene so clear in his mind. 'Yes,' he whispered.

'He killed his whole family. I think we all thought it was sad, that we wished we'd known he was capable of such evil. I never considered how deeply Megan's death impacted you. I should have. You'd been close in junior high. I'm sorry for that, David. I was so wrapped up in getting by after your dad died . . . and you were always so strong and steady. I never saw you were hurting. I'm sorry for that, too.'

He lifted his eyes to hers. *She* was sorry? She'd done nothing wrong. *Not like me.* He cleared his throat, hoped his voice would be level. 'Why bring all that up now?'

She sat back in her chair. 'Because I've thought about this for a long time and have wanted to ask you so many times. It never seemed like the right time, so I left it alone. I don't suppose you understand that.'

He thought of Olivia, of how he'd put things off far too long. 'More than you think.'

She leaned forward, covered his hand with hers. 'For years I watched you donate your time and your talent to worthy causes. But during those same years I watched you be so alone it's made my heart break. But you're a man grown, so I kept my counsel.'

'And now?'

'Now . . . you look like you're trying to start your life again. So I come to visit, hoping to find you settled. Instead I find an empty apartment and a son who's still alone. Who still volunteers every waking moment of his time to others.'

David squared his jaw, looked away. 'That's not wrong.'

'Not when it's for the right reasons. I'm not sure your reasons are the right ones. If I didn't know better, I'd say you were doing penance.'

He met her eyes, helplessly miserable. He wanted to deny her words, but could not.

Her eyes filled with tears. 'I thought so. Sometimes, when you think no one can see, you get this look in your eyes. Like you carry the world on your shoulders. Why?'

His chest was too tight. But she was waiting. *I can't tell her the truth. Not all.* So he carved away enough of the truth to make the pain on her face go away. 'I saw it. The crime scene.'

Confused, she blinked, sending the tears down her cheeks. 'What?'

'I was coming home from my friend's house. You all were at Mass that morning. I saw police cars in front of

Megan's house, and I ran up to see. And I saw them. Dead.'

His mother blanched, horrified. 'Dear God. Megan, her mother . . . they were . . .'

He nodded, kept his voice steady. 'Beaten to death. Yes.'

She sat across the table, stunned. 'Why didn't you say anything?'

Because I was ashamed. I still am. And I don't want you to ever know what I did.

He shrugged. 'I guess I was in shock. I was eighteen, Ma. Boys that age don't get all emotional about things like that.' Which was a lie. He had been emotional. He'd nearly lost his mind. 'But I remembered it. And I needed to do something to keep it from happening again. I can't help the women themselves, but I can help the shelters.'

His mother blinked again, struggling for composure. 'David, I wish you'd told me then. I can't imagine what you saw. We should have gotten you help. Therapy.'

'I was eighteen, Ma. I wouldn't have gone to therapy.' Hell, he hadn't even told his priest. 'So stop blaming yourself.'

She nodded uncertainly. 'Well, that does explain a lot.' She looked at him, her eyes intense. 'You do know there's nothing you could do to make me not love you.'

And he realized she knew he lied still. 'Yeah. I know.'

She reached for his hands, squeezed them fiercely. 'I'm proud of you. Never forget that.' She sat back briskly. 'Now, about where I'm going to stay.'

'Here,' he said firmly, relieved that was over. 'You're going to stay here. You need to check out all the apartments, get a feel for colors.'

'That would be best. I'm going carpet shopping,' she

said. 'If you're going out tonight, you should get some rest.'

'Drive carefully, Ma.' He kissed her cheek. 'I'm glad you're here. I love you, too.'

He watched her leave, then sagged into a chair, his eyes closed, drained. But it would be fruitless to try to sleep. His mind was churning along with his gut. It happened every time he remembered that day. Today it was worse, lying to his mother.

He rose wearily. He had time to lay the floor in 2A. He could have the girls' new fridge put in the living room until the floor was set. But first he sent a short text to Olivia with the address of Glenn's fishing cabin. It was quiet there. They could talk.

I should have done it earlier. I've been a coward. He supposed after tonight there would be one less mystery in his life.

At least I'll know exactly what I did the night I spent with Olivia Sutherland.

Chapter Seven

Monday, September 20, 2:25 P.M.

Olivia frowned at the address David texted. It was a rural area twenty minutes away from the city. Why there?

'What's wrong?' Kane asked.

'Oh, nothing.' She put her phone away and went back to studying the map of the lake. 'We've covered the cabins with views of the condo. Nobody saw Tracey Mullen.'

'Or will admit to it. Something's going on at the condo. Give me the field glasses.'

Olivia patted her pocket, then groaned. 'I forgot them earlier. I handed them to David and forgot to get them back. I'll get them for you tonight.'

He started to speak, then thought better of it. 'I think the dog is here,' he said instead.

Olivia strained to see across the lake. 'I wonder if it's the arson dog or the SAR.'

They'd told Barlow the girl had been with a man before the fire started. He'd already called for the state's arson dog but said he'd get a search-and-rescue team, too.

'Since we have no field glasses,' Kane said, 'let's drive over and find out.'

When they got to the condo, a search-and-rescue team stood ready to work. The dog was a German Shepherd and its owner a tall woman whose red hair hung down the middle of her back like a flame. Olivia knew only one person with hair that color.

'Barlow called Brie,' she said, satisfied. 'I wasn't sure he would.'

'That's your doggy-day-care friend?' Kane asked, surprised.

'Yeah. Her real business is training dogs for search, rescue, and detection.' She sped up her pace. 'Barlow and Brie and I all graduated from the academy together. For a while, we were all close.' The three of them and Barlow's best friend, to be accurate. 'Barlow and Brie used to be a couple. Engaged, actually.'

'Them, too?' Kane asked carefully. He rarely referred to her failed engagement and never referred to Doug by name, which was just fine by her.

'Them, too,' she said. 'Engagement didn't work out for them either. But Barlow knows Brie's good. She did SAR before she left the force. Her dad's a vet.'

'Dog vet or army vet?'

'Both. Takes care of the dogs in her training center and the day care in addition to his own practice. Mojo loves him, even when he's getting a shot.' She waved. 'Brie!'

Brie Franconi waved back. 'Get a move on. GusGus is missing his soaps.'

When Olivia got close, she made the introductions and Brie shook Kane's hand with a warm smile. 'I've heard so much about you,' Brie said. 'Good to finally meet you.'

'Likewise,' Kane said. 'I seem to have heard a lot about you. Especially today.'

'Our female victim had a cochlear,' Olivia told her quietly.

Brie's bright brows went up. 'That's interesting.' Her speech was clear, mostly because she'd been deafened as an adult, but partly because the implant allowed her to continue hearing. Not as well as she had before, but well enough to function in the world she'd made for herself after leaving the force.

It had cut Brie deep, resigning her badge. Olivia couldn't even fathom it. But she'd been there for her, as had Paige, who Olivia had drawn into their circle back in the academy days. *I'm lucky*, Olivia thought, thinking of Paige that morning. *I have good friends.* They'd gotten each other through many a tough patch. She thought about meeting David Hunter tonight. If it went badly, she might need her friends again.

'That's how we ID'd her,' Kane said. 'Serial number on the device. Very handy.'

'Good to know,' Brie murmured. 'Just in case I ever get caught dead without ID.'

Kane grimaced. 'Sorry. I didn't mean . . . hell. I'm sorry.'

Olivia elbowed her, hard. 'She's *teasing* you, Kane. Leave him alone, Brie.'

Brie's brown eyes twinkled. 'Sorry, Detective. I couldn't resist.' Then Barlow walked up and Brie's expression went bland. To strangers, they appeared professional, but Olivia knew that under Brie's veneer, resentment toward Micah Barlow still brewed. 'Sergeant Barlow says we may have another victim in the structure,' Brie said briskly.

'Perhaps. We're not sure if he got away. If so, we want

him as an eyewitness. If not, we need to identify his remains as well,' Kane said.

'But if he got away and we can track where the girl came *from*,' Brie said, 'then you may be able to track your eyewitness.'

'Exactly.' Olivia looked at Barlow. 'Did you get her clothing from the morgue?'

Barlow held up an evidence bag. 'Can we check for the unidentified male's remains first? One of the investigators is inside, Brie. He'll walk you through.' His smile was tight. 'Wouldn't want you and GusGus to fall through any of the holes.'

'Thanks,' Brie said, whipping her bright hair back into a ponytail. She tightened her hold on the dog's leash. 'GusGus, time to work.'

She and the dog started into the building and Kane's brows went up. 'GusGus?'

Olivia smiled. 'Yeah, like the mouse in the Cinderella cartoon. GusGus. He's certified as a cadaver dog and SAR and a list of other things as long as your arm.'

Kane sighed. 'She's addicted to cartoons, too? What were they serving in the academy canteen when you all came through?'

'Cartoons can be brilliant social commentary,' Olivia said archly, knowing Kane was teasing. Mostly anyway. 'And sometimes,' she added quietly, 'it's just escape.'

'That I'll buy,' he replied, just as quietly.

Some women craved ice cream. When Olivia was stressed, a few episodes of the Road Runner relieved her tension. Something about that anvil crunching the Coyote's umbrella made her laugh, every time.

She'd watched a lot of the Road Runner over the last seven months. It had become habit during the weeks of informing the families of the victims they'd found in the lime pit. Come home, walk Mojo, slide her 'Best of Road Runner' DVD in the machine, then sit and stare at the screen until she'd fallen asleep.

Their killer had kept their driver's licenses as souvenirs, making initial identification a lot easier. The killer had been quietly murdering women for decades.

Sometimes the families had moved. But focusing on details like tracking next of kin kept Olivia from focusing on the horror of finding the remains of victim after victim. At times it ran like a slide show in her mind. Bones, bones, and more bones.

The bones actually weren't so bad. It had been the first bodies they'd pulled from the pit that had been the worst. Lime decomposed a body in a matter of days. But the killer had killed too many at the end. Decomposition was slowed for those final victims.

She briefly closed her eyes, remembering the rotting flesh. How it would simply . . . fall off the bones as the body was moved.

If there was a body in the burned-out condo, there wouldn't be much left. It would look like *them*. Her anxiety returned in a harsh wave and with it, the fierce need to run away. But she didn't, forcing herself to stand her ground. It would get easier. It had to.

She wondered how Kane coped, but he'd never shared, so she'd never asked. He'd just done his job. *Like me. Because that's what we do.*

'We know where the arsonists exited,' Barlow said. 'The arson dog sniffed a trail of accelerant to that door.' He pointed to a stairwell door, on the same side of the building as the window on which David had first spotted the girl's shiny handprints.

'Did you find footprints?' Olivia asked, but Barlow shook his head.

'Only smudges. The arsonists stepped in the carpet adhesive and tracked it to the door. Unfortunately, the adhesive on their shoes picked up dirt, so the impressions aren't crisp. No tread, no feel for shoe size even, although there do appear to have been two individuals.'

'So if we find their shoes?' Kane asked.

'You'll find traces of the accelerant and the glue,' Barlow said. 'If there's any ash or dirt still mixed in with the adhesive, we'll be able to match the composition to what we found here, so we can place them at the scene. The dog tracked the accelerant trail across the construction yard to that cut in the fence.' He pointed to one of the three slices in the fence that Micki had told them about, the one closest to the road.

'So they escaped by the road,' Kane said, frowning. 'Not by the lake. Henry Weems's killer shot him while standing between Henry and the lake.'

'I thought of that. The handler took the arson dog around the condo, including the area on the other side of the building where Henry Weems was shot. No accelerant on the ground, anywhere. His shooter might have left by the lake, but it's equally possible he walked back around the building to join the others, escaping by the road.'

'So,' Olivia said, 'whoever shot Henry didn't step in the adhesive or was never in the condo to begin with.'

'Could have shot Henry, then gone into the condo to set the fire,' Kane theorized.

'If Weems inhaled no smoke, that's a possibility,' Barlow said. 'But if Ian finds smoke in his lungs, it would have to be after.'

141

'Ian's doing the cut this afternoon,' Olivia said. 'If Weems was killed after the fire started, and there were two arsonists inside, then we have at least three arsonists. The question is, were Tracey and her sex partner involved with them?'

'And is her sex partner still alive?' Barlow added.

'And if the arsonists came out through that side door,' Kane continued, 'did they go in the same way? How did Tracey Mullen get in?'

'The side door lock hadn't been tampered with,' Barlow said, 'but that doesn't mean anything. On a construction site, people prop doors open all the time.'

'That should have been something the guard checked, right?' Olivia asked.

'It was on his route. First stop would have been the camera console in the construction trailer, then a check of all the doors from the outside, then a walk around the perimeter. But Weems was struck as he exited the back door. He never got a chance.'

Olivia looked at Kane. 'We gotta check him out,' she said. 'Weems.'

Kane nodded. 'I know. We can't ignore that he might have known they were coming and they killed him to keep him quiet. Let's pull his financials. But discreetly.'

'No need to add any more grief to the family unless we have to,' Barlow murmured. 'Did you catch Weems's daughter on the news?'

In his eyes Olivia saw the compassion she'd seen so often in the past. *Except when I needed him most, and then he was an arrogant bastard.* 'What did she say?'

For a bittersweet moment it was like they were still friends. 'She sang our praises, Liv.' He met her eyes then, held them. 'She was stronger than I might have been, considering she'd just lost her father. I wouldn't want to do anything I'd . . . regret.'

Olivia nodded. She'd lost her own father the same night her friendship with Micah Barlow had crumbled into pieces. *Because Barlow had been an arrogant, meddling bastard.* Today, his words might be an apology, or the start of one. She'd have to see.

'We'll be careful,' she said. 'We just want to rule him out as an . . . accomplice.'

She could see he got her double meaning, just as she'd gotten his.

'Good enough.' Barlow looked away. 'It'll take Brie's dog a while to cover the whole structure. I've got the personnel files for Rankin and Sons' construction personnel in my car. We can go over them while we're waiting. Maybe something will pop.'

Monday, September 20, 2:40 P.M.

'Thank you for coming, Mrs Dent.' Mr Oaks, the principal, signed to his mother, then threw Austin a harsh look. All three of them were deaf and their signing flew fast and in his mother's case, very furious. 'Your mother drove a long way.'

'Three hours,' his mother signed. 'But this is a mistake. Austin doesn't smoke.'

'The dorm RA smelled smoke this morning,' Oaks signed, 'after the smoke alarm started flashing. When he went in Austin's room, Austin had the lit cigarette in his hand.'

His mother's face went pale. 'Why, Austin? Just tell me why.'

Because I took Tracey to that condo. I wanted to take care of her.

Now she's dead. And it's my fault. The stairwell had been full of smoke. *She was behind me. I know she was behind me.* He'd made it outside, but Tracey hadn't.

'Sorry,' Austin signed. But it wouldn't bring Tracey back. She was gone.

Oaks frowned. 'Austin is suspended for five days. He can return next Monday.'

Austin closed his eyes. He hated this, lying to his mother. But if he told her . . . He remembered the man in the boat. He'd shot that guard. *If he knew I saw . . .*

Austin had been ready to tell the truth so many times. But as the shock over losing Tracey had worn off, he started remembering the way the guard's face looked as he fell. And the way the shooter's teeth had gleamed in the moonlight as he'd smiled.

And every detail of the shooter's face when he'd pulled off his ski mask.

He'd been ready to tell. But if he did, the man might kill him, too.

People who get involved, who tell the truth, get hurt. What do I do?

His mother stood up, her back hunched over. 'Get your backpack,' she signed.

His backpack. He'd left it behind, in the fire. It had some of his books, his papers. Tracey's things. *My hearing aid.* He only hoped the fire had been hot enough to burn all the papers up. He didn't want anyone to know he'd been there. But he needed his hearing aid. His mom didn't have the money to buy a new one and they'd lost their insurance a long time ago. *What am I going to do? For now, nothing.*

He stood. 'Lost it,' he signed back carelessly.

His mother looked at him, defeated. *Not again*. He knew she wanted to say it, to scream it. But she just shook her head, her signing weary. 'Let's go home.'

Monday, September 20, 3:25 P.M.

Brie stopped at Barlow's car where Olivia, Barlow, and Kane read personnel files. 'He must have escaped,' Brie said. 'There were no human remains in the structure.'

'Then we have a witness to the fire at least,' Olivia said. It was more than they had after reading through Rankin's personnel files. There were a few performance reviews. One or two drug tests. Nothing popped. So knowing Tracey's partner hadn't died with her was the best news they'd had all day.

Barlow handed Brie the bag containing Tracey's clothing. 'Can we track the girl?'

'Of course,' Brie said formally.

Olivia put the file she'd been reading in the box in Barlow's car. 'Can I watch?'

Brie smiled at her. 'Of course,' she said, her voice substantially warmer.

Kane dropped his file in the box. 'I'm in.'

Brie pulled Tracey's shirt from the bag and let GusGus sniff it. 'GusGus, it's time to work.' The two set out, the dog's nose to the ground.

Olivia and Kane followed, Barlow a few paces behind them, video camera in his hand. GusGus led them to the other side of the condo, where Weems's body had been found. He picked up the scent, winding through the trees, stopping at the chain-link fence. It was another one of the three slices in the chain link that CSU had found.

'We can keep going,' Brie said.

'Please do,' Barlow said. 'I'd like to see how they accessed the property. From here, you can't get to the dock. Lots of thorns.'

Brie nodded. 'If you pull back the fence, Liv, we can move through.'

Olivia did and GusGus and Brie kept going and they followed. A few times the dog lost the scent, but Brie would let him sniff the shirt again. Finally the dog sat, abruptly.

They stood on a bank of the lake. A deep crease in the mud ran into the water.

'They had a boat,' Kane said, crouching to examine the track in the mud. 'Small. Wider than a canoe. Probably a small rowboat.'

'Somebody had to know about this little stretch of beach,' Olivia said. 'The shoreline between here and the dock is covered in thorn bushes, just like you said, Barlow. This is the closest place to land a boat, other than the dock.'

'Tracey wasn't local,' Kane said, 'but the guy she was with might have been.'

'Or at least has stayed at one of these cabins at some point.' Olivia strained to see across the lake. 'For now, let's assume Tracey's guy is local. If we can't find him, we can broaden the search to cabin renters – permanent and the holiday crowd.'

Brie was staring at the mud. 'He pushed this boat into the water, but I don't see any footprints. We got a good crease of the boat's keel. We also should have a shoe impression. Unless he came' – she handed the dog's lead to Olivia and walked a wide half-circle around them – 'from this way,' she finished. Gingerly she moved the thick bushes aside. Then looked up with a grin. 'Shoeprint. Score.'

Kane followed her path and looked over her shoulder. 'Size ten shoe. Nice.'

The single word was high praise from Kane. Brie turned to search the area. 'See the path, the trampled twigs and leaves that stop ten feet farther than he wanted to be?'

'He was scared,' Olivia said quietly. 'Running from a burning building. I wonder if he knew Tracey hadn't made it out.'

'Oh.' Barlow put down his camera and stared at Brie's profile. 'I know what else he was.' He walked to Brie's side and bent slightly, his gaze focused on her ear.

Stiffening, Brie pulled away and glared at him. 'What?'

Barlow straightened and looked at Olivia. 'Cochlear processors worn behind the ear don't have ear molds,' he said. 'I can't believe I forgot that.'

Olivia frowned. Then understood. 'Oh. God. You're right. As many times as I've seen you hook that on your ear, Brie . . . I can't believe I forgot, too.' She glanced up at Kane. 'Brie's processor is held in place by a little hook that grabs here,' she explained, touching the topmost fold of her ear. 'Not a pink mold like David found in the rubble.'

'Molds are used by hearing aids, not implants,' Brie said. 'You found a pink mold?'

'In the rubble,' Barlow told her. 'The ear mold was still recognizable.'

'She wouldn't have a hearing aid and an implant at the same time?' Kane asked.

'Perhaps,' Brie said, understanding now as well. 'Some people use both, depending on the kind of hearing loss they have. What kind did the victim have?'

'According to mom, Tracey was profoundly deaf, but her father refused to consider the cochlear implant. They'd tried hearing aids with Tracey, without any benefit.'

'He's deaf, the father?' Brie asked. 'The controversy against implanting kids isn't as hot as it used to be, but it still exists. Many deaf people don't see their deafness as something that needs to be "fixed." They're protective of their culture, their language, and many see implants as a threat.'

'I got that when I talked to the dad,' Kane said, 'even through the relay operator we had to use. He was angry, especially at his wife. Of course he was grieving, too, and it was almost impossible to get any nuance over the phone.'

Brie's mouth curved ruefully. 'It gets easier, with practice. Next time, use a videophone operator if you can. If the father has a videophone, he can sign to the operator instead of typing into the TTY. That way the interpreter's voice can give you some of the emotion, because they're seeing the signer's face. I'll show you how to connect.'

'I'd appreciate it,' Kane said.

'Getting back to the mold?' Barlow asked impatiently. 'Was it the girl's or not?'

'If she was born profoundly deaf,' Brie said, 'and wasn't wearing it before the surgery, chances are good it didn't belong to her. You'll have to confirm that.'

'If it wasn't hers, the backpack we found may not have been hers either,' Kane said. 'And the hearing aid may belong to whoever she was with before the fire.'

'We know from the hair he left on Tracey's body that he's Caucasian with dark hair. He's probably local, probably deaf or hearing impaired,' Olivia said. 'Narrows it down.'

Brie nodded. 'And if he's her age, you're in more luck. He'll be enrolled in school, and the district will have paperwork on his disability.'

'Where should we start?' Olivia asked.

'I'd start with the school for the deaf.' Brie checked her watch. 'School's out for the day. Some of the kids live in the dorms, so you could check there, but you're going to want to go through the principal, whose name is Oaks. I've found him very helpful.'

'You went there?' Kane asked. 'I thought you lost your hearing as an adult.'

'I did, so no, I didn't go to that school. I work with the school's vocational program, teaching a vet-tech class. When they graduate, the kids have a skill.'

'So you know these kids,' Kane said.

'Some of them. They also have classes in cooking, mechanics, and farming. A lot of teens think they want to be a vet, but transfer when they have to sweep out kennels. Those kids usually go into cooking.' Brie smiled. 'It's sugar to shit, just in reverse.'

Kane chuckled. 'So can you help us talk with these kids?'

Brie hesitated. 'My signing is slow. You should get an interpreter and try on your own first. It's possible the male you're looking for isn't local or is graduated already, but the deaf community is close-knit. If he still lives here, somebody will know him. You just may need to be patient. They're sometimes protective of their own.'

'Kind of like cops,' Kane said.

'Exactly.' Brie looked at Barlow, her brows lifted. 'Anything else, Sergeant?'

'No,' Barlow said, his manner as stiff as hers. 'Thank you and your dog.'

'You're welcome. Call me, Liv. We can grab Paige and go to Sal's for a drink.' She took the dog's leash from Olivia with a pointed look. 'Like old times.'

149

Like old times. Before Pit-Guy. *Before I started avoiding my friends.* 'I promise.'

'I have witnesses,' Brie warned. 'Come on, GusGus. Let's go home.'

Olivia turned to Barlow, who looked grim. And as tired as she felt. Earlier he'd extended an olive branch . . . Well not a branch. More like a twig. She'd up the ante a bit. 'You did the right thing by calling Brie. I know it wasn't easy.'

Barlow's smile was tight. 'I didn't at first. The first four SAR teams I called weren't available.' He let out a breath. 'How do you want to go forward?'

'We'll look for Tracey's partner,' Kane said. 'You keep working the inside angle, checking the personnel. See if any of the employees were suspicious.'

'Or deaf or hearing impaired,' Olivia said. 'What if the guy Tracey was with worked for Rankin and Sons? What if he was letting her hide there? He may have had a key.'

'Good point,' Barlow said. 'What about the Feds? Did Abbott hear from Agent Crawford?'

'If he had, he would have called. Hopefully he'll hear something by five,' Olivia said. 'What about the size ten shoeprint in the mud?'

'I'll get CSU to take a plaster cast of the print and the keel crease,' Barlow said.

'And we have just enough time to check with Ian before our five o'clock meeting,' Kane said. 'He should be done with Weems's autopsy by now.'

It was a few minutes till four. A trip to the morgue, an afternoon command meeting, back to the morgue to stand with Tracey's father during the official ID, then . . .

Up to David, who would be waiting at a cabin on a different lake, a half hour away. Why there? *Because he wants to take up where we left off.*

150

Which was damn appealing, both for her bruised ego and her lonely libido. Still, she clearly remembered the single name he'd groaned that night they'd spent together. *And it wasn't mine.* If he did want a rerun, she wasn't anywhere close to knowing how she'd respond. *Well, girl, you've got about two hours to figure it out.*

Monday, September 20, 4:35 P.M.

'Can I get you anything else?' he asked the lady at the counter while he kept watch on the rest of the shop from the corner of his eye.

She looked up from her BlackBerry, a dreamy smile on her face and a twenty in her hand. 'No, this will be fine. You have a nice day.'

He made change that she didn't bother to count. 'You do the same. Buh-bye.'

He watched the woman go, no doubt in his mind what had put the dreamy smile on her face or where she was headed. He wondered if her husband knew that she was cheating on him or that the phone she clutched in one hand held her lover's e-mails expressing his undying ardor, demonstrated at the local motel every Monday after work.

Breaking into her e-mail had been child's play. Every time she waited in line, she checked her e-mail, just like three-quarters of his customers did. Everyone seemed to have one of those handy smartphones these days, and the lure of free Internet was too sweet to pass up as they waited in line.

Of course, anyone logging in to the 'free' wireless Internet service he offered also received a sweet little Trojan that mined all of their e-mail passwords, bank account passwords, contact lists, anything they had stored on their cell phone or laptop.

He'd latched on to several of his current clients by stealing their e-mail info and logging into their accounts. My, my, the e-mails people sent, and *kept*. They were enough to make him blush. Hot, hot, hot. And perfect blackmail fuel. *Cheating on your wife? For shame. Pay me and no one need ever know*. It was so damn easy.

It had taken him only a few of Eric's e-mails to realize he'd hit a gold mine. Eric and Joel had already been e-mailing back and forth about their anger over the condo development and how it encroached on the wetlands. Eric hadn't seemed the type to care about wetlands, but through their e-mails, he could see how Joel had reeled him in.

Joel was an enthusiastic do-gooder, but he also knew which of Eric's buttons to push. *For once in your life, live*, Joel had written. *Take a risk. Be a champion. Do something that will make a difference. My father says you're boring and safe. Is that how you want to live your life? Do you want to become like our fathers?*

Who were both incredibly, stinking rich.

Too bad Joel had a conscience. He could have become a great salesman. Eric, on the other hand, had little imagination but a very thorough mind. Once led to a point, he'd run with it, just as he'd run with the idea of being a hero for once in his life.

Eric had become the leader, and quickly the plan had taken form. He'd enlisted help from Albert, his lover who'd gone along for the ride, probably for lots of reasons, most of them selfish. Then Joel brought in his own lover, *a name that stopped me in my tracks*. Mary. It was a name he hadn't seen in some time. One he could have gone a lifetime without seeing again.

He might have left her alone forever if she'd stayed put. Worked her little job. Taken her frivolous little classes. But she hadn't stayed put. She'd met Joel and had gotten involved in this delightfully escalating disaster. As soon as he'd seen her name in Joel's e-mail, he'd known this was far bigger than blackmail. This was revenge.

And that the girl in the window had died? It made the pot all the sweeter.

Unfortunately, though, the girl's death was bad for business today. He'd had the normal crowd at the counter and the register had been ringing almost nonstop, but the fire and the girl's death were dominating all the 'private' conversations. People said the damndest things in public, believing no one could hear them, that no one paid attention.

But I'm always paying attention. That's why I'll be rich. Nonchalantly, he drew his remote from his pocket. It looked like an iPod, from the circular thumb wheel on the device to the earbud he wore in one ear.

It wasn't anything so frivolous as an iPod, although he, too, enjoyed his tunes. Just not when he was working. He spun the wheel with his thumb, rotating through all the hot zones. He'd wired the whole place and with his handy surveillance gadget could listen to any conversation. It was like an auditory zoom, an indispensable piece of equipment for any blackmailer, and a real steal on eBay.

He got most of his tips through listening in on conversations. Then he hacked into their e-mail to get the real goods – the documentation that would make his marks pay and pay again. Unlike Barney Tomlinson, the majority of his marks paid.

But like Tomlinson, when they didn't, he took care of them. Permanently.

His shift would be over soon and he could take care of Tomlinson, then pick his spot to watch the College Four Minus One in action. He leaned down to close his laptop and jumped, startled when his pocket buzzed. It was one of the disposable cells in his pocket. It was Eric, he saw, once he'd found the right phone. He flipped the phone open to read the text.

Joel is dead. There are only three of us. Job on schedule.

Eric was taking him at his word, afraid the video would be leaked if all four of them didn't show. The boy was afraid. That was good. By tomorrow, he'd be terrified. That was better. For now, he'd play with them a little bit, get that hook set in even deeper.

how do i know you're telling the truth? he typed. *prove it.*

Chapter Eight

Monday, September 20, 4:40 P.M.

Eric needed to prove Joel was dead. He glanced at Albert, who was studying the map of the street where Tomlinson's warehouse was located. He could ask for proof, but they'd agreed not to speak of it. Besides, Albert was still angry with him.

Eric remembered the ridiculous note that had popped into his mind that morning. *Please excuse Joel from extortion-related arson, because he is dead.* He logged on to the local TV news' website. Earlier, the account of Joel's 'accident' had said only that the victim had been a Minneapolis university student. Hopefully they'd updated.

They had and the article listed the victim as Joel Fischer, aged 20. *Twenty.* He should have had his whole life ahead of him. They all should. *And we would have if we hadn't listened to goddamn Joel.* Quickly he texted back, including the article's URL.

Here is proof. He waited for a moment, then read the return text.

my condolences.

Yeah, right, Eric thought, tossing the phone to his sofa. 'How's it coming?'

Albert looked up from the map with a cold look. 'You do your part. I'll do mine.'

They'd split the duties, engaging Mary in the planning as little as possible. The one thing they agreed on was that they didn't quite trust Mary. They would pick her up tonight, right before it was time, giving her no opportunity to leak their plan.

Before, the situation had been different, the four of them going over details again and again, here in his living room. Eric had hacked into the construction company's server and found everything they'd needed – blueprints, the guard's route, the schedule that had told them the adhesive was staged on floors one through three.

What were we thinking? They hadn't been. They'd been so caught up.

Tonight, Eric would take care of the dog, disable the electronic alarm and the video systems, and get them inside. Albert would procure gas and matches, and, along with Mary, set the fire. A drive-by check had shown there were only simple recording cameras. They'd wear ski masks to hide their faces.

And if they were caught? *Big deal.* How much would arson add to their sentence? Life plus a few years. *Big deal.* If they didn't get caught, they'd bought time. They'd lure the fucking texter out and kill him, quickly and cleanly. It was the only way to break free.

'It's almost five,' Albert said. 'Tomlinson's warehouse will be closing soon.'

'Then I'd better call.' With the texter's phone, Eric dialed Barney Tomlinson's warehouse and a woman answered. 'Hi,' Eric said, 'my name is John Davis and I'm with Airtight Security. We make video security systems.'

'If you'll leave your number, I'll have the manager get

back to you,' the woman said in a bored tone. 'I'm not authorized to listen to sales pitches.'

Bitch. 'We're offering a special. We'll install the cameras, then hook up a wireless router for free, then store and back up all your feeds on our servers here.'

'We've got a system and it works fine. Old-fashioned video, pop in a new tape every month. Nothing fancy to break. Look, kid, leave a number or I'm hanging up.'

'Wait,' Eric blurted. 'Don't hang up, please. You're my first call. My first job. I really need the money to pay for school. Just let me practice my pitch. Please?'

She sighed dramatically. 'Go ahead. God, I'm a sap.'

'Thank you. Are you sure your system works fine? Have you checked the video quality lately? Extreme temperatures can damage the sensors.'

'The recorder's inside,' she said. 'No temperature problems.'

Damn. He'd hoped for an outside unit. 'You might think that, but if it's near a loading dock or an external door, you're letting in Mr Freeze several times a day.'

'Mr Freeze? Look, it's not near an external door. It's in the electrical room, right next to the john. Your pitch sucks. Better work it or you're going to be very poor.'

She hung up and Eric breathed a sigh of relief. 'The videotape will be in the electrical closet next to the bathroom. We'll take it with us. That way we don't need to worry about disabling the cameras. Although we should still wear masks, just in case.'

Albert still didn't look up. 'What about the alarm?'

'He's got a dog. I'm betting his alarm system isn't that advanced.'

Albert's jaw clenched. 'Don't bet. Be sure.'

Eric wondered how he could make things right. Then

dropped his eyes to his laptop where he'd been trying all afternoon to hack into Tomlinson's system. 'I'll do my best.'

Monday, September 20, 5:00 P.M.

David studied the face in his bathroom mirror. Laying the floor in 2A hadn't taken long, and wound with nervous energy, he'd done 2B as well. Now he was showered, cleanly shaven, and wearing a Sunday shirt and the trousers that went with his suit. He'd even picked out a tie. He hated this feeling. This unsure, unsteady, oh-God-what-if-I'm-a-monster feeling. He hated not knowing. At least that would soon be over.

He didn't look in the mirror very often. Usually he shaved in the shower. For a long time after Megan died, he'd forced himself to look in the mirror. Forced himself to come to terms with the man he was, not the man everyone saw.

People saw what they wanted to see, he knew. On the surface, he'd been blessed with a nice face. What could he say? He'd be lying if he denied it. He knew women gave him second and even third looks. Sometimes he was even flattered.

But most of the time it was a pain in the ass. Nice women assumed he was a player or that they'd never have a chance. There had been so few who'd taken the time to look beneath the face. To find out who he really was. Who he'd made himself to be.

'So who are you?' he murmured. But he had no good answer.

He wandered through his apartment, empty save the

absolutely necessary pieces of furniture he'd brought with him from Chicago. A table, a few straight-backed chairs, the easy chair that sat in front of his TV. And the bed he'd bought right after moving in. A new bed. A big bed. Hopefully for a new beginning. *Please*.

He could tell himself not to worry, but it was folly. Looking for distraction that wouldn't get him sweaty again, he grabbed his laptop and dropped into his easy chair.

He'd thought about the glass ball off and on all day. David believed in fate, divine providence. That the ball had slid so neatly into his glove had been no accident.

In his mind he saw the dead girl's waxen face, her wide eyes staring up at them. In a few hours her father would have to identify her body. Her life was ended, so young.

Just like Megan's. He'd thought about Megan more today than he had in a long time. Nothing could bring her back, just like nothing could bring the girl from the condo back. It was a waste. An evil, senseless waste.

For Megan, it had been because a selfish bastard wanted to control those weaker than himself. For today's victim, it was because a group of radicals wanted to save the environment. They might talk passionate, even selfless rhetoric, but under it all they were selfish bastards, too. Seemed to be a common theme.

He wondered if they'd known the girl was there. He hoped not. Still he hoped Olivia found them, and quickly. He hoped they went to prison for a very long time.

The ball that had slid into his hand had been their signature. He typed *glass ball* and *environmental arson* into Google and settled back to read.

He found an article on the group known as SPOT, then another. He found the account of how an innocent woman had died twelve years before, during the last fire for which they'd claimed responsibility, and his heart chilled. Surely they didn't know the girl was there last night. He thought about the guard, shot through the heart. That had been no accident. The arsonists were no idealists. They were murderers.

David found a link to a man recognized if not as the leader, then as their inspiration. Preston Moss. He'd been a university philosophy professor. Hadn't been heard from in twelve years. But before Moss had disappeared, he'd been prolific in his writing.

Someone had captured Moss's articles on a website. Reading Moss's words, David could almost hear the man's voice ringing in his mind.

'David? You here, boy?'

Abruptly David jerked his eyes from his laptop screen, blinking to refocus on his front door, which was opening. Glenn Redman stuck his head in. 'David?'

'Yeah, Glenn, I'm here. Come in.'

Glenn did, frowning. 'I knocked three times. I saw your truck outside, so I knew you were here. You okay? You look like you've seen a ghost.'

David's mind was still caught up in the stirring words of Preston Moss. Stirring and frightening, the barely veiled advocation of violence to make their voices heard if arson did not succeed. David rubbed his palm over his chest. His heart was still beating hard.

'I was reading,' he said distractedly, then blinked again. 'What do you need?'

Glenn's frown deepened. 'You tell me. You left me a note.' He produced it from his pocket, the sight instantly bringing David back to the present.

'Right. I knocked earlier, but thought you might be resting.' Propping his laptop on the arm of his chair, he brought one of the kitchen chairs into the living room, motioning for Glenn to sit in the easy chair. 'I wanted to talk to you about what you told my mom today.'

Glenn's eyes narrowed. 'Which thing?'

The way he said it had David's brows shooting up. 'About me catching the ball in that condo fire.'

'Oh, that.' Glenn's frown eased, making David wonder what else Glenn had told his mother. 'Heard it was a hell of a save.'

'It was. And it turned out to be important. The cops don't want us talking about it.'

'To who?'

'Well, to the press for sure, but to each other, also. Loose lips and all that.'

'All right.' The older man regarded him steadily. 'You're looking pretty clean behind the ears. Sunday clothes. You going out tonight?'

David's cheeks warmed. He'd hoped he didn't look that obvious. 'Yeah.' He returned the old man's stare. 'You're looking pretty clean yourself, old man.'

'I was thinking your mama might like to see the town, but if you two got plans . . .'

David wasn't sure if he should laugh or frown. 'You got designs on my mom?'

'No,' Glenn said forcefully. Indignantly, even. 'I just thought she might like to . . . Never mind.' He struggled to get out of the deep chair and David waved him back.

'Sit. I'm not going out with my mother tonight. She's out shopping.'

'You're leaving her alone, her first night here?'

'Just for a little while.' Maybe. He was afraid to hope for longer than a little while with Olivia. 'Where did you want to take her?'

Glenn shrugged, embarrassed. 'Dooley's maybe. They got good wings.'

David shook his head. 'My mom's better than a place with big-breasted waitresses. Besides, you changed your shirt and shaved. That calls for something special.'

'Like I can afford anything special,' Glenn groused. David shook his head again, saying nothing, and Glenn blew out a frustrated breath. 'Martino's has tablecloths.'

David chuckled at his discomfort. 'She'd like that. And you might see Lacey from 2A. Martino hired her. You like my mother or something?'

Glenn's cheeks went red. 'She's a nice lady. Back off, boy.'

'It's just that . . . she doesn't date.' It was true, he realized. 'Not since my dad.'

'How long ago did your dad pass?'

'I was eighteen, so eighteen years ago. She was so strong, never complained. She was always there for us. I guess I never thought of her ever . . . dating again.'

'It's just Martino's,' Glenn said in an overly patient voice. 'I'm not gonna marry her.'

David looked at him, slyly now. 'She's awful pretty, my mama.'

'Don't make me get out of this chair, Hunter.'

'Like you could without a winch. Just be nice to her, okay? She's a good person.'

'That I could tell, straight off.' Glenn cleared his throat. 'So where are you going?'

It was David's turn to fidget in his chair. 'Your cabin.'

'Dressed like that? You even spit shined your Sunday shoes.'

'I don't spit. I have to talk to someone about something that happened a while ago.'

'What's her name?'

He sighed. 'Olivia.'

Glenn's brows went up. 'The one you slept with and whose sister you slept with? I also have ears like a bat. Just so you know.'

David closed his eyes. 'I didn't sleep with either of them. I think.'

'You think? You *think*?'

'That's what I said.' And he'd said too much. 'What time is it, anyway?'

Glenn glanced at the computer screen. 'Ten to six.' Then he squinted, looking closer. He looked up, his eyes gone angry. 'Why are you reading about Preston Moss?'

David leaned forward. 'You know Moss?'

'Not personally. I remember him. They left a glass globe at each of their fires,' Glenn said slowly. 'That ball you caught today. The cops think Moss is back?'

'They don't know,' David said. 'They're trying to keep it out of the news.'

'I can see why. This guy was bad, Davy. He wore this veneer of sincerity, but in the end, he was just a thug.' His voice trembled. 'No more than a thug.'

'What happened, Glenn?'

Glenn closed the laptop. 'They talk about the woman who died, who fell asleep in that building and couldn't get out. How she was charred black. They don't talk about the firefighters who were hurt trying to knock that fire down. The building went up, taking the buildings on both sides. We were lucky we knocked it down as quick as we did.'

'Who was hurt?' David asked, and saw pain flicker in Glenn's eyes.

'Two young guys. One is scarred to this day. The other's forty and pulls an oxygen tank behind him like he chain-smoked for fifty years. They got caught inside. Ran out of air. Both of 'em nearly died. It was big news when it happened, but now . . . just one of those historical footnotes. That poor lady died, and we were really sorry about that. But we lost two good men that day. And Preston Moss just disappears. Lousy coward.'

'Lousy coward who could really stir up a crowd.'

'That he could. I can't believe he's back.'

'Maybe he's not. But I need you to keep quiet on this. Not a word, Glenn.'

Glenn pursed his lips. 'All right.'

The outer door downstairs slammed. 'David?'

David jumped to his feet and looked down the stairs to the entryway where his mother stood, arms laden with grocery bags. 'I'll get those, Ma.' He tossed a look over his shoulder. 'And you mind your Ps and Qs, old man. She's my mom.' He jogged down the stairs and took the bags from her hands. 'You gonna feed an army?'

'Just you. And Glenn.' She followed him up the stairs. 'And the new mothers in 2A.'

'The Gorski sisters in 1B planted a garden. Kept me in tomatoes all summer.'

'Then we shall feed them as well. But aren't you going out tonight?'

His front door had closed again, and he nudged it with his hip. 'Yep. But Glenn has a yen for Italian, don't you, Glenn?'

She smiled when she saw Glenn. 'I make a fantastic carbonara. You'll love it.'

David shook his head, and Glenn cleared his throat. 'Can't cook in the boy's kitchen. He just laid that medallion on the floor. But we could go to Martino's.'

David put the grocery bags on his table and dropped

a kiss on his mother's cheek. 'They have tablecloths,' he said, then grabbed his laptop. 'Don't stay out past eleven. You need any mad money in case the old goat gets fresh?'

She swatted at him, laughing and blushing prettily. 'Get out of here.'

Monday, September 20, 6:10 P.M.

Abbott's afternoon meeting had been mostly a rehash of what Olivia had already known. The only new information was that Ian had found smoke in Henry Weems's lungs, but not that much, indicating Weems was probably not in the building while it was burning. Still, that negated the theory that the gunman had shot him, then set the fire.

Which meant they had at least three arsonists. Barlow had background checks on the Rankin construction company employees. Six had felony records, none for arson, and eight in ten appeared to be teetering on the verge of bankruptcy.

So much for narrowing down the motive. Barlow had asked for help processing the employees and Abbott said he'd free up Noah Webster. That made Olivia happy. Noah was a damn good homicide detective and easy to work with.

Abbott told them Special Agent Crawford of the FBI had finally returned his call. Crawford was up north, on reservation land, but would be back and in their office by oh-eight tomorrow. Crawford had been extremely excited to hear about the glass ball.

Now she sat next to Kane in Ian's office in the morgue. Tracey Mullen's father had arrived, but their sign language

165

interpreter had not. They'd wait to start the ID until they could clearly communicate with the girl's father.

'Whose turn is it?' Kane asked.

'Yours. I told Mrs Weems, and we each told one of the Mullens this morning. So it's your turn to take the lead with the dad.'

'I figured as much,' Kane said glumly. 'What do you have going on tonight?'

'I'm getting your field glasses back,' Olivia said dryly and Kane's brows went up.

'Good,' was all he said and Olivia was relieved.

'I heard from Mr Oaks at the school for the deaf,' Olivia said. 'Apparently he was using one of those videophones Brie told us about, because the conversation went a lot faster. Oaks said that he'd be glad to work with us in asking the kids what they knew. Offhand he couldn't think of anyone we should be looking at, though.'

'It's possible Tracey's partner doesn't go to the school,' Kane said.

'True, but it's a place to start.'

'Just like the Gators nail art,' Kane said. 'That was nicely done, by the way.'

She smiled. 'You're just trying to butter me up so I'll take the lead, aren't you?'

'Did it work?'

'No.' They came to their feet when a woman knocked on Ian's office door.

'Hi, I'm Val Lehigh. I'm looking for Detective Kane.'

'That's me,' Kane said. 'You're our interpreter?'

She had a few streaks of gray in her hair and was firmly built, comfortably capable, and dressed completely in black. 'I am. Have you ever worked with an interpreter before?'

166

'I have,' Olivia said.

'Yes, but a long time ago,' Kane said.

'Good. Then I'll cover the bases quickly. I'm here in an official capacity and have taken an oath of confidentiality. Nothing I hear or see will be repeated. I will voice everything the deaf individual signs, even if it is an aside, meant only for me. I will sign everything you two voice, even if you mean it only for each other. Any questions?'

'Yeah,' Olivia said. 'Have you done a corpse identification before?'

'Yes. Didn't like it, but we don't get to pick where we go, any more than you do.'

'Tracey Mullen's body is in pretty good shape,' Olivia said and watched some of the tension leave the woman's shoulders. 'Except of course, that she's dead at sixteen.'

Mr Mullen jumped to his feet as soon as the three of them entered the waiting room. His face was haggard, his eyes red from weeping. His signing seemed frantic, but Val didn't seem fazed.

'I'm John Mullen. I'm here to see my daughter. Where is she?'

'I'm Detective Kane and this is my partner, Detective Sutherland,' Kane said, glancing from the corner of his eye at the interpreter, then returning his gaze to the grieving father. 'We are very sorry for your loss.'

'What happened?' he signed. 'I need to know what happened to my child.'

'She was in a condo when it caught on fire,' Kane said. 'We're not sure why she was there. She was trapped inside and did not survive.'

'She didn't burn,' Olivia added and Mullen's shoulders sagged, as close to relief as one could expect under the circumstances. 'She died of smoke inhalation.'

'She was alone at the time of her death,' Kane said gently, 'but not before. We're wondering if you might know of any boyfriends, anyone she knew living in this area.'

Bewildered, his signing slowed. 'No, no one. She lived in Florida. She was supposed to be safe in Florida. Who was she with?'

'We're trying to find that out, sir,' Kane said. 'Can you tell us if your daughter wore a hearing aid, in addition to her cochlear implant?'

Still bewildered, he shook his head again.

Then the hearing aid belonged to the male she'd been with. 'When was the last time you physically saw your daughter, sir?' Olivia asked.

'This summer for four weeks. I get . . .' He clenched his fists, then relaxed them to begin signing again. 'I got every other Christmas, Thanksgiving, spring break, and six weeks in the summer.'

'But she stayed only four weeks?' Kane asked.

Mullen hesitated. 'She went to camp for the other two weeks.'

Okay. 'Which camp, sir?' Olivia asked.

'Camp Longfellow, in Maryland.' His face crumpled as his steady stream of tears became sobs. 'Please, please, let me see my daughter.'

Kane glanced at Olivia and she nodded. She had no more questions for now. They'd definitely check Camp Longfellow as soon as this ID was done. Olivia touched Mullen's shoulder and led him to the family viewing room. The green light was on in the room's uppermost right corner, the sign that the ME was ready on the other side.

Kane pulled the curtain, and it took only seconds for Mr Mullen to numbly nod. Then he closed his eyes and cried, silently rocking himself. All alone.

Kane pulled the curtain closed while Olivia swallowed hard. There had been no viewings with Pit-Guy's victims. There hadn't been enough left of the victims' bodies and DNA had been used for identification instead. Now, standing with Tracey's father, she realized that had been the one positive in the entire nightmare. She hadn't had to watch the impotent grief of the families as they gazed on their loved ones through a sterile window.

She touched Mr Mullen's arm again, gently, as she'd learned to do when Brie wasn't wearing her processors. He struggled for control, then met her eyes.

'I'm sorry,' she signed. It was one of the few signs she knew, a tightened fist rubbing over her heart, as if to soothe the pain. She signaled to Val. 'I have a message from the firefighter who brought her out. He wants you to know that they're very sorry. They tried to save her, but by the time they arrived, it was too late.'

'How long before they arrived?' Mr Mullen signed, his chin lifted. Olivia would have taken it for belligerence if she hadn't seen it before, on too many grieving parents. It was the rush of anger, the need to blame. It was human.

'Five minutes from the time they got the call,' she said. 'The ME thinks Tracey was gone before the firefighters even got the call. The firefighter who brought her out risked his own life.' Olivia thought about the gaping hole that went four floors down. If David had stepped the wrong way when he climbed through the window to get Tracey . . . She couldn't think about it. 'Everyone did everything they could.'

'Thank you. When can I take her home?'

Val voiced his question and Olivia wanted to sigh. She hated child cases, but the heartache was made worse when there was shared custody of a minor child.

'Your wife will arrive tomorrow,' Kane said, stepping in. 'You two will have to decide the final arrangements.'

Mullen's face went as hard as stone. 'I understand.' Then he marched from the room, his body trembling, from grief or fury Olivia didn't know. Probably a mix of the two.

'Will you be available tomorrow?' Olivia asked Val. 'We'll want to ask the parents a few more questions, when they're sitting together in the same room.'

'You can request me,' Val said. 'I'll let the office know.'

'We may need you all morning,' Olivia said, thinking of their visit to the deaf school. 'We'll have some interviews to conduct.'

'I'll clear my calendar.' Val sighed heavily. 'Now, if it's all right, I'd like to leave.'

Olivia knew the feeling. The morgue was not her favorite place. 'Sure.'

When they'd signed out both the interpreter and Mr Mullen, Olivia turned to Kane. 'She went to camp.'

'He hesitated before he told us that,' Kane said. 'What is Camp Longfellow?'

'Let's find out.' They went to Ian's office and found him coming out of the cold room, having put Tracey's body away. 'Ian, can we use your computer for a minute?'

'Sure,' Ian said. 'What's up?'

Olivia slid into the chair at his desk. 'Tracey Mullen went to camp this summer.'

Ian nodded. 'Where she could have met a boy her parents didn't know she knew.'

'Oh, the things parents don't know their kids know,' Kane murmured.

'I know I gave my mom a million gray hairs,' Olivia said ruefully as she paged through the Google results for

Camp Longfellow. 'Here it is. It's a camp for deaf high school students. I wonder why Mullen hesitated about that.'

'Maybe Mrs Mullen didn't know he'd sent Tracey,' Kane said. 'Sounds like they didn't agree about much when it came to raising her. Ian, how long ago were those fractures made and the damage you mentioned to her left hand?'

'Sometime in the last three months, I'd guess.'

Olivia sighed. 'So it could have been dad, mom, mom's new husband, anyone at camp, or anyone Tracey met on her way to Minneapolis. No help toward finding who beat her or in finding our eyewitness either. Tomorrow should be an interesting day.'

And tonight an interesting night. The day was finished. She'd been anticipating and dreading this moment in equal measures. *Get up. Go. At least you'll know.*

Ian cleared his throat. 'As much as I know you *love* my morgue, I'm going to have to run you out. I still have one more autopsy before I can go home. So be gone.'

Embarrassed, she pushed to her feet wearily. 'Sorry, Ian.'

Kane waited until they were at the front door before speaking. 'I do want my field glasses back,' he said mildly. 'Just in case you were thinking of canceling on Hunter.'

Her cheeks heated. 'I wasn't. Exactly.'

'Look, I don't know what happened and I don't need to. But if you need to talk . . .'

Touched, she patted his shoulder. 'I'm okay, but thanks.' She was almost to her car when she heard him yell from the other side of the morgue's parking lot.

'Don't forget the lipstick,' he called, and made her smile.

Chapter Nine

Monday, September 20, 8:30 P.M.

David's jaw clenched as he cast his line off the end of Glenn's dock. With quick, vicious jerks he reeled the line through the dark water of the lake, knowing he was never going to hook a fish as angry as he was, and not giving a damn.

Olivia hadn't come. Hadn't called or texted. Nothing.

Maybe this was her way of getting back at him. If so, he deserved it.

Sweat dampened the back of his shirt, despite the cooler temps of the fall night. He'd rolled his sleeves up his forearms, tossed his shoes into the dirt at the other end of the dock, and now stood in his bare feet casting for a walleye he'd never catch, going over each minute of that one night again and again, and trying very hard to stay calm.

Then his shoulders jerked forward. He'd hooked one. A damn big one. Reflex had him reeling – just as he heard the low roar of a vehicle approaching. He kept reeling as he listened, wondering if it would keep going, like all the cars had up until this point.

It didn't. It stopped out front, the engine idling. Minutes

ticked by and the engine continued to idle. *Turn off the car, Olivia.* Then he let out the breath he'd been holding when she did. A door slammed in the stillness of the night.

Two very long minutes later he heard the gentle slam of the back door and let out another breath. His hands continued to reel as he heard the crunch of fallen leaves and, finally, detected the faint aroma of honeysuckle. *She was here.*

'I didn't think you would come,' he said, not turning around.

'I said I would,' she said quietly.

He turned then, looking into the face that had captured his imagination the moment he'd seen her. But it had been her eyes that had drawn him that first night. He found they still did. Round and blue, they'd been by turns sharp and intelligent, soft and understanding. And, later, hot and needy as she'd looked up at him, her head on his pillow. He swallowed hard.

'I'm glad,' he said simply and her lips turned up. Not quite a smile. He dropped his eyes to her throat and could see the pulse beating there, fast. Nervous, he hoped. Not scared. *Please don't let her be scared.*

'I'm sorry I'm late. I needed to pick up my dog and go home. Clean up a little.'

His eyes dropped to the dress she wore. He'd seen it before. The first night he'd met her, at Mia's rehearsal dinner. The night they'd sat and talked about everything under the sun until the small hours of the morning. He had to wonder if she'd chosen the dress on purpose, or if it was simply a favorite.

Blue like her eyes, it was made of something diaphanous that gave him teasing glimpses of her curves as the fabric rippled in the breeze. She'd left her hair down, as he liked it best. He wanted badly to touch, but his hands were filthy, so he kept them where they were, clutching his rod and reel for dear life.

He looked at his own clothes ruefully. 'I was. Cleaned up, that is. Sorry.'

'It's my fault. I should have called. Time got away from me. It sometimes does that.'

He stared another long moment, wondering how to ask the question that had burdened him for two and a half years. *Why did you leave? What did I do?* 'I've hooked a fish. Hook's set hard in his mouth. If I cut the line . . .'

'He'll suffer. So reel him in. It's nice out here, with the lake. Who lives here?'

He reeled, impatiently now. He wanted to wash his hands so that he could touch her. 'A friend who's staying in my apartment building. The one I'm rehabbing.'

'I didn't know you'd opened it for tenants already.'

'I didn't plan to. They just needed a place to stay. Now I'm half full.'

Something moved in her eyes and he wished he could interpret it. 'That was kind.'

'So is your work with runaways. That night in Chicago, you said you wanted to do something, to give kids like your sister a chance before they ruined their lives. Lots of people talk about making a difference, Olivia. You do. You're there at the teen shelter almost every weekend.' Even at the height of her work with the victims in the pit, she'd kept her commitment. That had profoundly impressed David.

Her eyes widened. 'Wait a minute. How do you know what I do in my spare time?'

'I've . . . paid attention. Since I've been here.'

Now her eyes narrowed. 'You've been *watching me*?'

He focused on reeling. *Yes.* 'Kind of.'

'*Kind of?* What the hell kind of answer is that?' Her hand was plunked on her hip. Her very curvy hip. Her blue eyes flashed dangerously.

'Not a terribly good one, I'm afraid,' he said.

She pursed her lips, fixing her gaze on his fishing line. 'Do you have a better one?'

'I think so, but it's hard to concentrate right now.'

She huffed. 'So hurry up. What are you going to do with it anyway?'

He assumed she meant the fish. 'Depends. Do you like fresh fish?'

'Depends. Who's cleaning it?'

His mouth quirked up at her disgruntled tone. 'Me.'

'Then I like fish. I couldn't help but notice the table you'd set. Is the fish for dinner?'

He'd stopped by the home store for a tablecloth, candlesticks, and some plain white china. Nothing fancy, but better than Glenn's chipped plates. He'd turned Glenn's gouged-wood table into something halfway presentable, in case things went well.

'Depends. I've got steaks marinating. I didn't know if you'd have had a chance to eat.'

Some of the starch seemed to leave her sails. 'I don't really do steaks. But the fish sounds wonderful and I didn't have dinner. So thank you.'

He had the fish now, lowering the rod and reeling fast. 'Did the father ID the girl?'

'Yes. Her name was Tracey Mullen. We have no idea why she was in that condo, but it looks like she played mom against dad. Each thought she was with the other.'

'Divorced then?'

'Yeah. Mom comes tomorrow. Not gonna be fun. I gave the dad your message.' She hesitated. 'Told him you'd risked your life to save her. He thanked you.'

'I've been thinking about him, all afternoon. Thinking of you, having to tell him.' The fish was close now. 'Back up. This boy's coming out.' She skittered back and he gave a final pull, landing the walleye on the dock where the fish slapped around frantically. 'Big one.' He looked up, saw her face droop. 'Should I throw him back?'

'Would I seem silly if I said yes?'

He met her eyes. 'No,' he said gently and she relaxed. 'This boy's lived a long time. Seems a shame to end his roll.' Pulling on gloves, he took the hook from the fish's mouth and put him back into the water, holding on until the fish gathered enough strength to swim away on his own. 'I catch and release most of the time anyway. Only so many fish one man can eat. Let's go inside. I'll clean up and then we can talk.'

'And I'll get better answers?'

'Yes.' And he hoped he got answers, too. Ones he could live with.

Monday, September 20, 8:45 P.M.

Barney Tomlinson sat at his desk in his office at the back of his warehouse, blearily staring at the P&L statement on his computer screen. Blindly he reached for the glass on his desk and, finding it empty, reached for the bottle he kept in his drawer.

It was empty, too. With a throttled oath, he chucked the bottle across the room where it bounced harmlessly against the wall. Cheap liquor in plastic bottles.

That's what his life had come to. Cheap liquor, and no more of that. *I'm ruined.*

His wife had put a hold on their funds. Some fancy lawyer was going to become rich . . . *on my money*. He dropped his head to his hands. 'My goddamn money.'

I hope the little whore was worth half your money, his bitch of a wife had sneered. She'd probably get what she was asking. Half of his money. His own lawyer didn't seem hopeful. When there were pictures involved . . .

Those damn pictures. *He'd* sent them. That damn blackmailer. *Who ruined my life*. He peeked between his fingers to look at the pictures her lawyer had given his lawyer. Barney remembered that night. The sex had been good. Not great, but good. More than anything, Shondra had listened to him. Made him feel . . . important. Young.

Now that his money was gone, Shondra was gone, too. His bitch of a wife had gotten a good chuckle out of that. He wished she were dead. Shondra *and* his bitch of a wife. He'd thought it through, looked at all the angles, but every way he looked at it, he'd be the first suspect. At least when the dust cleared, he'd have half of whatever was left.

'Excuse me.'

Barney looked up, brows crunched. A man stood in his doorway, hands in his pockets. He looked familiar, but Barney couldn't place him.

'We don't allow soliciting here,' Barney said. 'You'll have to leave.' He started to stand, then sank back into his chair when the man casually pulled a very large gun from his pocket. He was wearing black gloves. Barney's heart began to beat like all hell. His eyes darted around, finding the phone at the edge of his desk. Too far away to grab.

No one was here. His employees had gone home. Nobody would hear him scream.

'W-we don't keep cash here,' Barney stammered. 'B-but

I have a watch.' He started to take it off but the man lifted his gun higher.

'I don't want your watch, Barney,' the man said mildly. He rounded the desk, shoving the gun's barrel against the back of Barney's head.

'Who are you?' Barney demanded, then he knew. '*You*. You took those pictures. You fucking blackmailed me.'

'Well, technically it was only attempted blackmail. You never paid me, after all.'

'What do you want? I have no more money. You ruined me.'

'No, Barney. *You* ruined you. You stick your cock in places it ought not go, you gotta accept the consequences.' The man actually sounded amused. 'Buh-bye.'

Buh-bye. He'd heard it before. Now he knew who this guy was. 'You're—'

He stepped back from Tomlinson's body, now face-first on the desk. What was left of his face, anyway. He searched Barney's pocket, finding keys, his BlackBerry, and the disposable cell he'd provided. Pocketing the keys and BlackBerry, he walked around the desk, careful not to step in any of Barney's brains. Pausing at the door, he snapped a picture with the disposable cell, then checked to be sure he'd gotten a good one.

He had, indeed. Barney was well centered and the blood contrasted well with the white papers strewn over the desk. It would make a nice visual aid for the next bozo who ignored him. And for the College Four Minus One if they balked.

He hoped the cops would find the hollow-point bullet that had exited Barney's head and tie it to the dead cop-turned-security-guard. It would let him pull the noose a little closer around the necks of Eric and his friends.

He pulled Barney's office door closed and, pulling the ski mask over his face, left the way he'd come in. He wasn't too worried about the cameras. After listening to Albert and Eric discuss their plans, he'd concluded the two had the cameras covered. Besides, the only video that would matter after tonight would be the video he took.

On his way out he unlocked the cage that held Tomlinson's dog, just as Tomlinson did every night when he left. The dog didn't like Tomlinson at all. The warehouse manager handled the hound, feeding it and putting it back in its cage where it would pace all day. He hoped Eric and Albert didn't plan to kill it. It was a beautiful animal.

He closed the back gate and yanked on the twine Tomlinson kept tied to the door of the dog's cage, just as Tomlinson did every night. The dog bounded out with a ferocious growl, jumping at the fence, teeth bared. Truly a magnificent animal.

Buh-bye, he thought as he got into Barney's car and drove away. He'd park it a few blocks over, then retrieve his own vehicle. That way when Eric and the gang arrived, they wouldn't see the car and think anything was amiss – like that Tomlinson was dead inside. They'd start the fire, and by morning, his grip on them would be even tighter.

Monday, September 20, 8:57 P.M.

'I'm in.' Eric was hunched over his laptop, staring at Tomlinson's company server.

'About time,' was all Albert said, his gaze glued to the

television set. He'd been watching the news to get a feel for where the cops were on the condo investigation.

Eric let Albert's words roll off his back. He couldn't worry about the two of them right now. He had to figure out how to get past the alarm or there would be no 'them' to worry about. It had taken a lot longer than he'd expected to break into Tomlinson's server, but he was nervous and not thinking, which explained most of the delay.

Opening a folder labeled 'Maintenance,' he nodded. 'The alarm's an old design. The documentation here is from a system they bought ten years ago.'

Albert's jaw clenched. 'I don't care about the make and model. Can you turn it off?'

'Yeah. It'll be easy. I just have to—'

Albert held up his hand. 'Shh. It's nine.'

On the television, the anchor looked grim. 'Good evening. We have an update on the fire that destroyed the lakefront condo last night. Police have identified the female victim as Tracey Mullen. Tracey was just sixteen years old.' The screen split, a photo of a pretty young girl with big brown eyes appearing next to the anchor's face.

Eric's stomach turned inside out and he was glad he'd eaten nothing for hours. *Tracey Mullen*. He stared at the face on the screen, but what he saw was her face pressed against the glass, her mouth open on the scream that echoed in his mind. Next to him, Albert had tensed and Eric wondered if the guilt was eating him like acid, too.

The screen changed to a video of a woman with bright red-orange hair wearing a jacket with SAR printed on the back and holding the leash of a German Shepherd. The woman and the dog entered the burned-out condo while three others looked on – a blonde woman, a dark-haired man, and a tall guy wearing a fedora. Hat Squad, Eric thought. The guy with the hat was a homicide detective.

'This was the scene this afternoon as a cadaver dog searched for additional remains in the building,' the anchor's voice said. 'Fortunately, they found none.'

Eric released a breath. At least they'd killed no one else. The girl was a tragedy, but she shouldn't have been there to begin with.

The video changed abruptly, now grainy and far away. 'News 8 has obtained this video, taken with a bystander's cell phone. You're looking at the cadaver dog, who, after searching the burned building, continued tracking on the other side of the property, ending up at this stretch of beach. Police captain Bruce Abbott had no comment as to the relevance of the dog's find to the ongoing investigation.'

The anchor reappeared. 'In other news, a fatal car accident claimed the life of Joel Fischer early this morning. Joel's car ran off the road between his home and the university, where he was a prelaw student. No one else was injured. Funeral services will be tomorrow afternoon . . .'

'The dog found where the blackmailer left after killing that guard,' Albert said coldly.

'But they'll still think it was us,' Eric said, fear in his voice.

'They don't know about us. Yet. We need to make sure they don't find out.'

Monday, September 20, 9:02 P.M.

Olivia rubbed her hands over her arms briskly. She was partly cold, partly nervous. Mostly nervous, she admitted. She stood in the cabin's living room, which was dominated by a wooden table covered in linen, candles, and china. The man knew how to set a nice table. And he planned to cook for her.

And then what? Nothing, she decided firmly. *Nothing, until I get some answers.*

He'd been 'paying attention.' *Watching me.*

She caught a flash of white from the corner of her eye and turned to follow it. It was his shirt, she realized, thrown from the bathroom into a waiting basket. Which meant that right now, the man was half naked. Olivia drew a breath, her arms no longer cold. None of her was cold. She knew what he looked like half naked.

She knew what he looked like all the way naked. Therein lay the problem. The water started to run and Olivia started to walk, her feet having a mind of their own, stopping in the open bathroom doorway.

He was washing up in the sink, his head bent to the water. He still wore his trousers and she told herself that was a good thing. Otherwise, she would have had serious trouble keeping her resolve. *Must have answers before . . .* well, just before.

She leaned against the door frame undetected and simply watched him. If anything, he looked better than he had that night, stronger, muscles more defined . . . just better, which really wasn't fair. At the moment though, she found it hard to complain.

The dark hair at his nape was wet and curled just a little, and her fingers itched to reach out and touch, but she silently stayed where she stood. He still hadn't seen her. Razor in hand, he lifted his eyes to the mirror, then froze, watching her reflection. When she said nothing, he straightened and started to shave, meeting her eyes in the mirror every time he rinsed his blade.

It was an intimate thing, watching a man shave. She'd watched Doug shave, all the months they'd been engaged. She'd missed this, the intimacy. She missed the sex, too, but the intimacy most of all. That sense of belonging to someone, that he belonged only to her. She'd thought she'd had that with Doug, but had painfully learned she had not.

She drew a breath, steadying herself. She wouldn't have it here either. David Hunter would never belong to her. She knew that. She wondered if he knew it, too.

As she watched his muscles move, his eyes meet hers, and she felt everything inside her go liquid and needy . . . she wondered if belonging, the exclusivity of it, even mattered. Too soon he was finished with the blade. But he didn't turn, still watching her in the mirror.

'Why have you watched me?' she asked huskily.

His throat moved as he swallowed hard. 'I needed to be sure you were all right. You were working that case . . . all those bodies coming out of the pit. You were pale and stressed. Evie said you weren't sleeping. Not eating. I worried.'

She lifted her chin. 'So if you were so worried, then why didn't you call?'

He turned then and the room seemed a whole lot smaller and the air seemed a whole lot thinner. His silver gaze was piercing, yet uncertain.

'Well?' she pressed and had only a second to prepare before he stepped forward and slid his fingers into her hair, lifting her face.

'I'm sorry. I need to know,' he said harshly, and then she couldn't breathe at all. His mouth was on hers and it was exactly the same. Exactly as she remembered. Hot and necessary. All the reasons that she shouldn't kiss him back

183

vanished like mist as she stood on her toes, her palms flat against his chest, touching all that bare skin and hard muscle. *Mine. For this second, mine.* Then her arms were around his neck, winding tight, pulling herself higher. Closer.

He made a sound deep in his throat, rough. Needy. One hand tightened in her hair and the other roved her back and sides impatiently as he deepened the kiss and she remembered how it felt. His mouth on her. His hands on her. God, the man had amazing hands. *Touch me.* She wanted to scream it, but there was no air. Her dress fluttered against the back of her legs as he grabbed a handful of fabric at her hip and twisted it in his fist. Visions of him ripping her dress over her head taunted. Tempted.

Just like last time.

He pulled away abruptly, his chest swelling as his breath beat hard and fast against her hair. But although his grip gentled, he didn't let go. His one hand cradled the back of her head, pulling her cheek against his bare skin. The other hand splayed firmly against her lower back, as if he'd keep her from bolting.

Just like last time.

She eased from her toes, her hands sliding down his skin, finding a natural resting place on his back. And she held on, because she needed to. If she pushed away, he'd let her go, but she didn't. Couldn't. He rested his cheek on the top of her head.

'It was real,' he murmured, sending a shiver down her spine. 'I didn't imagine it.'

She thought of how she'd left him, sprawled in his own bed, snoring softly. He'd had way too much champagne at Mia's wedding while she had been one hundred percent sober. For long months she'd wondered what he'd remembered. If he remembered what they'd done. What he'd said.

'It depends,' she said cautiously, 'on what you think you imagined.'

'I remember Friday,' he said quietly. 'Everything about Friday. Saturday, not so much.' Friday had been Mia's rehearsal dinner. The first time she'd seen him. Saturday had been the wedding, and Saturday night . . . Well, that's why she was here.

His fingers began moving against her scalp, gentle circles that made her eyes drift closed. 'I was sitting on the steps of the church,' he said, 'dreading going in.'

'Another wedding you'd leave alone,' she murmured.

He stiffened, his fingers going still. 'I told you that?'

'Saturday night, after the reception. After a couple glasses of champagne you told me . . . quite a lot. I wondered how it could be true. How a man who looked like you could possibly be alone.'

'It's just a face, Olivia.'

She leaned back to look up at him, at the face that made women everywhere swoon. His gray eyes were sad. And alone.

She ran her fingertips over his jaw, felt it twitch, and realized how tautly he held himself. 'It wasn't just your face. I kept thinking, he's got to be mean, proud, stupid, *something*. I kept looking for a flaw, but never found one.'

'I have a lot of flaws. Believe me.'

She leaned against his chest again, her words defeated. 'Not that I could see.'

His fingers resumed their slow massage and she could feel herself melting against him. 'You wore this dress at the rehearsal dinner. I was hoping that was a good sign.'

'I wondered if you'd remember.'

'Like I said, I remember everything about Friday. I was sitting on the steps and you almost fell into my lap.'

She felt compelled to defend herself. 'My heel hit a rock and I tripped.'

'One more reason to be grateful for a woman in high heels,' he murmured. 'You didn't hear me complaining, did you?'

'No.' He'd been sweet and funny, tending to the knee she'd skinned when she'd fallen. He'd helped her into a side entrance of the church, his arm around her as her heart cantered. Then he'd found her a chair, crouched at her feet, and tenderly cleaned the blood from her knee as she'd stared down into his face. Which was far from 'just a face.' She'd been all but mesmerized. 'You put a Little Mermaid Band-Aid on me.'

'My niece, Grace, had skinned her elbow that afternoon.' He still sounded faintly embarrassed, charming her now as he had then. 'I had them in my pocket.'

'So you said.' As he'd looked up with a boyish, bashful grin. *And that was the moment he had me.* He never had to be smart or funny or thoughtful or polite. But he'd been all those things, too. He'd been perfect. 'Friday was a nice night.' *Perfect.*

'It was. I didn't want it to end.' Neither of them had. After Mia's rehearsal dinner, they'd ended up at Moe's, a restaurant run by his friends, where they'd had pie and coffee and talked until the owners swept up around them and finally turned out the lights.

'I don't think I ever closed a restaurant down before.'

'When Moe knew I was moving out here, he asked me to tell you hello.' He said nothing more for a long, long moment, still holding her. Then he sighed quietly. 'Hello, Olivia. I should have said that months ago.'

She pulled back, met his eyes, her own hardening. 'Then why didn't you? Why did you move here in the first place?'

He didn't blink. 'Because of the next night. Saturday night.' He paused, his gaze unflinching, and her cheeks grew hot. 'There's a lot I don't remember about that night after Mia's wedding, Olivia, but I remember enough.'

Her chin lifted a fraction. 'Such as?'

His eyes changed, shifted. 'Like how you felt when I danced with you, holding you against me. How your bridesmaid dress dipped low in front.' He slid his hand from her hair, gently tracing the edge of her bra through the thin dress she wore, sending current charging all over her skin. 'How I wanted to know what you looked like without it.'

He dipped his head, brushing his lips over the curve of her shoulder, his fingertips teasing the fullness of her breast. 'But somehow,' he whispered, 'I know how you look without it. I shouldn't. But I do, don't I?'

She was trembling now. *You have to make him stop*. But she couldn't. Didn't want to. 'Yes.' It was barely audible, but from the sharp intake of his breath, she knew he'd heard. *Touch me*, she wanted to plead, but once more there was no air in her lungs.

Abruptly he slid both hands down, covering her butt. Her whimper of relief was muffled as he took her mouth again, hot and demanding. A shudder shook him and he tore his lips away.

'God. I remember how you felt in my hands,' he muttered, kneading her flesh and she lifted on her toes, up into him. He was already hard.

She knew how it felt to press against that hard ridge, to feel it throb against her. She needed to feel it again. Now.

She made a frustrated noise and he finally lifted her, pressing her into the door frame, his body hard between her thighs.

Almost, but not nearly enough. Just like last time. She rocked against him and heard him utter an oath, then his hands found the bare skin of her legs, trembling as they caressed.

Unsteadily, he feathered kisses up the side of her neck to her ear. 'I remember how you taste, Olivia.' It was a harsh whisper, wringing a moan from her lips. He ground into her and her head lolled against the door frame as she let the memories in. *This*. This is what she'd craved, all those months. All those months he'd stayed away. 'Don't I?' He kissed her neck, hard. 'Do I know how you taste?'

She nodded, every muscle clenching.

'And I know how you sound when you come.'

'Yes.' The word was nearly a sob.

'And then . . .' He was breathing hard, his fingers digging into her inner thighs, pulling her wider, rocking up into her, so close that if it weren't for their layers of clothing, he'd be inside her. She met each thrust, so damn close. Almost there, just from a few whispered words and the thrust of his hips.

She swallowed hard. 'What?' she whispered, her voice raspy. Desperate.

'Your mouth . . . I can still feel your mouth on me. Hot and wet.' He shuddered. 'I wasn't sure if I'd dreamed it. Tell me I didn't dream it.'

'You didn't.' The memory hit her hard and she jerked her face away from him. *Stop this now*. 'Why?' she asked roughly. 'Why didn't you call? If you remember all of it, why have you stayed away all this time?'

His hips stilled. 'I woke the next morning with a hell of a hangover. Alone. The last clear memory I had was the reception, drinking champagne. Dancing with you. Then I woke up in my bed.' He swallowed. 'Naked. I wasn't sure how I'd gotten home. What was reality and what I'd fantasized. Then I smelled you on my pillow.' He turned his face into her hair. 'I knew you'd been there. You'd gone without a good-bye or a note.'

He lifted her head and she opened her eyes. His gaze was intense. She saw confusion swirling there, and hurt. And something else she couldn't define.

'Why did you leave?' he asked urgently. 'I need to know.'

'Let me down.' Instantly he did. Her knees were weak, but her feet were solidly on the floor, *where I should have kept them all along*. She wanted to look away, but forced her eyes to remain on his face. 'When I . . . when I came,' she said, 'what did I say?'

He frowned slightly. 'My name. Why?' His frown deepened, his eyes narrowing when she said no more. 'Why? What did I say?'

She drew a breath. She'd never done a one-night stand in her life before David Hunter, not that he'd believe it. And rarely had she done *that*, even with men she'd known for years, but . . . *God*. She'd been caught up in some kind of evil genie spell, because not to take him into her mouth had never entered her mind. His body had bucked and bowed and he'd been so goddamn . . . beautiful. Then he'd thrown his head back, clenched his teeth and . . . said the word that had said it all.

She realized her own teeth were clenched. 'Dana,' she said tautly. *My sister's best friend*. Who was married to someone else.

His gray eyes abruptly shuttered, becoming unreadable. 'And?'

Olivia's mouth fell open. '*And?* That's all you have to say?'

He shook his head hard. 'No. That's not what I meant.'

And? Like it was nothing. *Like I was nothing.* 'Let me go.'

'Olivia, wait.'

She shoved at his shoulders. 'No. Let. Me. Go.' She twisted, her dress falling back down around her legs. He reached for her and she smacked him away.

'Olivia, wait.'

A sob was building but she'd be goddamned before she let him see her cry. She made it out of the room, grabbing her purse from the kitchen counter, him on her heels. He made it to the door ahead of her and slapped his palm against it.

'Listen to me.'

'I did,' she spat. 'That's the problem. Let me go or I swear to God you'll be sorry.'

Slowly he backed away. 'I am. I am sorry.'

'Yeah, right,' she scoffed and yanked the door open. She stopped herself, forcing herself to calm down. Driving when she was this angry was dangerous. She stared straight ahead, not trusting herself to look at him again. 'I don't do one-night stands, David. Believe it, or don't. I don't care. But hear this clearly. I don't play second-string. When I'm with a man, I want him to be thinking of me. Only me.'

'Olivia, please. I . . . don't have any excuse except I'd had too much to drink.'

'And?' she asked sardonically. 'From now on, stop watching me. Please.'

'All right,' he said hollowly. 'I won't bother you again.'

190

'Good.' She got to her car and out to the main road, then the shakes hit and she pulled over. This always happened when she got emotional. That's why she didn't like to get emotional. She groped for her cell phone in her purse and hit speed-dial one.

'Well?' Paige asked, bypassing greeting.

'Sal's Bar,' Olivia said darkly. 'In thirty.'

'Then . . . it didn't go well?'

'Y'think? I'm gonna text Brie, see if she can meet us.'

Paige sighed. 'Are you okay?'

'Oh, sure. I'm just peachy. See you in thirty minutes.'

David stood in the doorway of Glenn's cabin, knuckles pressing into his throbbing temples. And? *And?* His stomach was churning. He'd blown it again. And he'd hurt her. Again. 'You stupid, dumb fuck.'

But standing here wouldn't help anything. Shoulders heavy, he closed the front door and started to clear the unused table when his cell phone rang. It was Paige.

Of course it was. 'What?' he asked wearily.

'You know, for a gorgeous guy with a really sharp brain, you are a stupid SOB.'

He closed his eyes, too tired to fight. 'Thank you, Paige. See you tomorrow night at the dojo. You can rip me a new one then.'

'I'm on my way to Sal's to meet her and Brie for major mojitos. What did you do?'

'This is none of your business. Really.'

'I'm going to have to tell her you know us both. I've never lied to her. I won't start.'

Terrific. 'Go ahead. Not much you can tell her that'll make it much worse.'

'That bad?'

'Oh yeah.' *I don't play second-string*, she'd said. 'Paige, who hurt her?'

'You mean, besides you?'

He flinched. 'You know, you're not helping here.'

'I'm sorry. I just hate to see her this upset and I'm going to have to make it worse by saying you and I are friends.'

'Well, at least we're still friends,' he said morosely.

'God. David, I'm sorry. I don't mean to twist the knife. You want to know who hurt her? Most recently, it was her ex-fiancé.'

David's eyes narrowed. 'Micah Barlow?'

'You know Micah? Oh, wait, he's in Arson now, so you would. Well, yeah, Micah was in it, but he wasn't her fiancé. That would have been Micah's best friend, Doug.'

Second-string. 'He left her for someone else, didn't he?'

There was a pause. 'Yeah. And it almost killed her.'

Good going, Hunter. 'Just do what you need to do to make her okay. Say what you need to say. Call me anything you want. I won't bother her anymore.'

'David . . . Dammit.'

'Tomorrow at the dojo, just let me know that she's all right.'

'We'll think of something. Just hang in there.'

I hung on too long. That was the problem. But how could he fix it?

Monday, September 20, 11:15 P.M.

'It's easier when the stuff is already here,' Albert muttered. Like Eric, he carried a gas can in each hand. Mary quietly brought up the rear, carrying the spool of fuse line. Her eyes were still red-rimmed and swollen.

I should be grieving, Eric thought. *Joel was my friend*. But all he could think of was getting this job done and getting the hell out of Dodge.

'Last time we got lucky,' Eric hissed back. 'The glue was there. I told you, the fork trucks here run on propane and the tank is out back. We can't use it to light the fire.'

Dressed all in black, each of them wore gloves and this time, ski masks over their faces. They stepped over the dog, who'd finally gone to sleep after eating the steak they'd injected with a narcotic Mary had left over from a back injury. She looked back.

'He's breathing,' she said. 'Good. I don't want anyone else hurt.'

'He's a dog, not an "anyone,"' Eric muttered, putting his gas cans down next to the back door. *Not a girl*. Whose face he could still see every time he closed his eyes.

'Let's dump the gas outside,' Albert urged. 'Don't risk triggering the alarm.'

'We have to destroy what's inside.' Eric sliced a hole in the door's window and broke away enough glass so that he could crawl through. 'Plus the video from the security cameras is inside. We need to take that with us. Give me a boost.'

Grumbling, Albert did so and prepared to come through himself.

'Wait,' Eric said, staring at the alarm panel. 'The alarm's not set. Whoever was last out must've forgotten.'

'Or we're about to get caught,' Albert said. 'Open it. I want to do this and get out.'

Eric opened the door and took his gas cans, then stepped aside to let the others through. 'I'll get the video first, then I'll pour my gas. Mary, you start laying the fuse.'

The video was where Tomlinson's secretary said it

would be. Eric imagined she'd remember his phone call when the police began asking questions, but that was okay. He'd used the bastard's disposable phone. Let it lead the cops to the real bad guy.

He popped the tape from the recorder, then spread his gas among the boxes stacked near the loading dock before meeting Albert and Mary at the back door. 'Got the video. Mary, light the fuse.'

'For Joel,' she said, then touched the flame to the fuse. 'Let's go.'

They ran to their car, Eric looking over his shoulder, watching for the moment flames became visible inside. When they did, he snapped a photo using the texter's cell.

'What was that for?' Mary asked as they drove away. 'Why did you take a picture?'

Eric and Albert shared a glance. 'Let's get out of here,' Eric said. 'Then we'll talk.'

Albert drove quickly, then pulled onto a side road where they'd be shielded by trees. They jumped out and replaced the license plates they'd taken from Eric's car, then got back in and took their ski masks off. Once they'd climbed back in, Albert started driving again and Eric turned back to Mary. 'It's like this,' he began.

Her face went pale as she listened. 'Oh my God. We just . . . Oh my God. The guard . . . He's dead? Are you sure?'

Eric nodded. 'He was shot in the chest.'

She closed her eyes. 'I can't do this.'

'You must,' Albert said harshly. 'Until we find this guy and kill him ourselves.'

Her eyes flew open, widened. 'Kill him? Us?'

'How else can we be sure he won't leak those pictures to the cops?' Eric asked.

She shook her head, hard. 'I can't kill anyone else. I can't.'

'You already did,' Albert said again, more harshly. 'Don't even consider running away, unless it's to off yourself like Joel did. He saved us a hell of a lot of trouble.'

Her jaw clenched. 'I hate you.'

'The feeling is mutual,' Albert said. Then silence fell over the car as the three of them drove back to the city.

Thoughtfully he tapped the steering wheel of his unobtrusive white panel van. *Interesting*. The three of them had turned on one another but seemed to be sticking together – for now anyway. He'd have to see how that played out over the next few days and whether or not they decided to run away.

He'd waited until they were out of sight of Tomlinson's warehouse before pulling out behind them. Now he stopped on the side road, just as they had and changed his plates, too, in case he'd been caught on the security cameras of the other warehouses.

Back behind the wheel, he reached for his video camera. He'd been parked at the fourth warehouse down from Tomlinson's, sitting in the back of his van, filming the three of them going in, then coming out. They'd worn black ski masks tonight, but he got their eyes – especially Mary's as she looked back to check on the dog. He'd even gotten Eric on tape, taking a picture with the disposable cell.

The video would provide some excellent clips to send to Eric and his pals. Now, home. He still had work to do. It wasn't like Eric and the gang were his only concern. No, sir. He hadn't gotten to where he was by putting all his eggs in a single basket. Nor had he gotten to where he was by being afraid of sacrificing a few eggs. What was left of Tomlinson was frying up right now. It was time to start a new omelet.

Monday, September 20, 11:55 P.M.

Olivia pushed her glass to the middle of the bar. 'I'm done.'

'I thought you were going to drown your sorrows,' Brie said, sitting on her left. 'You've nursed that one glass all night.'

'Maybe you just need time to process whatever happened,' Paige said quietly from her right and Olivia gave her a sharp look. Usually Paige egged her on, fanning the flames of ire at the injustice of men, but she'd been uncharacteristically muted tonight.

The three of them sat at the bar, morosely looking at their reflections in the mirror behind it. A redhead, a blonde, and a brunette, all in a row. 'The two of you could be on magazine covers,' Olivia said. 'But between us, we can't find a decent guy. Why?'

'Because men are dogs,' Brie said disgustedly. 'And you're beautiful, too.'

Olivia smiled at her in the mirror. 'And you're drunk, babe.'

Brie sighed. 'One of us needed to be.'

'It wasn't easy seeing Micah today, was it?' Olivia murmured.

Brie's eyes closed. 'No.'

Paige's black brows winged up. 'You saw Micah today?'

'It's an arson case,' Olivia said. 'Barlow's assigned. We needed cadaver dogs.'

'That's surprising,' Paige said. 'I thought he'd die before asking Brie for anything.'

'He called everyone else on the list first,' Olivia admitted. 'But he knows his job.'

'His job was never the problem,' Brie muttered. 'But we're talking about you. I can't believe you had sex with a fireman in Chicago and never told me. I'm still mad at you.'

'No, you're not.' Olivia sighed. 'And I didn't have sex. Exactly.'

Brie leaned forward, chin on her fist. 'What did you have, exactly?'

'Maybe she doesn't want to talk about it,' Paige said uncomfortably.

Brie frowned. 'Whose side are you on anyway?'

Paige flinched. 'Why would you even ask me that?'

Brie leaned forward more so that she could see Paige. 'What's with you tonight?'

Olivia turned toward Paige. 'Yeah, what's with you?'

'Nothing. I just think that sometimes there's more to it than meets the eye.'

Olivia sighed. 'He obviously didn't think there was anything wrong with screaming someone else's name . . . in the throes of passion.'

Brie patted Olivia's hand. 'Although, sometimes "*And?*" means more than "*And.*"'

Olivia shook her head. 'We need to get you some coffee.'

'No, I don't wanna be sober. I was just wondering what *he* thought he'd said.'

'Or what he'd done,' Paige added. She signaled to the bartender. 'Sal, can we get a cup of really strong coffee for our friend, here?'

Brie frowned. 'Spoilsport. When did you become the responsible one?'

Sal put three steaming cups of coffee in front of them. 'You need a cab, Brie?'

'I guess so,' Brie said glumly. 'Dammit.'

'I'll drive her home,' Paige said, then drew a breath. 'Liv, I just think you should reconsider. This guy's nice. From what you said, I mean.'

Brie was still frowning. 'No, he's not nice. Focus, Paige. He's a jerk.'

Paige hesitated, then blurted, 'Look, Liv, I need—'

Olivia's cell phone buzzed in her pocket. 'Wait a minute.' She checked the caller ID. 'It's Barlow. I have to take it.'

'He's a jerk, too,' Brie muttered.

'Shh,' Olivia hissed. 'Sutherland. What's up?'

'Another fire,' Barlow said. 'You should come.'

She slid off her stool. 'Where?'

He gave her the address. 'We've also got another homicide. Guy looks like he was shot in the head, then left in the building to burn. And Liv, we've got another ball.'

Olivia's pulse started to race. 'I'll call Kane and we'll be there as soon as we can.' She hung up and put enough cash on the bar to cover her tab. 'Gotta go, girls.'

Chapter Ten

Tuesday, September 21, 12:10 A.M.

The garden behind David's apartment house was his hideaway. The Gorski sisters kept it up beautifully, and for that he cut them a deal on the rent. The seventy-two-year-old identical twins had identical green thumbs and the air was fragrant with the last roses of the season. At least it wasn't honeysuckle.

Behind him a sliding glass door opened, then closed. A minute later Glenn settled himself in the chair next to him and drew a deep breath. 'God bless the Gorskis.'

David lifted his mug of hot tea. 'Hear, hear. Did I wake you?'

'Nah. Couldn't sleep. Saw the light from your laptop.' He gestured to the computer on David's knee. 'You still reading that asshole's shit?'

David glanced at the Preston Moss speech he'd been rereading. 'Somebody copied this guy last night at the condo fire, by design or smoke screen.'

Glenn looked amused. 'And you're playing detective?'

Annoyance prickled because he'd been trying to do exactly that – to understand the motive behind the arson that had killed that young girl. To understand how it had

199

morphed into the cold-blooded murder of the guard. 'That, and wondering if these environmentalists would quote Preston Moss after pulling a few dead bodies from a fire,' he said, then shook off his mood. 'Did you and my mom have a nice dinner?'

'Yeah, except that Martino flirted with her shamelessly.'

David chuckled at Glenn's sour tone. 'What time did you get her home?'

'A little earlier than you rolled in, *Dad*. Thought you'd stay out longer.'

David's smile faded. 'Yeah. Well, it didn't work out that way.'

'Sorry, boy.'

David sighed. 'Me too.'

For a while they were silent. 'So what did you do to your pretty blonde cop?'

David leaned his head back to stare at the stars. 'Did you ever mess up, Glenn?'

'With a woman? Time or two,' he said easily. 'How bad did you mess up?'

It was something about Glenn, something about the night, or maybe David was just damn desperate for advice. 'I, uh, said someone else's name when we . . .'

'Oh.' Glenn's face creased in a prolonged wince. 'You didn't just mess up, boy. You royally fucked up.'

'I got that,' David said dryly. 'Thank you.'

'You're welcome. Was the other woman current or past?'

'More like never.' He stared at the sky again. 'I believe they call it unrequited love.'

'Ah. Well, that sucks.'

'Indeed it does.'

'So, why did you do it? Say the other woman's name, I mean.'

'Got drunk on champagne,' David muttered.

'Why'd you do that?'

'It was a wedding. I hate weddings.' But he didn't get drunk at weddings, no matter how miserable he'd been. Hell, he hadn't even gotten drunk at Dana's wedding. So why at Mia's? Why in front of Olivia? He'd been asking himself that for two and a half years.

'Did your lady cop buy the champagne excuse?'

'No,' he said grimly.

'Didn't think so. So what are you gonna do?'

'Talk to her again.' He'd promised not to bother her again, but sitting among the Gorski sisters' roses, he'd decided that was a stupid promise to have made.

Glenn's gray brows lifted. 'Planning to wait another two and a half years for that?'

David huffed a surprised chuckle. 'No.'

'You know,' Glenn mused, 'I've never seen you drink more than one beer.'

'I don't get drunk,' David said flatly, then amended it. 'Hardly ever, anyway.'

'What happened the last time you got drunk? Before the lady cop?'

David closed his eyes. *Someone I cared about died.* 'Something very bad.'

'But you got drunk again that night at the wedding anyway. I think you need to figure out why before you try to smooth things over with your lady cop.'

'I know,' he said. 'I just don't know how.'

'Yeah, you do.' He met David's eyes. 'I've watched you for seven months and you don't sit still, boy. You run all the time, doing for other people. According to your mama, over Martino's lasagna and a couple of glasses of red wine, that's the story of your life. St David, defender of the helpless, fixer of broken stuff.'

David gritted his teeth. *Not again.* He couldn't have this conversation again. 'There's nothing wrong with doing for others.'

'There is when it keeps you from facing yourself. You've been running from yourself so long, all you see is your own ass. Eventually, that's all anybody else will see.'

David started to get up. 'Good night, Glenn.'

'Sit your ass down, boy,' Glenn snapped, and, rolling his eyes, David obeyed. 'Do you care about her?'

David crossed his arms over his chest. 'Who?'

Glenn huffed his displeasure. 'Your pretty blonde cop.'

David pictured the hurt in Olivia's eyes and his anger abruptly fizzled. 'Yes.'

'Why?'

David drew a breath, letting the scent of roses calm him as he considered his answer. 'I felt like I'd known her forever the first night I met her. There was something there. I can't explain it, but it was like . . . home.'

'Yet, knowing you shouldn't, you drank too much and said something that hurt her. You wanna know what I think?'

David stole a glance at Glenn's craggy face. The old guy was staring at him with a mixture of pity and wisdom that he missed so much since his father passed. 'Why not?'

'I think you recognized something special and you got scared. You'd been pining for this other woman for so long that being alone had become comfortable.'

'But I don't like being alone.'

'Didn't say you liked it. Said you were comfortable. Big difference there. One thing I learned in all the years I was married is that good relationships take time. They take heart. And they take trust. Maybe you didn't want to give her that.'

David swallowed hard. 'How long were you married, Glenn?'

'Almost forty years. Miss her every day. She made my life . . . good. And a man can't ask for more than that.' He started for his apartment, but looked back. 'Heard buzz on the scanner before I came out. Warehouse fire. Might be arson. Definitely homicide. And they found another glass ball.'

David came to his feet. 'They mentioned that glass ball on the scanner?'

'Nah. Your captain's there, at the scene. He tried to call your cell, but it went to voice mail, so he called me. Asked me to tell you to call him.'

He shoved his hand in his pocket, looking for his cell. Then remembered it was inside his apartment, charging. 'Why didn't you tell me that first thing?'

Glenn shrugged. 'Your mama is worried about you, so I wanted to say my piece. Your pretty blonde cop will be at the fire scene. Be careful.'

David waited until Glenn had his hand on the back door. 'Thank you, old man.'

Glenn looked over his shoulder. 'You're welcome. Don't fuck it up again.'

Monday, September 20, 11:59 P.M.

Sitting in his easy chair, he reached for the cell he used with Eric when it beeped. There was no message with Eric's text, only an attachment. It was grainy, but he could see the flames consuming Tomlinson's warehouse. They'd taken a while before sending it to him, as close to a 'fuck you' as they dared. Part of him had to admire their pluck.

you almost missed your deadline. wait for your next assignment.

He closed the phone and went back to his nightly task of combing through his customers' e-mails, working through potential clients who were ready for first contact. Ah, here was one who was almost ready for the plucking.

An office flirtation he'd been following seemed to have taken the next step, the man sending the woman a link to a quaint bed-and-breakfast off the beaten path. There was no invitation, no details, yet. But there would be, he was quite certain.

At the beginning the two had come in for lunch, talking about nothing but their office project. But the moment he'd seen them together, he'd known. He could always pick the couples who'd end up together. Sure enough, after a few weeks they were sharing personal details. A few weeks later, she told the guy she was unhappy with her husband, and then the guy was covering her hand with his. Whether they'd started out intending to have an office affair or not, it didn't matter. That's where they were headed.

And once they did the nasty, he'd be in business. *Ka-ching*.

He could always spot the philanderers and the ones who were up to something more. Doers of the naughty often realized it was better to conduct their illegal business in plain sight, rather than to skulk in the shadows, drawing attention to themselves. Sometimes they got away with being naughty in plain sight, *but not if I'm listening*.

He logged into his offshore account and smiled. Right on schedule. He studied each line of his statement and nodded. Most of his clients paid regularly and on time. Except one. Dorian Blunt had missed a second payment. He'd been patient last month when Dorian had complained of mounting medical bills for his child and his out-of-work wife. He'd begged for more time.

And I gave him more time. Once. Grabbing a new disposable phone from the box next to his easy chair, he texted Dorian Blunt's personal cell phone.

you're late. While he waited, he checked Dorian's checking account. The man did have a lot of bills. His balance was disturbingly low. Still, a deal was a deal. After a few minutes, he got a response.

I'm broke. 100K will have to be enough. No more.

He sucked in both cheeks, annoyed. *Broke?* Hardly. Dorian simply hadn't dipped into his illegally gotten gains for fear of getting caught. If the man didn't want to play by his rules, he shouldn't have embezzled company funds. *And he definitely shouldn't have left a paper trail that I could have found blindfolded.* He knew where Dorian kept his stash of embezzled cash. He could take it at any time. But that would be stealing.

He looked at blackmail as a kind of poetic justice with a twist of irony. *That makes me rich.* If people didn't want to get blackmailed, they shouldn't do bad things. *Or they should be smarter about it.* Calmly, he texted back.

i would reconsider. you have 12 hours. watch the news and be 'plumb' afraid.

That should do it. If Dorian didn't pay, the College Three would have their next assignment. Then, he'd go in and clean out Dorian's stash of cash, leaving Dorian's life insurance for his grieving widow. Whenever possible, he always left something for the widow, grieving or no. It was the right thing to do.

Tuesday, September 21, 12:20 A.M.

Olivia was one of the last ones to the warehouse, having gone home to change her clothes first. No way she was arriving on a scene dressed like she'd been for David.

And? Sonofabitch. The fact he'd screamed another woman's name when she'd been giving him . . . Well, he was an ass. She slammed her car door then stopped abruptly, realizing she was at the scene. Her gut had been so churned up over David, she hadn't had any churn left to worry about the body she was about to view.

Like Wile E. Coyote suddenly realizing he was standing in midair, Olivia's stomach dropped and she leaned against her car, momentarily weak-kneed. Now she had dead-body churn on top of David churn. And there was a mojito rolling around in there, too, along with some greasy chicken fingers from Sal's Bar. She swallowed hard.

Throwing up at the scene would not be good.

Move your body. Find Kane. She took a deep breath and immediately regretted doing so. Acrid smoke hung heavy in the air, burning her lungs. *Fuck this night.*

She made her feet move. At least David wouldn't be here. He didn't work again until Wednesday. As always, she found Kane easily in the crowd, his 'fire fedora' pushed to the back of his head. He waved her over when he saw her headed his way.

'We have another one,' Kane said. He stood with Barlow and Captain Casey, from the fire department. Casey wore his gear and looked grim.

'Appears they used gasoline this time,' Barlow said. 'They left four empty cans inside the building. Entered through a broken window in the back door.'

'The victim?' Olivia asked, focusing on the words, not the churn.

'Probably Barney Tomlinson, the owner of the company,' Kane said.

'Probably?' The warehouse's concrete walls still stood. 'Was the fire that bad?'

'Pretty bad,' Casey said. 'But there's a good bit left inside. Lots of melted chrome.'

'Tomlinson sold plumbing fixtures,' Barlow explained. 'No known connection to KRB Corporation or Rankin and Sons' construction – not yet anyway.'

'So the fire burned Tomlinson up?' Olivia asked.

Casey shook his head. 'No, ma'am. He was shot. He's still in his office, sitting at his desk. Most of his face is gone. He was shot in the back of the head.'

Her stomach pitched. 'Who discovered the body?'

'One of the firefighters out of Company Forty,' Barlow said. 'The office was in the center of the warehouse, self-contained with walls and a separate eight-foot ceiling. Inside was the victim, facedown on his desk. The team tried to keep the scene as intact as possible while putting the fire out.'

'When you called, you said they found another glass ball?'

'Covered in gel,' Barlow answered, 'like before.'

'When the firefighters saw it, they told their captain, who called me,' Casey said. 'They'd all heard about the glass ball Hunter caught yesterday. Nobody plans to talk to the press, although I'd be surprised if we kept it secret for too much longer. When they saw the ball tonight, they called me. I called Barlow.'

'I asked him to bring Hunter over,' Barlow said and Olivia's gaze shot to his face. 'I wanted Hunter to walk through and tell me how the place looked compared to last night's fire. I needed the info fast, before they'd let me go in. Hunter's in there now.'

'All right,' Olivia said calmly, although her heart had started to pound with the first mention of David's name. 'What about video surveillance?'

Kane pointed to a man standing next to the uniformed cops on duty. 'That's the warehouse manager. I haven't talked to him yet. There was also a guard dog.'

Olivia grimaced. 'They killed it?'

'No,' Barlow said. 'Appears the animal was drugged. The warehouse manager dragged him to the edge of the fenced area, then called 911. The dog was unconscious when the firefighters responded. I called a vet. I think the warehouse manager is more worried about the dog than his boss. Tomlinson didn't seem very well liked.'

'We'll want to talk to Hunter and the firefighters who discovered the body,' Kane said. He looked at Olivia. 'But first the manager.'

She nodded. 'Let's go.'

'I didn't know Hunter was here until just now,' Kane murmured as they walked toward the now-pacing warehouse manager. 'Did you, um, get my field glasses?'

'No. I . . . left early. I'll get your damn glasses later, all right? You want me to lead with the manager?'

'Knock yourself out, kid.'

The warehouse manager stopped his nervous pacing when they approached. 'I'm Detective Sutherland. This is my partner, Detective Kane. You are?'

'Lloyd Hart. Is that vet here yet?'

'I don't think so,' Olivia said. 'But I know he's been called. Is the dog yours?'

'No, but I'm the one who takes care of him. Have for five years. His name is Bruno.'

Olivia wrote it down. 'I'll make sure the vet knows you're the contact, Mr Hart. You can tell him Bruno's medical history and make sure he gets the best care.'

'Thank you.' He swallowed hard. 'You probably think I'm a horrible person, being more concerned about the dog than Tomlinson, or this fire.'

'I have a dog, too. So, what can you tell us about this fire and Mr Tomlinson?'

He rubbed his hands over his face. 'I left at my usual time, about six. Barney was still here. He was doing the books. They said he was shot. How?'

'We don't know yet, and we haven't been in there. So Mr Tomlinson was doing the books. Was the business in any trouble?'

Hart rolled his eyes. 'Oh, yeah. Tomlinson and the missus were in the middle of a messy divorce. He'd been cheating and she had pictures. She made sure everybody knew she had pictures and who Barney'd been doin' it with. Young woman he'd hired as a temp. Nobody was surprised because we all knew why he'd hired her. The girl never did a lick of work except on him.' He winced. 'Sorry, Detective.'

'It's okay. Was the divorce the reason the business was in trouble?'

'Not the whole reason. We were hurting before, with construction slowing. Most of our customers buy for commercial building. But Weezie had just ordered an audit of the books, and all of our spending had to be approved. I guess she figured he'd been buying things for the other woman from the business accounts.'

'Was he?' she asked.

209

'Yeah. I tried to tell him to stop, that he was gonna get fried, but he didn't listen. He was a fifty-year-old man with a twenty-year-old on the side. They never listen.'

'Mrs Tomlinson's first name is Weezie? Short for Louise?'

He nodded. 'It's a real shame. I like her. She didn't deserve this.'

Olivia met Hart's eyes. 'But Mr Tomlinson did?'

'No,' he said. 'Nobody deserves that. But I won't lie to you. Barney was a prick. He cheated on Weezie, he was rude to employees. Never made eye contact, always either on his cell phone or using it to surf the Internet. Probably looking at porn. And he hated Bruno,' he finished, as if hating the dog was the most egregious sin of all.

'What about you, Mr Hart?' she asked. 'Did you hate him?'

'Sure. He was racist, sexist, every bad "ist" you can name. But he was my boss, and I said "yes, sir" when he gave an order. The only time I ever held my ground was over Bruno. And before you ask, I was with my wife and some friends playing bridge when the fire started. I can give you their names.'

'That would be great. We can cross you off quickly. Sergeant Barlow said you were the one to call 911. How did you know to come here?'

A sheepish expression stole over Hart's face. 'I installed a smoke detector in Bruno's run. Just in case. It sends an alert to my cell phone. We were just finishing our last game when my phone went off. I got here, saw the fire, called 911. I dragged Bruno beyond the fence. I didn't want him to get burned or trampled on by the firemen.'

'Why the dog?' Kane asked. 'Did you have a problem with theft?'

'We used to store porcelain fixtures out here and had some vandalism. Kids, with too much free time. They'd break up porcelain, that kind of thing. Barney got the dog, hoping Bruno would bite one of them. The kids went elsewhere and Bruno stayed.'

'Video security?' Olivia asked.

'Cameras outside, none inside. Feed goes straight to a recorder inside. Old-fashioned. Barney didn't think he needed anything fancy as long as he kept Bruno.'

'We'll need a list of your clients and employees,' Olivia said.

'Talk to Jake Mabrow. He does our IT. I convinced Barney to set up an outside server about a year ago so that we'd have a backup. Jake will have access to our files. So will Weezie. She came in and made copies of everything on Barney's computer the day before she filed for divorce. He didn't know she knew about the temp.'

'What about you?' Kane asked. 'What will you do now that this place is gone?'

'Retire. I'd been planning to anyway. Weezie promised me Bruno.' Hart's head whipped to the side, focusing on a minivan that had just arrived. 'Vet's here.'

Olivia recognized the vet immediately. 'Barlow called Brie's dad,' she told Kane. 'He's a good vet,' she told Hart. 'He takes care of my dog. Bruno's in good hands.'

'I can go?' Hart asked and was gone with Olivia's first nod.

'We need to get Tomlinson's customer list,' Kane said. 'See if KRB Corp or Rankin bought plumbing supplies from them.'

'We also need to pay a visit to the Widow Tomlinson. Sounds like she won't be so grieving. This one shouldn't be as hard as Mrs Weems. It's my turn, isn't it?'

'It is. You did good with Mr Hart, by the way.'

One corner of her mouth lifted. 'You're just saying that so I'll give you my turn.'

His brows lifted. 'Did it work?'

'No.'

'Damn.' Then his eyes narrowed. 'Firefighters at your six.'

Olivia looked over her shoulder at Barlow and three firefighters coming their way. David was one of them. That her breath backed up in her lungs and her stomach rolled was an annoyance she'd just have to get used to. David Hunter was handsome. Gorgeous. Total eye candy. And a jerk. *So live with it and do your job.*

By the time the men reached them, she was steady.

'I'm Cunkle and this is Sloan,' one of the firefighters said. 'We're with Company Forty. And this is Hunter. He's with Company Forty-four. Barlow said you wanted to talk to us.'

'We do,' Kane said. 'Tell us what you saw inside.'

'Fire was fully engaged,' Cunkle said. 'The office walls were burning and the ceiling crashed in. Sloan and I pulled the walls down and there he was.'

'He wasn't alive. He'd been shot.' Sloan pursed his lips hard. 'Face was gone.'

'What about his desk?' Olivia asked. 'What did you see?'

'A bunch of papers, splattered with his blood. They hadn't completely burned, so I checked with my flashlight. They were hard to see, but they looked like sex pictures.'

'Sex pictures? You mean, like porn?' Olivia asked and Sloan shook his head.

'No. Looked like the guy was him. Pudgy, lots of white skin. Really white.'

'This time they brought their own fuel,' Barlow added. 'They found gas cans.'

'Pour patterns were similar to the ones we saw in the condo,' David said. 'They spread the gas on the floor in a line, then dumped what was left into a puddle. Looks like they came from the east and west sides of the warehouse and met in the middle.'

'And the ball?' Olivia asked and he met her eyes, his unreadable.

'Propping open a side door, just like you thought they'd done in the condo. The ball is covered in gel. I got a picture of it. Look where the ball touches the floor.' He handed her his camera and Olivia turned it so both she and Kane could see the view screen.

'What am I looking at?' she asked and David looked over her shoulder, his chin almost touching her ear. Her lungs stopped working as he pointed at the screen.

'There. Piece of a fuse. They used the ball to hold one end of the fuse in place.'

David moved back, and Olivia breathed again. 'When can we go in?' she asked.

'An hour or two,' Barlow said, 'when it's cooled. I'll call you.'

'Thanks,' Olivia said, then gave Barlow a small smile. 'Thanks for calling Brie's dad. He'll take good care of Bruno, and that'll make Mr Hart more cooperative.'

Barlow nodded. 'Hart's got an alibi?'

'Yes, but we'll check him out. First stop is the widow. She had motive to kill Tomlinson and to burn the place down. Supposedly she copied her husband's files, so we'll see if we can get customer and employee lists from her.' She turned to the firefighters. 'Thanks for the information. We'll be in touch.'

She walked away without a word to David Hunter, feeling him watch her back. Kane matched her stride, checking over his shoulder.

'He's watching you, Liv.'

'He'd better stop,' she said through her teeth, then made herself chill. 'I've been thinking. What if Barlow was right yesterday morning, that this has nothing to do with the SPOT environmental group?'

'That the glass ball is just a smoke screen?' Kane asked.

'Yeah. What if somebody really wanted to kill a person they hated and set the first fire to establish a false pattern? That killing Tomlinson was their plan all along?'

'I've been thinking the same thing. Sounds like Tomlinson's wife really hated him.'

'Let's find out how much.'

Sloan and Cunkle went back to their duties, leaving Barlow standing next to David. For a moment neither of them said anything, then Barlow said, 'Ouch.'

'What?' David muttered. 'She was nice to you.'

'For the first time in a couple years, but I wasn't talking about me.'

David hesitated, then shrugged. 'Who was Doug?'

Barlow shot him a surprised look. 'My friend, then and now. Used to be engaged to Liv. I introduced them, actually.'

'He left her.'

Barlow sighed. 'He did. And I helped, which is why I'm persona non grata.'

David thought of Paige's words. *He was in it, too.* 'How did you help?'

'Doug had a fiancée long before Liv. They'd been college sweethearts, then she left him. He never got over her, but he met Liv and I thought they had a shot together. Time passed, they got engaged. They set a date. I was going to be the best man. Everything was fine. Then, a couple weeks before the ceremony, Doug's old fiancée showed up. She begged Doug to take her back.'

'And he did?'

'Not right away. He came to me, asking for advice, and unfortunately I got involved. One of the stupidest things I've ever done.'

David frowned. 'You told him to dump Olivia?'

'No,' Barlow said forcefully. 'I just told him to imagine himself at eighty and see who he thought he'd be happiest with. He went off for a few days, thought it through, then chose Angela. Olivia was' – he sighed – 'a lot more crushed than I ever thought a woman could be.'

I don't play second-string. 'How did she find out what you'd done?'

'That would have been me telling her, another stupid thing I did. See, a week after Doug left her, her father died. He was a cop, too, apparently. In Chicago.'

'Yeah, I know. I'm friends with Olivia's half sister Mia. They share a father.' David's shoulders sagged. Now the second-string statement made even more sense.

'You knew Liv's father?'

David thought about Olivia and Mia's father, the animal that he'd been. Which always brought back memories of Megan's stepfather and what he'd done to Megan and her family. Which always made him mad enough to kill. Carefully, David relaxed his fists. 'Not personally. Thank God.'

Barlow looked down at David's hands, then back up, warily. 'That bad, huh?'

'Olivia's father was a miserable sonofabitch who didn't

deserve the air he breathed. Mia didn't know Olivia existed before their father died. Olivia only knew another family existed, that her father had chosen to live with them and not her and her mother.'

Barlow briefly closed his eyes. 'Shit. And then Doug left her for someone else.'

And then I said another woman's name when she was in my bed. 'Hell.'

'I saw Liv the day she found out her father had died. She was packing to go to the funeral in Chicago. I didn't know about her dad, and I thought she was packing to leave permanently because of Doug. I tried to get her to calm down, telling her not to do anything drastic, and somehow, I told her what I'd done.'

'What did she do?'

'Just looked at me, with those big blue eyes. Like I'd stabbed her in the gut.'

Like she looked at me when I said 'and.' He sighed. 'I know the look.'

Barlow's eyes narrowed. 'What did *you* do to her?'

David was tempted to say it was none of his business. *But I might need some help.* God knew he wasn't being too successful on his own. 'She thinks I wanted someone else, but she doesn't understand. I wouldn't have hurt her for the world, but I did. Then I tried to fix it, and . . .'

'And you dug yourself in even deeper,' Micah finished. 'Are you going after her?'

David's gaze shot over to where she and Kane stood with the warehouse manager. 'What, you mean right now?'

Barlow rolled his eyes. 'No, not now. Are you going to make this right?'

'Yeah. I am.'

Barlow nodded. 'Good. Now, let's get back to work.'

They headed back to the warehouse. 'This was no environmental arson, Micah. There was nothing in that warehouse worth burning, except for the guy without a face.'

'I know. Something's connecting these two arsons. You've got a good eye. You ever think of going into investigation?' he asked.

David shook his head. 'Took me a while to find fire-fighting, but now I can't see myself doing anything else.'

'You like walking into fires,' Barlow said, a touch of envy in his voice.

David grinned. 'It's a rush like no other. At the same time, I do like a good puzzle. Olivia's brother-in-law is an arson guy, too, back in Chicago. I like to think I've picked up a thing or two.'

Barlow slung his tool kit over one shoulder and pulled his camcorder from his coat pocket. 'Then let's see what our non-environmental arsonists left behind.'

Chapter Eleven

Tuesday, September 21, 12:55 A.M.

'Knock again,' Kane said when Mrs Tomlinson didn't answer the door.

Olivia raised her fist to knock again when the door opened, revealing a very tall, statuesque woman wearing a silk robe. Even without makeup, she was very beautiful and not at all what Olivia had expected a woman named Weezie to look like.

'Yes?' the woman asked.

'We're looking for Mrs Louise Tomlinson,' Olivia said.

'Well, I'm Louise, but not Mrs Tomlinson for much longer,' she said.

'I'm Detective Sutherland and this is my partner, Detective Kane. We're here to talk to you about your husband.'

Louise's perfectly tweezed brows lifted. 'What has he done now?'

'He's dead, ma'am,' Olivia said. 'He was murdered tonight.'

Quite unexpectedly, Louise Tomlinson's haughty expression slid away. Growing pale, her mouth dropped open. 'He's dead? Barney's dead? No.' Not waiting for an answer, she began to weep. She lowered her chin to her chest, hugged herself as she stood in the doorway and wept her heart out.

'Can we come in, ma'am?' Olivia asked.

Louise allowed herself to be led to a sofa in an ornately decorated living room, where she sank into the cushions, her face in her hands. 'How did this happen?'

'He was shot while he was in his warehouse.'

Louise looked up, her eyes wild. 'He didn't kill himself, did he?'

'It doesn't appear so, ma'am,' she answered. 'Why?'

'He was so angry with me. Very upset. I'd had our assets frozen.'

'We heard that you two were going through a messy divorce,' Olivia said quietly.

'We were. He cheated on me.'

'That had to make you angry,' Kane said smoothly.

Louise's wet eyes flashed. 'Of course it did. We'd been married for almost thirty years. I wanted him alive to suffer, not dead. Am I a suspect?'

'Right now we're just talking to people who knew your husband,' Olivia said. 'But just so we can check you off our list, where were you tonight?'

'Here. Alone.'

'Was Mr Tomlinson living here?'

'No. He had an apartment downtown near the university. Our son is a student there and lives in the dorm. Oh God, I have to tell him his father's dead.'

Olivia put a gentle hand on the woman's wrist. 'We'd like to tell him.'

Louise turned stark white. 'You think my son had something to do with this?'

'I think it would be best if you'd come with us, until we

can get this all sorted out.' Olivia stood. 'I'll go up with you while you change your clothes.'

Tuesday, September 21, 2:35 A.M.

'Well?' Abbott asked.

Olivia stood at the window looking into Interview Two and shook her head. Louise Tomlinson sat at the table, numb. Her lawyer patted her hand from time to time.

'She was angry with her husband and she stands to benefit financially from his death and the fire,' Olivia said. 'But unless she paid somebody to kill him, I don't think she was involved. No gunshot residue on her hands. The neighbors we talked to didn't see her leave her house. The engine of her car was cold. None of that is definitive innocence, but at this moment we can't place her at the scene.'

'The son's in Interview One,' Kane added. 'He was at a party all night. At least fifty people saw him. No GSR on his hands either.'

'Then cut them loose,' Abbott said. 'Find out who had cause to kill Tomlinson, besides his wife and son. Find out how they connect to the condo. See you at oh-eight.'

Olivia shot Abbott's back a baleful look. 'Why is it always oh-eight?'

'Go home, Liv,' Kane said kindly. 'Get some sleep.'

'I will, after we talk to the Tomlinsons. I'm hoping if I talk sweetly enough, she'll hand over the copy she made of her husband's hard drive. Otherwise we have to go to the IT guy, and he'll want a warrant.'

'You think you can sweet-talk her after hauling her ass downtown?' Kane asked.

Olivia raised a brow. 'I got ten that says I can.'

Kane smiled sharply, sensing an easy win. 'You're on.'

Olivia took a minute, putting herself in the mind of the older woman. Her grief had been real, as had her rage. She'd been entitled to both. Unless of course she paid someone to do her dirty work for her, but if that was the case, they'd find a money trail.

'Mrs Tomlinson,' Olivia said when she'd closed the door behind her.

Tomlinson's lawyer jumped to his feet. 'How long will you keep her here?'

'Not much longer,' Olivia said. 'Your son is coming. I'd like to talk to you both.'

Louise glared. 'I don't want to talk to you. You treated me like a criminal.'

Olivia sat across from her. 'No, ma'am. I was doing my job, as respectfully as I knew how. I'm so sorry that your husband is dead. I can't pretend to know how you're feeling right now, but I work homicide. My responsibility is to your husband. I have to find who killed him. I hope you and your son want the same thing.'

Louise swallowed, her lips thin. 'You fingerprinted me. You fingerprinted my son.'

'So we could tell your prints from anyone else's in his office or his apartment. It's standard procedure. Again, I'm sorry this had to happen tonight, but every hour that passes is an hour his killer goes free.'

Still pale, Louise closed her eyes. 'Someone shot him.'

'Yes, ma'am. It looks like he was at his desk, working. He was shot from behind.'

Louise flinched, then snapped her gaze to the door when her son entered. He looked even angrier than his mother had. He folded his mother in his arms and she began to cry again. Seth Tomlinson glared at Olivia. 'How dare you?'

'Please,' Olivia said. 'Please sit down.'

Still furious, Seth did, taking his mother's hand protectively. 'It's bad enough we have to go through this.'

'You're right,' Olivia said and Seth narrowed his eyes.

'You're the good cop. Where's the bad cop?'

Olivia returned his furious gaze with a sympathetic one. 'Right here in this chair. I can be either or both, depending on who's sitting in your chair. I need your help.'

'No,' Seth said. 'I'm not helping you.'

'You're entitled to your anger and your frustration. Right now, I need you to be angry at the person who put a bullet in the back of your father's head. The fire destroyed a lot of the things we'd normally look for – signs of a struggle, for example. Signs that someone forced their way into his office. Did he know his killer? Or was he simply in the wrong place at the wrong time? Did he keep money in his office?'

Louise shook her head. 'No. None of our sales trans-actions were cash. All of our customers paid by check or bank transfer. Anything Barney had in the office was strictly for personal use, and he was running short. I'd made sure of that.'

'Mom,' Seth said in a low voice, but she patted his arm.

'She's doing her job, Seth. I imagine she'll look at my finances to be sure I didn't hire a hit man.' Louise looked Olivia dead in the eye. 'I didn't. I wouldn't know how.'

'Yes, ma'am,' Olivia said. 'You still loved him.'

'Yes. He hurt me, so badly. But I never could have taken his life.'

'Who could have?'

Louise looked lost. 'I don't know. You'd need to talk to Lloyd Hart, our manager. He knew all the customers.'

'I did talk to him, for just a little while. He was pretty worried about his dog.'

'Bruno,' Louise murmured. 'Did they hurt the dog, too?'

'Drugged him. There's a chance he'll make it. Mr Hart said that the employees didn't care for your husband.'

'That's not true,' Seth bit out, but once again his mother patted his hand.

'Yes, it is.' She turned to Olivia. 'It wasn't always like that. Barney used to know everyone's name. He made sure everyone had benefits, pensions. As he got more successful, he changed. We had warehouses in three states and he started to travel. Buy fancy cars.' She lifted her chin. 'Fancy women, too, even though I didn't know it then. He wasn't the man I married anymore. Then business started to go down and Barney got scared. And mean. We were fighting all the time.'

'No, you weren't,' Seth protested. 'Mom.'

'We didn't fight in front of you. We didn't want you to know.' She turned to Olivia. 'I hadn't paid attention to the business in a long time. When I found out about Barney's affair, I made copies of all his files. I wanted my lawyer to have as much ammunition as possible.'

'Do you still have the copied files?' Olivia asked.

'On a couple of CDs, yes.'

'The fire destroyed so much. We could get started so much faster if we knew who to investigate.'

Louise looked at her attorney who gave a little shrug. 'It's up to you, Weez. I've seen the files. There isn't anything on them that you haven't already told them.'

'They're in my fire box at home.' Louise's lips twisted. 'Ironic, no?'

Olivia sighed. 'We get a lot of sad irony in this business. I know you're tired, but a few more questions, please. How did you find out about your husband's infidelity?'

'I hired a private investigator. One of my friends had gone through something similar, so I met her for lunch and somehow found the courage to ask for the name of her PI, and I hired her. She had incriminating photos in less than a week. I was devastated.' She swallowed hard. 'I went into Barney's office the next day when I knew he'd be out playing golf and copied the files. Then I filed for divorce that afternoon.'

Seth was studying his mother's worn profile. 'Can we go now? She's helped you.'

'Yes, she has and yes, you can go. Mrs Tomlinson, thank you. I'll personally keep you updated on the investigation. Can I take you home?'

'I'll take care of them,' the lawyer said. 'You'll want those CDs tonight, I take it?'

Olivia flicked a glance at the clock on the wall. It was almost three a.m. Surely the warehouse had cooled enough for her and Kane to see Barney in his office now. 'That would be ideal. My partner and I will follow you home.' Then she and Kane could double back to the crime scene.

Olivia found Kane in the observation room, a ten-dollar bill in his hand. 'Nice.'

'Keep it. She was going to help us all along. You ready to roll?'

'Yep. I'll drive. You can nap on the way.'

Tuesday, September 21, 3:58 A.M.

The three of them sat in Eric's living room, watching the muted television. It was tuned to the local twenty-four-hour news station, as it had been for the last day. Mary sat curled in the corner of the sofa, her expression like stone. Albert sat in an armchair, looking like the very angry captain of a starship.

Eric straddled a dining-room chair backward, his chin propped on the chair's carved back, having just been snapped at by Albert to stop pacing and sit his ass down.

'Turn it up,' Mary said flatly and Albert grabbed the remote.

'Top of the news this hour is another fire, this time in a warehouse north of the city,' the anchor said. 'News Eight has just learned that not only is it another arson fire, but also police have found another body inside.'

Shock had Eric surging to his feet. 'What the fuck?' he yelled.

Albert leaned forward, waving his arm. 'Shut up.'

Mary sat up straighter, her expression gone flatter, if that was possible.

'The body has been identified as Barney Tomlinson, the owner of the warehouse,' the anchor said, and a photo of a middle-aged man with a comb-over appeared on screen. 'We have Joseph Bradshaw live at the scene. Joseph, what are you hearing?'

The screen switched to the reporter, a fire truck in the background. 'The fire is out, but the activity here at the fire site has not slowed. Homicide detectives and medical examiners went into the building twenty minutes ago and have not yet come out. No one is giving any details of the circumstances surrounding Barney Tomlinson's death, but the presence of Homicide suggests the owner of this warehouse met with foul play.'

'Joseph,' the anchor said, 'is anyone indicating a link to the condo fire?'

'Not yet, but the homicide detectives who just went in are the same ones who were on the condo scene – Kane and Sutherland.'

Albert muted the television. 'So this is his game,' he said darkly. 'He murders and sets us up to take the fall.'

'We destroyed the tape,' Eric said. 'We wore masks. Nobody will know it was us.'

Albert's chuckle was without mirth. 'Do you truly think so, *mon ami*? I give him five minutes, perhaps ten. He'll send you another text with another link to another video.'

It was less than two minutes. Eric's personal cell phone buzzed. He checked the text and flicked a glance at Albert. 'It says "welcome to my employ."'

'And the video?' Mary asked, her voice barely a whisper.

Eric clicked the link. 'It's us,' he said when the video began playing. 'We're wearing masks.' He watched as the texter's camera closed in on Mary as she looked back to check on the drugged dog. Then the screen filled with a still shot of Mary's face, covered by the mask. Successive shots closed in on Mary's right eye until her iris was all that could be seen, then the video cut to a picture of Mary at the condo. Again the camera closed in, again the close-up of her iris.

Eric didn't even blink when he saw himself pause to snap a photo of the burning warehouse. 'He was there,' he said woodenly and passed the phone to Albert. 'He's basically saying he can put Mary at both scenes through her eyes.'

Albert replayed the video, his jaw going taut. 'Where was he? Goddammit.'

'He got Mary when she stopped to see the dog, so he had to have been hiding to our left.' Eric sank onto the sofa, opposite Mary. 'This is unbelievable.'

'This isn't what I planned,' Mary said thinly. 'I can't believe you didn't tell us, Eric. You had no right to keep this from us.'

'I said I was sorry.'

'Sorry doesn't help. If you had any idea . . .' She closed her eyes. 'Damn you.'

'Another text,' Albert said, then drew a sharp breath. 'It's Tomlinson. Or what's left of him.' He passed the phone back and Eric flinched.

Tomlinson lay facedown on his desk. There was a helluva lot of blood.

Eric passed his phone to Mary and waited for her to watch the video. 'So now what?'

'We draw him out,' Mary said coldly. 'And then we kill the sonofabitch.'

Albert raised a sarcastic brow. 'I thought you said you couldn't kill anyone.'

'I was wrong,' she said. 'The game just changed.'

'That's all well and good,' Eric said, 'but as I said before, now what?'

'He had to have had some beef with Tomlinson,' Albert said. 'Who knows, maybe he was blackmailing him, too.' Albert got up and paced. 'Somehow he found out about us. I can't figure out how. We never met together, except for here. Never in public. So how did he find out? How did he know Tomlinson? What's the connection?'

Eric felt an icy chill slink down his back. 'Could he have this place bugged?'

Albert stopped pacing, his expression grim. 'As crazy as that sounds, maybe.'

'But he still had to know about us,' Mary insisted. 'He's not going to just pick out rich boys at random and bug their apartments.' She lifted her chin defiantly. 'Hear that, asshole? We're talkin' about you!'

'Sshh,' Albert hissed. 'You'll wake the neighbors.' Then he stilled, his gaze swinging around to collide with Eric's. 'Eric.'

Eric had the same thought in the same instant. 'The neighbors. These walls are thin. Somebody heard us talking. Which one?'

'The walls aren't that thin,' Mary scoffed, but Albert looked away, rolling his eyes.

'One of the neighbors complained one night when we were . . .' Eric felt his cheeks heating. 'You know.'

'Oh.' Mary shrugged. 'Same thing happened to us. Joel and I . . .' She stopped suddenly, her lips pressing tight as tears filled her eyes. 'Dammit,' she whispered. 'For just a second I forgot. How could I forget?'

'It's part of grief,' Albert said quietly. 'You live in the dorm. A quad, right?'

'Yes. We all get our own rooms.'

'Did you and Joel discuss this in your room?' he asked.

Mary shook her head, hard, then slowed. 'Maybe, once or twice. But softly.'

'Those walls are thinner than these,' Eric said. 'That's why we never did anything in Albert's dorm room. Your roommates could have heard. But how do they connect to Tomlinson?'

'We need to find out more about Tomlinson.' Albert pointed to Eric's laptop. 'You got into his company server. What did you find?'

'Only what I was looking for – the maintenance files on the alarm system.'

'I Googled him while you were trying to hack into his server,' Albert said. 'I found a few general things. Tomlinson played golf in a charity tournament last year, but his business was bad – lots of layoffs. His wife is divorcing him. You're better at the computer, so dig deeper. Find out everything you can.' Albert grabbed his jacket.

'Where are you going?' Eric asked.

'Back to my dorm. It'll be daylight soon. I'm going to change and shave and then go have a talk with Mrs Tomlinson and find out what her husband was up to.'

Mary stood up. 'You can't just waltz into her house and talk to her.'

'As a reporter, I can.'

Eric rose slowly. 'Albert, wait. What if she checks up on you? You don't exactly fade into the woodwork. Especially with your accent.'

Albert's smile was grim. 'What accent?' he asked in a perfect Minnesotan tone.

Eric stared, his mouth open. 'You . . . Which is real?'

Albert met his eyes, his gaze cold. 'Does it matter anymore?' he asked. 'Start digging on Tomlinson. We need everything we can get.'

Well. As always, they were an interesting bunch. *So Mary wants to kill me? Right back atcha, girl. And Albert, not really French? Say it isn't so.* He'd seen that one coming a mile away. For a nerd, Eric was really very stupid.

He sat back in his easy chair and frowned. But Albert going to talk to Louise Tomlinson? He needed to think about that one. Louise didn't know anything to tell. He'd made sure of that. What harm could Albert do?

Conversely, how can I use this to dig their graves a little deeper? And how long can I keep the leash tethered so tightly? He didn't plan on watching them so closely forever. When their useful life was over . . . their lives would be over.

Besides, he might have a bigger worry at the moment. He rewound the recording he'd made of the nine o'clock news. It was a grainy video, taken by a cell phone. A search-and-rescue dog and its handler stood on the bank of the lake, a few hundred yards from the dock at the condo. He knew that shoreline like the back of his hand. The only way to that patch of open beach was by boat, but he saw no boat in the video.

He might have assumed that patch of beach was how the girl had come to be in the burning building to start with, but if so, the boat would still be there, would it not? Which could mean someone had been with her, someone who had not died in the condo.

Which could mean trouble for me. He needed to know what the police knew. If a witness existed, that person needed to die.

Tuesday, September 21, 5:30 A.M.

Austin Dent sat on his bed hugging his knees to his chest. His mom would be coming home from her job soon. She worked hard, his mom. He hated the worry he'd put in her eyes.

He hated that he couldn't forget the fear in Tracey's eyes when they'd both smelled smoke. Or the look on that guard's face when he'd been shot, the way he'd crumpled to the ground. But mostly he hated that somewhere out there a killer walked free.

Austin's hands clenched into fists. *I have to do something.* But he was afraid.

I owe it to Tracey. I promised I'd protect her. She was there because of me.

But what did he owe his mother? If he told, he'd put both their lives in danger. That man shot that guard in cold blood. He couldn't lead the guy straight to their lives.

But I can't do nothing. I can't live this way, wondering if he's going to shoot me, too.

If he called from a phone nearby, the cops would trace it. Everybody in town knew he went to school down in Minneapolis. A smart cop would connect the dots in no time.

So he'd have to contact the cops from Minneapolis. *Kenny will help me.* He'd text Kenny, tell him what to write in the letter and Kenny could mail it from downtown. That way the cops would know about the shooter, but nobody would know he'd told.

It could work. It would have to.

Tuesday, September 21, 5:45 A.M.

Olivia blinked hard as she drove the road to her house. The last forty-eight were catching up to her. She was going to walk Mojo, then fall into bed. . . .

She slowed as her front porch came into view. A familiar form slowly rose from her front steps and her tired brain wanted to scream foul. Carefully she pulled around the red pickup truck he'd parked on her curb and drove into her garage. For a moment she just sat in her car, her forehead resting on the steering wheel.

Then her door opened and she could feel the warmth of

his body as he crouched next to her. 'Olivia?'

'I'm all right, David,' she said, not looking at him. 'You promised not to bother me.'

'I know. I lied.'

'What do you want from me?'

'A chance to explain. Please.' His hand dipped under her braid, closing over her neck. His palm was warm, his fingers strong as they began massaging her skull.

A little whimper escaped her throat. She was so tired and his hand felt so good. *Focus, girl*. She grabbed his wrist and pulled his hand away. 'What's to explain?'

'A lot. Come on.' He urged her from the car, pulling her to her feet. 'You're about to fall flat on your face.'

'I was about to go to sleep.'

'Then I won't take long.' She let him lead her to her front door, not complaining when he took the keys from her hand and unlocked her front door. Mojo came bounding, crouching into a snarl when he saw David.

'Down,' Olivia commanded and Mojo instantly dropped to his stomach, eyeing David suspiciously. *Smart dog. Good dog.*

David closed the door behind them, walking around the dog as if he weren't there. Mojo craned his neck, watching. Cursing her own weakness, Olivia did the same. David looked as good going as coming. She followed him into her kitchen, Mojo at her heels.

'What are you doing?' she asked.

Standing in front of her open fridge, he looked over his shoulder. 'Making us breakfast. Your eggs are about to expire.'

'Sorry?' she said, shaking her head, then tilting it sideways on a silent sigh when he bent over to check out her vegetable bin. Too nice. Way too nice. *And so not fair that all the sexy ones are jerks.*

Abruptly he straightened, pointing to the bar stools at her counter. 'Sit, please.'

Mojo sat obediently, wagging his tail, looking up at David adoringly.

'Traitor,' she muttered to the dog. 'I want you to leave, David.'

He deposited all the cooking materials on her counter, ignoring her.

'I'm not hungry. Stop that,' she snapped when he broke eggs into her mixing bowl with the finesse of a chef. 'What the hell are you doing?'

His jaw clenched. 'I cook when I'm tense.'

'You're tense.' She made a scoffing sound. 'Please.'

'No, I'm actually scared to death.' He looked up, met her eyes. 'I'm not lying.'

He looked utterly serious and she felt her resolve weakening. 'Hell of a line,' she said. 'I must be the most gullible woman alive. Come on, Mojo.'

Her dog hesitated, staring up at David. Biting back a really vile oath, she tugged on Mojo's collar. 'I said, come.' Finally he followed, looking back over his shoulder as if to ask why the new guy wasn't coming. Olivia stood on her patio, tapping her foot impatiently. Finally Mojo padded back and she let him into the house. David was still there, inspecting a clear carton of mushrooms with a grimace.

'It's been a while since you shopped,' he said.

'I've been busy.' She slid onto a bar stool. 'Say your piece and then leave.'

He dropped his gaze to the cutting board, chopping the few vegetables that hadn't gone bad. 'I said someone else's name that night. I'm sorry. You don't know how sorry. But I need to know if I did anything else.'

She frowned at him, Brie's and Paige's words coming

back. *I wonder what he thought he'd said. Or done.* 'Like what?'

'Like, get rough. Or ask for something you didn't want to do.'

And? So it really hadn't been a statement of disregard. 'No,' she said softly. 'What did you think you did, David?'

He gripped the edge of the counter with both hands, bowing his head. 'I didn't know. At first I thought you were just embarrassed, but you never called and months went by. I wondered if I'd done something to . . . turn you off.'

'You did. You said another woman's name when I was giving you a great orgasm.'

He lifted his face, his eyes tense. 'Other than that.'

'That was enough. But to set your mind at ease, no, you didn't push me or try to force me to do anything I didn't want to do.'

His shoulders sagged. 'Good.' He turned from her, pouring the eggs into a pan.

He was still nervous, she realized. Unbelievable, but apparently true. She made coffee, then turned to watch him cook. 'Why didn't you call?'

He shrugged. 'I'd go from fear of what I'd done to fear that you had someone else back home to fear that what I *had* done hadn't been . . . good enough.'

'You're kidding,' she said and thought she saw a glimmer of a smile curve his lips.

'Okay, maybe not that last part. But I did worry.' He did something with his wrist and the omelet in the pan slid and flipped. 'And I did try to forget about you.'

'You did?'

'You were here, I was there. Then Evie called, asking for help with her leaky roof.'

Seven months ago. 'She said you dropped everything and came to help.'

'She thinks I'm some white knight, so don't tarnish my armor. The truth is, I dropped everything and came right away because it was what I'd been waiting for.'

She frowned slightly. 'What you'd been waiting for? What does that mean?'

He wasn't looking at her and she suddenly wished he would, that she could see his eyes. 'Do you believe in signs, Olivia? Fate? Miracles?'

'Once, I'd have said no. But now, yes, I do.'

His glance was sharp. 'What changed your mind?'

Olivia's answer took no thought at all. She knew the moment she'd begun believing in miracles. 'Meeting Mia when I did. I needed her and she needed me. I'd just come out of a bad relationship and a week later found out that our father, the father I'd never known, was dead. Mia was already in love with Reed. I was so jealous. She asked me if I was involved with anyone and I told her no. I didn't want to admit I was a failure.'

'I can understand that feeling,' he said ruefully.

She thought of the name he'd groaned, knew that Dana was happily married to someone else. If there had ever been a relationship between Dana and David, there wasn't now. 'I guess you can. Anyway, you remember when Mia was shot by that guy?'

'He was an arsonist,' David said, slanting her another glance. 'Ironic, huh?'

Or fate. 'Yes, very. The guy shot her just a few days after I met her, took out her kidney. She'd only had one.'

'And nobody was a match. I remember. We all got tested.' David turned to stare at her, his eyes narrowed. 'Then all of a sudden, Mia got a mystery donor. She never told us who it was. We all thought it was anonymous.' He leaned closer until he was inches from her face. 'It was you, wasn't it? You saved her life.'

Olivia's cheeks warmed. 'Your omelet's burning.'

He turned back to the stove. 'It was a damn nice thing to do, Olivia. You should be proud of yourself.'

'I didn't do it to be proud. I did it because she needed me. Nobody ever really had before. So to answer your question, yes, I believe in fate.'

He shut off the burner. 'Evie needed me, too. I wanted to help her, of course, but I'd been looking for some kind of sign. I'd told myself it was just one weekend, that you'd probably found someone else, but I couldn't get you out of my mind. Evie's leaky roof was the sign I'd been hoping for. "Go to Minnesota," in blinking neon. I wanted to see you again, and find out if you did have someone else. And to find out what I'd done.'

'And then you got in a killer's way and ended up in the hospital.' She put plates on the table and looked back to find him staring at her, his eyes no longer unreadable. They were hungry and hot and for a moment she had to concentrate on breathing.

'I knew it was you the moment you walked into my hospital room,' he said fiercely. 'I could barely see a thing, but I could smell you, just like I'd smelled you on my pillow, and I wanted you then. But it was the wrong time.'

She swallowed hard. 'And?'

'And . . . after that it never seemed like the right time. Evie got taken and everything was crazy. Then you and Noah found her.'

'And the body pit,' she murmured.

'Then you were busy, stressed. Pulling bones out of that

236

damn pit. I didn't want to make it worse, but I guess I did.' He brushed the backs of his fingers across her cheek, a fleeting touch that made her want more. 'I couldn't let another day go by with you thinking I didn't want you, that you didn't matter. That you were just a substitute for someone else. I'm sorry I hurt you.'

She held his eyes, hoping she wasn't a total fool for believing him. 'I could have called, too. I should have.'

He smiled and her heart rolled over in her chest. 'Sit down. You need to eat.'

She did, not realizing how hungry she'd been. She thought about what Paige had said the morning before, about taking a risk. What's the worst that could happen? Dana. He'd said her name. There had to be a reason. There had to be some feelings still. A man didn't love for that long and just turn it off because he met someone else.

You did. It was true, she admitted. When she met David, all thoughts of Doug had fled, as if he'd never been. *But I said David's name. He said Dana's.* And if at some point his lost love was free? *Been there, done that.* She was gullible, but she hoped she wasn't a fool.

She looked up to find him staring at her expectantly. He looked like he wanted to say something but didn't, rising to clear the table. Mojo stuck to his heels, hoping for a handout, but all David gave him was a scratch behind the ears. 'He's a nice dog.'

'Not as smart as the average bear, but he's mine. He keeps this place from getting too lonely.' She wanted to look away, but wouldn't let herself. 'So. Now what?'

'Now, I believe you said you were going to sleep.' His words were mild, but his eyes were still hot. Shivers danced across her skin.

'That had been my plan, yes.'

'Then come on.' He led her to her sofa and pulled her down in his lap. 'Go to sleep. I'll wake you up in time for your meeting.'

It was surreal, sitting there cradled in his arms, but it felt natural to rest her head on his shoulder, so she did. 'I have to leave early, take Mojo to day care,' she mumbled.

'I'll take him.'

'Okay. I need to be downtown at oh-nine. Was oh-eight, but CSU needed more time to process Tomlinson's office.' She yawned. 'It was a nasty scene.'

'I know,' he said quietly and she knew that he did.

'Maybe Tomlinson was the target all along. Maybe the condo fire was just a red herring, to distract us from Tomlinson's murder.'

'Maybe. Except they weren't trying to hide his murder.' His fingers gently unwound her braid, combing through her hair.

She pulled back to see his face. 'They weren't?'

'No. Barlow and I went back in to look at the office again. There were no signs of gas around or on the walls of the office. If they'd meant the fire to hide Tomlinson's murder, they'd have destroyed his body to destroy the evidence of his gunshot, right?'

'Right.'

'They should have dumped gas on his body, his desk, his papers. But they didn't.'

'You're right. Why didn't they?'

He pulled her head to his shoulder. 'You'll figure it out after you've had some rest.'

'You're tired, too. How will you wake up?'

'I set my cell phone alarm.'

'When did you do that?'

'When I was sitting on your front porch waiting for you.'

So he'd planned this. She wanted to be annoyed, but his hand was massaging her scalp again. She closed her eyes, drifting. 'That should be illegal. Feels too good.'

He kissed the top of her head. 'There is no such thing as feeling too good, Olivia.'

She wanted to know what that meant, but fatigue dragged her down. 'Promise?'

'Oh yes.' His words rumbled against her ear. 'I definitely promise. Now sleep.'

Chapter Twelve

Tuesday, September 21, 6:45 A.M.

Eric woke up with a start. He'd been dreaming of the girl in the window. Her name was Tracey Mullen. She'd only been sixteen. He hadn't wanted to know that. Of all the dead, she was the one he owned. Her blood was on his hands. But he'd be blamed for the other two as well. The guard and Tomlinson. *If we're caught, that is.*

He lay staring up at the ceiling, hating the goddamn blackmailer, hating goddamn Joel. Hating himself. And he might as well throw Albert in there, too. He'd been taken. Duped. *Played for the fool I am.* He'd cared for Albert, but he'd been used.

And Albert actually thought he could draw this blackmailer out. *Idiot.*

Eric knew better. The moment he'd seen the video sent to his phone last night, he'd known it was useless. Albert had stalked off, intent on his own plan after telling Mary that Eric had first considered running to France. Mary had followed Albert in a huff.

They were angry that Eric had the money to start over, anywhere in the world. Mary and Albert didn't. Albert wanted to play hockey, and he couldn't do that as a fugitive.

Mary . . . Who knew what that chick wanted? One minute she wanted the blackmailer's blood. The next, she was sobbing over poor Joel. She was an emotional basket case.

And I'm not much better. His hand heavy with dread, he picked up the disposable cell. There were no new texts, but there would be. It was just a matter of time.

I have to get out of here, while I still can.

Tuesday, September 21, 6:55 A.M.

He had a few minutes before he opened the doors for the morning's first customers, so he logged in to his offshore account. No payment from Mr Dorian Blunt. Well, he had given the man twelve hours. Dorian had until noon to pay up.

He checked on Dorian's account, just to make sure it was all there. It still was – two million, cleverly embezzled over five years, Dorian's employers none the wiser. *And I might never have been the wiser had Dorian not felt the need to log into his account while eating his lunch, staring longingly at the zeroes and commas on his screen. He'd obviously thought himself unobserved, but no one ever goes unobserved in my shop.*

He was about to open the shop doors when an e-mail alert popped up on his screen, making him frown. *Eric, you sly dog.* He'd made a rather sizeable bank-card purchase of a specific amount, $1,322.65, but to whom? He quickly logged on to Eric's account.

Air France. Dumbass. And only one ticket. He wondered how Albert would take that news. He logged out and stowed his laptop beneath the counter.

The bell on the door jingled, signaling his first customers of the day. 'Good morning. How can I help you?'

Tuesday, September 21, 7:50 A.M.

Fell asleep in the Gorskis' garden again, David thought groggily, breathing in the scent of flowers. Sweet, but a little smoky. Abruptly he woke, realizing in the same moment that he sat on Olivia's sofa and that she was straddling him, her hands in his hair and her mouth busy on his. Arousal smacked him like a club and his hands streaked under her shirt, roaming her back, drawing her throaty murmur of approval.

In a flash he had her on her back, her surprised laugh breaking into a strangled groan when his mouth found her breast through her thin cotton blouse.

'God. Don't stop.' Her hands pulled his head closer. 'Please.' It was a gasp as her body arched like a bow, the staccato jerks of her hips against him begging for more.

His blood pounding in his head, he yanked at the buttons on her blouse. 'Hurry,' was all she said as he managed the front clasp of her bra.

Mine, was all he could think as his mouth closed over her breast again, sucking hard as she twisted against him, making reality out of what had been a damn frustrating vague recollection. He pulled at the button on her waistband, unzipped her slacks and, his own hand shaking, touched her and groaned. She was wet, dripping wet.

He worked a finger up into her, her little whimper of relief stoking the fire in his blood. God. She was tight. Wet and tight and he wanted nothing more than to drive himself into her, feel her around him. But he'd fucked up twice before and he wasn't going to make it three times. When he took her, it would be the right way. Slow and sensual, so that she'd have no doubts about being first string.

But now . . . now her hips were lifting, reaching. Needing. *Needing me.*

'David. Please.' The harsh plea made him smile fiercely as he took her other breast into his mouth, suckling as he worked her higher. The cries coming from her throat sounded exactly as they had in his dreams. He added a second finger to the first, pressed his thumb hard against her and she wrapped her arms around his head, pulling him closer to her breast as she went taut, completely silent as she came.

Her breath came shuddering out and she collapsed. In his pocket, his cell phone buzzed three times. His alarm clock. Her body tightened and he knew she'd felt it, too.

'Good morning, Olivia,' he murmured and she laughed breathlessly.

'Oh God.'

Ignoring the throbbing of his own body, he took the time to admire what he'd enjoyed. Her breasts were full, round. Perfect. Her skin was pale, flawless. Except for the red areas his beard had scratched. He kissed those places, softly. 'I was rough.'

Eyes still closed, she hummed contentedly. 'I liked it.'

'I'll shave next time.'

Her knuckles slid across his jaw. 'I liked it. I like this. Makes you look like a pirate.'

He smiled at that. 'Open your eyes.' She did and in them he saw sensual satisfaction. 'You're beautiful.'

Her eyes flickered, surprising him. 'So are you.'

He pressed a kiss to the valley between her breasts. 'You were wet,' he murmured.

'I was dreaming. Then there you were.' Her eyes grew troubled. 'But you didn't . . .'

'Not yet. There isn't enough room or enough time for me to do what I want to you.'

He could see the pulse pound at the hollow of her throat. 'To me?'

'To you.' He kissed her mouth, then nipped her lower lip lightly. 'With you, for you. In you.' He brushed his lips over her throat. 'I didn't get to that last time, did I?'

'No. I, um, then you . . . fell asleep.'

He winced. 'I've got a lot to make up for. Good thing I've got fantasies saved up.'

She shivered. 'Like what?'

'Most are better shown than told, but there is one . . . No. I don't know if I should tell you. You might never sit at your desk the same way again.'

He could feel her pulse hammering. 'Just tell me it doesn't involve handcuffs or butter,' she said and he laughed softly.

'No butter.'

'But handcuffs?'

'Mmm. And your Hat Squad fedora. And my very big bed with the wrought-iron headboard. And nothing else.'

'How cliché.' Her cheeks were red as flame.

'But effective.'

She swallowed hard. 'When?'

'Tonight would be good.'

'I don't know when I'll be done.'

'That's okay. I've waited this long, I can wait a little longer.' He slid back down, resting his head between her breasts. It felt right. Comfortable. Like he belonged.

For a long moment she was quiet, her fingers toying with his hair, then she sighed. 'I have to get up and shower. Go into work. It's not going to be a fun day.'

He wondered what would make one day as a homicide

detective less fun than any other. He thought all the days would pretty well suck, which was why he respected her for doing it every day. 'Why not?'

'The girl you pulled out of the condo? Her mother comes today and she'll want to see her. I hate that part.'

He'd thought of it, wondered how she and the other cops managed it. 'I'm sorry.'

'Me too. But I do have to get up, and as good as you feel, you've got me pinned.'

David made himself move, rising from the sofa and pulling her up with him. 'I don't have to report back to the firehouse until tomorrow morning at eight. I'm at the dojo till nine tonight, but if you get done before then, call me and I'll bow out early. Otherwise, I'll be at my apartment house, probably picking out carpet with my mom.'

She pulled the edges of her blouse together self-consciously. 'I met your mom at the wedding. Mia thinks the sun rises and sets on her.' She was halfway up the hall when she turned. 'Did you say dojo?'

Paige. Had she said anything? 'Yeah, I go a few times a week.'

She tilted her head, considering. 'You told me about that, back in Chicago. You were a brown belt then. You helped with karate classes for the kids at the local Y.'

That she'd remembered made him feel foolishly proud. 'I made black belt last year.'

She smiled at him. 'And you still work with the kids?'

'Yeah. It gives a kid confidence he might not get anywhere else. And teaches them how to protect them-selves.' *Sometimes from the very people who are supposed to protect them. If Megan had been protected . . .*

'My friend Paige teaches a self-defense class for women at the Y. I should introduce the two of you. I have to jump in the shower now or I'm going to be late. Can you take Mojo out in the backyard?'

He watched the bathroom door close and snapped his fingers for the dog to follow. Out on her patio, he dug his cell from his pocket and called Paige.

'You didn't tell her,' he snapped when she picked up.

'Where are you, David?' Paige asked cautiously.

'On Olivia's patio. You said you'd tell her we were friends and you didn't.'

'Why are you on Liv's patio? I thought she dumped you.'

'She thought so, too, but I managed to change her mind.'

'Oh. Exactly how far did you change her mind?'

He thought of Olivia going taut in his arms and clenched his teeth against a new wave of need. *Not nearly far enough.* 'None of your business,' he said. 'Look, she offered to introduce us and I didn't know what to say. Now what?'

'I tried last night, but she was so mad,' Paige said miserably. 'I was about to blurt it out when she got called to that fire. I thought you were history, and I had more time.'

'Well, I'm not and you don't.' At least he hoped he wasn't. She hadn't taken kindly to his watching her and he couldn't really blame her. 'I'll tell her.'

'Tell her I was duped. Or you could just blame it on Rudy. Everybody does.'

'Tempting, but no,' he said dryly. 'I'll see you tonight.' He whistled for the dog and went back inside. The shower stopped and he couldn't help but think of Olivia wearing nothing more than drops of water. Trying to push the picture from his mind, he wandered her living room, satisfying at least a small portion of his curiosity.

He'd wondered how she lived. Very modestly, he could see, most of her money going into the posters on her wall. She collected animated art cels, she'd told him the night they'd talked until the sun came up. He could see them now, hanging in her living room – Daffy Duck and all the other characters from the cartoons he'd loved as a kid. Road Runner, it seemed, was her favorite. A giant poster of the Coyote holding his little umbrella hung over her TV and on top of her set was a stack of Road Runner DVDs.

There were pictures on the mantel over her fireplace. An older couple smiling from a faded snapshot that he assumed were her grandparents. A pair of teenagers mugging for the camera. He leaned closer, recognizing a young Olivia and Paige, arm in arm. There was another of a woman he thought was her mother. In another a stunning redhead sat on the grass, surrounded by puppies. And finally, a more recent picture of Olivia with Paige and the redhead at a restaurant, lifting glasses in a toast.

'That was my birthday,' Olivia said from behind him. 'The big three-oh. Last year. Those are my friends Brie and Paige.'

She'd dressed in what seemed to be her work uniform, slacks and a blouse. Her face was free of makeup, the way he liked it best. She was braiding her hair and for a moment he just let himself watch.

'I know,' he finally said and she frowned.

'What?'

'I know your friend.' He held the picture out as if that explained it. 'Paige.'

Slowly she lowered her arms. 'How?'

He explained how he'd met Paige, how he'd gleaned information on Olivia over the past seven months, how

Paige had been unaware. Olivia's eyes went flat and David got the uncomfortable feeling that this was how she approached suspects. 'Are you mad?' he asked when he was done.

'I don't know,' she said honestly. 'I'll have to think about it.'

'While you're thinking, think on this.' He cradled her face in his hands and kissed her hard. 'All these months, all I thought about was you. About this. Now, go to work.'

'Mojo—'

'Can ride in my truck. I'll drop him off. Just tell me where.'

She gave him the address and backed away, studying him in a way that made him want to squirm. 'Who are you?' she asked him quietly.

I wish I knew. 'What do you mean?'

'Who are you, that you want me? A man like you could have anyone.'

A man like you. 'Tonight,' he said. 'I'll tell you everything you want to know about me.' With one very big exception. *That* he couldn't share. 'I'm not that complicated.'

Her smile was grim. 'If you think I believe that, you're not as smart as I thought.'

Tuesday, September 21, 8:55 A.M.

Kane was at his desk when Olivia dropped into her chair. Her cheeks flamed as soon as her eyes fell on her fedora, rakishly adorning the head of her goddess statue as it always did. She'd mulled over David's words all the way in and, God help her, could see herself in nothing more

248

than her fedora, cuffed to his bed. She leaned over and pulled the hat so it covered the goddess's face. Foolish, she knew. 'Hell,' she muttered.

Kane's brows went up. 'Anything you'd like to share with the class?'

'No.' Most definitely not. 'What are you doing?'

He shrugged, disappointed. 'You never dish anymore. Where's the excitement?'

'You couldn't handle my excitement, old man,' she said dryly and made him chuckle. She noted the breakfast-sandwich wrappers on his desk. 'Jennie's gonna be mad. You know you're only allowed one egg and pastrami every two weeks.'

'Jennie won't find out.' He crunched the wrappers and threw them in her trash can. 'There, problem solved.' He handed her a thick folder from his desk. 'I've been going through the CDs Tomlinson's wife gave us. Those are Tomlinson's paying customers.'

'All these? How come he was going bankrupt, then?'

Kane lifted another folder, twice as thick as the first one. 'These are the customers who owed him money.'

Olivia began scanning pages. 'Rankin and Sons?'

'In the nonpaying folder.'

'So there's a connection. Condo contractor owes plumbing supplier money.'

'But not a lot. Rankin owed a lot less than a lot of these other guys. Certainly not enough to warrant killing Tomlinson to make the debt go away.'

'Maybe the debt was more than money.' Olivia checked her watch. 'It's nine. Let's go.' Kane ambled while she walked quickly, as usual.

'Can you at least tell me if you got my field glasses back?'

249

She winced. 'I forgot again.'

'No glasses and no dish. This day sucks already.' Then he stopped abruptly in the door of Abbott's office.

Olivia craned her neck to see around him. A man in a black suit and shiny black shoes sat at Abbott's round conference table, looking serious and slightly sour. 'Who's that?' she murmured, but she knew.

'Come in,' Abbott said. 'Meet Special Agent Crawford. Crawford, these are the lead detectives on the case, Kane and Sutherland.'

They shook hands with the federal agent and Olivia looked at Abbott from the corner of her eye. 'Morning meeting?'

'In here,' Abbott said. 'Crawford will be joining us. On a consulting basis.'

Crawford's jaw tightened, but he said nothing, sitting back down in his chair.

'Bruce,' Olivia said gingerly, 'we need to talk to you. Outside?'

Abbott rose wearily. 'Of course.' Olivia felt a stirring of pity as her boss closed the door of his own office behind them and leaned against the wall. 'Don't give me shit, please,' he said. 'I've had enough already.'

'From who?' Olivia asked.

'My boss's boss, who doesn't want to be caught playing cowboy if this is domestic terrorism. Can you tell me that it's not?'

He sounded so hopeful that Olivia hated to burst his bubble. 'I don't think we can say with a hundred percent certainty yet.'

'Great.' Abbott sighed. 'Crawford's already put in a request for jurisdiction.'

'My ass,' Olivia said.

'I know. But we have to share the sandbox. Prove the glass ball is just a ruse and Special Agent Crawford goes away.' Abbott leaned closer. 'Please make him go away,' he whispered. 'He is a major pain in the ass and I've only known him an hour.'

Olivia patted his arm. 'We'll do our best. You want us to spill all in there?'

Abbott shrugged. 'For now.'

They went back in the office where Crawford was still scowling sourly.

'Arson and CSU are en route from the scene,' Abbott said. 'I expect them to be here soon. You can go get yourself some coffee if you like.'

'It's okay,' Crawford said flatly. 'I'll wait here.'

Abbott shrugged. 'Suit yourself,' he said, then looked relieved at the appearance of one of his detectives. 'Come in, Detective Webster.'

Olivia was always glad to work with Noah, who was solo for the time being. His former partner was Jack Phelps, who'd returned to Homicide a few months ago after taking a medical leave. It was common knowledge that Jack had been through rehab, but nobody had mentioned it since his return. Jack's new partner was rookie detective Sam Wyatt. Olivia suspected Noah had cut Jack too much slack when they'd been partners, hoping Jack would work out his addictions on his own.

Olivia also suspected she and Noah would be assigned together once Kane retired at the end of the year. It was one of the sparkles of silver in a dark cloud.

Noah came in, looking warily at Crawford. 'Good morning. The meeting's here?'

'It is. Detective Webster, this is Special Agent Crawford, FBI.'

Noah sat down next to the Fed. 'You investigated Preston Moss.'

'I did,' Crawford said, his tone inviting no chitchat, so Noah turned to Abbott.

'I got the list of the condo contractor's employees from Faye. She's pulled backgrounds on the ones who were financially strapped, which was damn near all of them. Anything special I'm looking for?'

'Probably,' Abbott said, 'but let's wait for the others. I don't want anyone missing anything.' They sat in awkward silence for another two minutes until the arrival of Barlow, Micki Ridgewell, and the shrink, Jessie Donahue.

Abbott did the introductions. 'Ian called to say he won't be here,' he said. 'He's started Tomlinson's autopsy. He did say that the man's blood alcohol was nearly point two. No evidence of any narcotics in the urine. He hasn't done the cut, so he didn't yet know if there was smoke in Tomlinson's lungs. So, Barlow? You want to get started?'

'The arsonists came in through a back door,' Barlow said, 'and left the same way. There was no sign the alarm had been tampered with. They drugged the guard dog. I spoke with the vet this morning, who said the dog was still unconscious. The vet drew blood and sent it to the lab for testing, to see what drug they used. The fire was set with gasoline, a long fuse, and probably a match. They kept it simple.'

'Security video?' Abbott asked.

'The warehouse ran on an old video system,' Barlow said. 'The video should have been in a recording unit in the electrical closet, but the unit was empty. The manager, Lloyd Hart, said they kept four videotapes in cycle, changing the tape once a week. We found three melted tapes, but the one inside the recorder is gone.'

'Inside job again?' Olivia murmured.

'Maybe.' Barlow held up a sketch of the warehouse layout. 'They poured the gas around the stacked boxes, but none near the office.'

'They didn't mean for Tomlinson's body to burn up,' Olivia said, remembering what David had told her.

'He was shot execution style,' Kane said. 'Maybe we're looking at a message of some kind. Rankin and Sons construction was one of Tomlinson's customers and they did owe him money.'

'Or maybe it's about money, but not the way you think,' Crawford said in an overly paternal, condescending way. 'These activists have torched insurance companies that sell policies to animal labs and construction companies. Why not threaten a construction company's supply chain? Terrorize enough vendors and they'll think twice before selling to a company building in a controversial area.'

'It's possible,' Kane said. 'That's why we're looking at both arsons individually, as well as establishing connections.'

'But,' Barlow put in, 'these two fires lack an important hallmark of environmental terrorism. Nobody's claimed credit – and SPOT always did.'

'But,' Crawford said, too patiently, 'you have two glass balls. Globes, just like SPOT left behind. That's signature enough.'

'We also have two gunshot vics,' Micki said. 'We found the slug in a fragment of Tomlinson's wall. Ballistics says it came from the same gun that killed Henry Weems.'

'SPOT never shot anyone,' Crawford admitted. 'Preston Moss was very anti-gun.'

'Did you bring any photos of the glass balls SPOT left behind?' Micki asked.

'One better.' Crawford reached into his briefcase and pulled out a small evidence envelope. He shook out a box and took off the lid. 'This is one of the actual balls.'

Olivia reached for the box, but Crawford held it back. 'Look only, please.'

She frowned at Abbott, who looked beleaguered. 'This is Super Ball-sized,' she said. 'Ours is larger. This one's continents are embedded in the glass. Ours are etched.'

'Maybe they couldn't get the original model,' Crawford said. 'We were never able to trace the maker of this ball. We had it narrowed to three companies. I've got the list.'

Olivia took the folder he offered. 'Two of them have online catalogs. Let's see if they sell an etched globe.' She let him see she was surprised by his gesture. 'Thanks.'

His nod was stiff. 'I spent a career chasing Moss, Detective. I want him gone.'

'Tracey Mullen was only sixteen years old and Henry Weems was a good cop,' Olivia responded briskly. 'We want whoever killed them gone, too.'

'I noticed you didn't say anything nice about Tomlinson,' Crawford said dryly.

'From all accounts, he was a royal jerk. But he's a victim and we want his killer.'

'Tomlinson was a very flexible, royal jerk,' Micki said. 'There were photos on his desk when he was shot. We've pieced together some of the fragments from the rubble. There's a lot of water damage from putting out the fire. Reclaiming them won't be easy.'

Micki placed copies of three pictures on the table. All were missing pieces, like a puzzle in process, but there was enough remaining for everyone to wince.

'Ouch,' Kane said. 'How did he do that?'

Olivia tilted her head. 'I was a gymnast in college, and nobody I knew could do that.'

Beside her, Olivia could hear Noah clear his throat, as if swallowing a laugh that would have been entirely inappropriate.

Abbott shook his head. 'People,' he admonished. 'Who's the woman?'

'Her name is Shondra,' Kane said. 'She's on Tomlinson's list of employees, even though the manager said she was a temp. When Tomlinson's wife found out about the affair and got a restraining order on his corporate checkbook, Shondra walked.'

'Give me a copy of Tomlinson's employee list,' Noah said. 'I'll do a cross-check against Rankin's list. See if anything pops.'

Micki started to gather the photos, but Olivia stopped her. 'When was this taken?'

'There were no time stamps that we could see,' Micki said. 'The originals appear to be printed on photo paper on a printer, not at a photo shop. Why?'

'Well, just that Hart, the manager, said Tomlinson golfed,' Olivia said slowly. 'He should have tan lines on his upper arms from his golf shirt, but he's white as a ghost. All over.' She glanced at Kane. 'When did Louise Tomlinson say she filed for divorce?'

'She didn't, but the files she copied from her husband's computer were dated June fifteenth. Hart said she filed the very next day.'

'That must be it,' she murmured. 'He wouldn't have had time to get much sun.'

'Why is that important, Olivia?' Abbott asked.

'I don't know. It just doesn't feel right with what the wife told us.'

'Then we dig deeper into Mrs T,' Kane said simply. 'Anything from the gas cans?'

'A few prints,' Micki said. 'We're running them through AFIS, but they could belong to anybody. The gas cans were old and rusted. If you find the arsonists' car, we may be able to match rust residue from the cans, putting them at the scene.'

'Speaking of cars,' Barlow said, 'we recovered Barney's. It was parked about a half-mile away, keys in the ignition. We didn't find any prints on the keys.'

'So his killer took his keys?' Kane asked. 'Then drove his car away?'

'Took his BlackBerry, too,' Micki said. 'The manager said Tomlinson never went anywhere without it. We found footprints all around the property, but with so much foot traffic, they could belong to anyone, like the gas cans.'

'What about the shoeprint we found in the mud near the lake?' Olivia asked.

'The lab matched the tread to Converse high-tops, male, size ten,' Micki said.

'So, Tracey's partner wore shoes when he ran from the condo fire, but Tracey didn't,' Olivia mused. 'Why? They'd just had sex. Why did he have shoes on?'

'Maybe he was getting ready to leave when the fire broke out,' Barlow said.

'Which meant he wasn't squatting with her,' Olivia said. 'He had someplace else to be, but she was hiding out. More weight to the theory that he's local. We need to find him and find out how he got access to the building to start with.' She checked her watch. 'We're meeting the sign language interpreter in half an hour. We're going to the deaf school to see if anyone knows this boy. The principal promised total support.'

'What about the girl's parents?' Abbott asked.

'Mom's supposed to call when she and stepdad get to the airport,' Olivia said.

'We met with the dad last night,' Kane said. 'He ID'd Tracey and told us she'd gone to a Camp Longfellow this past summer. It's in Maryland. We're wondering if this could be where she met the boy.'

'So get a roster,' Abbott said. 'See if they had any campers from the Twin Cities.'

'I can take that,' Noah said, 'while you're out at the deaf school.'

'It might not be that straightforward,' Kane warned. 'I checked out the website last night and I couldn't find a contact name. There are some e-mail addresses and one toll-free number, but there's a note on the page that says, "Leave a message and we'll call you as soon as possible." I'm thinking the camp's not staffed year-round.'

'Wonderful,' Noah muttered. 'Well, I guess I'll have to dig.'

'I need to see the condo and the Tomlinson warehouse,' Crawford said.

Barlow slanted a look at Abbott, who nodded. 'You can ride with me,' Barlow said.

Crawford's jaw had tightened at Barlow's double check. 'Thank you,' he said coldly.

'You've been quiet, Jess,' Abbott said to the shrink, ignoring the Fed. 'What are you thinking?'

'That there is a very big disconnect,' Dr Donahue said. 'The fires were set to burn stuff, not people. But in both, a person was shot – Weems in the heart and Tomlinson in the back of the head. You're right, Kane, Tomlinson was an execution. Weems . . . not. It's like the shooter was caught unaware by Weems, but shot anyway. And accurately. Like target practice. But Tomlinson . . . that was revenge. Neither mesh with the fire. Right now, there seems to be a very divergent set of personalities in this group.'

'Or divergent agendas,' Olivia said.

Donahue nodded. 'Quite possibly. The question is, are the divergent agendas acceptable to all the group members, and if not, when will they splinter?'

'How many people are in this group?' Abbott asked.

'At least three,' Barlow said. 'We found two sets of footprints mixed with accelerant at the condo door. But whoever killed Weems did not set the fire. So at least three.'

Donahue nodded again. 'The shooter not only brought a gun to the condo, but he procured hollow-point bullets. He planned to kill, if he fired.'

'He killed Tomlinson from behind,' Olivia said. 'He had to walk through the office door and around his desk. Tomlinson didn't happen on him like Weems did. He went there to kill Tomlinson. But why? And assuming this isn't really about environmental arson, why hide behind it?'

'Go find out,' Abbott said. 'Keep me informed. Be back at five. Be careful.'

Everyone stood to go, then halted when the office door opened and Faye, their clerk, stuck her head in. 'Turn on the TV. Channel Eight. They know about the ball.'

With an oath, Abbott turned on the television, where a reporter stood in front of the wreckage of Tomlinson's warehouse, holding an orange in one hand.

'Sources tell us that the ball was about the size of this orange. They also tell us that a similar ball was found in the condo fire. The ball is solid glass, with the map of the earth etched on its surface,' the reporter said. 'This is important, as it links these fires to the infamous SPOT organization, which destroyed an office building twelve years ago, leaving one woman dead. SPOT's leader, Preston Moss, is still wanted for the fire and the woman's death. Moss disappeared and has not been seen since.'

Abbott muted the sound when they rolled old footage. 'Goddammit,' he snarled.

'It was all over the fire department, Bruce,' Olivia said. 'I told you yesterday it was just a matter of time.'

'I know, but I was hoping for more time. This changes nothing about our plans, so go do what you were going to do. I'll deal with the press. Barlow, please impress on all the firefighters the importance of keeping quiet on this story.'

'They know, Captain,' Barlow said. 'If the leak came out of the fire department, I'm sure they'll deal with it appropriately. But I'll tell them again.'

'That firefighter,' Abbott said, 'the one who caught the ball. What was his name?'

'David Hunter,' Olivia said. 'I'll call him, warn him.'

'Fine.' Abbott waved them to the door. 'Go, get me some answers.'

Chapter Thirteen

Tuesday, September 21, 9:25 A.M.

David pulled his pickup truck in front of a big sign that read K-9 TRAINING, and below it hung a much smaller sign in a child's script that read ... AND DOGGY DAY CARE.

'Come,' he said and Olivia's German Shepherd jumped from his truck and ran to the door. Assuming the dog knew the way, David followed. He knocked, but there was no answer. The door was unlocked, so he went in, setting off a beep and a flashing light overhead.

'Hello?' he called. He could hear dogs barking from somewhere behind the wall. There was a reception counter, but no receptionist. Then he heard it – a small moan of pain. He looked down at Mojo, saw the dog's ears had pricked up. He'd heard it, too.

David saw a woman, facedown on the desk, red hair hanging down her back, her arms dangling uselessly at her sides. 'Ma'am?' he said but she didn't respond. He took her arm to check her pulse, then jumped back when she leapt to her feet, fists clenched.

'Who are you?' she demanded and once he'd recovered his composure, he immediately recognized her from one of the pictures on Olivia's mantel.

'David Hunter,' he said. 'You're Brie, Olivia's friend.'

She narrowed dark brown eyes. 'You're the jerk.'

David rolled his eyes. 'Not anymore,' he said.

'Wait.' She stumbled to her desk, finding what looked like two hearing aids. Popping one behind each ear, she squinted at his face. 'Did you say "not anymore"?'

She was hearing impaired, he realized, and hadn't heard him come in. 'I did. See, she even trusted me with him.' He patted the dog's head, and Mojo licked his hand.

'You must be a sweet talker to have earned a second chance after what you did.'

Embarrassed, his cheeks heated. 'I heard someone moaning.'

She sank into her chair. 'That would have been me. Dying. Don't talk so loud.'

He smiled. 'You must have been in on the major mojitos last night.'

She put her face back down on the desk. 'Don't say that word ever again.'

'I might be able to help,' he said.

Blearily she looked up at him. 'You have a gun?'

'Give me your hand.' He put pressure against the base of her forefinger.

'Voodoo?' she mumbled.

'Acupressure. It should help the nausea.'

'Oh. Paige does that.'

'I know.'

One brown eye opened, then narrowed. 'How do you know?'

'Because I know her from the dojo. We train together.'

'Ohhhh. So that's what was up with her last night. I bet Liv's mad.'

261

'Jury's still out on that. Any better?'

'Maybe. Why *did* you scream another woman's name when Liv was doing you?'

For a moment the question left him speechless. 'Because I'm a jerk.'

'Very good answer,' she mumbled. 'For a jerk, you have really good hands.'

'Thank you,' he said dryly. 'Next time, maybe you shouldn't have so many mojitos.'

'And maybe next time you should lay off the champagne,' she shot back.

He winced. 'Touché. Can I leave the dog with you?'

'Of course. What are your intentions toward Liv?' she asked.

'Honorable.' He thought about what he hoped would happen later. 'Mostly.'

One side of her mouth lifted. 'All right. But she's been hurt before. Don't hurt her.'

'I'm trying not to.'

'I believe you. But even if you didn't mean to, you hit her where it hurt the most.'

'I know. I know her fiancé left her for an old lover. And then I said . . . what I said.'

'Which was bad. But your being friends with Paige first was just the cherry on top.'

He frowned. 'Why?'

'Because Paige is like a honey bee. It's a little ego deflating, walking next to her. Worse for Liv, because she doesn't see herself like everyone else does.'

'Why?'

'From what I've seen, some of it was her mom. She was . . . demanding.'

'She told me her mother died the year before her father,'

262

David remembered. 'But she talked like she'd loved her mother.'

'She did. But life was tense in their house. It can't have been easy raising a kid alone – and an illegitimate one at that – back then. Her mom was always, "Get an education, get a scholarship. Don't depend on your face, use your brain."'

'Good advice,' David said cautiously. 'Isn't it?'

'When it's balanced. From what I've gathered during past mojito sessions, and what I saw myself, Liv's mom put down her looks and nothing she did was good enough.'

'Olivia strongly resembles her father, just like Mia,' David said. 'That must have been hard for her mother, too, to look at her daughter and see the man who'd tossed her aside. Still, that doesn't make it less wrong or any easier for Olivia to get past.'

'True. But I'm sure you'll find a way to make Liv feel really pretty. Just say *her* name this time. Olivia. Say it with me now. O-li-vi-a.'

David's cheeks grew warm again. 'I'm going now. What about the dog?'

'I'll keep Mojo with me. He was mine first, you know. But he flunked training academy and needed a home. Olivia needed company after Doug left. It worked out. Hey, I heard you made a damn good save at the condo.'

'How did you hear that?'

'My dad was at the warehouse fire last night. He's the vet taking care of that drugged guard dog. He said it was all the gossip. So, you play ball?'

'Went to school on a baseball scholarship.' For one disastrous semester. 'Why?'

'Because I play on a league and we need a fielder. One

of our guys broke his foot. We're headed to the play-offs, but without him it won't be easy. If you wanna come . . .'

He knew a 'welcome to the group' when he heard one. 'Thank you. I'd like that.'

'We practice Thursday night.' She scribbled an address. 'Here.'

'If I can, I will. Thanks for the history. Hope the head stops exploding soon.'

'From your mouth to God's ears. Don't slam the door on your way out.'

He was back on the main road when his cell buzzed in his pocket. It was his mom. 'I'm sorry, Ma. I should have called you this morning, but I wanted to let you sleep in.'

'Where are you, David?' she asked, a tension in her voice he didn't like.

'North of town. Why? What's wrong?'

'The news reported on that glass ball. You weren't mentioned, but word's gotten out. A dozen reporters were here, wanting to interview you on your "save."'

'A girl died in that fire and a man was murdered. And they want the scoop on my catching a ball?' He blew out an angry breath. 'I'll be home to take care of it.'

'No, don't come home. That's why I'm calling. Glenn told them to go away, that you didn't live here. Glenn said for you to go to the cabin for the day, that he'd drop off a change of clothes for you at the firehouse.'

'It's not a bad idea. But what about you? I hate to leave you alone all day.'

'I've got a building full of people to keep me company. I got up early and made fresh bread. The Gorski sisters are adorable, and those babies in 2A? Well, I got my grandma fix for the day. Don't worry about me. I'm having lunch with Tom and dinner with Evie, so I'm too busy for you anyway.' She said it lightly, but it didn't fool him.

'Tom never has time for lunch with me. He's always too busy studying.'

'He has to make time for me. I'm his grandma. You're only the uncle. Just don't worry about me. If you stay away, maybe this'll blow over in a day or so.'

He sighed. 'From your mouth to God's ears, Ma.'

He'd no sooner hung up when another call came in. Olivia. Hopefully calling to tell him he'd been outed as the ball catcher and not to tell him she was still mad and not coming back tonight for what would hopefully be stimulating conversation and more stimulating sex. 'Hello?' he answered cautiously.

'It's Olivia. The news picked up the story about the glass ball.'

'I know. My mom just called. I had a yard full of reporters, so I'm going to the cabin. So if – when – you get done . . .'

'Understood,' she said stiffly and he realized she couldn't speak freely. Still, there was a huskiness in her voice that encouraged him. 'My boss wants me to tell you not to talk to the press, but it seems like you have that covered.'

'There are a lot of things I'd like to cover,' he said, dropping his tone to a caress.

'Understood,' she said again, then cleared her throat. 'I have to go.'

David hung up, then let go and grinned. Things were looking up.

Tuesday, September 21, 9:45 A.M.

Olivia pocketed her phone as she and Kane stood in line at the Deli, hoping her cheeks weren't too red. No chance, because Kane was grinning at her. 'You shut up.'

'I didn't say a word,' he said. 'I could continue not saying a word for a pastrami.'

'I'm not supporting your pastrami habit. You already had two this morning.'

'That was hours ago,' he grumbled.

'Fine. I'll split one with you. I'm not that hungry anyway. I had an omelet already.'

'Who made you an omelet?' His eyes narrowed. 'The firefighter who you left early last night came back, huh? Come on, Liv,' he whined. 'Tell me.'

Annoyed, she looked to the front of the line. 'What is taking so long this morning?'

'Avoidance has always been your go-to defense. This time of the morning Kirby's always slow. It would go faster if he didn't stop to chat with everyone.'

'You don't like him because he flirts with you,' Olivia said slyly.

Rolling his eyes, Kane looked over the crowded tables. 'The interpreter isn't here.'

'She texted me ten minutes ago. She's looking for a parking place. Relax. You're awfully tense today.'

'Too much coffee.' The bell on the door jingled and he turned to look. 'She's here.' Val was dressed all in black, exactly as she had been the night before. She lifted a travel mug, indicating she had coffee and would just wait at the door. 'Is the black a uniform or a fashion statement, I wonder?' Kane murmured.

'Uniform, of sorts,' Olivia said. 'It provides contrast for

her hands. Dark solids are good. Bright crazy prints, very bad.' They made it to the front of the line and Olivia spouted her order, but the barista behind the counter didn't respond. His gaze was locked on the television mounted in the corner, his forehead furrowed in a frown.

'Yippee,' Olivia muttered. Channel 2's reporter was talking about the glass ball. 'Kirby.' She knocked on the counter. 'Hey, Kirby.'

The barista blinked, then turned to her. 'I'm sorry, Detective. That's some story. In fact, unless I'm wrong, that's your story. So what's the sitch?'

She gave him a back-off look. 'The *sitch* is a detective who really needs her coffee. Can I get two coffees and a pastrami and egg?'

Kirby looked over her shoulder to Kane. 'Three in one day? I'm flattered,' he cooed, all but batting his eyes. Behind her, Kane tensed and Olivia's lips twitched, knowing Kirby only baited Kane because it made her partner uncomfortable.

'Just fill the order, please,' Olivia said with a sigh. She paid him, dropped her change in his tip jar and took the coffees.

'Buh-bye, Detective,' Kirby sang, waving at Kane as he grabbed the sandwich.

Kane shook his head. 'Good-bye, Kirby,' he said and Olivia chuckled.

Sutherland and Kane met the woman in black as he surreptitiously turned the wheel on the microphone tuner he'd clipped to his waist. Now he could hear them at the door.

'Sorry I'm late,' the woman said. Kane called her an interpreter. Sutherland said her black shirt provided contrast with her hands. *That says sign language to me.*

'Principal Oaks texted to say he's ready for us,' the interpreter murmured as Olivia held open the door. 'I told him we were running late.'

The door closed behind them. Oaks, principal, interpreter . . . *Call me crazy, but I think they're going to a school. For deaf kids.* And then a piece of the puzzle fell into place. He'd wondered why the girl in the condo hadn't run before she'd been trapped. Eric and Joel had certainly made enough noise to wake the dead.

But not the deaf. She hadn't heard them, and she'd died. If the girl was deaf, the person who'd taken the boat may be, too. Sutherland and Kane obviously thought so.

He smiled at the next customer. 'How can I help you?'

He filled the order while glancing up at the television. He'd seen the report on the glass balls the first time it aired but had pretended to be absorbed to keep Kane and Sutherland waiting – and chatting – a few moments longer.

So glass globes had been found at each scene. *I'll be damned. Who's got the nostalgic streak?* He might have guessed Joel, but Joel hadn't been at Tomlinson's because Joel was quite dead. Not Albert, because he never went into the condo. Eric? Maybe, but unlikely. Nostalgia was not the boy's style. No, it had been Mary.

She'd just changed the game. The cops may have considered environmental terrorism as a motive, but the glass ball cemented it. Now the Feds would get involved.

A lot of things made sense now.

The FBI wouldn't take too kindly to knowing about Eric's plane ticket to France. Still, Albert was likely to take Eric's fleeing a lot more personally. He couldn't wait until the morning rush was over so he could tell him.

As for Mary, he had a pretty good idea of what her end game was. It would be damn entertaining. He snapped lids on the coffees for the waiting customer. 'Now, you have a nice day,' he said with a smile. 'Buh-bye. Who's next?'

Tuesday, September 21, 9:45 A.M.

Eric carefully laid out his black suit and chose a dark, sober tie. Mary had called to say that Joel's funeral would be at two this afternoon. He'd have just enough time for the service. He'd need to be at the airport two hours early for an international flight.

He'd land in Paris at 9:30 tomorrow morning, local time. That would be 2:30 a.m. here in Minneapolis. If the texter had no plans for tonight, he'd be fine. No one would miss him until he was gone. But if they were commanded to set another fire tonight with a midnight deadline, that left two and a half hours for the texter to post the video and for the police to find him and where he'd gone. All it would take would be a phone call and the police in Paris might be waiting for him at the gate. It was possible, certainly. But not probable. Right now, improbability would have to be good enough, because if he did nothing, capture and prison were guaranteed.

He'd only pack a small bag. Albert would notice things were missing if he packed too much. He had packed a few of the belongings he wouldn't want to end up in police hands when he became a fugitive. He'd mail the box to an uncle who had been the family bad boy in his youth and was unlikely to turn it over to the cops.

Behind him the television news murmured and his

heart skipped a beat when he heard the words that now represented his worst fear. *Breaking news.*

'Breaking news on the two arsons we've been covering,' the newscaster said and Eric slowly turned to watch. Then frowned. *A glass ball?* What the hell?

He heard *SPOT* and *environmental arson* and *ongoing FBI investigations* into some guy named Preston Moss that he'd never heard of. But Joel would have. Joel read all that shit. 'Joel, you fucking idiot,' he muttered.

But it couldn't have been Joel. He wasn't there last night. And it couldn't have been Albert, because he never entered the condo. *And it wasn't me.* Mary. *But why?*

He grabbed his phone to dial her number, then stopped. Mary had left those glass balls. What if she'd left fingerprints, too? He didn't want any more communication between the two of them. *If they caught her, they'll trace her to me.*

He'd see her at Joel's funeral and he'd ask her then. Unless they were caught before then. He drew a breath, closed his eyes, and forced himself to use the logic that had ruled his life until two fucking days ago when he'd decided that once, just once, he'd be a damn crusader.

The news reporter had said it was the signature of some radical environmental group back in the nineties. That Joel would know about them was certainly possible. That he would want to leave something behind to honor his hippie hero, Preston Moss, was certainly possible. That he and Mary had planned it behind his and Albert's backs?

Totally possible. Joel and Mary had wanted to leave a signature and Eric had refused, saying that stopping the threat to the wetlands was enough. Albert had sided with him, and Joel and Mary had sulked. *Looks like they decided to do it anyway.*

He thought of Mary's words as she'd lit the warehouse fuse. *This one's for you, Joel.* That she'd continue with the signature they'd planned made perfect sense in a totally insane way. She hadn't known about the murders and he himself had told her Joel would have wanted Tomlinson's place torched.

So now what? Keeping Mary un-arrested was critical to his own protection, at least until he made it to France. Then everything would hit the fan and the three of them would be on their own. Using the texter's disposable cell, he sent Mary a text.

Ball on news. WTF?

He hit SEND and waited, wondering how the hell to go about getting a fake ID. If the cops found out about them, there was no way he was making it to France on his own passport. Unfortunately, Albert was the only one he knew unsavory enough to know people who could get him false papers, and Albert would not be the best person to ask.

Then who? Eric pinched the bridge of his nose. He'd had a headache for days. He needed sleep, but every time he closed his eyes he saw that face at the window.

We killed her. But we didn't mean to. It didn't matter. *She's still dead.* Visions of turning himself in taunted. But he wasn't going to prison. *I'd rather die.*

If Albert finds out I'm leaving the country, I just might.

Tuesday, September 21, 10:30 A.M.

Steven Oaks, principal of the school for the deaf, had a fatherly face that was currently creased with worry lines. He gestured to a table where another man waited.

'I'm stunned, Detectives,' Oaks signed and Val voiced.

271

'To think that one of our students could be involved in the death of that young woman. But I'll help in whatever way possible. This is Dr Haig. He's our staff psychologist and knows all the high school students. I invited him to be part of this meeting. I hope you don't mind.'

'Not at all,' Olivia said and Val signed. 'I want to be clear from the start, we don't know that the young man we're looking for has done anything wrong. We think he escaped from the building that burned. He might be able to help us.'

That seemed to set the two men a bit more at ease.

Olivia handed Oaks a photo of Tracey Mullen. 'This is the girl who died in the fire. Her name was Tracey Mullen and she lived in Florida with her mother. Do you know her?'

Oaks studied the photo, then passed it to Haig and both shook their heads.

'She's never been a student at our school,' Oaks signed. 'I can't help you.'

'We think Tracey came here because of the male she was with in the condo,' Olivia said. 'Our best guess is that he's got dark hair, Caucasian, and wears a size ten shoe.'

'We have a lot of young men who could fit that description,' Haig said aloud, signing at the same time. He was hearing, Olivia realized. 'Can you give us more?'

'He wears a hearing aid, but I guess that doesn't narrow it down much either,' Kane said. 'He may have attended a Camp Longfellow this past summer.'

Both men raised their brows. 'Some of our students do attend that camp,' Oaks signed, Val's voice quietly following. 'I know a few who did last summer, but I wouldn't know them all. If their parents made the arrangements, we wouldn't know about it.'

'Did you contact the camp for their roster?' Haig asked.

'That's in process,' Kane said. 'It's off season.'

Haig sighed. 'A few went on scholarship, so I had to write a recommendation for them. I have a list of those students. We can bring them up for you to talk with first.'

'That would be great,' Olivia said. 'The boy we're talking about had a relationship with the victim. If he escaped the fire, he might be very emotional. Can you think of any of your male students who seem overly upset recently?'

Oaks gave them an incredulous look. 'This is a high school, Detective,' he signed. 'They're all overly upset, every single day. They're teenagers.'

'Right,' Olivia said ruefully. 'This boy would be familiar with boats – rowboats, that is. And he was in the condo at about midnight on Sunday.'

Haig considered. 'Nothing's triggering for me with the boats. But if he was in the condo on Sunday night, he's a day student. Versus living in the dorms,' he explained. 'Residential students return from the weekend with their families on Sunday afternoon and the dorms are locked down at ten each night. Staff do room checks. If he was in the condo at midnight, he would have been missed.'

'Can we borrow copies of your yearbooks for the past few years?' Olivia asked.

'Of course,' Oaks signed as the two men stood. 'I'll have my secretary get the yearbooks and I'll get a day-student roster.'

'And the residential roster?' Olivia asked and Oaks frowned. 'Please.'

When they were gone, Olivia turned to Kane. 'He could be right, but kids are going to get out if they want to badly enough. This kid was meeting a girl he'd have sex with.'

'He'd find a way,' Kane agreed. 'Val, are you ready for a bunch of defensive teenagers who aren't likely going to want to talk to us?'

The interpreter shrugged. 'I've got two at home. I'm used to that.'

Tuesday, September 21, 10:50 A.M.

He needed a break, but he was alone behind the counter. Buster was late. Again. It was hard to get help that would be on time. Damn college kids. No responsibility.

He checked his customers, found them all absorbed in their own business, so he opened his laptop. First, Eric's bank account. It was all still there. With a few clicks, he wiped Eric's rather sizeable account, transferring the money to his own holding account. He left eleven hundred behind, so that if Eric stopped to get his customary thousand-dollar withdrawal, he wouldn't be turned away.

Wouldn't want him to suspect. That would spoil Albert's little surprise.

On his cell phone, he typed in Albert's number, which he'd harvested from Eric's cell phone. One could learn a lot from an individual's address book. Phone numbers of contacts, addresses, even personal info like birthdays, passwords, and bank PINs.

your birdie is about to fly the coop, he typed. *au revoir. 5:30, lindberg terminal.*

He closed his phone. That was that. He wondered what Albert would do. Would he beat Eric up? Force him to stay? Kill him? Mercy, this was more exciting than TV.

Next on the agenda was the embezzling accountant, Mr Dorian Blunt. Dorian owed him two months' payment.

274

He'd been duly warned. He logged in to Dorian's account and saw that only half of one month's payment had been rendered.

He frowned. The man honestly thought that would be enough. *He is a fool.*

He wiped Dorian's account, sending it to his offshore holding account. Now, what to do about Dorian? He had no issue with Dorian's wife and child, so torching the family home just wouldn't do at all. Dorian didn't have a convenient warehouse like Tomlinson's where he could be dealt with alone. He'd have to think on that one for a while. These things had to be handled delicately.

The bell on the door jingled and part-time help Buster hurried in. 'Man, I'm sorry.'

'You're late.'

'I know. I should have called.'

'Yes, you should have.' He closed his laptop. 'I have to do some errands. Darren is coming in at noon. You think you two will be okay to handle the lunch rush?'

'Is Manuel caught up on the sandwiches?'

He'd been lauded by the community for providing immigrants with jobs. Truth was, he was happy to have people around who didn't speak English. Made for a much smoother operation that way. 'Yeah, he's ready.' He stepped aside so that Buster could man the register. 'I should be back before dinner.'

'I could use the hours. I can work the evening, even close up if you want.'

'No, I won't be gone that long. I'll close.' God forbid if Buster actually cleaned anything. He might find his microphones. But so far, they were safe. The mikes were hidden very well indeed. Factor in that Buster, Darren, and his other counter help were as lackluster as Manuel and the kitchen help were hardworking, and he had no concerns about leaving his shop. Together they all worked like a song.

Kane and Sutherland had been at the deaf school for hours. He wondered if they'd found who they were looking for. He wondered what if anything that person had seen. He wondered if he could be identified. That would be bad.

So he'd have to somehow figure out what Kane and Sutherland knew. Luckily, he had a plan. Laptop under his arm, he left, the little bell on the door jingling behind him.

Tuesday, September 21, 12:15 P.M.

Eric hung up the pay phone, glad he'd made the effort. Pay phones were difficult to find these days, but he hadn't wanted to use his own phone to call the synagogue. He'd been angsting over whether he should go to Joel's funeral. If the cops were on to them, they might be waiting for him there.

But if no one suspected, it would be suspicious for him not to go. They'd been friends since kindergarten. But his quandary had been solved. Joel's funeral would not happen today, which he suspected had thrown the Orthodox Fischers into a real tizzy. He remembered Joel telling him once how important it was for them to bury their dead within twenty-four hours. But Joel's body would not be ready for burial until tomorrow.

And I'll be in France by then. Au revoir, Joel.

He'd already mailed the package of his keepsakes to his uncle. Now the only thing to do would be to go back to his apartment and wait until it was time to leave for the airport.

His flight was at 5:30 out of Lindberg Terminal. He didn't plan to be late.

It wasn't until he'd turned the key in his front door that he realized something was very wrong. There was a fire roaring in the fireplace. *Someone's here*.

The door was yanked open, but all he saw was a hand. Holding his own gun. 'I found your gun, Eric. I also found your bag. One really should pack more clean underwear when fleeing to France.'

Chapter Fourteen

Tuesday, September 21, 1:15 P.M.

David woke abruptly, but didn't move a muscle. Tensed, he listened, then heard it again. The rustling of papers out in the living room of Glenn's cabin.

Someone is here. The sun was high in the sky outside his bedroom window. He'd only been asleep a few hours. Rolling soundlessly to his feet, he crept to the door and looked out. From here he could see nothing, but he could hear the opening of drawers.

Call 911. But Glenn had only one land line, in the kitchen. *And my cell's sitting next to it, charging. Stupid.* Glenn had a rifle, but it was out in the living room. *Where it does me no good at all.* He stood in nothing but his boxers, no weapon and no phone.

A robber? Then his mind finally fully woke. *That glass ball. Goddamn reporters.* One of them must have found out where he was. He tilted his head to better hear. More drawers were opened, more papers rustled. Whoever it was, was looking for something. But what?

He slipped through the door, grateful that the carpet on the floor muffled his footsteps. His heart was racing as his mind pictured what could be waiting.

The living room came into view and he stopped, assessed, barely breathing.

A man stood at Glenn's desk, rifling through papers. He was at least as tall as David, lean and wiry. It was hard to tell his age, but he wasn't very young, nor old. Most importantly, there was a gun tucked into the man's waistband. *Shit*.

David's laptop sat on top of a stack of mail he'd forgotten to take back to Glenn last night. *Shit*. The realization was like a swift kick in the gut. The laptop had been on the table next to his bed. The man had been in his room while he slept.

Intent in his search, the man hadn't heard him yet, which was a good sign. Watching the man going through Glenn's things, David visualized what he would do, then moved, closing the distance between them in two swift leaps.

The man reached for his gun at David's first footfall. But David got there first, taking him down, his hand capturing the man's in a wristlock. The man flailed, but David tightened his hold. It was a painful hold, as he well knew, from all those times Paige's self-defense students had practiced it on him.

'If you move, I will break your hand and then your fucking neck,' David hissed, his heart pounding to beat all hell. 'Who are you and what are you doing here?'

The man's eyes were wild. Crazy wild. 'Get off me. You bastard.'

'No fucking way.' He took the gun, appalled that his hand shook, while the man bucked wildly. David reversed the wrist hold, bending the guy's arm behind him. A string of vile curses spewed and David held the lock.

He was breathing more evenly now, the initial terror over. 'Who are you?'

'Go to hell,' the man gasped, quivering now. This close David could see he was in his thirties. 'You bastard.'

David leaned in farther and a howl burst from the man's throat. 'Stop!' he cried.

'Who are you?'

'Lincoln.'

'Lincoln who? Dammit. I don't want to break your shoulder. Who the hell are you?'

'Lincoln Jefferson.'

Lincoln Jefferson? David almost laughed. The name was almost definitely fake, but it was something. He held the pressure firm. 'Why are you here?'

'You're lying bastards,' Lincoln sobbed. 'You lied. You lied. You lied.'

'I don't lie.' Not in a very long time anyway. 'Who sent you?' Lincoln said nothing, and David tightened the hold with a jerk that made the man moan. 'Who sent you?'

'The earth is our mother. *Valla Eam,*' Lincoln whispered, then started to chant it, again and again. '*Valla Eam.*'

David had read those words, recently. *Valla Eam.* 'Defend her,' as in defend Mother Earth. '*Valla Eam*' was the way Preston Moss ended every speech. It had been the rallying cry of his followers.

Relaxing his hold a hair, David studied the man, wondering if he was looking at the person who'd created the website on which he'd found Moss's speeches. Could Lincoln have helped Moss set his fires? Twelve years ago, Lincoln would have been in college.

'You followed Preston Moss,' David said quietly. 'Why are you in my house? Did Moss send you?'

Lincoln's laugh was muted, strangely disturbing. 'No.'

David bent closer, careful not to increase the pressure. 'How did I lie? Tell me.'

'You said you caught the ball.'

'I did. I caught the ball.'

'You didn't. You couldn't.'

'But I did. I don't lie.' He thought of the girl, Tracey Mullen, of the gel on her hands. Of the dead guard and the faceless Tomlinson. 'I was there,' he murmured. 'At both fires. I saw the bodies.' He saw Lincoln flinch. 'I caught the ball, Lincoln.'

'No. You didn't. Not his. You put it there. You *planted* it there. You *bastards*.'

David blinked, surprised. 'Why would you think I planted it, Lincoln?'

Lincoln shook his head hard. 'I'm not talking to you.'

Yes, you will. David put more pressure on Lincoln's arm. 'I think you should reconsider that. Look, I'm a good guy. I pay my taxes and I put out fires. I even save old ladies' cats from trees. Why would I lie about your damn ball?'

'It wasn't his ball! You want to bring him down, *again*. But I won't let you.'

'You think that I, a tax-paying, cat-saving firefighter, planted a glass ball in a burning building to make your crazy leader look bad? You're more insane than he was.'

Lincoln's laugh was brittle. 'Oh yes. Crazy I am. Crazy I am,' he said in a singsong. 'Doctor says it, mother says it, brother says it. Lincoln's crazy. What happened to Lincoln? Why don't you smile, Lincoln? Lincoln, why are you *so fucking crazy*?' Lincoln yelled the last three words and lunged, but David subdued him.

'Why are you crazy, Lincoln?' he asked softly.

'She was black,' Lincoln murmured. 'Black. All black.'

Oh God. David remembered what Glenn had told him

281

about the victim of SPOT's blaze, how the woman had been burned. 'You were there, twelve years ago. You killed that woman in the insurance building. You came back. Saw her body.'

'Burned up. All burned up. Took her away, but she's always there. Always there.' He shuddered and went still. 'Always there,' he whispered.

A shiver raced down David's spine. Seeing a dead body could push someone to insanity. He studied the man, an unwelcome thought intruding into his mind. *There, but for the grace of God, go I.*

'Why did you come here, Lincoln?' he asked, his voice rough with a compassion he didn't want to feel. It was a betrayal of the real victims. 'What were you trying to find?'

'The letter with the lies. From the bosses. All made up.'

'You think my bosses told me to lie? You think they wanted Moss's name dragged into this? To accuse him?'

Lincoln just sighed. David wanted to do the same. He'd get no further.

David gripped Lincoln's gun. 'I have your gun pointed at you. If you try to run, I'll just take you down again. I don't want to hurt you anymore. Do you understand me?'

Lincoln made no response. David released him, stepping several feet back in the same movement, relieved when Lincoln stayed put. He needed to restrain Lincoln until the police could arrive. David looked around for something to tie him with, finally cutting the pull cord from the blinds at the window.

Quickly he tied Lincoln's hands and feet, then called 911.

Then he called Olivia. It went to her voice mail. 'Olivia, it's David. I've caught an intruder you're going to want to meet.' He hung up and crouched next to Lincoln, who lay with his eyes closed. The man looked a little green.

'You okay?' he asked Lincoln.

'Go to hell,' Lincoln said wearily.

'I hope not,' he said honestly. 'You need to understand something, if you can. I really did find a ball Sunday night. I saw another last night. Nobody's lying to you.'

'No.' He said it simply, like a child. 'Preston Moss can't kill.'

But he had. Even if he hadn't meant to, Moss caused the death of an innocent woman. *So did you. St David, the killer. Megan was an innocent and now she's dead.*

No. It wasn't the same. It was not *the same. You go on believing that if it makes you feel better.* David sat on the floor, Lincoln's gun in hand, and prepared to wait.

Tuesday, September 21, 1:15 P.M.

In two and a half hours, they'd talked to twenty teenaged boys and so far not one knew anything. Or so they claimed. Olivia watched turbulent teen number twenty saunter out of Oaks's office. 'How many more?' she asked.

'Legions,' Kane said morosely. 'Or six. Seems like the same thing.'

From across the table Val, the interpreter, chuckled, but said nothing. Olivia liked her. Val had done her job reliably and without a single complaint.

Principal Oaks appeared with the next boy. 'This is Kenny Lathem,' he signed, Val voicing. Oaks had been present for every interview and Olivia was sure that had hampered their results. But the kids were minors, so there wasn't much choice.

Kenny was sixteen, his hair sandy blond. He was a dorm student and once again Oaks had protested that a dorm student would have been missed on Sunday night. But Kenny had gotten a scholarship for Camp Longfellow, so he was of special interest.

'Hi, Kenny,' Olivia said. 'Do you know why we're here?'

Kenny nodded, then signed while Val voiced, 'I heard it from the other kids. You're looking for whoever saw the girl who died.'

The kid's eyes were as defiant as the twenty pairs that had come before. Except . . . except there was a flicker of something else there. Fear. This kid knew something.

Olivia slid Tracey's photo across the table. 'Do you know her?' she asked.

He watched Val interpret, glanced at the picture, then shook his head.

'Kenny?' Olivia still saw the flickers of fear as he fixed his eyes on Val. 'She died, Kenny,' Olivia said. 'She was murdered.' Kenny looked away from the interpreter.

Oaks stepped forward but Olivia warned him back with a glance. She tapped the table again, waiting until Kenny looked at Val. 'Kenny. Somebody set the building on fire with her in it. She was sixteen, Kenny, same age as you. Somebody was with her, but they left her there. Left her there to *die*. She died from the smoke. *Suffocated*.'

'I don't know her,' he signed, but his hands trembled, ever so slightly. 'I swear.'

I don't believe you. Olivia flipped through the yearbook to his picture. 'You lettered in track. I lettered in gymnastics. Now I biathalon. You know what that is?'

He shook his head, seemingly bored.

'It's cross-country skiing combined with marksmanship.

I tried rowing, but I got seasick.' She tapped the yearbook page with her finger. 'This says you're a rower.'

He shrugged, uncomfortably. 'I do okay,' he signed. 'So?'

'So, do you ever boat on the lake? Canoes, rowboats, that kind of thing?'

'Sometimes.' It was tentatively signed.

'Like at Camp Longfellow?'

Kenny nodded warily.

'You were there, last summer. So was she.' Olivia pushed Tracey's photo back to him. 'Maybe you met her. Maybe you liked her. Maybe she liked you.'

He pushed the picture back. 'I don't know her.' Each sign was deliberately made, spaced apart. Val's voice became clipped. Impatient. She was good.

'I wonder what the camp counselors will tell us, Kenny?' Olivia tilted her head, studying him carefully. 'Did you have a summer romance?'

'No.' This word Kenny voiced harshly and signed at once.

Val's voice trailed behind. 'No.'

That Olivia actually believed. 'But you wanted to. Did she not like you?' Kenny looked away. Patiently, Olivia tapped the table again until he looked back at Val. 'I asked you a question. Did she not like you?'

'I said I don't know her.' His signs were dramatic. 'What do you want from me?'

'I want the truth. This girl deserves the truth. She deserves justice. The person who killed her needs to pay. So from you, I want the truth. We know she met someone Sunday night at the condo. They had sex. Was it you?'

He looked straight into her eyes then, his tormented. 'No. Not me.' He voiced it thickly, signed it forcefully, then

285

lurched to his feet and ran from the room.

Oaks started to follow him, but Olivia held up her hand. 'Let him go.'

'Could he be protecting someone?' Kane asked and Oaks let out a long sigh.

'Maybe. Kenny's one of those boys who gets in trouble, but basically has a good heart.' He signed it, then looked hopefully at Olivia. 'Do you know what I mean?'

She nodded with a smile. 'I was one of those girls, I'm afraid. What about his friends? Does Kenny have any friends he might be protecting? Anyone with dark hair?'

'He's friends with his roommate, Austin Dent,' Oaks signed, 'but Austin has red hair, not dark brown. Kenny's pretty social, but you've already met his good friends.'

'Five more on the list,' Kane said. 'I need to take a break, stretch my legs.'

'Me too,' Olivia said. 'I just let a call go to voice mail. I didn't want to stop Kenny. Let's break for lunch. Mr Oaks, we'll be back in forty minutes to talk to Kenny again.'

'Of course,' he signed, standing to open his office door.

In the hall, Val flexed her hands and Olivia looked at her in concern. 'You okay?'

Val smiled. 'When I work in the school systems, I sign all day long with only a lunch break. This is easy. I'll meet you back here in forty minutes?'

'You didn't drive here. How will you get to lunch?'

'There's a sub place about three blocks down. I eat there whenever I come here.'

When Val was gone, Olivia closed her eyes. That little nap on David's lap had helped, but she needed a night's sleep. Maybe tonight. Then she thought of her fedora and handcuffs. Maybe she'd get that night's sleep tomorrow night.

She checked her messages. Noah Webster said he hadn't yet heard from Camp Longfellow's staff, and Faye said Tracey Mullen's mother had called and said her connecting flight was delayed in Atlanta. The last message was from David. She listened to it, then, heart beating harder, called him back, relieved when he answered normally.

'What happened?' she demanded.

'I was asleep and heard a sound. It was a man digging through my friend's desk.'

'A reporter?' Olivia asked with distaste.

'Oh, better. This man followed Preston Moss. Says his name is Lincoln Jefferson. I subdued and restrained him, then called 911. Olivia, I think this guy was with Moss when he set that last fire.'

'Oh my God.' She heard some banging and voices and shrieking. 'Who is that?'

'Local cops. Lincoln's not real happy right now. What do you want done with him?'

'Hold him. We're coming up right now.' She relayed instructions to the officer, then hung up just as Kane came around the corner. 'You are not going to believe this.'

'Nothing good ever follows that statement.'

'Today, you are wrong.' She told him and his brows shot up.

'I guess we should tell Principal Oaks we won't be back in forty minutes. Of course, we could just call Barlow and let him deal with the intruder.'

'Yeah, right,' Olivia scoffed and he grinned.

'I thought you'd made up with Barlow.'

'We are a long way from being made up. But he's trying. Still doesn't mean I'm going to bring him in until I know what this is about. Especially since he's got that Crawford tagging along with him today. Guy gave me the creeps.'

'Same here,' Kane admitted. 'I'll tell Oaks we'll be back in a few hours.'

'I'll call Val and let her know.'

Tuesday, September 21, 1:50 P.M.

After careful consideration – and a drive-by inspection – he'd decided what to do with accountant Dorian Blunt. It was time to rally the troops. He sent a text to Eric.

new assignment.

He hit SEND, then sent the address, followed by the intel he'd picked up on his drive-by.

no dog. no alarm. no cameras. consider it a gift.

He lifted his eyes to the building he sat watching. No one had emerged in the hour he'd sat here, but they would. He could be patient. It was a beautiful day, after all. But the minutes ticked by and he began to frown. There was no response from Eric.

Could the kid have changed his travel plans? Escaped? That would be disturbing. And annoying. He'd actually have to release the video and he was far from ready to do that. He'd given Albert all the information necessary to stop Eric's escape. He was disappointed in the big guy. He'd thought that Albert would have the situation well in hand by now and that Eric would be toeing the line.

He shook his head and began a new text to Albert's phone, when one came through from Eric's disposable. He read it and his eyes widened.

It appears Eric has left the building.

There was a photo attached and his eyes widened more. Eric lay on his bed, nude, an empty baggie on his nightstand. Out of all the possible scenarios, suicide was the one he'd least anticipated from good old Eric. He didn't think the boy had had the nerve.

He thought about his earlier text to Albert and suspected Eric hadn't gone willingly.

Damn. I would have liked to have heard that conversation. But he'd been out of range of the planted microphone's transmitter, doing his drive-by intel for tonight.

who is this? he typed.

Moi. You will deal with me now. I want to meet.

He laughed softly. *no*, he typed, hit SEND, then tossed the cell back in the console. And none too soon. The front door to the building opened and a woman came out, dressed all in black.

She was alone. He couldn't ask for much more than that. Until he had her in his hands, of course. Then he'd ask a great deal more. And she'd answer every question.

He hoped she'd give up the information he sought easily. He didn't mind putting a bullet into someone who deserved it, like Tomlinson, or who was a direct threat, like the condo guard. Torture, though . . . always left him queasy.

But, it was unavoidable. She had info and he wanted it. *Sucks to be her. Oh well.*

She was walking west, probably to grab a bite of lunch. He put his van in gear and slowly followed. A little ether on a handkerchief and the element of surprise would do the job nicely. He did like his gadgets, but sometimes it paid to keep it simple.

Tuesday, September 21, 3:50 P.M.

'You should have called me,' Barlow said between his teeth. He and Olivia stood looking into Interview Two, where Lincoln Jefferson sat in a chair at the table, his hands cuffed and his legs shackled. He hadn't asked for an attorney yet. Olivia wasn't certain that enough of his mind was present to do so.

'I did call you,' she said calmly. 'That's why you're here.'

Barlow's jaw clenched. 'You should have called me right away.'

Olivia glanced to her left. Special Agent Crawford stood beside her, his intense gaze fixed on Lincoln Jefferson, as if willing him to speak. She didn't like the FBI man but knew better than to fight his presence. 'You were processing a crime scene. I called you when we'd confirmed this man's identity.'

'I can't believe his name really is Lincoln Jefferson,' Kane said.

'His brother is Truman Jefferson,' Olivia added. 'The mother confirmed it.'

'I want Moss,' Crawford said in a low, angry voice. 'Let me talk to this shit. He'll know where Moss is hiding.'

'That'll be up to our captain,' Kane said carefully. 'But nobody sees him until our shrink gets here. Lincoln may have no bearing on our case, but we can't assume that. Dr Donahue will assess him and advise the best way to question him.'

'He's not crazy,' Crawford said with contempt. 'He's an arsonist, plain and simple.'

'The behavior David Hunter described makes him

sound pretty crazy,' Olivia said. 'Either way, we do nothing until Donahue gets here and does the psych eval.'

'We're wasting time,' Crawford hissed. 'You may not feel the urgency of this situation, Detective, but I do. Every minute he sits there is another minute Moss is free to plan his next attack. I'm going to talk to him, before it's too late.' He started to move into the interview room and Olivia grabbed the lapel of his black suit.

'Cool your jets, Agent Crawford,' she warned sharply, releasing his lapel. 'This is not your investigation.'

'It will be,' he said. He left the viewing area and Barlow sighed.

'Thank you. He's been breathing down my neck all day.'

'Which is a major reason we didn't call you,' Kane said reasonably. 'We didn't want Crawford going off on Lincoln in David Hunter's living room.'

'Where is Hunter?' Barlow asked wearily.

'Filling out a complaint,' Olivia said. 'He followed us. His promising to come to the station with Lincoln was the only way we could keep him calm enough to transport.'

'We thought we were going to have to request a tranquilizer gun,' Kane said, only half joking. 'Lincoln went wild when the uniformed cops showed up to cuff him. It was only when Hunter talked to him that he calmed down. Bizarre, considering.'

'Yes, it is.' Jessie Donahue joined them at the window, watching in silence for a minute. 'What's that he's chanting?' she asked. 'I can't make it out.'

'*Valla Eam*,' Olivia told her and Donahue nodded.

'"Defend her,"' she murmured. 'SPOT's rallying cry. What can you tell me?'

'Just what his mother told us,' Olivia said. 'She said he

291

was diagnosed as a schizophrenic at twenty-one, when he was at the university. With meds, life is better.'

'But he doesn't take his meds,' Dr Donahue said.

Olivia nodded. 'According to his mom, that's true. She said Lincoln has been in and out of psychiatric care for the last ten years.'

'You think he really was at the last SPOT fire?' Donahue asked.

'He was a student in Moss's university class twelve years ago,' Kane said. 'It fits.'

'He was in the home of the firefighter who caught the ball. Did he say why?'

'Conspiracy theory. The fire department was dragging Moss's name through the mud.' Olivia eyed Donahue. Since joining the team, the shrink had made no reference to Olivia's three mandated visits. Or the fourth that she'd rescheduled six times. 'Is Lincoln crazy?'

Donahue met her eyes and Olivia had the sense the woman was reading her mind. Discomfiting. 'If he's diagnosed schizophrenic, then yes, he's certifiably crazy. But that doesn't mean he can't be held accountable for what he did today or twelve years ago.'

'Special Agent Crawford wants to talk to him,' Kane said. 'Dig Moss's whereabouts out of his brain.'

Donahue frowned. 'I don't think that's a good idea.'

The door closed sharply behind them. 'It doesn't matter,' Crawford said smugly. He was standing next to Abbott, who looked worn out.

'We are to cooperate with the FBI,' Abbott said stiffly. 'So let the man through.'

What followed made them all cringe. Crawford was twice as belligerent with Lincoln as he'd been with them, repeating his demand, 'Tell me where Moss is,' again and again. Within minutes Lincoln was cowering and rocking in his chair.

Donahue crossed her arms over her chest. 'What is he doing?' she asked angrily.

'Crawford's an old-fashioned sink with two spigots,' Barlow said. 'One hot, one cold. This morning we got cold. A few times during the day, he went hot. It was not fun.'

'But you're not a schizophrenic off his meds,' Olivia said. She looked at Abbott, frustrated. 'Don't let him break Lincoln's brain before we can talk to him.'

A few seconds later, Crawford himself gave Abbott an official out when he grabbed Lincoln's collar and yanked him so that he sat up in the chair. 'You will answer me.'

Abbott stepped into the room. 'Special Agent Crawford, you have a phone call.'

'I'm busy. Take a message.'

Abbott shook his head. 'I'm sorry. You need to take this call. Please.'

Crawford thrust Lincoln away in disgust. 'I'll be back for you,' he said angrily, then followed Abbott into the observation room. 'What the fuck?' he exploded as soon as the door was closed. 'How dare you? I was going to break him.'

'We don't want him broken,' Abbott said. 'He is our witness.'

'He's wanted for a goddamn federal crime,' Crawford said, getting in Abbott's face. 'Are you going to give him milk and cookies? What kind of department do you run?'

'A successful one,' Abbott said quietly, not moving a muscle, not backing down. 'Now, we will question him, but we'll follow the advice of our psychiatrist.'

Crawford's expression became one of blatant disrespect. 'And she'll say he's crazy, that he can't be held responsible,' he said sarcastically. 'Then be my guest. Try the milk-and-cookies approach. See if you can *cajole* a confession out of him.'

'Under this kind of duress,' Donahue said, 'no confession you pull from him will hold weight in court anyway. His defense attorney will leap all over this. I don't think you want that, Special Agent Crawford.'

'I don't want him. I want Moss,' Crawford uttered slowly as if they were all stupid.

'Then we need to calm Lincoln down,' Kane said. 'Liv, you up to try?'

'We both tried to calm him down back at David's,' she said. 'The only person he listened to was David Hunter.'

'The firefighter?' Crawford asked, narrowing his eyes. 'What did Hunter tell him?'

Olivia looked at Abbott, purposely ignoring Crawford. 'David's been reading Moss's speeches since he caught the ball. The uniforms had cuffed Lincoln and had him facedown on the carpet. David started quoting Moss's speeches, word for word.'

Abbott's brows lifted. 'Some memory.'

You have no idea, Olivia wanted to say, but swallowed it back. 'Apparently so. He thinks Lincoln might be the guy who built the website shrine to Moss.'

'Where is Hunter now?' Abbott asked.

'Filling out a complaint,' Kane said. 'You want him in there?'

There was a crash in the interview room. Lincoln had rocked his chair until he tipped and hit the floor. Now he lay on his side, rocking and chanting, *'Valla Eam.'*

Abbott sighed. 'Go get Hunter. What can it hurt?'

'We're not going to get back to the deaf school before school's out,' Kane said, 'but I want one more go at Kenny.

I'll bring Hunter, then tell Oaks we'll be back after dinner.'

'Val sent me a text saying she had a three o'clock interpreting commitment when I told her we were running behind,' Olivia said. 'She'll be busy for a while longer. I'll tell her to be back at the school around seven.'

'I'll get the fireman,' Kane said. 'Don't do anything exciting without me.'

Chapter Fifteen

Tuesday, September 21, 4:45 P.M.

David stood at the window looking at Lincoln, who was rocking in his chair. 'What do you want me to do?'

'Go in and talk to him,' Olivia said. 'Like you did at the cabin. Calm him down. Then I'll come in and try to find out if he knows anything about these two fires. After that, we want to know if he knows where Moss is.'

'How long has he been schizophrenic?' David asked.

'Why does that matter?' Special Agent Crawford demanded.

David already didn't like him, but that wasn't his business.

'Since he was twenty-one,' Donahue said. 'A common age to manifest.'

'And right about the time he met Moss,' David said. 'Lincoln was ripe for the picking by a radical cultlike leader, wasn't he?'

'Likely,' Donahue agreed. 'He would have been frightened and confused by what was happening in his mind and reached out to a group that helped him stay grounded.'

'SPOT?' Crawford snorted. 'A radical environmental group kept him *grounded*?'

'They probably welcomed his zeal,' Donahue answered, as if Crawford hadn't dismissed her. 'When he was "up," he would have been quite an asset.'

'And seeing a charred body that he'd helped kill?' David said.

'Would have pushed him over the edge, putting horrific images in his mind.'

'Understandable,' David murmured. 'I've seen a few charred bodies and it's an . . . unforgettable sight.'

'Hunter,' Crawford said mockingly. 'Do you feel *sorry* for this man?'

David looked him in the eye, gratified he had to look down several inches to do so. 'This man killed a woman and permanently damaged the lives of two good firefighters. I don't feel sorry for him.' Which was true when he thought about it like that. 'Satisfied?'

Crawford had a sour look about him. 'Yes.'

'Then I guess I'm ready to go in.' He walked into the room, pausing at the table. He had to remind himself that the pathetic man before him had violated Glenn's belongings, was going to steal his laptop, and had been armed with a lethal weapon. Still, he couldn't push Lincoln's eerie whisper from his mind. *Always there. Always there.*

Did he feel sorry for the man? When he thought about the whisper, yes, David found that he did. But he struck all pity from his voice. 'Hi, Lincoln.'

Lincoln's rocking slowed, but it didn't stop, nor did his chanting of *Valla Eam*.

David sat and began reciting one of Moss's speeches, as he'd done before. Within a few minutes the chanting had slowed. After another few minutes, Lincoln was reciting along with him. Finally David stopped. After finishing the paragraph, Lincoln fell silent.

'Lincoln, the police wanted me to talk to you. You got upset. What happened?'

Lincoln scrunched his eyes closed. 'He yelled. In my ear. In my head. It was loud.'

'I'm sorry,' David said quietly. 'I don't like it when people yell at me either. Lincoln, you know you're in trouble, right?'

Lincoln nodded, saying nothing, eyes still squeezed shut.

'Detective Sutherland drove you down here. Can she talk to you now?'

The man didn't open his eyes. 'No.'

'Then, you have a problem,' he said, keeping his voice calm. 'You broke into my house. You had a gun. The police want to know why.' And after the adrenaline had settled, David realized he wanted to know who'd told Lincoln he was there. 'Detective Sutherland won't be loud in your head. You need to stay calm.'

David rose when Olivia came into the room. 'Hi, Lincoln.'

Lincoln still didn't open his eyes. 'He stays. Cat-saving fireman stays.'

Olivia's blond brows rose. 'He saves cats?'

'Little old ladies' cats in trees. He stays.'

She motioned to a seat and David sat. She sat next to him, across from Lincoln. 'He's not your lawyer, Lincoln,' she murmured. 'I read you your rights. You have the right to an attorney. David Hunter is not your lawyer.'

'I know. He stays. He understands.'

She met David's eyes, a frown in hers. 'What does he understand?' she asked, but Lincoln was silent. David shrugged, unsure of what to say in front of the man. Unsure what he'd say were he alone with her. Yes, he understood. But he wasn't proud of it.

'Okay,' Olivia said softly. 'I want to talk to you about the glass ball.'

'No. He's listening.'

'Who?'

'The loud man. Where is Moss? Where is Moss?'

'No, he's not. Special Agent Crawford had to leave. He's not listening.'

David wasn't sure if she was lying or not. Apparently Lincoln wasn't either. Lincoln opened his eyes, searched her face plaintively. 'He wants Moss.'

'Yes, he does,' she said. 'But I want to talk about the glass ball.'

'It was Mother Earth,' Lincoln said dreamily. 'Defend her. *Valla Eam.*'

'You left them at fires, these balls,' she said.

'Yes. Marked. *Valla Eam.*'

Olivia leaned forward. 'How were they marked?'

'On the pole.'

She frowned slightly. 'On the pole?'

'On the pole. *Valla Eam.*' He sang it and Olivia tilted her head, watching him.

'Okay. Did you mark the big glass ball that was left at the condo?'

Lincoln blinked, seeming genuinely surprised. 'No.'

'How did you know about it?'

'News.'

'Where were you last night?'

'Blue Moon.' He sang again, this time singing the melody to the old song.

Her eyes sharpened. 'The bar? On Hennepin? When did you leave?'

'Bells. Last call.' He called it, like a train conductor.

'I understand. Lincoln, how did you know it was David who caught the ball?'

'Firemen. But the old man said he didn't live there in the old house.'

'How did you know he was in the cabin?'

'The girl told me. Baby smiled.'

The girls in 2A. 'One of my tenants,' David whispered to Olivia and she nodded.

'Lincoln, do you know where Preston Moss is?'

Tears filled his eyes. 'He left but she stays. Always there. Always there.' And then he began to rock again, his eyes clenched tightly.

'Who stays?' she asked, but Lincoln was gone again, back into his own mind.

'The woman he killed,' David murmured. 'She's always there, in his mind.'

'I think we're done here,' she muttered. The two of them went to the observation room and David closed the door. 'I don't think he's involved in our fires,' she said.

David searched the room. Crawford was indeed absent. 'Where's the FBI guy?'

'He got pissed when you said you were sorry he yelled at Lincoln,' Kane said. 'Stomped out. What did he mean by "marked on the pole"?'

'The pole of the world?' Barlow said, frowning. 'But there was no mention of that in any of the documentation I've read on SPOT.'

'Let's see if our glass ball has a mark,' Abbott said. 'As for this guy, psych ward at the jail. Fifteen minutes till our five o'clock. I'll see you all in my office. Mr Hunter, thank you. We appreciate your help this afternoon.'

'You're welcome.' Abbott and the others left, leaving

him alone with Olivia who had been watching him carefully since they'd left the interview room. 'What?' he asked her.

'What did you understand, David?'

He wanted to sigh. Wanted to run. Wanted to look away, to lie. Instead he answered as honestly as he could. 'I guess that what he saw that night still haunts him.'

Her gaze hadn't wavered. 'I'll see you later. I have to finish an interview after our meeting, so it'll be nine before I'm finished for the night. Where will you be?'

His heart rose from his gut to slam against his ribs. 'Where do you want me to be?'

She hesitated. 'The cabin was nice. I'll call you when I'm on my way.' She turned to go, then turned back. 'You promised to answer my question tonight.'

His heart kept rising. Now it was in his throat, choking him. 'Yes, I did. Who am I?'

'Exactly. That's what I want to know. Come on, I have to sign you out.'

Tuesday, September 21, 4:55 P.M.

He stepped out of his van and took a great gulp of fresh air. The interpreter's screams still rang in his ears and his stomach still churned. If only they'd just *tell*, it would make it so much easier.

She'd tried to stay silent, begged for her life, sobbed about her children, but in the end, *thankfully for both of us*, the interpreter hadn't held out all that long.

He had a name and a description. Kenny Lathem, sixteen, sandy blond hair, brown eyes, about five ten, wearing blue Converse high-tops. He wasn't the boy they'd been looking for, though. They were looking for someone with dark hair and size 10 shoes.

But Kenny knew something and the cops were going to try talking to him again tonight to find out just what he knew. *I have to find him first.* Trouble was, the kid lived in a dormitory, in a damn school. *How am I going to get him out? How will I communicate with him?*

The interpreter was quite dead, but he wouldn't have trusted her. He'd use paper and pen. But first he needed access to the kid.

He flipped open the woman's phone and smiled at the latest text she'd received. Olivia Sutherland was tied up, wanted to meet back at the school at seven.

I'm so sorry, he typed back. *I can't help you. I have a commitment tonight.* That would keep the cops from worrying when she didn't show at seven. Then he found the most recent text she'd sent to her sons. That wasn't hard to find. She'd told them to do their homework before watching TV after school. *Have an appointment tonight*, he typed. *Dinner in the fridge.* He had no idea if there was dinner in the fridge, but she'd sent texts like this in the past. The kids were teenagers. They wouldn't starve.

Now, nobody would be looking for her for hours, maybe till morning. In the meantime, he didn't want the interpreter's body found. It would tip off the cops that he knew about the boy they sought and that wouldn't be constructive at all. He dragged her body into the trees and rolled it into the shallow grave he'd dug while she slept off the ether with which he'd drugged her. He covered her up with dirt and drove away.

Tuesday, September 21, 5:10 P.M.

When Olivia got back to Abbott's office everyone was already seated – except for Special Agent Crawford who stood staring out Abbott's window. The room was very tense and Olivia was sure Crawford was the reason.

'Okay,' Abbott said, ignoring the Fed. 'So where are we?'

'Lincoln is on his way to the psych ward,' Kane said. 'When we're done here, Liv and I can hit the Blue Moon bar and check his alibi. I don't think he did our fires.'

'But he did give us something,' Barlow said. He took one of the large etched globes from an evidence envelope, turning it until the north pole pointed toward them. 'VE, scratched into the glass, so light you'd miss it if you weren't looking for it. *Valla Eam.*'

Crawford slowly turned, his face expressionless. 'What did you say?'

'VE,' Barlow repeated. 'Where Lincoln said it would be. Scratched into the pole.'

Everyone was watching Crawford and the Fed clenched his jaw. 'When did the suspect say that?'

'After you left,' Barlow said.

Crawford was at the table in three steps. 'Give it to me.'

Barlow snatched the ball. 'I'll show you mine, if you show me yours,' he said coldly.

His jaw clenching even harder, Crawford grabbed his briefcase from the floor and set it on the round table with a bang. 'I don't like the tone of your voice, Sergeant.'

'And I don't care,' Barlow said evenly. 'You held back information.'

'We didn't want copycats, so we kept that detail from

the press.' Crawford passed the small evidence box he'd shown them that morning to Barlow.

'We aren't the press,' Barlow snapped. 'We're investigating three homicides. You should have told us. We could have checked this out this morning.'

'*I* looked at your damn ball this morning,' Crawford bit out. 'I already knew.'

Abbott's brows rose. 'That's simply . . . unpleasant, Crawford.'

Barlow shook his head, likely at a loss for words. 'Can I see your glass, Micki?'

Micki gave him the small magnifying glass she carried and Barlow removed the smaller globe from its box and studied it. 'Identical,' he pronounced.

'When did you plan to tell us, Crawford?' Abbott asked mildly. Oh, he was pissed.

'When we took someone into custody. Until then, I was under orders to share that information on a need-to-know basis.'

Abbott was visibly trying to control his temper. 'So, based on your need-to-know info, you'd already determined our arsons were connected to yours.'

'I have been searching for these bastards for twelve years. That drooling psycho down there is guilty as hell,' Crawford said between his teeth. 'He knows where Moss is. He can identify the others who set my fire. Doesn't that *matter* to you people?'

'It matters a lot,' Olivia said. 'He and others caused the death of an innocent woman twelve years ago and he should pay. But make him pay for what he did. If he's not guilty of setting our fires, we're wasting valuable time arguing.'

Crawford's jaw closed with a loud clack. 'Give me back my evidence.'

'After we photograph it,' Abbott said calmly. 'I wouldn't argue if I were you.'

Crawford seethed. 'We are wasting time here.'

'Indeed,' Abbott said, deliberately misunderstanding. 'Micki, what do you have?'

Micki glanced at the rigid Crawford from the corner of her eye. 'Pictures from Tomlinson's desk,' she said and spread them out. 'We recovered a few more pieces.'

'I'd hoped not to have to see Tomlinson having sex again,' Olivia said and sensed Micki was waiting for them to discover something she'd already found.

'These weren't taken at the same time,' Kane said. 'Look at Tomlinson in this second one. He's skinnier. Has muscle tone in his torso. He was working out. Buffing up.'

'The timeline's wrong,' Olivia said. She blinked hard, trying to make the pieces fall into place. 'Mrs T said she found out about her husband's infidelity and hired a PI.'

'On the recommendation of her friend,' Kane supplied.

'Right. She hired the PI and said she had photos . . .'

'A week later,' Kane murmured. 'She said she copied her files the next day and that was June fifteenth according to the time stamp on the files she gave us. So the earliest these pictures could have been taken was June eighth.'

Olivia placed the before and after pictures of Tomlinson side by side. 'So he's white and doughy and then he's white and toned. It must have taken him months to get this toned. In this "after" picture his skin should be tanned because the PI would have taken it a few weeks ago at the latest. Tomlinson played golf all summer. These "before" pictures were taken long before June eighth. That means Mrs Tomlinson is lying.'

Micki looked impressed. 'Wow. I didn't see that.'

Olivia looked at her, surprised. 'Then what did you see?'

'The mistress's shoes.'

Noah chuckled. 'It's always the shoes with you, Mick.'

Micki arched a brow. 'I was right on your case.' Micki had correctly predicted the Pit-Guy's shoe fetish by studying victim photos. 'And I'm right again.'

Olivia gave both pictures another look and sighed. 'Yes, she is. Look at the pile of clothing on the floor. You have to squint unless you're the shoe queen.'

Micki pretended to buff her nails. 'The shoe queen rules. Those are snow boots on top of her parka and long underwear. It was too warm for those clothes in June.'

'Let's talk to Louise Tomlinson,' Kane said. 'And find out what's really true.'

'Nice job,' Abbott said. 'What else, Micki?'

'We pieced together some papers from the backpack the firefighters found at the condo. It's a page from a book. I Googled the phrases. It's from *Ethan Frome*.'

'Required reading for high schoolers,' Abbott said. 'My daughter has to read it. Any scraps with a student's name?'

'Not yet. We're still sifting through rubble. We took soil samples around the path the arsonists took away from the condo. It's strange. We found two sets of foot smudges coming out of the condo. The arson dog picked up the accelerant close to the fence where they escaped, but found evidence of only one pair of shoes.'

'One of them took off his shoes?' Olivia asked.

'Don't know. That's why we took the soil samples. We're back to shoes again.'

Abbott's mouth turned up. 'Keep me updated. Noah?'

'No news on Camp Longfellow,' Noah said. 'I contacted the state troopers to check the campsite, but it's not staffed right now. I left voice mails all over. I'll keep trying.'

'What about the background checks on the condo construction workers and Tomlinson's employees?' Kane asked.

'No one common to both,' Noah said. 'I tracked the girl Tomlinson was having the affair with. He had the deed for one of his properties transferred to her name, a house out in Woodview. The bank started foreclosure on the property last month.'

'When did Tomlinson transfer the deed?' Olivia asked.

Noah's brows went up. 'Last December.'

'The shoe queen rules,' Micki crowed. 'Snow boots do not lie.'

Abbott's grin was quick, but genuine. 'You go, Mick. Noah, keep working on the camp. We need to know who that girl might have met at camp this summer.'

'Kenny, the sixteen-year-old at the school, definitely recognized her,' Olivia said. 'We're going back tonight to talk to him again.'

'Check Lincoln's alibi first,' Abbott said, looking at Crawford who stood like a statue. 'I want to either connect Lincoln or clear him. And I want that eyewitness to the condo fire.' He waved them out. 'Tomorrow, here, oh-eight.'

Back at her desk, Olivia checked her cell phone, then frowned. 'Val texted. She's got another commitment. We have to get another interpreter. Dammit.'

Kane sighed. 'I'll call in the request on the way to Blue Moon.'

'This will set us back hours,' Olivia grumbled, straightening up her desk. Her fedora still covered her goddess statue's face. After a moment's hesitation, she picked up her hat and placed it on her head. 'Well?'

'Looks good.' He adjusted it on her head with a critical eye. 'Very Ingrid Bergman.'

'She *vanted* to be alone, right?'

Kane sighed. 'No, that was Garbo. Bergman still had Paris with Bogart. Someday you're going to stop watching cartoons and start watching grown-up movies.'

'Not any time soon, old man.' The phone on her desk rang. 'Sutherland.'

'It's Ian. I have something down here you need to see.'

Tuesday, September 21, 5:25 P.M.

David's mind was still spinning as he climbed the steps to his loft apartment. He was happy to see no reporters out front but suspected they'd be back. He wasn't sure what it mattered anymore. He was happier to see his mother's car parked out front.

He paused at the first landing, a sudden thought making his knees go momentarily weak. His mother. What if Lincoln had come here first? He exploded up the stairs but was stopped again by the voice of Mrs Edwards, who stuck her head out from 2A.

'Thank you, David. They delivered the refrigerator this morning. We appreciate it.'

'Are the girls all right?' Lincoln had talked to one of the girls in 2A and David hadn't checked to be sure everyone was all right. *What the hell was wrong with me?*

'Lacey and Tiffany? Why wouldn't they be all right?'

'I'll explain later.' He charged up the stairs, unlocking his door and shoving it open in one motion. Then he stopped once more, stunned.

Glenn and his mother stood close together. His mother held her hair off her neck as Glenn fumbled with her necklace. They twisted toward the door like guilty teenagers.

Glenn's face was the color of a ripe tomato. 'She's going out to dinner. Asked me to help with this confounded thing.' But he hadn't moved, his fingers still clutching his mother's necklace. And if David wasn't mistaken, the expression he'd worn when David barged in had been uncharacteristically tender.

Hell. Glenn was falling for his mom.

'I can do it.' David managed the clasp and stepped away. 'You look nice, Ma.'

'Thank you. Glenn stopped by to make sure I heard the latest news.' She gave him a pointed look. 'Before it hit the news. I hear you had another eventful day.'

David grimaced. 'I'm sorry. What did you two hear?'

Glenn glared. 'That somebody broke into my cabin. Were you going to tell me?'

'Of course I was. I should have called you both. I'm sorry, okay? Who called you?'

'The local sheriff's office. Told me not to worry, that you had it all under control. That you'd taken the gun away from the guy. And I said, "What guy? What gun? What the hell?"' He looked at David's mother. 'Excuse me, Phoebe.'

She nodded. 'No problem. I said the same thing. So what the hell, David?'

David sank into his easy chair and pulled his hands over his face. 'It's like this. . . .' He told them the story, watching his mother's face. She was scared, but handling it. Glenn, on the other hand, grew angrier with each word. 'And that's all of it,' David finished.

'Where is this Lincoln Jefferson now?' Glenn asked, very carefully.

'In the psych ward at the jail. He'll be charged with B and E on your property and assault on me. The Feds will have their go at him for the arsons twelve years ago. Olivia and her partner were going to validate his alibi tonight for the latest fires.'

'And he never gave up Moss?'

'No. I don't think he knows where Moss is.'

'Let me get this straight,' Glenn said acidly. 'He heard about the glass ball on TV, so he asked firefighters who caught it and, not suspecting he was a fucking lunatic, they told him it was you. He made it out here in time to hear me tell the reporters that you didn't live here. Then he talks to one of the girls in 2A and they tell him about my cabin. He gets the address for my *unlisted* property, breaks in and searches the place. And all before two o'clock. I'd say we have a damn smart schizo.'

David pinched the bridge of his nose, trying to think through the headache that had started to pound. 'He's been under psychiatric care for more than ten years, Glenn. He is schizo.' *Always there. Always there.* David fought a shiver. 'But you make a good point. That's a pretty organized line of logic for a man with a mental illness.'

Glenn folded his arms over his chest. 'Did he have help?'

'I guess it's possible. Maybe even probable.'

His mother sat on the arm of his easy chair and patted David's shoulder. 'You're okay, and that's the important thing. I'm glad you can take care of yourself.'

'No, the important thing is that someone else might have helped this vile piece of murdering shit,' Glenn said and his eyes narrowed. 'Who you seem to *pity*, David.'

'No.' David shook his head in denial. 'Okay, yes, I felt pity, but not like you think.'

'Then explain it to me,' Glenn growled.

'Glenn,' his mother said, rebuke in her tone.

'Phoebe,' Glenn shot back. 'This so-called schizo could

have come up *here*. You would have been here, not your black-belt son who can defend himself. That guy had a goddamn gun and he would have gone after *you*. Did you even think about that, David?'

Glenn stood, fists clenched, chest heaving from his outburst. Wordlessly David rose from his chair and motioned Glenn to sit, but Glenn shook his head hard.

'What kind of pity did you feel?' Glenn asked, more quietly, but no less intensely.

'How many bodies have you seen? How long have they haunted you?'

'Too many and too long,' Glenn answered levelly. 'But *I* didn't kill them.'

'Exactly. He killed her and he didn't even have his full sanity to get him through it. Should he be held accountable? *Hell, yes*. But he is not the man he was. Twelve years ago he was an undiagnosed schizophrenic, vulnerable, looking for something. Now, he's pathetic. I didn't want to feel anything for him, but I did. Maybe that makes me weak, I don't know, but I did feel.' He was inches from Glenn's face and backed away, drawing a breath. 'I'm not necessarily proud of that, but there it is.'

'I think I'll sit now.' Glenn took the easy chair and briefly closed his eyes. 'I shouldn't have lashed out at you. You have nothing to be ashamed of.'

Oh yes, I do. 'It's all right. You were right about the danger to Ma. I wasn't thinking straight. I should have come straight here from the cabin to check on her.'

'*She* is right here,' his mother said pointedly. 'And *she* is fine,' she added kindly. She patted Glenn's arm as she'd done to David's. 'I have to go to dinner. I'm late.'

'I'll drive you,' David said, raising his hand to silence her protest. 'I know you're a good driver, but Glenn is right. The more I think about it, Lincoln had to have help finding me. Until we're clear on who that was and why, I'm going to be more careful with you.'

'All right, son. Are you going to be here tonight?'

He hesitated. Olivia was meeting him at the cabin. If the night ended as badly as last night had, he'd be back. If it ended like this morning . . . But that was selfish. He couldn't let himself think about what might have happened had Lincoln come up here first. His mother's safety was the priority until this was sorted.

Still, there were things he and Olivia needed to discuss. 'Yes, but I'll be out until maybe ten or eleven. What time will you be finished with Evie and Noah?'

She studied him carefully. 'It would be easier if I stayed with Evie tonight. That way they don't have to drive me back after dinner. I'll pack a few things.' She rose, looking down at Glenn. 'Invitation's still open. You're welcome to join us for dinner.'

Glenn shook his head. 'Thanks, but I'm beat. And I want to talk to the boy here.'

David waited until his mother had left the room. 'And the boy wants to talk to you. But I have to run down to 2A and find out which of those girls talked to Lincoln and give them a talking-to. Drive with me to drop off my mother and we can talk on the way back. I've got to be at the dojo at seven and after that, I've got a . . . something. Maybe a date.'

'The pretty blonde cop gave you another chance?' Glenn asked, amused. 'You must be one hell of a smooth talker.'

'I have my moments.'

Chapter Sixteen

Tuesday, September 21, 5:55 P.M.

Olivia and Kane found Ian staring at skull X-rays on the morgue's light board.

Olivia winced. The skull shown was crushed in several places. 'What'd he hit?'

'His steering wheel, his windshield, the frame of his car as he rolled down an embankment, and then, I think, three trees. He was brought in on Monday.'

'Why are we looking at him?' Kane asked.

'You remember last night, when you were checking that camp and I told you to leave, that I had another autopsy to do? That was this guy. Joel Fischer. No history of smoking. Then I did the cut. He had damage to his upper airways. Smoke inhalation.'

The hairs rose on the back of Olivia's neck. 'What kind of smoke?'

'First I thought he'd inhaled smoke at the accident scene, but I checked – there was no fire. Then his urine tox came back loaded with oxycodone. I'm surprised he was even able to drive the car. On a hunch, I ran a blood test. Traces of cyanide.'

'He was poisoned?' Kane asked and Ian shook his head.

'Not in this case, especially because he's also got high levels of carbon monoxide. He inhaled burning plastic.'

'A structural fire,' Olivia said. 'Oh my God. And Tracey Mullen's blood screen?'

'Acute cyanide toxicity. It doesn't mean they were in the same fire, but they were in the same type of fire. A burning building with carpet, furniture, something polymer based.'

'He was there,' Kane said. 'Sonofabitch. So how does the X-ray fit in?'

'Glad you asked.' Ian put another skull X-ray next to Joel Fischer's. The second film showed a single crack at the base of the skull. 'Look at the same place on Joel's skull.'

Kane leaned forward. 'Same crack, although it gets lost in all the other damage.'

'Which is why I didn't catch it the first time,' Ian said. 'This second X-ray belongs to Henry Weems, the security guard. It's not conclusive, but I'd say it's highly possible they were struck by the same weapon, by the same person.'

'Did Joel Fischer have gunshot residue on his hands?' Olivia asked.

'No. I checked,' Ian said. 'He could have cleaned it off, but I found no trace.'

'Do you still have this Fischer kid's body?' Kane asked.

'I do, and it's causing me quite the headache. The Fischers are Orthodox Jews and had his funeral and burial set up for this afternoon. They had to cancel because I wouldn't release the body until I got this blood test back. They are very upset with me.'

'They'll be more upset with us,' Olivia predicted grimly. 'This is good, Ian. Gold.'

'Here's the Fischer kid's info,' he added, handing her a

printout before she could ask. 'I've released Weems's body and it's gone. What's the status on the Mullen girl? Her dad ID'd her last night. She's free to go.'

'Mom was supposed to claim her today. Last I heard, her flight was delayed,' Olivia said. 'I have a cell number. I'll find out where she is. There's still the question of who caused Tracey's abuse injuries. I don't want to lose that in all the rest of this.'

'I never thought you would. The mom might come straight here from the airport. You want me to stall her until you two can get here?'

'Definitely,' Kane said. 'We need to see her and her new husband's faces when we tell them about her injuries.' They said good night to Ian and left the morgue. 'So which first? Blue Moon for Lincoln's alibi or Joel Fischer's house?'

'Blue Moon. Then we can get Crawford off Abbott's back.'

'All that's going to do is show if Lincoln was involved in our fires,' Kane disagreed. 'Crawford's not going to give up that our fires are domestic terrorism until we prove that they're not. Which they could still be. These arsonists knew about the mark on the North Pole. And if a university kid was there . . .' He opened the morgue door for her.

'Yeah, except for the fact that Tomlinson's missing his face,' she said, drawing a deep breath of fresh air. She took her hat off, sniffed it. 'Morgue stink is in my hat.'

'It'll pass,' Kane said. 'Otherwise Jennie would make me keep all my hats in the garage. We're going to want to search Joel's room.'

Olivia looked at Joel's personal info. 'Lived with his folks. I'll call the assistant DA. Hopefully what we have will be enough for a warrant.'

Tuesday, September 21, 6:10 P.M.

David's mother waved at Evie and Noah, who were standing outside the restaurant. 'I hope they haven't been waiting long.'

'I don't think they minded, Ma,' David said dryly, parking his truck. The couple had been holding hands, smiling sappily into each other's faces and the sight hit David with a wave of longing. He didn't begrudge Evie a single moment of happiness. She'd been through so much. She deserved to be happy with Noah forever.

David just wondered when it would be his turn.

'You have to meet them, Glenn,' she declared. 'Help me down, David. I don't want to twist my ankle jumping out of this truck in these silly high heels.'

But Noah helped her from the truck before David could get out. He glanced at David curiously, then kissed her on the cheek. 'Phoebe, you're looking beautiful tonight.'

'And you're a charmer,' she said. 'Evie, come here. Meet Glenn.'

Evie looked different tonight. She smiled a lot since meeting Noah, but tonight her smile was brighter. Something good was brewing. Friends for years, David and Evie were more like siblings. Evie had been brought into the family through his brother Max's wife, Caroline. Through whom he'd met Dana and fallen head over heels in love.

Which seemed like a lifetime ago, now. Thoughts of Dana, images of her in the arms of another man, used to make his heart physically hurt. Now, nothing.

Time did heal wounds. And sometimes it revealed that what a man thought he wanted so desperately wasn't necessarily the thing he should have.

His mother had her arm around Evie's shoulders. 'Glenn, this is Evie. I told you about her. And this is Noah, her boyfriend. Evie, this is Glenn. He rents from David.'

Glenn had extricated himself from the backseat of the truck and shook Evie's hand. 'I've heard a lot about you, young lady.' He then lifted her hand higher, a broad smile on his grizzled face. 'Is this rock what tonight's all about?'

Evie met David's eyes. 'We were going to tell you first, but you've been busy.'

He had to swallow the lump in his throat as he grabbed Evie up in a bear hug. 'Congratulations,' he managed gruffly. 'I couldn't be happier. Really.'

'Thank you,' she whispered fiercely. 'Really.'

He put her down, the grin still on his face. 'Congratulations, Noah.'

His mother was crying, hugging Evie so hard he thought she might break her. Because this wasn't simple joy over an engagement. His friend had suffered so much, surviving attacks on her life, brought back from the edge of death twice. She'd almost given up. But not quite. Here she was, beaming like a star. David felt his own eyes sting.

'So when's the date?' he asked Noah whose eyes were also suspiciously bright.

'We don't know yet,' Noah said. 'Eve just wants to be passed around and fussed over for a while, which is fine with me.' Noah shifted his weight so that he leaned closer to David while the women chattered happily. 'Why did you drive Phoebe?'

Noah was no fool, as David had quickly realized seven months before when the dark, brooding detective had led the investigation against the serial killer who'd murdered so many. He'd trusted Noah almost immediately and they'd become friends. That Noah and Olivia were also friends was damn convenient, too. Noah had been one of David's best sources on Olivia over the last seven months.

'Glenn and I were talking about Lincoln, the guy who broke into the cabin.'

'I heard about him.'

'He did some complex thinking to find me. We're wondering if he was alone.'

'I wondered the same thing as I was driving home. You want me to drop Phoebe off at your place later?'

'She's going to stay with you tonight, if that's okay.' David took her bag from the backseat. 'I'm going to be a little late tonight and I'm on shift tomorrow at eight. I keep thinking that if Lincoln had gone up to the loft first . . .'

'Well, he didn't,' Noah said practically. 'Do you or Glenn have any thoughts on who might have been helping this guy?'

'No. Do you?'

'Not yet. I'll make sure Olivia knows about this.'

David hesitated, then shrugged. 'I'm supposed to see her tonight. I'll tell her then.'

Noah gave him an impatient glance. 'It's about damn time, Hunter.'

'I know, I know. I've gotta go. Just keep an eye out for Ma.'

'You know I will.'

David started to go, but Evie stopped him. 'Wait.' She wrapped her arms around his neck in a big hug, then whispered in his ear, 'You pushed me to take a chance on Noah and on myself. Told me the chance might not come again. Do you remember?'

He did. She'd challenged him to stop watching his own life go by that same night seven months ago. 'Yes. It was my fee for fixing your roof.'

'You fixed my life instead. Now I'm returning the favor.

Do not let this opportunity get away. Promise me you will tell Olivia how you feel. And soon.'

He started, surprised. 'How did you know?'

'Noah made me sign up for another self-defense class. Rudy told me.'

David laughed. 'That guy's a damn weasel.'

'No, he's not. He's a sweetheart, and the best source of gossip in town.' She sobered. 'Promise me, David.'

'I promise.' He let her go and waved to Glenn. 'Let's go. I've got an appointment to get my ass kicked at the dojo and I'm going to be late.'

Tuesday, September 21, 6:20 P.M.

He'd decided how to get Kenny out of the well-secured residential dormitory. Except the timing was wrong. If he could have set his plan for Kenny in motion later, say around midnight when the cops and rescue teams would be busy at the fire Albert was planning, success would be virtually guaranteed.

But Sutherland and Kane were due back at the deaf school at 7:00 p.m. He needed to get his hands on Kenny before the cops got him to talk. Even though the timing was wrong, he didn't have a choice.

Make the call. He'd dialed the first few digits of the school's main phone number, wondering who would pick up this time of the evening. Campus security, most likely.

And then the interpreter's phone jingled a little tune. Detective Olivia Sutherland, once again. Abruptly he canceled the call he was about to make. Sutherland wasn't at the school yet, because he was, sitting down the street in his van. Why was she calling?

He held his breath, waiting for the call to go to voice mail. He gave it a minute, then dialed the interpreter's voice mail and listened.

He let out the breath he held in a whoosh of relief. Something else had come up. They wanted Val back here tomorrow at 10:00 a.m. Everything would be totally fine now.

Smiling, he typed a text. *10 is fine. will see you then*.

He needed to get back to his shop. This was the third Tuesday of the month, when the local book club met. Luckily they talked more about their own lives than the books they'd read. He'd managed to snag quite a few new clients based on their gossip alone.

Tuesday, September 21, 6:30 P.M.

'That was nice,' Glenn said quietly.

David glanced over at him before returning his gaze to the highway, where traffic was stop-and-go. He'd been so lost in his own thoughts that he hadn't realized the older man had been as well. 'Yes, it was.'

'Your mother just took that girl under her wing. Evie, I mean.'

'That's how it is back there, in Chicago. Our family is bigger than just blood relatives. And we take care of each other.'

'And yet you left.'

'Yeah. I did.'

'Because of the name you said during . . . you know.' Glenn cleared his throat. 'The unrequited thing.'

David found himself smiling at Glenn's embarrassment. His own father would have been the same way. 'You ready to talk about Lincoln Jefferson?'

'I think that's wise,' Glenn said, relief in his voice. 'Your cop friend back there didn't have any ideas?'

'No. But I was wondering why someone would want to help Lincoln. What would they get out of it? Lincoln said he broke into your place to find proof I'd been paid or commanded to lie, to set Moss up.'

'Which is crazy.'

'It is, because Lincoln is. Who else would be upset that we'd sullied Moss's name?'

'Moss, for one. If he's still alive. Or one of his other followers. There were a hell of a lot of them,' Glenn said. 'You'd have to find the one who had contact with the schizo.'

'One might have that,' David said slowly, 'if one had checked Lincoln's cell phone.'

Glenn's brows shot up. 'And who might have done a thing like that?'

'Me. I checked his pockets after I tied him up. I was making sure he didn't have any other weapons while I waited for the cops.'

'Prudent.'

'I thought so. I found Lincoln's cell, checked the log, and wrote the numbers down.'

Glenn laughed. 'I stand corrected, boy. You did good.'

'We'll see if the numbers yield anything. The other thing I was thinking about was the Moss website.'

'That piece of trash,' Glenn muttered.

'True, but somebody put hours and hours into building and maintaining that site. Somebody who treasured Moss and wouldn't want to see him linked to two gunshot murders. I'm wondering how to track ownership of that site.'

'Wouldn't the FBI already have done that?'

'I would have thought so, but Lincoln seemed to have passed under their radar.'

'True. Didn't you tell me your friend Evie did website work? A little hacking?'

'Yeah, but I don't want to drag her into this. She's finally got her life steady.'

Glenn waited a full minute while David frowned. 'And? Who else, boy?'

David sighed. 'I know someone in Chicago who's great with Internet spying, but I hate to ask him for anything.'

'Why?'

'Because he's the husband of the unrequited thing.' Who, to David's constant consternation, was a hell of a nice guy. He'd always wanted to hate Dana's husband but had never been able to summon it.

Glenn winced. 'Oh. What about that nephew of yours? He goes to college. I bet he knows something about the Internet.'

'I'm sure Tom knows quite a lot, but he's not the hacker type. He might know someone who is, though. I'll call him.'

'You do realize you aren't going to make your karate class tonight?'

David sighed. Traffic was snarled. 'I got a decent workout this afternoon with Lincoln, so I can miss once. I'll call Paige and tell her I'm not coming.'

'Then we can work on those phone numbers and the website.'

'I was thinking that.'

Tuesday, September 21, 6:30 P.M.

Austin Dent paced his bedroom floor, checking his phone every few minutes. School had been out for three hours.

Three hours. Where the hell was Kenny? All he had to do was get to the mailbox in the middle of town and drop a goddamn letter in.

Getting to town was no problem. The two of them had done it dozens of times when they'd been given off-campus public-library passes. That was one of the perks of being in high school. You got more freedom than the little kids who lived on campus.

He stopped pacing, raked his hand through his hair. Why hadn't Kenny texted?

Trying to calm down, Austin slumped onto the worn-out sofa in the living room and turned on the television news. And frowned. The closed-captioning sucked on this channel. They used some kind of computer speech detector and it was always getting the words wrong. Half the stories made no sense.

He switched to the national cable station where the captioning was more consistent. It was annoying to have to depend on the captioning. A lot of kids he knew didn't bother with the news. But Austin wanted to know what was happening in the world because one day he'd go to college, make something of himself.

He shook his head. College? *Yeah, right.* There was no money for college. And after this suspension? He could kiss the scholarships he'd been trying for good-bye. *If they think you did that fire, you'll go to jail and nothing else will matter.*

But I didn't do it. I was only trying to protect Tracey. His chest hurt to even think of her, which meant it hurt all the time. *She trusted me. I promised to help her.*

Why didn't I do something? He remembered the bruises with vivid detail. He'd picked her up at the Omaha airport and had wanted to kill someone.

'Let me take you to a hospital,' he'd begged her but she'd refused.

'They'll make me go back.' Her eyes had been so determined, even as she signed with one hand, because her hand was sprained. *Sprained.*

Austin had never felt such hate before, but he did when he thought of a monster twisting her arm until it fractured and her hand until it sprained. Someday, when all this died down, he'd make sure the monster paid. But it wouldn't bring Tracey back.

And then, there she was. Her picture on the news. A scream rose from deep within him, but he kept it chained. Silent.

She was only sixteen. A runaway from Gainesville, Florida, the captioning read. But she'd been so much more. She'd been sweet and smart and funny. And scared. She'd been so scared. *I promised her she'd be safe.*

A second picture joined Tracey's on the screen and Austin flinched. It was the guard he'd watched get shot in cold blood. Henry Weems.

Fuck, he thought, his heart plunging as he read the captioning flowing across the screen. A retired cop. *They'll want revenge. They'll take it out on me.*

He jumped to his feet, turning his back, unable to watch any more. He turned off the television, then went back to pacing. *Kenny, where the hell are you?*

Tuesday, September 21, 6:50 P.M.

Olivia brought the car to a stop. 'I thought the Fischers' house would be bigger.'

'Me too,' Kane said. 'Mr Fischer is a rich man.'

She bit at her lip thoughtfully. 'I wish we had a warrant. They're going to be mad enough that Ian put the skids on Joel's burial. I don't think we'll find them terribly cooperative. I'll call the ADA one more time.'

'He's gonna yell,' Kane said glumly.

Olivia's lips twitched as they did whenever he used that tone. 'Let him yell.' She dialed Brian's phone, prepared for the yelling.

'No,' the assistant DA said without preamble. 'Judge said no.'

'No way,' Olivia whined. 'Really?'

'Look, I'm sorry. You need to get more before we have cause to search.'

'Okay. Thanks for trying.' She hung up and looked at Kane. 'No warrant.'

'I got that,' Kane said dryly. 'At least we can tell Abbott that Lincoln's clean of these two fires.'

'Luckily Blue Moon had video showing Lincoln there until closing both nights. I don't think Crawford would have believed the bartender's word on it.'

'We'll still want him for B and E and attempted assault on Hunter, but on the fires, Lincoln is the Fed's problem. Joel Fischer is ours.' Kane got out of the car, tossing back a careless, 'It's your turn.'

'It is not. I did Louise Tomlinson. The Fischers are yours.'

Kane made a face. 'I was hoping you'd forget.'

'Have I ever?' she asked as they walked up the Fischers' driveway.

'Not once.'

Olivia stopped him before he knocked on the door. 'Wait. Take off your shoes.'

Kane frowned. 'Why?'

'They're not sitting *shiva* yet, because the burial was

325

delayed. But the house may be prepared. No leather shoes. It's just respect.'

'How do you know this?' Kane asked, toeing off his shoes.

'Our next-door neighbors growing up were Orthodox. When they had a family death, my mom and I visited, took food. Take off your hat.' She did the same.

He obeyed. 'Look, Liv, if you know all this, maybe you should take this one. It'll go smoother if I'm not bungling it out of ignorance. I'll take the next two. I promise.'

She shot him a disgruntled look. 'I hate it when you make sense. All right.' She knocked and waited, dread mounting. Informing parents was never easy. When the deceased was a potential suspect . . . This wasn't going to be pretty.

The door opened, revealing a man with a full beard, wearing a black suit. 'Yes?'

'I'm sorry to intrude. I'm Detective Sutherland and this is my partner, Detective Kane.' She flashed her badge. 'We'd like to speak to Mr and Mrs Fischer.'

'They are in mourning. They cannot be disturbed.'

Olivia put her hand on the door as it began to close. 'Excuse me,' she said. 'This isn't a social call. We realize they are in mourning, but we must speak with them. Now.'

Displeased, the man opened the door. 'I am Rabbi Hirschfield. Come in.'

'Thank you.' Olivia sat down on the love seat the rabbi indicated, Kane at her side. In a moment a red-eyed couple joined them, sitting on the adjacent sofa. The rabbi stood in the doorway to the kitchen, almost as if standing guard.

'We're the Fischers,' the man said indignantly. 'Are you going to release his body now? We'd like to bury our son.'

'I know this is difficult,' Olivia began. 'The medical examiner found something in your son's autopsy that required further investigation. That's why we're here.'

Mrs Fischer lifted her chin. 'We've already been told about the narcotics supposedly found in our son's body. We don't believe it.'

Oh, great, Olivia thought. *They're going to believe this even less.* 'We are very sorry for your loss, ma'am. The medical examiner has no reason to lie.'

Mrs Fischer flinched slightly. 'I didn't say he lied. He made a mistake. My son was not some druggie. He was a good boy. With a good family.' Her voice broke and tears rolled down her cheeks. 'He was the champion of causes, not some junkie.'

'What kind of causes, Mrs Fischer?' Olivia asked gently.

'All kinds. He raised money for AIDS – ten thousand dollars in his senior year of high school. All by himself. We said we'd give him the money, but he said he wanted to raise it himself. He worked for charities. He volunteered in Temple.' She was sobbing. 'He wanted to make the world a better place and I won't let you tear him down.'

Her husband gathered her close and frowned at them. 'You have to leave.'

'Not yet,' Olivia said soothingly. 'Please, try to listen to me. I need your help.'

'With what?' Mr Fischer snapped as his wife tried to stifle her sobs.

'Sir, was your son involved in any on-campus groups? Clubs?'

'No.' Mr Fischer looked confused. 'Why?'

'Did he ever talk about wanting to save animals, wetlands, the environment?'

'Of course.' Mr Fischer was patting his wife's shuddering back. 'He cared about all those things. Why?' he repeated, more suspiciously.

'The thing the medical examiner found was lung damage to your son's airways. He'd been in a building fire. Recently. Within twelve hours of his death.'

There was a moment of tense silence, then Mrs Fischer pulled away from her husband, her eyes now wide, horrified, and angry. 'He was *not*. I know what you're saying, that he somehow started that fire that's been in the news. Where that girl died. But he didn't. He was *not* in a fire.'

Olivia stayed calm. 'Yes, ma'am, he was. The medical examiner wanted to be very sure. He tested Joel's blood and found traces of cyanide. That happens when someone breathes in burning plastic, as in a structural fire. We'd like to understand what happened. Did Joel seem upset Monday morning?'

Mrs Fischer was shaking her head. 'He was not in a fire. He was *here*. With us.'

'All night?' Olivia asked.

Mrs Fischer's chin lifted again. 'All night,' she insisted. But Mr Fischer's eyes had skirted away.

'Is that right, Mr Fischer?' Olivia asked quietly.

'Yes,' he said. But it wasn't a firm reply.

Olivia glanced at the rabbi, who now looked more worried than affronted. 'Would it be all right if we looked in Joel's room?' she asked.

'Leave,' Mr Fischer demanded. 'Or I'll report you for harassment.'

Olivia and Kane stood. 'My partner has been very patient with you, sir,' Kane said sternly. 'Denying the facts will not change them.'

'If he set that fire in the condo, we'll get to the bottom of it,' Olivia said, still quietly. 'I can't begin to understand what you're feeling, but if it were my son, I'd want to know. We will find out, with or without your help.'

'A girl died in that fire,' Mr Fischer said unsteadily. 'You want our help pinning her death on our son? What do we look like to you?'

Olivia glanced at the rabbi, then turned to look at the mirrors covered with black scarves, the low stools set to the side in preparation for *shiva*. 'You look like people who would do the right thing. The moral thing.' She let the comment stand for a moment. 'Last night I stood beside the father of the girl who died while he identified his daughter's body. He cried, too. He wants answers and I will get them for him.'

'We will be back,' Kane promised. 'With a warrant if necessary.'

'You said your son was a good boy,' Olivia said. 'A good man. It's possible he started out wanting to do the right thing and it got away from him.' Uncertainty shadowed both Fischers' faces and Olivia knew she'd hit a nerve. 'Were he here, I'm sure he'd want to do the right thing. Do *Teshuva*.'

Mr Fischer met her eyes. 'But he's not here.'

'But you are,' Olivia said with a sad smile. 'You've spent your life following the law, honoring the Talmud. If your son were a child and did a sin, you'd be guiding him through the steps of *Teshuva* right now. Admit he's wrong, ask forgiveness. Make amends. He can't do that, but you can. Let us look at his room. We need to find out what happened – for the girl who died, for Joel, and for your family.'

Mr Fischer appeared to be wavering. 'But the guard. He was shot.'

'The medical examiner checked for traces of gunshot residue on Joel's hands, but found none,' Kane said, his tone a shade gentler. They'd honed their partner rhythm well. 'It doesn't appear Joel fired a weapon.'

'The medical examiner also found evidence that Joel was struck in the head with a blunt instrument. He might not have known . . .' A detail clicked in her mind. Two sets of prints leaving the condo, only one at the fence. Her own voice echoed in her mind, in response to Donahue's profile of the arsonists. *Different agendas*.

'He might not have known what?' Mrs Fischer asked, her voice strained.

'He might not have known what the others had planned,' Olivia said.

Mr Fischer paled. 'Joel would never kill. Not on purpose. I know my son.'

'But you don't know what he actually did. It'll be worse, not knowing,' Olivia said. 'Please. We need to see his room.'

Mr Fischer looked at his rabbi. Rabbi Hirschfield shrugged. 'It's your choice.'

'And if it were your son?' Mrs Fischer asked him, crying again.

Hirschfield's shoulders sagged. 'Then, God help me, I would hope I'd say yes.'

Mr Fischer let out a long breath. 'All right. You can look.'

Olivia met his eyes. 'Thank you. We'll try to be quick.'

Chapter Seventeen

Tuesday, September 21, 7:30 P.M.

'Hi, Tom.' It was squealed by two pretty college girls outside the university gym, where David and Glenn had found David's nephew Tom finishing basketball practice. Glenn's head turned as he watched the girls' heart-arresting, hip-swinging departure.

'Put your eyes back in your head, old man,' David said, amused. 'I don't carry a defib around on my back, you know.'

'Youth is wasted on the young,' Glenn grumbled and Tom chuckled.

'Sorry about that,' Tom said. 'Let's get away from the gym. Draws the groupies.'

David knew Tom was aware of his star-athlete status, but he was relieved that his nephew tried to stay humble.

'I don't know,' Glenn said. 'I kind of like drawing the groupies.'

Tom's grin flashed as he led them down a sidewalk toward his dorm. 'Me too.'

'As long as you only look,' David advised, as he always did. 'Don't touch.'

'I know, I know,' Tom said. 'I'm not stupid, David.'

'Never thought you were.' He'd met Tom when the boy was fourteen and terrified. His mother, Caroline, had gone missing and Evie had just been rushed to a Chicago hospital, fighting for her life. Tom's biological father, a true monster, had found them after Tom and Caroline had successfully remained hidden for years. David's older brother, Max, in love with Caroline, had saved the day and later adopted Tom, loving him as if he'd always been a Hunter. They all did.

What David always remembered most about those horrible hours when they feared Caroline dead was the almost unnatural maturity Tom maintained. When the adults around him were losing it, Tom stayed calm, focused. Since then, David had watched him grow into a young man who made the family proud.

They stopped at a picnic table and Tom perched on it, propping one of his huge feet on his basketball. 'So, beyond ogling girls, what brings you two here?'

David sat on the table, Glenn on the bench. 'We need a hacker,' David said baldly.

Tom laughed, then sobered. 'You're serious.'

'Oh yeah.' David told him what happened and Tom paled.

'I had lunch with Grandma at the Deli and she never mentioned any of this.'

'It hadn't happened yet,' David said. 'It was at about two.'

'When she was back at your place.' Tom shook his head. 'My God, if she'd been in your place and if that crazy guy had gone there.'

'Exactly,' Glenn said, all of his prior levity gone. 'That's why we're here.'

'We want information on the Moss website,' David said. 'Who designed, owns, maintains it. Who's visited it. Do you have any geek friends who can help us?'

Tom nodded grimly. 'Hell, yeah. You're looking at him.'

David's eyes widened. 'You? No way.'

'Me.' He aimed a sidelong glance at David. 'I told you I was bagging groceries last summer when I went home for summer break. And I did, part-time. The rest of the time I worked for Ethan. I actually worked for him the past few summers. He pays really well. I made double working for him compared to bagging groceries, in half the time. Sorry.'

David sighed. 'Why didn't you tell me?'

'Didn't see much need to. Salt in the wound and all that.'

His shoulders sagged. 'You knew?' Who *hadn't* known he was in love with Dana?

'Sorry. It was kind of obvious. Only if you were looking, of course.'

David's face heated. 'Well, hell.'

Glenn cleared his throat. 'I take it Ethan is the husband of the unrequited thing?'

David rolled his eyes, thoroughly embarrassed now. 'Yes. God. Back to our point. You can find out all we want to know about the Moss website?'

'And nobody will even know I've been there.'

'What is this Ethan?' Glenn asked. 'Some CIA spy guy?'

'Kind of,' David said uncomfortably. 'Does network, shadowy, PI kind of stuff.'

'Ooh.' Glenn winced. 'Tough competition.'

David scowled down at him. 'Thank you.'

'Just getting back for the defib comment,' Glenn replied cheerfully. 'So, young man, you won't get caught?'

'Nope. I've got a study date at eight, but I'll do it when I'm done and call you.'

'Thanks, kid.' David stood up and met his nephew's solemn blue eyes. 'You're sure? I don't want to drag you into anything dangerous. Your mother would kill me.'

'Everybody says that, but Mom wouldn't. She was doing the dangerous work all those years, picking up families in bus stops in the middle of the night. Hiding them from abusive dads.' He shrugged. 'This is nothing compared to that.'

Glenn's eyes had gone wide. 'You have to tell me about this.'

'Unrequited Thing ran a secret shelter for battered women leaving their spouses,' David explained. 'Caroline, Tom's mother, was her right hand and Evie worked for her, too. Olivia's sister, Mia, was also in on it, but more discreetly, being a cop. They gave lots of women new starts – new IDs, job skills. Even money.'

'And what did you do?' Glenn asked.

David smiled, but sadly. 'I fixed the roof, her car, and anything else that broke.'

'I see,' Glenn said, quietly now, and David thought he probably did.

'Who's watching Grandma?' Tom asked.

'Noah and Evie.' David's brows lifted. 'And I've got news.'

Tom's face broke into the high-wattage grin that made college girls swoon. 'Noah finally popped the question, huh?'

'Yeah. And Evie's smiling.'

Tom's grin dimmed and he swallowed hard. 'Good. That's good.' Abruptly he hopped off the table and took off, waving good-bye over his shoulder. 'I'll call you.'

David watched him go, once again feeling his own eyes sting.

'And?' Glenn asked. 'That was?'

'Family,' David said thickly. 'Evie is Tom's oldest friend. They grew up together, in Unrequited Thing's shelter. Her happiness has been on his wish list for a long time.'

'Does Unrequited Thing have a name, son?' Glenn asked gently.

'Dana,' David said, then smiled. 'I used to dread hearing her name after she married Ethan, dreaded saying it even more.'

'And now?'

'Now . . . it's okay.'

'Sounds like this Dana was dedicated to serving others.'

'She was, to the exclusion of everything else. Used to make me nuts, her going after those families in the middle of the night at the bus station in downtown Chicago. Sometimes the husbands would come after her, threaten her, but she didn't seem to care if she lived or died. But that was then.'

'What changed?'

'She met Ethan. Figured out that there was more to life than . . .' He stopped, then sighed. 'Than helping other people.'

'At the exclusion of everything else,' Glenn murmured.

'I bet you think you're pretty clever, old man.'

'Yep.' Glenn stood, stretched his back. 'I do.'

Tuesday, September 21, 7:40 P.M.

It didn't take long to find Joel's shoes. They were in his closet, under a pile of dirty laundry. 'Kane,' Olivia said. She held up one of the shoes, sniffed it, then turned it over. 'Smells like smoke and looks like glue.'

'Then he was there,' Mr Fischer said faintly. He stood in the doorway. Mrs Fischer had stayed in the living room with the rabbi. Olivia couldn't say she blamed her.

'It looks like it, sir.'

'I don't see any pill bottles,' Kane said, looking through Joel's drawers and under his mattress. 'CSU can search for residue, but . . .' He let the thought trail. Usually a kid who did drugs left some evidence behind in his room and Kane was good at finding it.

'Did he ever stay anywhere else?' Olivia asked Mr Fischer.

'No. He wanted to live at the dorm and we said he could in his third year.'

Kane held up a thick textbook. '*Environmental Ethics.* What was his major?'

'Philosophy,' Mr Fischer murmured.

Kane leafed through the book and his brows rose. 'Did Joel have a girlfriend?'

'No. He was busy with his studies. He said he was waiting for a Jewish girl.'

'Who were his friends?' Olivia asked.

Fischer closed his eyes. 'The Feinsteins' and Kaufmans' sons, from Hebrew school. And Eric. Eric Marsh. They've been friends since kindergarten, first grade.'

Kane wrote down the names. 'Would these boys know about Joel's interests?'

'I don't know. Kaufman's son is going to school out

West somewhere. Feinstein's son is still in town. I don't know if Joel saw them often. Eric is an engineering student at the university. I think they had lunch sometimes. Eric was always the one to keep Joel steady. Showed him the problems in all the wacky plans he came up with over the years.' His face fell. 'I don't even know if anyone's told Eric about the accident.'

'Okay,' Kane said. 'Here we go.' He'd been going through Joel's stack of school papers and held up a bound folder. ' "Preston Moss – hero or monster?" On the last page Joel concludes he was a hero.'

A strangled breath came from Fischer. 'Son, what have you done?' he whispered.

Olivia looked around Joel's room. One wall was covered in plaques, honoring community service, which made her think of David's bedroom in Chicago. He hadn't had any plaques or mementos. David didn't do his service to be noticed. *Teshuva*. David was making amends, but for what sin? What about Lincoln had he understood?

She turned to Joel's father. 'I'm betting more than he originally bargained for.'

Fischer's eyes were anguished. 'Oh, God. He did this thing. This terrible thing.'

'I am so sorry, sir,' she said. 'We're going to need to bring in our crime scene unit.'

He nodded unsteadily. 'I understand.'

His color worried her. He'd turned gray. 'Can I get you anything?'

'No. Nothing.' He turned away then, his back hunched and Olivia heard the familiar muted howl of agony. It was raw grief and always tore at her gut.

'Dammit,' she muttered.

'You did all you could, Liv,' Kane said quietly. 'More

than most would. How did you know all that about the . . . What did you call it? Teshu . . . ?'

'Doing *Teshuva*,' she said with a sigh.

'You didn't pick that up from dropping by your neighbors for the occasional wake.'

'No. When I was in college, I had a few years of soul searching,' she admitted. 'You know, why are we here? I looked into a lot of religions. I really liked my neighbors. They were a happy family. I thought maybe it was their faith. So I went to Temple near campus for a long time. I was curious. Kind of like Joel.'

Kane held up the textbook. 'He did have a girlfriend. I found a note, with hearts, x's and o's. "Meet me by the library. Signed, *M*." '

She picked up one of the pillows on Joel's bed. 'Pink smudge. Lipstick.' She sniffed it and her mind flashed back to David's words. *I thought I'd dreamed you, then I smelled you. On my pillow.* Her heart fluttered. 'Perfume. Faint, but there.'

'Wouldn't be the first time boys and girls sneaked behind their parents' backs.'

'I'll give Micki a call, get a crew out here.'

'It's late,' Kane said, 'and I'm beat. It's been a long day. Once CSU gets here, let's go home, recharge, and come back at this in the morning.'

She thought of David, waiting for her at the cabin. Wondered again at what he might have done, then thought about all he'd done since and wondered what the past mattered. He'd proven the kind of man he was, time and again. He was waiting for her and he'd promised answers. She'd been waiting for two and a half years. 'All right.'

Tuesday, September 21, 8:55 P.M.

'It's about closing time, sir,' he said to Dorian Blunt, who sat alone at a table, his eyes on the door. The wayward accountant had been there for almost an hour, jumping every time the bell on the door jingled.

Poor Dorian was waiting for the man who'd contacted him via e-mail about an accounting position in a new company. There was just enough verifiable detail to make Dorian believe in the job and just enough promised to make him desperate for the position.

Because Dorian needed a new job very badly. Especially now. The job he'd taken after leaving his old firm after embezzling all that money had not been successful, and the Blunt household's finances were suffering. So much that Dorian might start dipping into his ill-gotten gains any day now.

Which wouldn't do at all. *Because I took every cent.*

Of course there was no job. *There is just me, playing with Dorian a little.* Not wanting to harm Mrs Blunt or their child, he'd needed a way to lure Dorian out of his house, and promising a job interview was better than most. Having him wait for an hour, watching the door?

Now, that was a strategy he'd learned from a real master. Honed right here in his shop. The serial killer unceremoniously dubbed the 'Red Dress Killer' by the press had lured his female victims from their homes with the promise of a hot date in a public place. He'd made them wait, demoralizing them, then when they'd given up on Mr Right, the killer had followed them home and performed his dastardly deeds.

He'd lured his third victim here. *Right under my nose and even I didn't suspect a thing.* Not until the police flashed the

339

victim's picture all over the media. He'd recognized her immediately then. He'd even chatted with her the night she'd disappeared. The police had tracked her here, asking for video of the dining area, but he'd lied, telling them he only had video of the cash register.

For a very brief moment, he'd considered blackmailing Pit-Guy but quickly decided against it. The man had been a serial killer, for God's sake. There was no way he was getting involved with that. And as for helping the police? He let them figure it out on their own. That's what they were paid for.

Eventually they had figured it out and Pit-Guy's full story had been revealed. He'd had more than three dozen bodies stashed in the pit in his basement. *So my instincts were right. Don't mess with a man with three dozen bodies in his basement.* The video of Pit-Guy watching his victim, following her out that night, was one of his treasures.

And whenever he needed a lesson in discretion, he watched it. Pit-Guy got cocky, then careless, then caught. Now he was dead. *I don't intend to get careless.*

I intend to hang everything on Mary and Albert. Especially Mary. He had a score to settle with her. But for now, he had a score to settle with Mr Dorian Blunt. *Pay me a fraction of what you owe.* Foolish. Between Tomlinson and Blunt, he'd have enough visual aids to convince his other clients to pay on time. And if not, he'd kill them, too.

He looked up at the clock. He needed to finish with Dorian so that he could deal with that kid Kenny at the deaf school and find out what he knew that he wasn't telling the cops. He'd snip those loose ends and then he could get back to business.

'Sir,' he called out. 'We're closed now. You have to leave.'

Dorian stood, his briefcase clutched in his sweaty hand. 'Just a few more minutes? This meeting is very important.'

'I'm sorry, sir. I'm ready to lock up. You may want to wait outside for a few minutes. Just in case.'

Dorian did just that, which he'd known he would. He locked up and went to get his van. Soon, Dorian Blunt would wish he'd just paid his bills on time.

Tuesday, September 21, 9:05 P.M.

David stood on the edge of Glenn's dock, his face lifted into the cool wind coming off the water. It was after nine and Olivia hadn't called.

He'd almost given in and called her, but stopped himself. The ball was truly in her court now, he thought. No pun intended. She could be busy. She could be tied up with a suspect and unable to call. Or, she might have simply changed her mind.

He looked down at his fishing rod and tackle box that lay on the dock, unused. He'd brought them out here, intending to try for another walleye, but had ended up standing here, contemplating. Everything.

He thought about what Evie had said about missed opportunities, about Glenn's paralleling his life to Dana's. Service, at the exclusion of everything else. Dana's had been penance for the guilt she felt over her mother's murder at her stepfather's hand.

Mine . . . Megan's death and the deaths of her entire family. Also at the hand of a stepfather. Funny how he'd never stopped to consider the parallels before. But they'd always been there, plain for anyone to see. If anyone knew the truth.

341

Which brought him back to Olivia's big question – *who are you?* He still wasn't sure what he'd answer, if she ever got here.

He turned his mind to Lincoln and his phantom helper, who might not even exist.

He hoped Tom was making more progress with the website than he had with the phone numbers he'd found on Lincoln's call log. The only calls that showed up in any of the reverse lookups he'd done were cell phones for Lincoln's mother and his brother, Truman. The other number Lincoln had called matched nothing. It might be a disposable cell. He'd gone as far as picking up a disposable cell phone of his own on his way up to the cabin, but he'd stopped short of calling the numbers.

If one of them was important, he wouldn't want to tip them off.

Whoever 'they' might be. Because even though he was pretty positive Lincoln had help, David still had to ask why? *Why would anyone not crazy want to find me? All I did was catch the damn ball.*

A noise caught his ear, faint, but it got louder and his heart began to pound. A car. Either Olivia had just forgotten to call again or someone else had come to search the place. He grabbed his fishing gear and jogged back up to the house, stowing his things on the back porch. He strode through the small living area. He'd set the table again and restored order to Glenn's desk. The house was ready for Olivia.

But was she ready? *Am I?*

Hands unsteady, he wrenched open the door, only to find her on his doorstep, her fist poised to knock. Slowly she lowered her fist to her side, her eyes locked to his, and he had to force himself to breathe.

She wore a beige trench coat, cinched tightly around

her waist. But peeking out from beneath it he could see the dress from last night. The one she'd worn the first night he'd met her. She wore ridiculously high-heeled shoes that made her legs look incredible. He lifted his eyes back to her face, hoping he was reading the right words between the lines, because on her head she wore a fedora, the brim pulled low.

'Can I come in?' she asked. He stepped aside and she entered, her eyes drawn to the table. She looked up, her mouth slightly curved. 'Just like last night.'

'I was hoping . . .' The words trailed away, his thought unfinished. She stood before him, looking good enough to eat and every muscle in his body clenched. He shoved his hands in his pockets lest he reach out and touch. 'I'd take your coat,' he said roughly, 'but once I touch you, I won't be able to stop.'

Her eyes heated and he could see her pulse fluttering at the hollow of her throat. She tugged at her belt, then pulled the buttons free, shrugging out of the coat on her own. She laid her coat across the arm of the sofa, carefully placed her hat on top of it, and looked back up at him. Deliberately she extended her hand. 'Hi. I'm Olivia Sutherland. It's nice to meet you.'

His eyes dropped to her hand and he swallowed. Hard. She was offering him the chance to start over. To get it right this time. Slowly he watched his hand take hers, his large and dark, hers small and pale. Nearly fragile. But he knew she was anything but. She was strong and kind and beautiful and he was shaking like a teenager.

'I'm David Hunter.' He leaned closer until he could see every eyelash framing her blue eyes. Until his mouth was a whisper from hers. 'And I want you more than I want to breathe.'

'Oh.' It was more an exhale than a word. Her eyes slid closed, her chest barely moving with the shallow breaths she drew, as if all the oxygen had been sucked from the room. He didn't know who moved first, and then he didn't care. Her arms were locked around his neck and his mouth was on hers, savage and bruising, but she met him full force, openmouthed and so damn hot.

His hands were everywhere, her back, her breasts, her round butt that filled his palms like she was made for him. 'What do you want?' he managed.

'You.' She punctuated her words with hard kisses. 'Now. Please.'

He should stop this. She'd wanted to talk. Needed her answers. But he didn't think he could stop this if his life depended on it. He lifted her dress, running his hands up her legs and then he groaned when his fingers went from silk to bare skin. She wore real stockings. 'Where's the zipper on this thing?' he rasped, searching her back.

'No zipper.' Her hands were busy on the buttons of his shirt. 'Just . . . take it off.'

He yanked the dress over her head and let it land where it would. And then he stared. Silk and lace covered very little. His eyes dropped to a minuscule thong. Very, very little. He thought his heart might explode. He was sure other parts of him would. He cast his eyes at the sofa, tempted, but she tapped her finger against his mouth.

'You said,' she said in a husky murmur that sent every drop of blood rushing out of his head, 'you needed more space for what you wanted to do to me.' She pushed the shirt from his shoulders and brushed his mouth with hers while his hands cruised the skin she'd bared. 'For me. In me. No sofa, David.'

He was going to die. 'Fine,' he ground out, and lifted her, wrapping her legs around his waist. He took two steps toward the bedroom when his mouth found her breast through the lace and she arched against him, her body lithe and beautiful. He stopped where he stood, sucking hard and making her whimper, loving the sound. He shifted her, claiming the other breast so he could hear it again.

'Hurry,' she urged. 'Please. Please.'

It was a desperate chant as he obeyed, laying her on the bed, then ripping the tiny panties down her legs, pushing her shoes off her feet in one motion. Before she could draw another breath his mouth was on her and she moaned, just like he remembered.

She tasted . . . just like he remembered. And her hands dug into his hair, pulling him closer, just like he remembered. 'Please, please.' She was chanting it again, begging for more, begging him to take her there, as if she wasn't certain he would.

So he sucked and nipped and licked, finally stabbing his tongue deep and her body went taut, her head flung back and a strangled cry ripped from her arched throat as she came with a force that stunned him.

But he didn't stop. Couldn't stop, and she shuddered again, his name on her lips.

He pushed to his knees, staring at her, his body throbbing. 'Olivia, look at me.'

She blinked, finally lifting her eyelids. She was beautifully dazed.

He placed his hands on either side of her face, leaning close. 'I am thinking of you. Just you. Only you. Olivia.'

She stared at him for a long moment. Then her lips curved. 'You're still dressed.'

Her hands reached for him, but he grabbed her wrists,

345

twining his fingers through hers. 'If you touch me, I'll come.'

'I want you to. I need you to.'

'I need to, too, but I want it to last more than thirty seconds. So give me a minute.' He dropped his brow to hers. 'I dreamed of your taste. You're better than I dreamed.'

She twisted up into him. 'David, please.'

He let her go, backing up before she could touch him. He peeled the stockings from her legs slowly, one then the other, then stood next to the bed and shrugged out of his shirt. 'Take off the bra.'

She sat up and unhooked the frothy lace that hardly covered enough to earn the term. She let the straps slide down her arms and quite suddenly, took his breath away.

'You're beautiful.'

She dropped her eyes to her hands as she worked his belt free. 'So are you.'

David's hands stilled. She knelt on the edge of the bed, her gaze dropping as she reached for the button on his trousers. He covered her hands with his, stopping her. 'No. Look at me, Olivia.'

She looked up until she met his eyes. 'What's wrong?'

'Nothing. Everything.' He cupped her face tenderly. 'Why do you think I'm here?'

'Because you want me more than you want to breathe.'

'And that's because you're beautiful. I couldn't get you out of my mind, Olivia. I tried. For months and years I tried and nothing worked. Nobody worked. I kept seeing your eyes when we talked and your face when you smiled.'

Something shifted behind her eyes and he knew he'd never convince her with words alone. He let his trousers drop to the floor and pushed his boxers down with them and felt a wave of satisfaction when her eyes widened, heating again.

She ran a fingertip down his length, then ran her hands down his sides, grasping his hips. He knew what was coming, but still nothing prepared him for how utterly incredible it felt when her mouth slid over him, wet and warm. His head fell back, his eyes closed and a guttural groan escaped his chest.

It was heaven. But he didn't want to come like this. Not tonight.

'Stop.' Summoning every ounce of strength, he dug his fingers through her hair and pulled her away so that he could see her face. 'To you, for you.' He dragged her up, ground his mouth on hers, fiercely satisfied when her arms came around his neck and she pressed her breasts into his chest, kissing him back. 'In you.' Blindly he reached into the bedside drawer for a condom. 'I want to be inside you.'

'Then hurry,' she whispered, yanking him down to the bed with her. Fragile she certainly was not. She snatched the packet from his hand and he had to clench his teeth to hold back when she slid it over him, her hands like little licks of fire.

He rolled her to her back, determined to do all the things he should have done before, praying he had the strength to hold back, to give her what she deserved. But when he pushed into her she was hot and wet and so damn tight. He stopped midway and shuddered, holding to his control by a thread. 'I don't want to hurt you.'

She met his eyes and he could already see the pleasure he'd hoped to put there. 'More.' She rocked up into him, pulling him deeper. 'God, please. David. More.'

His control snapped on the first *more* and he drove deep, making her gasp. But there was no pain on her face, only a growing sensual need as he moved, harder, deeper. Faster. She met each thrust as he watched her climax build. He could feel the orgasm tingling at the base of his spine and fought it back. *Not yet. Dammit, not yet.*

Then her short nails dug into his back and once again she went taut. He plunged harder, recklessly driving them higher until she screamed and the blistering wave hit and everything went black, her name on his lips as he fell.

Tuesday, September 21, 11:30 P.M.

All systems were go. He sat in his van a block away, watching the house Barney Tomlinson had purchased for his whore. Its destruction would mean more insurance money for Mrs Tomlinson and it was one last way to stick it to Barney, in memoriam.

Dorian was currently sprawled facedown on Barney's desk inside the house. Minus his face, of course. That would give the cops a fun puzzle to solve. How did Dorian and Barney connect? They didn't of course, *except through me.*

The beauty was that the money he took from both men had been held in offshore accounts that nobody would know to look for. No connection.

There were Albert and Mary. Right on time. They'd argued earlier about this job. Their voices had come through loud and clear via the mike he'd hidden in their phone.

Albert had been furious with Mary over the glass balls. Mary had been furious for his having lied to her about

Tomlinson being an environmental villain. Neither one seemed terribly upset over Eric's demise. Mary hadn't wanted to do this job. Albert had threatened to break her neck and throw her in the Mississippi River. It had been most entertaining. But after all that, here they were. And from the looks of them, still arguing.

He tuned the receiver clipped to his belt to their frequency and listened. Albert had the disposable in his shirt pocket, so his voice was loud. Mary held her own, though.

'Goddammit, woman, shut up,' Albert growled. He was speaking with his French accent. Maybe he hadn't faked it after all. Maybe he'd been trying to get back at Eric.

Given Eric's present state of death, I'd say he did that pretty well.

'This is stupid,' Mary hissed. 'We're just digging ourselves in deeper.'

'And if we refuse?'

'So he publishes the video. We'll say we were Photoshopped in. Besides, he's the one who has the girl on tape. It proves he was there, not us.'

Mary had a point, but Albert wasn't buying it. 'Just do what I say or the fishes will love you. Big nasty ones in that dirty river of yours.'

'I hate you.'

'Good thing you don't need to like me. You just need to do as you're told.'

You go, Albert. Somebody should have smacked that girl down a long time ago.

He videotaped them as they entered the house and were quickly out again. In minutes the fire was raging. The kids were getting pretty good at this. Albert pulled the cell from his pocket and snapped a photo, then the two of them ran for Eric's car.

They drove away and he started his van, taking off in the other direction. He needed to get to the deaf school. He had a date with Kenny that the boy didn't yet know about. He glanced behind him at the plastic dry-cleaner bag containing his costume. He'd have to do a quick change when he got there. His shirt was the wrong style, as was his hat, but he was betting Kenny wasn't familiar with the exact uniform worn by the Minneapolis PD.

Chapter Eighteen

Tuesday, September 21, 11:30 P.M.

Olivia woke slowly, sleepily contented. And totally naked. Her eyes opened abruptly, tensing when she realized where she was and whose hand possessively covered her breast. She was spooned against David, her back to his hard chest. And he wasn't asleep, if what she felt pulsing against her bottom was any indication.

'Don't leave,' he murmured in her ear, sending shivers over her body. 'Please.'

'I won't. But I need to get my phone, in case I get a call.'

'It's on the nightstand. I found it in your coat pocket.'

She lifted her head, her eyes becoming accustomed to the darkness. He'd arranged her clothes on a nearby chair, her purse on top. 'How long was I out?'

'Two hours. Thank you for giving me a chance to redeem myself. I did, didn't I?'

'I'd say you more than did,' she murmured.

He hesitated. 'Regrets?'

'No.' She still had questions, but no regrets.

'Good.' He kissed the top of her head. 'I needed this.'

'So did I.'

'I thought you would want to talk first.'

Her sigh was silent. 'So did I.'

'What changed?'

'Some of it was "I want you more than I want to breathe." Hell of a line, David.'

He shifted against her and she caught her breath. He was ready, again. *So am I.*

'That was no line, Olivia. I still want you more than I want to breathe. But now I can at least think. If that was some of what changed your mind, what was the rest?'

Joel Fischer's wall, she thought. 'We got a lead on one of the condo arsonists. It looks like one of them OD'd and drove his car off the road Monday morning. He's dead.'

'Guilty conscience?'

'I think so. I stood in this kid's room, looking at all the plaques on his wall, all for service to his community. He wanted to make a difference. I think he got in over his head and couldn't stand the guilt. I kept thinking that this kid did so much good, then one thing bad and it all unraveled for him. Then I thought about Lincoln, his guilt.' She paused. 'Which you understood.'

Tensing, he moved his hand from her breast to her stomach. Covering it with hers, she held on. 'I wondered what it was you'd understood,' she said. 'You said "And" last night when we argued about what happened after Mia's wedding.'

He swallowed. 'And?'

'You thought you'd done something else. Something worse. I wondered if I should have been more worried about that than I was. Then, I wondered what it mattered. You've more than proven the kind of man you are. I still wanted the answer to my question, but when I saw you . . . it seemed a lot less important. Because I wanted you more than I wanted to breathe, too.'

He drew a breath, let it out. 'So what is your question, Olivia?'

She rolled to her back, found his eyes guarded. 'Who are you, David Hunter?' She smiled up at him, trying to soften the words. 'Besides a cat-saving firefighter who volunteers more than ten people combined?'

He looked away. 'I don't know. I've been that man so long, I don't know anymore.'

She sensed honesty and frustration in his answer. 'Then who were you before?'

He flinched. 'Not so nice. I don't think you would have liked that me.'

'How old was "that you"?'

'Eighteen.'

Eighteen years then, she thought. He'd lived half his life with whatever it was that he'd done. 'And what did the eighteen-year-old you do?'

He rolled away suddenly, but she sprang to her knees, grabbing his arm as his feet hit the floor. 'Don't,' she said urgently. 'Don't you dare walk away from me. Whatever it was you did, or think you did, it kept you from coming after me for *two and a half years*. Whatever it was, it affected my life, too. That time is gone, David. Wasted. I don't want to lose any more. I'm here, right now, in your bed. I'm not afraid of you. So tell me.'

He sat on the edge of the bed, his back to her, shoulders hunched. 'I can't.'

Drawing on instinct, she took a chance. 'What was her name?' There was a long, long silence and she thought she'd try once more. 'Was it about Dana?'

He turned his head slightly, as if startled. 'No. I didn't meet her until I was thirty.'

'Mia told me about her, how she helped those battered women, running from their husbands. How you helped her do it.'

'No, I just fixed the roof.'

'Which meant a hell of a lot to the frightened women who had a dry place to hide with their children. Why did you do it? For Dana or for the women and their children?'

'Both. Dana was doing something concrete. She didn't just talk about the plight of these women and their children. She did something. I admired that.'

'You loved her. Dana.'

He'd turned back around now and she couldn't see his face. 'Yes,' he said and she felt the stab of envy and dismay. 'Or maybe the idea of her,' he added quietly. 'I always knew she didn't feel the same. Maybe that made her safe. Sounds stupid.'

'No, not at all.' For long minutes they sat in silence. 'What was her name, David?'

He shuddered out a weary sigh. 'Megan.'

'And she was eighteen, too?'

'Yeah.'

'Did you love her?'

The harshness in his laugh made her wince. 'Not as much as I loved myself.'

'What happened to her?'

'She died,' he said flatly. 'Murdered by her stepfather. Is my interrogation finished?'

'You said you'd answer my question,' she said quietly. 'I'm thinking that who you are now has a great deal to do with who she was then.'

She waited a long time until finally he sighed. 'I don't even know where to start.'

She ran a hand down his arm. 'How about, "Once there was a girl named Megan"?'

He swallowed. 'We met in junior high. She was my first dance, first date. First kiss.'

'So what happened?'

'Time passed. We went on to high school, drifted apart, but we were still friends. Then my brother Max went pro and everything changed. He got drafted into the NBA. His life changed, and so did mine.'

'For the better?'

'At the time I thought so. I was sixteen and already so full of myself. I played on my school's baseball team, my coach said I was a shoo-in for a scholarship. I was good-looking. Girls wanted me. Lots of girls. Then, that was everything.'

'What happened to Megan?'

'I'd left her way behind by then. I was an athlete. I needed the prettiest girl in class, the fastest. Megan couldn't compete. I felt sorry for her . . . social awkwardness.' He said it with self-recrimination. 'I shouldn't have, not for that anyway.'

'Then for what?'

'Her dad died when we were in junior high. She had a little brother and her mom worked hard to support them. Then when Megan was sixteen, her mom remarried. Life was supposed to get better for them, but her stepdad was a piece of work.'

'Oh no,' she whispered sadly, as if she already knew what was coming.

'He yelled at them, all the time. Nobody knew he hit them, but we should have. But I was busy,' he said scathingly, 'being popular. Having fun with the beautiful people.'

'It's just a face,' she murmured, understanding now. 'David . . .'

'I was busy,' he continued, as if she'd said nothing. 'Going to dances, playing ball, basking in being the brother of an NBA star. I never cracked a book. The smart girls did my homework. My mother prayed for me every day, begged me to straighten up, fly right. But what did she know? I had the world by the tail.'

'How did the tail break?'

'We were seniors and there was a party. One of the kids' parents were gone for the weekend and we were partying hard. Kegs, bottles, weed. Lots of girls. I got drunk. And Megan showed up.'

Olivia said nothing. His jaw was tight, his eyes staring straight ahead, unseeing.

'I was so drunk, so self-involved, that I didn't see she had a black eye. It was dark and the music was too loud and I assumed she'd come for the same reason the other girls had. For this face. I kissed her, and for a minute she held on. Then I pawed at her. Ripped her blouse and she tried to push me away. Nobody ever pushed me away.'

'It made you angry.'

'Yeah. Then she started crying. Said she needed my help. Needed my car. She needed to get away. But I was mad, so I pushed her away, told her to ask somebody that . . .' His throat worked as he tried to finish, but his voice broke. 'That cared. She was just Megan from down the street. I was David, Mr Perfect.'

Olivia rested her hand on his back, felt him flinch, but he didn't pull away. 'And?'

'The party went on. No one saw her come in or leave. She was a nobody. We were *popular*. I didn't give her another thought the rest of the night. I'd never been drunk before and the next morning I had a horrible hangover. All I could think was that I needed to get home before Ma got back from Mass or she'd kill me. And then I passed Megan's house.'

'You remembered what you'd done?'

His lips twisted. 'I had a vague recollection of what she'd said, that she'd cried. But I didn't understand until I passed her house. There was a cop car parked in front, lights flashing. My heart started pounding. I stopped my car and ran to the front door and . . . I saw her. The cop inside tried to block my view, but he was too late. I'd already seen.'

'She was dead?' Olivia murmured.

'They all were. Her mother was on the stairs. Her head . . . He'd beaten her head in with a bat. Megan was in the middle of the living-room floor.' He drew a shuddering breath. 'He'd beaten her, too. She was lying on top of her brother, shielding him. There were clothes everywhere and an empty suitcase against the wall.'

'She'd been running away.'

'She tried,' he said hollowly. 'He must have caught her. Flew into a rage. Killed them all, then shot himself.'

'What did the police do?'

'That day? They asked me what I knew. I said I didn't know anything. I never told them she'd come to me the night before.'

There was hatred and contempt in his voice, all for himself. Her heart ached for him, even as she struggled for the right words to say. 'And after that day?'

He shrugged listlessly. 'Then it was old news. There

was no mystery to solve, other than why the hell no one had stopped him before he killed three innocent people.'

'Did you ever tell anyone what happened?'

'No. I tried, a couple of times. I tried to tell my dad that summer, but I couldn't stand to see how disgusted he'd be with me. Dad was already hurt by my brother Max who was playing pro ball by then. Max had a new set of friends and hadn't been home in a while. He was living the high life and my folks were brokenhearted.'

He sighed. 'I couldn't even tell my priest. I went away to college that semester and failed miserably. I couldn't sleep. I kept seeing them, dead. I was losing my mind. I had to talk to someone, so I scraped my money together and bought a plane ticket to see my brother Max in LA. We'd always been so close and . . . I trusted Max not to hate me.'

Her heart cracked. 'What did he say?'

'I never told him. When I got to his place there was a real party going on. I saw all the booze and women, and I guess I snapped. I was thinking about the party that night, how stupid I'd been. I threw all Max's booze bottles out the window, told his guests to go home. Max thought I'd come to save him, make him go back home. I think he needed someone to set him straight and by accident, it was me. Max came home, reconciled with our dad, then that same night there was an accident. My dad died and Max was paralyzed. My mom was just devastated and Max couldn't walk. He needed help with his physical therapy. He needed me.'

'Like Megan had needed you.'

'Yeah. So I threw myself into helping Max and some days there were blocks of hours I didn't think about Megan. Everyone thought I was so noble. I was just trying to stay sane. I was just trying to make the pictures in my mind go away.'

'Like Lincoln. That's what you understood. You pitied him.'

He drew a breath. 'I keep thinking, "there but for the grace of God go I."'

'It's not the same at all,' she murmured. 'But I can see how you drew the parallel. Somehow Lincoln knew you understood. Maybe you were his first real human connection in a long time.' Olivia laid her cheek against his arm. 'That's a helluva secret to have carried around for eighteen years.'

'Isn't it, though?' he said wearily.

'But *you* didn't kill Megan and her family. Her mother was the adult and she stayed with a dangerous man. Why didn't Megan go to the police? Why did she come to you?'

'I guess in her mind, we were still friends. She probably still had a crush on me. I never shunned her and we'd sometimes talk in the hall, between classes. Like I said, I felt sorry for her. Looking back, I can see how isolated she'd become. How she walked around with her head down. I thought she was just sad because she wasn't popular.'

'You were a teenager, David.'

'I know, but still.' He drew another breath and she realized there was more. 'I went home after seeing her all . . . broken. I kept trying to remember what she'd said, wondering why she'd come to *me*. Then I remembered she'd rushed up to me between classes the day before the party, asked if I'd found the note she put in my literature book. I was busy so I said, "Sure." She asked if I'd do it. I had no idea what she was talking about and said, "Sure,"

359

without even stopping. I found the note the day she died.'

'What did it say?'

He pushed himself to his feet wearily to take his wallet from the pants he'd thrown over the chair and pulled out a worn, creased sheet of paper. Unfolding it with care, he silently handed it to her.

Olivia found it hard not to wince as she read the words of a girl who believed her old friend was still her best friend. 'Her mother wouldn't leave him and Megan didn't know who else to trust,' she murmured. 'She asked you to pick her up the next night.'

'That would have been the night of the party. She was taking her little brother and they were going to run. She just needed a ride to the bus station. I could have saved them if I had cracked the book to find her letter.'

She sighed. 'Okay, you might have saved them. Then again, you might have shown up with your car and the stepdad might have shot you all. The truth is, there were resources for Megan and her mother. Her mother was the adult. She should have called the police. It was a tragedy, David, but you didn't cause it.'

He refolded the letter, put it back in his wallet, then looked down at her, agony in his eyes. 'I still see their faces.'

'Because you've got a soul. If you didn't, it wouldn't matter. You didn't know how critical the situation was. If you had, you would have acted.'

He swallowed hard. 'How do you know?'

'Because you didn't "become" the man you are now overnight. Those values were in you, or you wouldn't have tortured yourself over this for eighteen years. David, you've helped so many. You turned a tragedy into a spirit of service. How long will you make that selfish boy pay?'

'I don't know. But that's why I worried about what I'd done that night with you.'

'You worried that you forced me? David, you didn't force Megan, even then. When she said stop, you did. You weren't civil about it, but you stopped. Didn't you?'

He nodded. 'Yes, I guess I did. But . . .'

'How many families did you help Dana save in her shelter?'

'Dozens, I suppose.'

'You support the work of the shelters all over town, so more families continue to be saved. Megan was a victim, but so many won't be. That has to be enough,' she said, 'because it never *can* be enough. There will always be wrongs in the world. We can't right them all. We just have to do the best we can.'

He sat back down on the edge of the bed. 'I know that.'

'But it's still hard. It's hard to see people in pain and not fix it. Thank you for telling me about Megan. I know it wasn't easy.'

'Does it change anything?' he asked tightly.

'You mean about what I think of you? Yes and no. You're a good person. That hasn't changed. But about what happened between us?' She shrugged. 'You said another woman's name when you were with me, then you moved here and it was like you didn't know I was alive. I wanted to hate you. Some part of me did.'

He didn't look at her. 'Do you still?'

'Hate you? No. I understand now what you were afraid you'd done. But I can't ignore the fact that you loved Dana at one time. That she was still in your mind when you were with me. I think putting that out of my mind is going to take time.'

'And heart,' he murmured. 'And trust.'

'Yes. You're going to have to give me time to trust you. And I still don't understand why you wasted two and half years of our lives. Why didn't you just ask me?'

'I was afraid of what you'd say,' he confessed quietly. 'I didn't want to think I could be a monster. Again.'

Her heart squeezed. 'You know, the night you had too much champagne you told me that you hated weddings because everyone else had someone and you were alone. I wondered how a man who looked like you could be lonely.'

His jaw tightened. 'It's just a face, Olivia. I did nothing to earn it.'

She brushed her fingers against his cheek. 'It's a very nice face. But more important is the man beneath. You're a good man, David. Honorable and kind. You make the world a better place.'

He looked over his shoulder, his eyes glittering. 'I needed you to think so.'

His eyes held hers. She couldn't look away if she'd wanted to. 'I do.'

'I still want you,' he whispered, 'more than I want to breathe.'

Her pulse quickened. 'Who needs to breathe?' Before she could blink, his mouth was on hers, ravenous and greedy, his hands setting fire to her skin wherever he touched. He tumbled her to the pillows and followed her down. Then she couldn't breathe and didn't care.

Wednesday, September 22, 12:25 A.M.

He snugged the knot of his tie, his cop costume complete. Neckties were uncomfortable. Never got how his old man could wear them around the house.

He climbed from the back of his van to the front and drove to a street that paralleled the school's rear parking lot. The lot was their evacuation spot, conveniently included on the school's Web page to give the parents a fuzzy feeling about their kids' safety.

It's showtime. Voice scrambler in one hand, cell phone in the other, he called the school's main switchboard, his message memorized.

Wednesday, September 22, 12:35 A.M.

Olivia was almost asleep when a phone rang. 'It's yours,' she mumbled. 'Mine plays Looney Tunes.'

David leaned over her and fumbled for his cell. 'Hunter.' He abruptly jumped out of bed and, shoving the phone between his shoulder and ear, pulled on his boxers. 'What happened?' He grabbed his pants, then his hands went still. 'I'm on my way.'

'What's wrong?' she asked. 'I thought you didn't have to report till eight.'

'Callback situation. Reinforcements needed on a residence fire out of control.'

'Why didn't they just call supporting firehouses?'

'They did. This is really bad and we have some men down. The fire spread to the next house and a propane tank blew. Took out part of the block.' He finished getting dressed then leaned down and pressed a hard kiss to her mouth. 'Go back to sleep. I may not be back for a while.' He hesitated at the door. 'Olivia . . .'

She knew what he wanted to say, but knew as well as he did that it was way too soon for words they'd both take very seriously. 'I'll be fine. You be careful.'

'Always. I'll call you in the morning if I'm not back.'

She switched off the light and slid back down under the blanket. Then on an impulse, switched pillows. She could smell him and it made her sigh. She'd nearly dozed off when her cell phone blasted the Looney Tunes theme. Loudly. 'Sutherland.'

'It's Kane. You need to get to the deaf school. Now.'

She swung out of bed, wincing. Her muscles had been sorely taxed. 'Why?'

'Bomb threat.'

Adrenaline cleared her brain and she dropped her dress over her head. 'When?'

'Ten minutes ago. They're evacuating the school now. The bomb squad and the fire department are already there.'

Her mind racing, she shoved her feet in the ridiculous heels. 'Where are you?'

'Just leaving my house. I'll be there in fifteen with my lights. Where are you?'

'David's cabin. I'll meet you as fast as I can get there.' She grabbed her keys from her purse and headed to her car where she'd left her overnight bag, still talking to him. 'Kane, why would someone bomb the school?' she asked, afraid she already knew.

'One, they're fucking nuts. Two, they have a beef with someone at the school. Three, someone wants the population evacuated from the dorms.'

'*Kenny*. We talked to twenty-one kids. Only Kenny lived in the dorms.'

'I know. I already told dispatch to have the first responders find him and watch him. I gave them Kenny's description, just in case there's confusion on the site.'

'How did they know about him?' She had her bag and

was running back to the cabin. 'He's our link to a potential eyewitness, but who told them we talked to him?'

'Could have been anyone at the school. I don't guess twenty kids kept it a secret.'

'Oh God.' The sick feeling was slinking down her spine. 'Kane, I never actually talked to Val. I left her voice mails, but she never did anything but text.'

'Shit. Get dressed and meet me here. I'll get a unit to check on the interpreter.'

Wednesday, September 22, 12:45 A.M.

It was controlled chaos, he thought. He stood in the trees beyond the back lot of the school, watching the children pour out of the dormitories, all in pajamas. There were more than he'd thought there'd be, ranging in age from five to eighteen, all scared.

They wore shoes, or at least carried them in their hands. His gaze moved to the oldest group of boys and watched for a pair of blue Converse high-tops.

The kids signed busily as the dorm staff herded them to their specified safe area. He was beginning to think he'd never find Kenny, when he saw him. Sandy blond, five-ten, wearing blue high-tops. Standing off to the side, looking miserable.

He took his notepad and scrawled two separate messages, then swaggered over to the boy as he'd seen countless cops swagger in and out of his shop over the years. He tapped him on the shoulder, ignoring the students and staff behind him.

Kenny read the note. *Kenny Lathem, the detectives want to speak with you again.*

For a moment, he thought the kid would run. But Kenny steeled his spine and nodded stiffly. He started to walk, Kenny in front of him.

'Wait.' It was one of the dorm staff who stood shivering in the wind. 'Where are you taking him?' The young man's speech was slightly slurred, but understandable.

Keeping his head down, he handed the note to the staff person, then took it back after the staff read it and nodded. He wore black gloves and had left no finger-prints, but there was no reason to hand evidence over to the cops. His hat covered enough of his face that if he kept his head down, no one would be able to clearly describe him.

And if they did, then so what? He looked like everybody. He had one of those faces that just blended in. Add to that the face putty he'd used to build up his cheekbones, chin, and nose, and he was unrecognizable.

He jerked his head, motioning Kenny to come. They rounded the building, out of sight. Then he drew his gun and watched the boy's eyes widen in fear. Stepping closer, he pressed the barrel of the gun to Kenny's gut and handed the kid the second note.

If you scream, I will kill you. Turn around and walk. Slowly. If you run, I will kill you. Then I will kill every member of your family. Nod if you understand.

Kenny's nod was tiny, but perceptible.

He patted the kid's pocket, found Kenny's phone, then shoved the phone in his own pocket and the gun into Kenny's kidney. They began to walk. He could see his van parked just beyond the trees.

Almost there. Almost home free. They were at the van and he slid the side door open and shoved the kid in. Then he heard it. The snap of a twig behind him. *Fuck.*

'*Stop. Police.*' It was a deep voice and loud. And coming closer.

Fuck. He yanked the side door closed and reached for the driver's door, wrenching it open. He had one foot in when a hand grabbed his collar and yanked.

'Get *out* of the *car*, goddammit,' the cop snarled.

His left hand clamped on the wheel and held on. His right hand still held his gun. He held it close to his chest so that the cop couldn't see it. The cop's hand left his collar, but grabbed his left wrist and twisted it behind him.

It hurt. A goddamn lot. The cop held him down and with his free hand opened the side door. Kenny scrambled out and ran. 'You're under arrest,' the cop said.

Hell no. He gave a huge shove back and twisted, firing as he did so. He heard the blast, felt the jerk of the discharge up into his shoulder, smelled the acrid odor of gunpowder, heard a little gasp. The hand on his wrist loosened and he fired again. The cop's body just fell away. He jumped in his seat, twisted the key he'd left in the ignition, and peeled out, zigzagging to throw his door closed as he sped away.

Then he looked back in his side mirror, saw a figure on his back on the ground. Not moving. It wasn't a regular cop. The man wore a suit. His fedora lay a few feet from his outstretched arm. He was big, dark, and . . . He knew him. *Detective Kane.*

He fixed his gaze forward, his mouth a grim line. 'Goddammit,' he hissed. His own hat was gone. His fucking hat was gone. *Relax. You wore gloves. It's just a hat.*

They might find a hair.

And? So what? *It doesn't tell them anything without something to compare it to.* And if he was careful, there would be nothing to compare it to.

I shot a cop. Maybe killed a cop. A retired cop had been hilarious because he'd pinned it on the College Four. Now the College Four was down to two. *And the cops have my damned hat. The cops won't rest until they find me.*

I'll cool it for a while. He laughed bitterly. *If I have to run, I can always go to France.*

He pulled into a side street, got out and changed the rear plate. He could already hear the sirens blaring. *They're looking for me.* He reached between the front seats and pulled out the magnetic sign he used for his business. THE DELI – WE CATER. They'd be looking for a plain white van. His sign made him invisible.

He applied it to the driver's side door and got back in. He pulled the putty off his face and yanked at his tie, pulled off the costume shirt, and pulled on a Deli polo shirt. His heart was pounding. He hated when his heart pounded. Dammit.

His hands were shaking as he put the van in drive and pulled out of the alley, onto the next block. He merged into traffic and headed for home.

I don't have Kenny. He patted his own pants pocket. *But I do have Kenny's phone.*

The evening wasn't a total loss.

Wednesday, September 22, 1:00 A.M.

Olivia was out of her car almost before it stopped, looking for Kane. *Officer down.* She'd heard it on the radio when she was five minutes out and her heart was pounding so hard she could barely breathe. *Serious injury. Shots fired.* She'd tried Kane's cell three times in the last five minutes, but nobody answered. He should have answered. He'd know she'd worry. He'd have hell to pay when she found him.

She scanned the crowd as she ran past the line of emergency vehicles and news vans. *Where's Kenny? Where is Kane?* She searched the crowd but didn't see Kane standing as he always did, head and shoulders over everyone else. She didn't see his fedora. Her heart was in her throat, choking her.

Two uniformed officers began to walk toward her and her pounding heart stopped. *No*. She knew that look. She'd worn that look.

No. She started to run. *No*.

'Sorry, ma'am, we can't let you through.' One of the uniforms grabbed her arm, stopping her, but she jerked free, flashed her badge and took off around them. There were people through the trees. She could see a gurney and the lights of a rescue squad on the access road behind them.

She was ten feet away when another uniform turned around. 'You can't—'

She bolted forward and shoved him aside. And stopped short.

Everything froze. 'Oh God. Oh God.' She could hear her voice saying it.

It was him. It was Kane. Lying on the ground. Blood on his white shirt. Too much blood on his shirt. Paramedics hovered over him, one on each side, lifting him to the gurney. One of them turned around, met her eyes.

And shook his head.

'No.' It was a howl, the same howl of pain she'd heard countless times before from the families. All those families. But it came from her. Her mouth. Her heart.

She stumbled forward, making her feet carry her alongside the paramedics as they lifted him into the ambulance. 'I'm going with him.'

The two medics glanced at each other. 'Okay,' one said. 'Stay out of the way.'

She climbed in beside them, numb. Sat where the attending medic pointed as the driver pulled away from the scene. Olivia glanced back through the rear window, saw the uniforms watching them. Saw Kane's hat on the ground.

'His hat,' she whispered.

The medic looked up. 'They'll keep it for you,' he said kindly.

For you. Not for him. 'Oh God.' Olivia pressed her hand to her mouth, trying to hold it back, this wave of pain that was ripping her in two. 'I need to call my captain.'

The medic nodded. 'He needs to get the family in.'

Numbly Olivia nodded. Her fingers seemed to belong to someone else's hand as she dialed Abbott's home phone. He answered on the first ring. 'What's happening?'

She couldn't speak. Couldn't form a word.

'Olivia? Olivia, are you there?' Abbott demanded.

'Bruce.' It was all she could say. It came out a whimper.

There was a moment of dead silence on the line, then a barely audible, 'Oh God.'

She looked at Kane, there on the gurney and she knew. He wasn't moving. Wasn't breathing. His face was already gray. Despite the medic's steady efforts, there was only a flat line on the heart monitor. She looked up at the medic who looked so damn sad.

He shook his head. 'I'm sorry.'

She bit her lips hard, made herself breathe. 'Kane's gone,' she said to Abbott.

'I'll meet you at the hospital. I'll bring Jennie.'

How can I face Jennie? 'I was too late,' she whispered. 'Ten minutes too late.'

'Do you know what happened?' he asked thickly.

'No. When I got here . . . it was done. He . . .' The words trailed away.

'I'll be there as soon as I can.'

She shook her head, watching the medic. All so slowly. Everything moving so slowly. 'It doesn't matter anymore.' She put her phone away. 'Can I hold his hand?'

'Sure. Detective, I'm so sorry. There was nothing we could do.'

She nodded dully. 'I know. You're sorry for my loss.'

The medic looked away, a muscle twitching in his cheek. 'Goddammit.'

She took Kane's big hand in both of hers and just held on. 'I know.'

Wednesday, September 22, 1:10 A.M.

He pulled into an all-night convenience store. Scrolling Kenny's texts, he smiled.

Where r u? Why haven't u txtd? Did u mail it?

It was sent from 'austin.' Mail what? He scrolled farther and muttered an oath. Austin had dictated a letter to Kenny. It was a description of what he'd done at the condo. *It's a description of me. He saw me.*

If Kenny mailed this letter and the cops got their hands on Austin . . . Well, it just didn't make sense to leave people lying around who could identify you in a lineup. Austin had to go. Where was he? *If he's in that dorm, I'm gonna shoot myself.*

371

He scrolled back farther and sighed with relief.

What happened w Oaks? Kenny had texted Monday afternoon.

Sent home. Suspended. Don't tell. Please. Back Monday.

Austin was at home, which would be where? He went to Kenny's contacts and *bingo*. Austin Dent. Lived in Duluth. He plugged the address into his GPS. Excellent. He had just enough time to get up there and back before opening the shop at seven.

Chapter Nineteen

Wednesday, September 22, 1:20 A.M.

David got out of the rescue squad that had brought him and Jeff Zoellner from the firehouse to the fire. Scanning the landscape, he tried to take it in. *Mother of God.*

The damage was already enormous in scale. Six houses smoldered, three on either side of a blank space that had been two more houses. Nothing remained but scraps of paper and wood.

Behind the three smoldering houses on the left were the charred remains of a small copse of trees. And beyond the trees, a six-story apartment complex still burned.

'Holy fuck,' Jeff breathed. 'Let's find Casey. He's probably with the truck.'

Their truck was a hundred yards away, the bucket high in the air. B shift was pulling residents out of windows. He could see more people at more open windows, waving frantically. He could see their mouths open, screaming.

But all he could hear was the rumble of emergency vehicles and the roar of the fire.

Captain Casey waved them over. 'Dalton and Myers are in the bucket. Relieve them. Station Forty-two is around the corner working the other side. Dalton and Myers will relieve them when they've rested. We'll work rotation until we're done.'

Their pumper was parked nearby and David could see the lines extended into the building. He pulled an oxygen can from the truck's storage locker. 'Who's inside?'

'Perry and Jacobs from B shift. Station Forty-two's also got a team in there with nozzles and Thirty-eight's doing a search on the inner units.'

Jeff pulled his hood over his head. 'Can we get support from out east?'

Casey shook his head. 'Bomb threat at a residential school.'

David stiffened. 'The university?' Where Tom was.

'No, a deaf school. Kindergarten through high school.'

The girl he'd pulled from the condo was deaf. *No coincidence.* 'Was this fire here set?' he asked tightly, already knowing the answer.

Casey nodded. 'Yeah. We've already transported half a dozen residents and two firefighters from this fire. ERs out here are strained, but the hospital out east is waiting for possible casualties from the school. Move out. Be careful.'

David jerked a nod, fury rising in him as he rushed to the bucket. He thought of the condo, of the dead girl's face. Tracey Mullen. These monsters had murdered her, just as if they'd shot her in the heart like the guard. In his mind he could see the faceless body of Barney Tomlinson. But this . . . this was devastation. How many would die tonight? How many were already dead?

Hundreds of kids went to the deaf school. What was so damn important that endangering *hundreds of lives* with a goddamn bomb was okay? He drew a steadying breath. The family coming down in the bucket was alive and they were his priority. *Focus*, he told himself sternly. *You can be angry later.*

When the bucket reached the ground, David helped a terrified woman and her three children to the ground and into the care of the paramedics. The woman grabbed his coat.

'My husband is still in there. Please get him out.' Her eyes were glassy with shock.

David nodded. 'Yes, ma'am.' He and Jeff traded places with Dalton and Myers.

'We were going to search the place for the husband on our next pass,' Myers said. 'Living room to the left, bedrooms to the right. These are all three-bedroom units.'

'Thanks.' David hooked on the belt, fixed his mask in place, and sucked in a hard breath to get the oxygen flowing. Jeff did the same and jabbed his thumb upward.

They rose to the fourth floor and David got an uncomfortable feeling of déjà vu, remembering how his legs had dangled into nothingness when the floor gave way. Brushing it aside, he followed Jeff through the window, his ax handle extended, checking for soft spots in the floor.

It was a child's bedroom. Mothers always went to their children's rooms before seeking safety themselves. *Okay, dad, where are you?* Left living area, right bedrooms. There was fire in the hall, licking at the walls from the inside out.

In front of him, Jeff turned right and shouldered his way through a door, then jumped back. Flames covered the far wall and in seconds licked across the ceiling.

Go back. The room was seconds from flashover. He reached for Jeff's coat, but Jeff was hunched over and moving forward. David followed, ax handle down. He hit something soft, but it wasn't the floor.

A body. 'Zell!' he yelled. He grabbed the man under the arms and started dragging him out into the hall. 'Get his feet,' he shouted to Jeff.

Jeff turned to get the man's feet when the room went up.

And the ceiling came down.

'*Zell!*' David dropped the man and lurched forward. A beam had come down, pinning Jeff's torso. Jeff lay on his back, not moving. David wedged his ax under the beam, lifting it so that Jeff could drag himself out. But Jeff wasn't moving.

'Firefighter injured,' David said into his radio. 'Need assistance in the bucket.'

David grabbed Jeff under his arms and dragged him out, around the unconscious man, until they were back in the child's room and at the window. He knelt beside him. His partner was breathing, but it appeared through the mask that his eyes were closed.

'I'll be back,' David shouted, unsure if Jeff could hear him or not. He went back for the woman's husband. The bedroom in which they'd found him was now fully engaged.

David got him back to the kid's bedroom to find Myers at the window.

'Zell's down,' he shouted, pointing to the floor. 'Unresponsive.' Together he and Myers lifted Jeff into the bucket and Myers laid him as flat as the small space allowed.

David knew they couldn't fit the woman's husband in the bucket as well. 'Take him down and come back for me and the victim.'

It seemed an eternity, watching the bucket descend.

Waiting paramedics moved Jeff to a stretcher. Then Myers started back up.

The entire hall was now engulfed in flames and the fire had licked its way into the kid's bedroom. Fifteen more seconds ticked by while the fire raced up the walls. Finally Myers was back and the two of them lifted the woman's husband into the bucket. David climbed through the window and into the bucket just as the room went up.

Myers maneuvered the bucket several feet from the building as he took it down.

'You okay?' Myers shouted.

David nodded mutely. His chest felt like it was going to explode. His fingers itched to rip off the mask now that he was out, but he quelled the need, breathing evenly.

They got to the ground and David opened the bucket door, letting the medics drag the victim out and to a waiting stretcher. David yanked his mask from his face.

'Zell?' he asked loudly and the medics pointed to a retreating ambulance.

'He's conscious but can't feel his legs. He said to tell you that you're even now.'

David's chest felt frozen. *Oh God*. Spinal injury. *God*. He thought about the way he'd dragged Jeff out but knew it had been the only way to get him out of the fire. *Please, don't let me have made it worse*. He looked back up at the building. Six more windows had terrified residents waving frantically for rescue. *Zell's in good hands. Those people are in yours. Do your job.*

He strapped his mask back on and looked at Myers. 'Back up?'

Myers nodded tiredly. David took the controls and sent them back up, casting worried glances at the ambulance as it screamed away.

Wednesday, September 22, 1:35 A.M.

'Olivia.' Noah Webster burst into the ER, pale. 'Abbott called me.'

She was leaning against a wall outside the room in which Kane lay. She looked up, met Noah's eyes. 'They called it.' Kane's time of death. As she'd stood and watched, helplessly. 'There was nothing they could do.'

Noah closed his eyes for a long moment. 'When?'

'Five minutes after we got here. I don't know the exact time.'

'What happened?'

'I was too late. I wasn't there.'

Noah grabbed her shoulders. 'Stop that. Right now. This is not your fault.'

'Fine.' In the minutes since they'd taken Kane from the ambulance, her mind had moved from chaotic to precise. Clear. Logical. Still, her heart pounded like hell. 'It doesn't matter now anyway.'

Noah pinched her chin, made her look up at him. 'You're in shock.'

'No. I'm not. I'm waiting for Jennie and then I'm catching a ride back to the scene.'

'No, you're not,' Noah said.

She jerked her chin from his fingers. 'I'll function. I owe Kane at least that much.'

'Olivia, you didn't cause this.'

'No, but I might have prevented it. And I know damn well who *could* have prevented it.'

'Who?'

'Kenny Lathem. That's who this guy was after. That's why he called in a bomb threat. One of the cops at the scene followed us in. He said when the evac started, the staff had all the kids together. One of the staff told him that a guy dressed like a cop gave Kenny a note that said the detectives wanted to talk to him again. He led him away and forced Kenny into a white van at gunpoint. And no, nobody got a plate,' she said before he could ask.

'And Kane?'

'Kane called ahead, told first responders to make sure Kenny was okay. It was the first thing we thought of when we heard about the evacuation. Kenny was the only dorm kid we talked to and he knew something. When Kane got there, dorm staff told him Kenny had gone with the cops. He chased and got to them just . . .' Her voice hitched and she sternly controlled it. 'Just in time. Kane got the van open, Kenny got away. Kane was shot twice, close range. He was probably dead before he hit the ground.'

Noah swallowed hard. 'Shit.'

'Yeah. And there's more,' she said wearily. 'You remember at the end of our five o'clock meeting yesterday, when I got the text from the sign language interpreter?'

'She had another commitment.' His expression twisted. 'Oh God, no. That's how this guy found out about Kenny?'

'I don't know, but that's my guess. Her kids say she never came home. Around ten they called a family friend who's been sitting with them. Val had texted them, too, saying she wouldn't be home for dinner. Her agency didn't have any record of any other assignments, so they filed a missing person shortly after midnight. Last I saw her was when we broke for lunch yesterday, right before K—'

She had to stop a minute. Breathe. Wait for the spasm in her chest to ease. 'Right before Kane and I went up to David's to bring back that Lincoln character.'

'Liv, were you with David tonight?'

She nodded, looked away. 'Yeah.'

'That wasn't wrong, you know. That had nothing to do with this.'

'If I'd been at home, I would have been there faster.'

'And maybe I'd be standing over your corpse right now,' Noah said sharply. 'You know it doesn't work like that. You could have been caught in traffic, Kane could have waited for backup. A million different things could have happened.'

'I know.' But that didn't change facts. If she'd been there, Kane would have had backup and he'd be alive. But she hadn't and he wasn't and she couldn't change that now. She could only do what he would have wanted her to do. Her damn job.

'Did you tell David you were all right?' he asked. 'He's going to hear an officer was killed. He's going to wonder if it's you.'

Yes, he would, she realized. And he'd worry. 'No, I didn't think to tell him, but I doubt he's heard about this yet. David was already gone when I left. There was a big fire. . .' She stopped and looked up, frowning. 'There was a big fire out in Woodview. Didn't you say something about Woodview at the meeting yesterday?'

'Yeah. That's where Tomlinson bought a house for his mistress. It's possible, isn't it? That they could have set one fire deliberately to divert attention from the evac?'

'It's possible. It was a bad fire with an explosion. Let's find out if Tomlinson's house was the target.' She straightened abruptly when the doors from the outside opened and Abbott entered, a small woman sobbing in his arms. 'Jennie,' she murmured.

'Remember you did not cause this,' Noah said quietly. 'She doesn't need your guilt. She needs your strength.'

Olivia nodded unsteadily and took a few steps toward them. 'Jennie.'

Kane's wife stumbled into Olivia's arms. She held Jennie, rocking her where they stood. 'Kane saved a boy's life tonight,' Olivia said helplessly.

'I know,' Jennie cried. 'Bruce told me. I can't believe this.'

'I know,' Olivia whispered. 'I'm sorry.' Jennie nodded against her and for a long, long moment they stood that way, until Olivia sighed. 'He's in there. I can go with you.'

Jennie pulled away, still crying but standing on her own feet. 'No. I need to be alone for a while.' She took Olivia's hand, patted it. 'He thought the world of you.'

Olivia could only nod. No words would come. She stood, frozen, while Jennie walked around her, through the door to where Kane lay. Abbott squeezed her shoulder.

'Go home, Olivia. We'll get through the night. That's all we have to do right now.'

She searched his face, saw he'd been crying. Abbott and Kane had known each other a lot longer than she had. 'I need a ride back to the school to get my car.'

'I'll take her,' Noah said. 'We'll be in at oh-eight.'

Abbott's nod was heavy. 'And we'll catch this bastard. I gave Jennie my word.'

'Come on, Liv,' Noah said, taking her arm. 'Let's go.' He led her to his car, put her in and got behind the wheel. 'Where to?' he asked.

'Back to the school.'

His brows lifted. 'For your car?'

'After. First, I talk to Kenny.'

'What about an interpreter?'

'There will be somebody there who can interpret, but if

not, I don't care.' Her jaw clenched. 'If I have to use a stone tablet and a chisel, that boy's gonna talk to me.'

'Okay.'

Olivia stared out the window as Noah drove, seeing nothing of the road that flashed by. She could only see Kane's body lying on the ground. 'What am I going to do, Noah?' The whispered question was out before she knew it was coming.

'What Bruce said. You're going to get through tonight. Then tomorrow. And you're going to find the guy who shot your partner and turn him into fucking hamburger.'

She turned to face her friend and saw his cheeks were wet. She reached out, grabbed his hand and hung on. He squeezed tightly and then she understood he needed her, too. She'd pushed Noah away over the last seven months, along with the rest of her friends. 'I need to make some calls, tell folks I'm okay.'

Wednesday, September 22, 2:20 A.M.

David walked away from the wreckage, so tired he could barely move his feet. Rotating their manpower, his and the other firehouses had gotten everyone out. They hoped. David hated to think of anyone still inside. The fire was largely knocked down, but in some areas it continued to flare and would for several more hours.

Beyond the woman's husband the paramedics had rushed to the hospital, they had four human fatalities – an elderly woman and an asthmatic child who'd died of smoke inhalation in the apartment blaze and two people known to have been in one of the houses when it exploded.

He hadn't heard anything about the other exploded house.

They'd seen dozens of injuries. Jeff had been the worst firefighter injury. David still hadn't heard anything about his partner's condition. He was trying hard not to worry.

Trying harder to contain his rage. Sonsofbitches. Why? What could they possibly hope to gain? How many lives had been devastated tonight? *And for what?*

'You okay, Dave?'

Their shift engineer was shaking a bottle of water, an empty packet of electrolyte mix in his other hand. He held it out and it was all David could do to lift his arm to grab it. He guzzled it down and held the bottle out for more.

'Just tired. Any news on Zell?'

'Not yet. Red Cross is set up over there. Go take a rest.'

He nodded and pushed away from the truck to trudge toward the Red Cross area. Thoughts of Olivia fluttered through his mind and he let himself steep there, pushing away all the rage, the devastation all around him. He let himself imagine her warm and soft in his bed, hoping he'd be able to get back to her before she left for work. He needed her, needed to hold her after a night like this.

The sex . . . He drew a breath. Had been unforgettable. *You could have been having sex like that for the last two and a half years if you hadn't been such an idiot.* He let out the breath in a sigh. He could have had much more than sex. He could have had her. In his arms. In his house. Someone to come home to. *Someone just for me.*

His feet stopped moving when he saw Barlow and Captain Casey standing off to the side, deep in conversation. Even from twenty feet away he could sense tension. And pain. Barlow looked like he'd taken a blow.

The two looked up, saw him and exchanged a glance.

David got a queasy feeling in his gut. 'What's happened?' David asked. 'I need to know. How's Zell?'

Casey looked old. 'I don't know. I'm waiting to hear. David, there was a shooting tonight. At that residential school.'

The queasiness turned to ice. *Oh God. Please. Not her.* 'Who?'

'Kane,' Barlow said quietly. 'He's dead.'

David felt his knees go weak. 'Oh no. How?'

'You know that hearing aid you found in the condo debris? Olivia and Kane were trying to track its owner, looking for an eyewitness at the deaf school. They found a kid who knew something. Somebody tried to snatch the kid tonight.'

'The bomb scare was a fake?'

Barlow nodded. 'They did a full sweep and didn't find anything, but it got the kids evacuated. Kane got there as the kid was being shoved into a van. He saved the kid, but there was a struggle and . . .' He trailed off. 'Poor Liv.'

David fought back panic. 'Was she there?'

'No. She got there about ten minutes later. Kane was already gone.'

Sadness settled on his shoulders, even as his body shuddered in relief that she hadn't been nearby, in danger. Kane had been more than Olivia's partner. He'd been her friend and, if David's instincts were right, a father figure as well. 'Where is she?'

'I don't know,' Barlow said. 'I'd heard there was an officer down. I didn't know it was Kane until a little while ago. She might still be at the hospital with Kane's family, but knowing Liv, she's gone back to the scene.'

Doing her job. As will I. He wanted to ask Casey for a few hours to go see Olivia, to see Jeff, but there was still hours of work to be done here. *And then I'm on shift for the next twenty-four.* 'I'll call her.' But what could he say?

'I heard about your partner, Zell,' Barlow said. 'I'm sorry.'

Fear, worry, and guilt rushed his mind, and he quickly turned it back. He couldn't let himself think about Zell now. He shouldn't let himself think about Olivia either, but that was impossible. She was there, in his mind. She was hurting, and he hurt, too.

'Thanks.' David surveyed the wreckage. 'Which house was the arson target?'

'Second from the left,' Barlow said. 'No glass ball that we've been able to find.'

'Was the gas tank targeted?'

'Doesn't appear to have been. Folks are just turning on their heat at night. They probably had a leak and didn't know it. The fire spread from one house to another and . . . boom.' The last word was said very wearily. 'We know two people were home in one of the houses, but the other house was for sale. Neighbors say it was unoccupied.'

'The condo was supposed to have been, too,' David said.

Barlow shrugged. 'I know. I thought of that already. I've called for a cadaver dog and they're supposed to be here soon. Then we'll start searching for remains.'

It was a grim prospect, but part of the job. 'They didn't leave a glass ball. Are we talking the same arsonists?' David asked and Barlow's eyes narrowed.

'House belonged to Barney Tomlinson's mistress. What do you think?'

The words hung in the air for a moment. Then Casey met David's eyes, his kind. 'Why don't you take off? Go see Zell and Detective Sutherland. You're back on in a few hours and you won't be able to then.'

David thought of Olivia, grieving alone. She shouldn't be alone. 'Thanks. I'll need to catch a ride back to the firehouse.'

'I'll ask one of the cops to drive you back,' Barlow said.

Wednesday, September 22, 2:30 A.M.

Olivia and Noah found Micki at the crime scene, staring at the flattened grass that was stained with blood. Kane's hat was still on the ground. It looked . . . lonely. And small. Nothing like the man who'd worn it.

Carry this picture in your mind, Olivia told herself sternly. *This is the monster you're chasing. This is what he took from you. From Jennie.*

Beside her, Noah let out a breath. 'Goddammit.'

Micki looked up, startled. 'I'm sorry. I didn't hear you coming.'

'Did you find the bullet?' Olivia asked harshly.

'Yes. Hollow-point. I had it sent to ballistics. They'll have results by morning meeting, but I'm betting it'll match Weems and Tomlinson.'

'Did he leave anything behind?' she asked. 'Did the cameras catch him?'

Micki's lips twisted bitterly. 'He was dressed like a cop. Kane must have knocked off the bastard's hat.' She pointed to it, flattened in the dirt on the shoulder. 'The shooter ran over it with his tires when he was escaping. Then the ambulance ran over it again, but it's folded over, so hopefully anything he left behind will be trapped inside.'

A hat, Olivia thought. Kane would see the irony in that.

'And the security cameras?' Noah asked.

'We got basic height and weight of the shooter. Angle was wrong for the license plates on the van. We can get a very basic make on the van, but that's it.'

Olivia pointed to Kane's hat. 'Can I take it?'

Micki shook her head. 'Not yet. I'm sorry, Liv.'

Olivia's nod was crisp even though her heart cracked. Micki was doing her job and she was damn good at it. *It's just that it's on the ground. It shouldn't be on the ground.* She cleared her throat and when she spoke, her voice was even and strong.

'It's okay. I just want to make sure Jennie gets it. I'm going to find Kenny Lathem now. Call me if you get anything.'

Micki just nodded, her lips pursed to keep from breaking down. Olivia turned on her heel and made her feet move, Noah at her side.

Oaks was waiting for them in his office. A woman sat in the chair next to his desk. He signed, then pointed at the woman who looked to be in her early twenties.

'He said he thought you'd come back, so he waited,' she said. 'I'm Danni Oaks. Principal Oaks is my dad. He asked me to come and interpret for him tonight.'

'Thank you,' Olivia said. She turned to Oaks. 'Were any children hurt tonight?'

'No,' he signed. 'Kenny is quite upset, as you might expect. We've called his parents to come get him.'

'We need to talk to him first,' Olivia said flatly.

Oaks hesitated. 'Detective,' he signed, 'I cooperated with you yesterday.'

'And we appreciate it,' Olivia interrupted the soft voice

387

of Danni Oaks, not bothering to hide her impatience in her face or her tone. 'But my partner is dead, Mr Oaks.' She watched him flinch. 'And Val, the interpreter from yesterday? She's missing. Somebody wants Kenny real bad. I want to know who and why. And I want to know now.'

'His parents should be here,' Oaks signed tiredly, Danni voicing.

'Kenny could be in danger, Mr Oaks,' Olivia said. 'He knows something that somebody doesn't want told. I don't want to have to explain to his parents why somebody murdered him, too.'

Oaks's shoulders sagged. 'I'll have him brought in.'

Chapter Twenty

Wednesday, September 22, 2:55 A.M.

Kenny shuffled in next to a man Oaks introduced as Roger Court. Roger was the dorm staff who had spoken with Kane's killer.

When they were all seated, Olivia began. 'Kenny, I know you're scared, but you have to talk to me.'

Kenny closed his eyes. 'I want to go back to my room,' he signed, his face stony.

Danni Oaks voiced it with a note of apology, sentiment Olivia knew was Danni's and not Kenny's. Olivia tapped the table, but Kenny's eyes remained stubbornly closed.

Olivia tapped harder, then banged her fist so hard the table jumped and shuddered. Still Kenny's eyes remained closed. Fury bubbled up, rattling her control and suddenly Olivia saw Kane again, lying on the ground. His blood soaking the ground. Dead. *Because this little shit wouldn't talk. Goddammit, boy, you'll talk to me.*

She grabbed the back of Kenny's chair, yanking it from the table and around so that he had nothing to lean on. His eyes flew open, went cold, closed again. 'Fine,' she said. 'We'll see how stubborn he'll be in the general population at the jail.'

'You can't,' Oaks signed. Danni's voice trembled as she spoke for her father.

'Watch me,' Olivia snapped back. 'Just watch me.'

'He's a kid,' Roger said aloud, signing at the same time. He was hearing impaired, but she could understand him. 'He didn't do anything wrong.'

'I don't know that. So I'm going to assume the very worst.' Olivia yanked her handcuffs from her belt and snapped one on Kenny's wrist.

Kenny's eyes flew open, stubbornness flashing to panic. 'No!' he cried aloud.

Olivia cuffed his hands behind him, then pushed him back in the chair. She had his full attention now. She turned to Danni Oaks, her temper close to breaking.

'Tell him he will talk to me or I will arrest him for hindering an investigation. Tell him my partner died to save his sorry ass and if doesn't start talking in the next ten seconds every cop downtown will know why he's there. Tell him I am sick and tired of his games and I want answers and I want them now.'

Danni signed rapidly, then Oaks stepped in front of Kenny and began to sign.

'What's he saying?' Olivia asked when Danni didn't immediately voice.

'To please cooperate. That his own life could be in danger.'

Kenny shot Olivia a look of impotent rage. 'Let me go,' he voiced thickly.

'Not until he talks,' Olivia said and Danni signed it, giving Olivia a fearful look.

'How?' Kenny roared.

'He can't talk if you've cuffed his hands,' Danni said quietly. 'Please let him go.'

'You'll cooperate?' Olivia asked him. Danni signed it and Kenny nodded furiously.

Olivia looked at Noah. 'Well?' she asked. 'Should I let him go?'

'He can't sign without his hands, Liv,' Noah said mildly. 'Let him go.' Olivia noticed Danni's expression softened when she interpreted for Noah. Kenny's did, too.

Olivia unlocked the cuffs. 'So talk to me, Kenny. First, what did this guy look like?'

Kenny rubbed his wrists resentfully. He deliberately turned halfway in his chair so that he answered Noah. *Good cop, bad cop*, Olivia thought, satisfied.

'Average,' he signed. 'My height, about my weight, average face. He wore a hat.'

Olivia looked at Roger. 'Anything you can add?'

Roger shrugged helplessly. 'He had a badge, a white shirt. He looked like a cop.'

Olivia nodded. 'I know. You told someone when he took Kenny away?'

'Yes. It wasn't right. He'd taken Kenny away from the cops, not to them. I couldn't leave my kids alone. I was trying to get the attention of one of the officers when the detective arrived with a piece of paper with Kenny's name. I pointed around the building. He went running after them and then another cop followed him.'

Roger touched his hearing aid with a tiny wince. 'I heard the shot and the second cop came back with Kenny. It didn't take long for the story to spread, that the detective was dead.' His eyes were stark. 'I'm sorry. I know he was your partner. I wish . . .'

The look she gave Roger was gentle, but inside she was screaming. 'I know, but your quick thinking helped

Detective Kane save Kenny's life.' She turned her gaze to Kenny sharply. 'My partner died protecting you. What. Do. You. Know?'

Kenny sagged. 'My friend saw something,' he signed, slowly. 'Sunday night.'

Olivia tapped Kenny's knee. 'Tell me,' she said softly.

'He was at the condo fire. He came back' – Kenny glanced at Oaks from the corner of his eye – 'through the window.' Oaks firmed his lips but said nothing.

'He was with Tracey Mullen,' Olivia said. 'The girl who died.'

Kenny nodded. 'He met her at camp. We were both there.'

'What's your friend's name, son?' Noah asked, his face kind.

'Austin Dent.'

Oaks frowned. 'Austin was suspended Monday morning. He was smoking in his dorm room. Now that makes sense. We sent him home.'

'Where is Austin's home?' Olivia asked.

'Duluth.' Oaks fingerspelled it. 'I'll look up his address.'

Noah wrote it down. 'At least our shooter doesn't know where Austin lives.'

Kenny looked sick, his hands trembling as he signed. 'The man . . . He got my cell phone. He has my texts. My phone list. He has Austin's address.'

Noah was already on his feet. 'I'll call the state police. They can pick Austin up. If the guy drove directly there from here, he's still two hours away.'

When Noah was gone, Olivia settled in her chair. 'What did Austin tell you?'

'Sunday night, he was so upset. I didn't know why. I

didn't know what he'd done.' Now that he'd started, Kenny's signs were frantic, but Danni kept up. 'He smelled like smoke.' Again he glanced at Oaks from the corner of his eye. 'I asked if what he'd done was worse than getting caught smoking and he said yes. So I gave him my cigarettes. We figured Roger would smell the smoke, but he'd think it was from the cigarettes.'

'So Austin got suspended,' Olivia said. 'And he never told you anything more?'

Kenny looked away. 'He texted me yesterday morning. Said he needed to tell the cops what happened, but anonymously. He asked me to send a letter for him. From a mailbox downtown. That way you wouldn't know it was him.'

They were just scared kids. But if they'd said something, Kane might . . . She had to take a moment, let the tightness in her chest pass. 'What did the letter say?'

'That he saw a man shoot that security guard. Then the man got in a boat that he'd tied to the dock and got away. That Austin was in the building when it started burning. He was with a girl. He thought she'd gotten out with him, but she didn't. He couldn't get back in. The door locked and he'd lost his key inside. He didn't think you'd believe him.'

'All right,' Olivia murmured. 'Kenny, I need to understand. Why, in God's name, didn't you tell us this when we asked you yesterday?'

Kenny looked away again and Olivia caught the clenching of his jaw. 'Because of Tracey,' he signed. 'She was supposed to be mine. Austin knew.'

Olivia closed her eyes, needing a moment to control the sudden rush of fury. 'You didn't tell us because you were mad at your friend for meeting the girl you liked in the condo?' She spoke very slowly. Kenny shot her an uneasy look as Danni interpreted.

'You said they had sex,' Kenny signed, his face anguished. 'She was mine. Not Austin's. I didn't know she even liked him. She pretended to like me. They must have thought I was pretty funny. Then Austin, wanting me to risk myself, mailing his damn letter. I figured, no.'

'So you never mailed the letter?' Olivia asked, still very slowly.

Kenny shook his head. 'Am I in trouble?'

Am I in trouble? Kane was dead and all this kid cared about was his own skin. *Self-centered, worthless, piece of—* She made herself stop. *He's a teenager. He was angry and scared. He didn't know this would happen. You can't blame him.* But she did.

'I don't know.' She looked away, ran a shaking hand over her hair.

Noah sat beside her. 'Breathe,' he murmured. He'd heard it all. He understood. 'Kenny, what did Austin say the killer looked like?'

'Tall, with brown hair.'

'Old? Young?' Noah pushed gently.

'Not too old, like not as old as our parents. But older than us.' Kenny shook his head. 'It wasn't very specific. I promise I'm not lying.'

Noah drew a breath, let it out carefully. 'Did he sound like he could be the man who grabbed you tonight?'

Kenny's shrug was pained. 'I don't know. I was too scared to look at him.'

'I saw him,' Roger inserted. 'He was maybe six feet tall, not really muscular, but not fat. He had a large nose.'

'We'll have the two of you sit with a police artist,' Noah

said. 'Kenny, do you know how Austin knew about the condo? How he got the key?'

'He had a summer job with a carpenter on the condo. That's how he paid for camp.'

'Do you know the carpenter's name?' Noah asked but Kenny shook his head.

Olivia frowned as a thought occurred to her. 'Does Austin have dark hair?'

'It's brown,' Kenny signed, 'but he dyes it red.'

'Why?' she asked.

'His dad left them,' he signed. 'Austin looks exactly like him and he knew it hurt his mom to look at him. So he changed his hair. It's been red since he was twelve.'

Olivia drew a breath. That emotion she understood. Her own mother had hated Olivia's face because she looked like the man who'd abandoned them. 'All right. We're going to leave a police officer outside the boys' dorm until we're sure it's safe.'

Oaks nodded, relieved. 'Thank you.'

When she and Noah reached her car, Olivia closed her eyes, drained. 'Hell. I can't believe that kid. Kane's dead because Kenny had a crush on a girl.'

'No, Liv. Kane's dead because a sonofabitch shot him twice while trying to kidnap a kid. Kenny's responsible for withholding information, but make him pay for what he did.'

Olivia winced. 'I said that yesterday. To that Crawford asshole.' When he'd lit into Lincoln Jefferson, who actually had done something wrong. 'You're right.'

'I know. So, where do we go from here?'

'Kane and I were going to track down Joel Fischer's friends. And we need to find out what Austin saw, see if he knew Joel or any of his friends. And we need to find Val.'

'She may be dead.'

'I know. But what if she's not? She said she was going to a sub sandwich place three blocks from here. We can start there in the morning, try to trace her last steps.'

Noah opened Olivia's car door and waited for her to get in, crouching next to her. 'How did this guy know about Val?'

She lifted a shoulder. 'I guess he was following us.'

'I guess that's possible. Go to sleep for a few hours. If you need me, call me.'

She nodded. Now that the conversation with Kenny was over, she was dreading going home. It would be too quiet. She wondered where David was, if he was all right. If he was back at the cabin yet. She didn't want to be alone.

She needed to sleep. She needed to be able to breathe again. She needed David.

She found her cell phone in her pocket. Saw that he'd called. That meant he was okay. That was good. Her shoulders relaxed a fraction, suddenly aware that some part of her mind had maintained a constant, nagging worry the words *bad fire* invoked. He was a good firefighter. He'd be careful.

Kane had been careful, too. And now he was dead.

She dialed David's number but got his voice mail. She hung up, unable to form the words she wanted to say. *I need you. Please come.* Simple words, but they opened up a world of hurt. His pillow. She'd been able to smell him there. For tonight, that might have to be enough. She turned her car north and drove.

Wednesday, September 22, 3:20 A.M.

WELCOME TO DULUTH.

Passing the highway sign, he glanced down at his GPS. Only another ten miles and all his worries would be eliminated, along with Austin Dent.

Well, not all his worries. He thought about Mary and Albert's conversation. She was right about their being able to claim he'd Photoshopped them into the video. If anything, the video showed there had been a fifth person there, who'd seen all. If she'd balked at the beginning, it might have made a difference, but Eric hadn't told her. Now he had them in too deep. Still, Mary might just balk if given any more assignments.

In the beginning, he'd planned to expose her naughty arsonist ways, humiliating her daddy. It would destroy the SOB, *like he tried to destroy me*.

But that wasn't enough anymore. Mary had tried to deal a different game, leaving those glass balls behind. She was no environmental activist, not that he'd believed for a moment she ever had been. Now she was a multiple killer. That fire had gone way wrong tonight. He'd listened to the story on the radio until he'd lost the signal. Innocent people had died.

The police weren't going to care for it too much either. Especially given the incident with Detective Kane. The cops would be looking for someone to pay. He'd much rather that someone be Albert or Mary. Or both.

Trouble was, he wasn't exactly sure how to make that happen. He glanced at his GPS again. Almost there. He'd get rid of Austin; then he'd consider his next steps.

Wednesday, September 22, 3:15 A.M.

David showered and changed at the firehouse, called Olivia again only to get her voice mail, then drove to the hospital where Jeff's fiancée, Kayla, sat in the waiting room.

He sat next to her, suddenly afraid to ask her about Jeff. 'Zell?'

'His back is broken, his hip is crushed.' She recited this as if reading a phone book. She was barely holding on. 'He's still in surgery. David, what do I do?'

'Be there for him, for now. Did you talk to him before they took him to surgery?'

'No. He wasn't conscious. He won't walk again, will he?'

'You don't know that. A broken back doesn't mean paralysis. And even if that's the case, people come back from injuries like that. My brother did,' he added.

'The same as before?' she asked through her tears.

'No,' he said honestly. 'Max was a professional athlete. It ended his career. But he found a new one and if Zell comes to that place, he will, too.'

She shuddered on a sob. 'God, I'm sorry.'

He slid his arm around her shaking shoulders. 'Why?'

'Because I'm sitting here, wishing he'd pulled you out.'

It startled him, but for just a moment. 'I can understand that. My . . .' *What is Olivia?* 'My friend's a cop. Her partner died tonight. I'm . . . I don't know. I can't believe he's gone, but I'm relieved she wasn't there when the shooting happened. So I understand.'

She wiped her face with her fingers. 'You're on shift soon, aren't you?'

He glanced up at the clock on the wall. 'In a couple hours, yeah.'

'Then get some sleep. I'll tell him you were here. Thank you. I do mean that.'

His heart heavy, he walked back to his car, checking his phone as he walked. He frowned, recognizing the number. Noah. Who was watching over his mother.

'Noah, what's wrong with Ma?'

'Nothing. As far as I know, she's asleep.'

'What do mean, as far as you know? Where are you?'

'Following Olivia who just exited north. I'm headed into the precinct. Did you hear?'

'About Kane, yeah. How is Olivia? I tried to call, but she wasn't picking up.'

'She's holding, barely. I told her to go home, but the exit she took wasn't hers. She's headed north.'

North. Relief flooded him. *She's coming to me.* 'I know where she's going.'

'I thought you might. Look, try to keep her from calling in.'

'Why? What's wrong?'

'We have the name of the kid we're looking for – the one who saw Weems get shot. Kid's supposed to be home in Duluth, but the state cops just called to say they can't find the kid. Looks like he saw them coming and bolted through a rear window. We hope.'

'You hope?'

'Olivia knows Kane's shooter has the kid's address. If she finds out he's gone . . .'

'She'll drive up there to look for him.'

'Exactly. She's hanging on by a thread. She needs to rest.'

'She's not gonna like that you decided that for her,' David said quietly.

'You gonna tell her?'

'If she asks, I won't lie, but I won't offer. If you're working, who's watching Ma?'

'She called that old firefighter friend of yours.'

'Okay, thanks.' This was becoming weird, his mother and Glenn. But his focus right now was Olivia. *She's coming to me.* He wanted to fix it so that she wouldn't leave any time soon. With a grimace for the late hour, he dialed Paige, unsurprised when she answered on the first ring. 'Where are you?'

'At Olivia's, waiting for her to get home. Where are you? Did you hear about Kane? Do you know where she is? I'm worried sick.'

'I'm headed up to the cabin. I think she's gone up there. And yeah, I heard. I don't know if she's got anything for work tomorrow. You know, clothes. Makeup. Stuff.'

'I'll pack her a bag,' Paige said. 'You want me to bring it up there?'

'No. Her house isn't too far out of the way. I'll swing by to pick it up.'

David hung up. He had one more call to make. He pictured Paige waiting for Olivia to come home and pictured his own mom, waiting by the phone. He hit the speed dial for Eve and Noah's house. Sure enough, it was answered almost before it rang.

'David?' It was his mother and her voice was shaking.

'I'm okay, Ma. Not a scratch.'

Her breath shuddered out. 'Thank God. I've been sitting here, trying not to worry. Glenn's been on his cellular phone, trying to find out what's going on.'

'I'm fine. My partner, Jeff, not so good.' And Olivia's

partner is dead, he almost added, but didn't. His mother had never met Kane, and Eve needed to hear that news from Noah. 'If you would, say some prayers for him.'

'Of course I will. Where are you going now?'

'Up to the cabin.' To Olivia. 'I'm going to try to get some sleep. You do the same. Love you, Ma.'

'And I love you. Thank you for calling me. I needed to hear your voice.'

Wednesday, September 22, 4:00 A.M.

This was bad. Really, really bad. The kid was gone. There had to be twenty police cars parked on the highway shoulder, on either side of the driveway that led to Austin Dent's tiny house. He'd passed by slowly, watching the action.

State and local cops congregated in groups and as he looked in his rearview mirror, he could see the crisscrossing beams of flashlights as search parties took to the woods. That meant they didn't have him either. Yet.

The boy was on the run, obviously not trusting the cops. Smart kid.

He kept going until he could no longer see the blue glow of flashing cop car lights, then pulled onto the shoulder, opened Kenny's phone, and started a text to Austin.

Cops grilled me all night in Oaks's office. He didn't know if that was true or not, but Austin wouldn't know it either. *They know about u. Want to arrest u. B careful.*

He closed the phone. That would keep the kid from trusting the cops a little longer. He could search for the kid, but who knew where he was? He did a U-turn and headed back the way he'd come. *I need to bring him to me.*

Wednesday, September 22, 4:05 A.M.

Olivia heard David's truck coming up the road but didn't get up. She sat at the end of his dock, her knees pulled to her chest. She heard his truck cut off and waited. Eventually he'd come outside. She wondered if he knew about Kane.

After leaving the school she hadn't had the energy to listen to any of her voice mails. She'd simply sat here, listening to the sounds of the night. After a few minutes she felt the dock rumble as he approached. He ran his hand over her hair. 'Hey.'

'Hey.' It came out a whisper.

He took her hands. 'Your hands are like ice. Why are you sitting out here?'

'I locked your house when I left earlier. I forgot I didn't have a key.'

'I can fix that,' he murmured. 'I wish I could fix everything else.'

'You can't. Nobody can.'

'Come inside. I'll get you warm.' He lifted her to her feet, his arm solid around her. 'I couldn't let you be alone.' In the cabin's living room he swung her up into his arms and settled her in his lap on the sofa, covering them with a blanket.

'I need to be in by eight,' she said. 'I have to go home and get clothes first.'

'No, Paige packed you a bag. Just rest.' He pointed the remote at the TV, and the screen came to life. It was her Road Runner DVD. Surprised, her eyes shot up to his and he kissed her forehead. 'I found it in your DVD player. That night we talked, you told me you watched cartoons to destress. I figured we could both use that tonight.'

She nodded once, but a sob barreled up and she had nothing left to force it back down. He pulled her closer, his cheek on top of her head, rocking her where they sat as the deluge poured out. Sobs and curses and vows of horrible revenge. Finally the storm ebbed and she was left shaken. Too hollowed out to feel anything but despair.

He threaded his hand through her hair, cradling her. 'Sleep now, baby.'

'In the morning Kane will still be dead,' she whispered.

'Yes, but your mind needs to be sharp to find the man who did it.'

'I want him dead. I want him to bleed and suffer. I want to watch while he does.'

'So do I.'

There was something in his voice. Grim certainty, but also pain. She pulled back far enough to see his face. He stared straight ahead, his jaw set. 'What happened?'

'Go to sleep.' He tried to urge her back against him, but she pulled free.

'What happened?' she repeated more forcefully. 'Tell me.'

'The fire tonight was set.'

Her mind clicked through the events of the night. 'Woodview. Noah said it was where Tomlinson's mistress lived. Was that the target? Did you find a glass ball?'

'No glass ball, but the mistress's house was the target. Except the wind shifted, taking houses on both sides. A gas-tank explosion leveled two more houses. Then the fire spread to an apartment building.'

403

'How many?' she asked quietly.

'Four dead.' Anguish flashed in his eyes. 'Including a child. She was only two.'

She pressed her lips to his jaw. 'I'm sorry.'

'Dozens more were hurt,' he said, his voice too even.

'Firefighters?'

'Zell,' he said roughly. 'A beam fell on him. He can't feel his legs.'

She flinched, seeing it all too clearly. 'Who got him out?' she asked, although she knew the answer and it scared her senseless.

'I did.' He closed his eyes. 'I dragged him out. What if I made it worse?'

'And if you hadn't dragged him out, he'd be dead.'

Now that she'd shed a layer of grief, she could really look at him. He was exhausted and heart sore . . . *just like me*. 'Let's go to bed. You need to rest, too.'

Wearily he followed her, taking her suitcase. 'Paige packed your Tweety PJs.'

On autopilot, she put them on in the bathroom, then found him in bed, their cell phones side by side on the nightstand. Drawing her close, his fingers pulled the band from her braid and started working her hair free. 'I like it loose,' he murmured, then slid his hand up under the nightshirt, cupping her breast as he'd done before.

Her heart still hurt and her chest was still tight. 'I needed you,' she whispered, finding it easier to say so in the darkness. 'Just to be with me.'

'That I can do.' He pressed a kiss to her shoulder. 'I have a question.'

'What?'

'Do you really wear these PJs or was Paige just causing trouble?'

Her lips tipped up sadly, so glad he was there. 'The second one. Unless it's below zero, I usually sleep in my skin.' He, obviously, did as well.

His fingers were already freeing buttons. 'I like feeling your skin against mine.' In less than a minute he had her naked and cocooned in his arms. 'Now I can sleep.'

Chapter Twenty-One

Wednesday, September 22, 4:30 A.M.

David couldn't sleep. He lay there holding her, pictures flashing behind his clenched eyes. Zell pinned, Kane dead. *It could have been her.* In the cacophony of his thoughts, it was the one that screamed louder than all the rest.

She wasn't asleep either. She lay stiff in his arms, her breathing shallow. She shuddered out a breath and he touched his lips to her cheek, wet with tears. 'Hey.'

'I keep seeing him there,' she whispered, her voice choked. 'In the grass. I can't believe this happened.'

He turned her in his arms and her fists clenched against his chest before her hands splayed flat, her fingers digging into his skin as another barrage of sobs tore through her. 'It's okay,' he murmured. 'Cry if you need to. I won't leave you.' He stroked her hair until her sobs quieted and her breath hitched.

She rubbed her palm over his chest, swiping at the tears. 'I got you all wet.'

'I don't mind.'

'I need to think.'

'No, honey. You need to grieve, and that's a long road. Kane was a good man, a good cop. He was your partner.

You spent more time together than most people do with their spouse. He had your back and you trusted him. You loved him.'

'Yes.' It was a hoarse whisper. 'I didn't cry like this when my mother died.'

He heard the guilt in her voice. 'You're not a bad daughter because you didn't.'

She lifted her head, peered at him in the darkness. 'What?'

'You're feeling guilty because you're grieving Kane more intensely than your mother, right?'

She nodded, tears falling again. 'She was my mother. I mean I cried, but this is different. I feel like my heart's being ripped out of me. What kind of daughter does that make me, if not a bad one?'

'That night in Chicago, you told me you missed her, that you loved her.'

'I did?'

'Yeah, you did. But I get the impression that things between you were never easy.'

She lowered her head to his shoulder with a sigh. 'No, they weren't. She loved me, I know she did. But I never seemed to make her happy. I could never do anything right. And sometimes she'd look at me like she hated me. I never understood why until I saw Mia for the first time.'

'At your father's funeral.'

'I rushed to Chicago as soon as I heard he'd died and got there just in time for the burial. Mia was wearing her dress blues, standing next to the coffin with her mother. The cops folded the flag and gave it to the wife, then she turned and almost shoved the flag into Mia's arms. I remember standing there, hating them both so much. Then Mia looked up and I couldn't breathe. It was like looking in a mirror.'

KAREN ROSE

'She was pretty shaken, too.'

'I know. It was at that moment I realized we must both look like our father.'

'You didn't know what he looked like?'

'I never even knew his name. My mother never talked about him. When I was little, I'd imagine what he was like. I'd wonder if he was walking around somewhere with amnesia or something. I couldn't understand why he didn't want me.'

David had to swallow hard, picturing her as a child. 'My parents loved each other and they loved us. I'll always be grateful for that. I'm sorry you didn't have that.'

'Thanks. I'm glad you're grateful. I used to get so mad at kids who hated their fathers for something stupid, like not getting a car or clothes. I just wanted to have a dad. When I got older, I badgered my mother to tell me about him. Finally accused her of not telling him I existed. That's when she lost her temper and told me that he was a cop in Chicago. He was married. He'd lied to her, said his wife had left him. That he'd promised to marry her when I was born. Then when I was, he decided to stay with his other family. His wife and kids. I didn't know his name or theirs, but I hated them all.'

'How did you find out he'd died?'

'From my mother's sister. I tried so many times to get my mother to tell me his name, but she wouldn't. It was a big area of contention between us. Finally, she died without telling me. I thought I'd never know. But then I got a call from my aunt, who saw his obituary. My mother had confided in her, years ago. Made her promise not to tell me, but my aunt knew I needed the closure.' Her voice hardened. 'Then I met Mia and found out I was better off

408

with no father than the father she'd lived with. I was glad he didn't want me then.'

'That was a hard few weeks for you,' he murmured and she lifted her head again.

'What do you mean?'

He hesitated. 'I know about Doug. How he left.'

'Who told you?' Then her eyes narrowed. 'Barlow. Damn his meddling.'

'I asked first. For what it's worth, he feels horrible. When I heard the story, so did I.' She looked down, saying nothing and he felt compelled to fill the silence. 'Olivia, your ex was an ass. But even though I know he hurt you, I'm glad he left. I'm glad I met you. I know you don't believe me, but I'd been waiting for you. Maybe my whole life.'

She finally looked up, her eyes filled with hurt. 'Then why did you say her name?'

He sighed. 'I don't know. Maybe I'll never know. I do know that I only drank too much twice in my life. Once eighteen years ago, and then, that night with you. Maybe I was scared. I met you and I knew. I knew you were special. Maybe too special. It was like you could see inside me, and I didn't want anyone that close.'

'Because they'd find out what you didn't want anyone to know.'

He nodded. 'Olivia, Dana was never more than a fantasy. She made things happen, she stood for the same people I'd been working to help for years. She was a crusader. But I never had anything else in common with her. We never stayed up all night talking about everything under the sun. I certainly never told her about Megan. I don't know why I said her name that night. I can only tell you that after I met you, I couldn't get you out of my mind.'

She held his eyes in the darkness. 'And if she were to suddenly become free?'

And come back, like her fiancé's old love had. 'I wouldn't go. Because I'm not free. I wasn't from the moment I met you.' He traced his fingertips over her cheek, her lips. 'You might not believe that now. But if you give me time, heart, trust . . . you will.'

Her lips curved, so slightly he might have missed it had he not been so focused on her face. 'Helluva line, David.'

'No line. You'll see. I'll show you.' He cradled her head in his palm and pulled her back to his chest. 'Go to sleep. I'll be here when you wake up.'

Wednesday, September 22, 6:25 A.M.

He pulled into his parking place behind the Deli, annoyed. Austin hadn't texted back and Kenny's cell phone account had been frozen. He entered through the kitchen to find his staff already at work preparing breakfast sandwiches. He grunted a greeting and they grunted right back, just as they did every morning. Important to keep a routine in case anyone became suspicious.

He'd left his hat behind. He still couldn't get over that stupidity.

He switched on the television behind the counter and stood watching the news. Last night's fire was big news. Four dead. Several injured, including a firefighter. Then came the bomb scare at the school and the death of Detective Kane.

He made a mental note to cut back on his pastrami order.

The next segment was Captain Abbott delivering a

message to Austin, complete with interpreter, begging Austin to contact them. *My priority is finding Austin before the cops do.* Using one of his disposable cells, he entered Austin's number.

It's Kenny. New account. Cops took old fon. Where r u? I have place you can hide.

He hit SEND, then started another. *Cops ?ed me all night. Know about u. I didn't tell, swear. They lie. Don't trust them.* And he hit SEND again.

He closed his phone, slipped it in his pocket. He wouldn't panic. If the cops knew about him, they'd have been here waiting in full SWAT gear. He clipped his mike tuner to his belt, put the bud in his ear and hoped Austin checked his messages soon.

Wednesday, September 22, 7:00 A.M.

Olivia must have slept because a trilling cell phone alarm woke her up. She lay spooned against David, not opening her eyes as he reached over her to silence the alarm. He ran his hand up her arm, cupping her neck and massaging the base of her skull with his thumb. 'We have to get up.'

The events of the night replayed in her mind and a wave of raw grief washed over her. 'I don't want to,' she whispered. 'This hurts.'

'He was a good man. A good cop. You loved him. It's going to hurt.'

Her eyes burned. Stubbornly she held them closed. 'Can we pretend it's not morning for five more minutes? Please?'

'Sure.' His voice was husky but sweet and suddenly not what she needed.

411

He'd put distance between their bodies and she knew why. She pressed back against him, feeling him hard and ready.

'I'm sorry,' he murmured. 'I can't help it, though. Not when I wake up with you.'

Last night she'd maneuvered around her own grief. Now she needed him to make the day go away, for just a few minutes more.

'David, if last night hadn't happened, how would you have woken me up?'

She heard the sudden intake of his breath. 'I'd be inside you.' And then he was, hard and full, stretching her, making her gasp. 'Like that.' He splayed one big hand across her abdomen to pull her closer, pushing deeper.

'And then?' she whispered.

'And then I'd ride you hard.' And he did, making her moan, writhe. Beg for more. His pace was fast and furious and when his thumb found her most sensitive place she went up like a rocket, light bursting against her closed eyelids. He followed with a groan, his body going rigid, his hands gripping her hips as he ground himself into her.

They lay shuddering together, panting like sprinters. Later she might worry over how he'd gotten so good, but for now she was grateful he'd pushed the day away a few more minutes.

Her breathing returned to normal, bringing with it the knowledge she could put the day off no longer. They both had jobs to do. She opened her eyes, their two cell phones on the nightstand the first thing she saw.

And something clicked.

'He takes their cell phones,' she murmured and felt David stiffen in surprise.

He leaned up on his elbow and stared down at her. 'Excuse me?'

She looked up at him urgently. 'This guy takes their cell phones. Tomlinson, Val, and now Kenny. He's taken all of their phones.'

'Why?'

'I don't know yet.' She pulled him down for a hard kiss. 'I have to go.' She rolled to sit on the edge of the bed, then stopped, another truth asserting itself. She looked over her shoulder, saw he'd realized it, too. 'We, um, forgot something this time.'

His gray eyes were intense, even though his cheeks had reddened beneath his morning stubble. 'You're safe with me, Olivia.'

Her own cheeks heated. It was an awkward conversation, to say the least. 'Me too. They checked me six ways to Tuesday when I donated my kidney to Mia, and there hasn't been anyone since. But . . . I'm not on the Pill. I should have been more careful.'

Still lying on his side, he ran his palm lightly down her arm, intertwining his fingers with hers. 'I waited for you for a long time. I'm not walking away.'

She swallowed. 'It's just . . . I grew up without a father. I should have been careful.'

'I understand that,' he said steadily. 'But I'm not walking away.' He pressed a kiss to her palm. 'Now go, get in the shower or we'll both be late for work.'

Wednesday, September 22, 7:30 A.M.

Austin Dent opened his eyes. The sun was up. He'd slept a little. Worried a lot.

413

His mom would be worried sick, even though she'd been the first and only text he'd sent when he got away. *I'm ok. Borrowed your car. Didn't do anything wrong. Sorry.*

His heart still thundered when he remembered watching the police car pull into his driveway. *Run.* Cell in hand, he'd grabbed a hoodie from a chair and escaped through his bedroom window. He'd run through the woods, not looking back until he'd come to a neighbor's house. The neighbor had left a bicycle outside and he'd taken it, riding as fast as he could to the truck-stop diner where his mother slung hash all night. Her car was there. Luckily, his keys and wallet had been in his pockets when he'd run.

He'd taken her car, driving north, intending to slip across the Canadian border.

But what good would that do? That was crazy thinking. He needed to find a way to make this stop. He needed to think. He'd needed to sleep. Luckily there were more places to hide up here in the northern woods than anywhere he knew. He'd tucked the car into a clearing and managed to get a little rest.

But now the sun was up and he needed to make some choices. *Where do I go? Who do I trust?* He picked up his cell phone. He'd removed the battery while he slept, not really sure if anyone could use it to find him.

He replaced the battery, then blinked when he saw all the texts. People had been trying to reach him for hours. His mother. *Trust the police.*

Kenny. *Believe the police.*

The police. *We're not going to hurt you.*

And Kenny again. *Cops took old fon. They lie. Don't trust them.*

Austin turned off his phone, scared and confused, but

knowing nothing was going to change if he sat here. Answers were in Minneapolis. So that's where he'd go.

Wednesday, September 22, 8:00 A.M.

David was surprised to find Tom waiting for him in the firehouse lounge. His nephew lurched to his feet, his face bent in a frown. 'Are you okay?' Tom asked.

David signed in and headed straight for the coffee. 'Hard night, but I'm fine.'

'I heard on the TV about Zell. Any news?'

'I called the hospital on my way in. They said he was unchanged.' David poured them both cups of coffee and handed one to Tom. 'I guess we won't know anything for a day or two. You remember Detective Kane, Olivia's partner?'

Tom nodded, his frown deepening. 'I heard it on the news. They said he was saving some kid from getting kidnapped.'

'Which is all mixed up in this glass-ball craziness.' And that a ball had not been found at last night's scene had been nagging at him.

'Poor Olivia. She's got to be crushed.'

'She is, but she'll stand.' *And so will I.* She'd turned to him that morning, needing him. He'd been afraid that in the light of day he'd see contempt in her eyes. But she'd taken the worst secret he owned and put it in the past. He'd find a way to do the same.

'I know. But still . . .' Tom sighed. 'I've got a nine o'clock class, so I don't have much time. I found a few things on that website we talked about. Can we talk here?'

It was very quiet in the firehouse that morning, the

mood depressed, common when one of their own was injured. Everyone was going about their business and nobody was paying attention to them. 'Good a place as any. What do you have?'

'The website's domain name is registered to a guy named Hubert Leeds, established ten years ago.'

'Two years after the last Moss fire. Who is Hubert Leeds?'

'Professor Leeds. Taught at the same university as Moss. They were pals, according to a few articles I found.'

'Taught? Leeds retired?'

'No, he's dead. Died of an aneurysm eight years ago.'

'So the website just lived on?'

'Not exactly. I'm not sure when the content was uploaded – you know, the speeches, the recordings, the pictures of Moss. But somebody has been renewing the domain registration. You can't just let your URL expire or somebody could snap it up and use it for their own website. It was last renewed six months ago – and registered out for nine years. That's the max.'

'Who paid for it?'

'Good question. That would have required a little deeper digging than I was comfortable doing. Credit cards and things like that.'

'So we're going to need help,' David said unhappily and Tom shrugged.

'Ethan's not a bad guy, David.'

'I know, I know. Never mind. What else did you find?'

Tom's brows lifted. 'You're welcome.'

David smiled. 'Thank you. What else did you find?'

'I got into the website pretty easily. I figured somebody had to be updating it and it was just as likely to be that Lincoln Jefferson guy as anyone. I played with usernames and passwords until I got it right. Didn't take long. His username is AbeThomas, all one word. And three guesses to his password.'

'*Valla Eam*,' David said.

'You got it. I'm betting Lincoln worked with Professor Leeds to build the site. The professor probably gave him access to all the admin stuff – the registration, the site itself. Then when he died, Lincoln kept it.'

'While he grew crazier and crazier,' David said. 'So this website has been sitting there all this time? Don't you have to pay for server space?'

'This one's hosted at one of these freebie places. The account's in Leeds's name. I checked hit activity and the site had a low level of visitors for the first half of last year. The real activity started last April, right about when the domain was renewed.'

'So who's been visiting?'

Tom drew a sheet of paper from his pocket. 'Names I was able to track. The rest are IP addresses I couldn't track. You're back to asking Ethan for help on those.'

David read the list, then frowned at a name that kept appearing over and over again. 'This name I know. Joel Fischer. Why do I know that name?' He closed his eyes, concentrating. 'Oh yeah, I remember now. It was Monday when I was listening to the news reports on the condo fire. Joel Fischer died on Monday. Car accident.'

'I remember him now, too.' Tom looked thoughtful. 'He went to the university. The heavy Web traffic in April was probably research for a spring semester class.'

He was at the fire, David thought. Then he'd driven his car off the road, unable to deal with the guilt. Joel's home was the visit Olivia had made right before she'd come to the cabin last night, before everything hit the fan. 'He's important.'

'And you're not going to tell me how,' Tom said flatly. 'Uncool, David.'

David leaned over, murmuring, 'He was at the condo fire, okay?'

Tom's brows shot up. 'Really? He doesn't seem like a smart criminal, then. He didn't try to hide his visits to this site and he visited a lot. Of course, hits to the site have gone off the charts since yesterday when the story of the glass ball broke.'

Olivia needed the information, but David wasn't sure how he'd tell her where he got it. He scanned the list again. There was a name that was noticeably absent.

'Lincoln's name isn't anywhere,' David said thoughtfully. 'No wonder that Fed was so pissed. Lincoln's been there, right under their noses for twelve years, keeping up the website. But they had to have known Professor Leeds had died. Why not investigate?'

'If no new content was added after Leeds died, they may have assumed it was a static site. Maybe they stopped checking it. That's all I got. Talk to Ethan about the credit card payment for the domain re-up. He has ways of tracking stuff.'

'I don't think all his ways of "tracking stuff" are completely legal,' David murmured.

'So? You want legal or you want to keep Grandma safe at your loft?'

'You're right. I'll give Ethan a call. Thanks for your help, kid.'

'Anytime.' Tom gave him a quick one-armed hug, then stepped back, amused. 'You need to lay off the honeysuckle perfume, David. People will talk.'

David's cheeks heated. Olivia had jumped into the shower without her shampoo. He'd pulled back the curtain to give it to her and found her crying, a new wave of grief having hit when she'd found herself alone. He'd held her while she cried, washed her hair because he knew the massage calmed her. Then one thing had led to another and he'd made the day go away one more time.

Tom barked a laugh. 'You should see your face. I have to get to class. Call me if you need me.' He handed David a card. 'Ethan's cell.'

David took the card. 'Thank you. I mean it.'

'No problem. Grandma's still with Evie?' Tom asked and David nodded.

'Yeah. Noah had to work last night, after Kane . . .' He sighed. 'Anyway, she called Glenn and he stayed there during the night. I assume he's still there.'

'I guess it's about time for Grandma, too. She's been alone a long time.'

It still made him wince. 'Yes, she has.'

Tom shrugged. 'Hey, I had to watch *my* mom fall for *your* brother.'

'But it turned out okay.'

'Sure it did. And this will, too. You shouldn't be complaining. If he's good enough to be your friend, then he's okay for your mom.'

'You're right. Hey, you know you could have called me with all this information.'

'I know,' Tom said. 'But I saw the fire on the news during the night and heard one of the firefighters was hurt. Grandma called me, told me it wasn't you, but—' he shrugged uncomfortably. 'Guess I needed to see for myself that you were all right.'

David felt his throat close once again. 'Well, I am. Get to class. And thanks.'

419

Chapter Twenty-Two

Wednesday, September 22, 8:00 A.M.

Olivia stood outside the doors to the police department, her fedora in her hand. On her way out of David's cabin she'd seen it on the sofa and picked it up on a whim. No, not a whim. A talisman maybe. But she hadn't been able to put it on her head.

She was late but couldn't make her hand reach for the door. She didn't want to go inside. Didn't want to see Kane's desk or Abbott's round table. Didn't want to see the looks of sadness on everyone's faces. *Just get through today.* Easier said than done.

'Good morning, Detective.' It was Dr Donahue.

Great. The department-mandated shrink smelled blood in the water. 'Good morning,' Olivia said and if she sounded a little curt, so be it. *I have stuff on my mind.*

'Contrary to what you think, Detective, I'm not here to analyze you. I'm here for Abbott's meeting.' She brushed by and, too late, Olivia realized her eyes had been red.

Olivia followed. 'Dr Donahue.' The shrink kept walking, face averted. 'Jess. Wait.'

Donahue stopped, dug in her pocket for a tissue. 'Can I help you, Detective?'

For a moment Olivia didn't know what to say, then searched her purse for a compact, handing it to Donahue. 'Damage control.'

Donahue swept powder under her eyes, but it was a token effort. 'Thanks.'

Olivia dropped the compact in her purse, then drew a breath. 'I can't go up there.'

Donahue's gaze was level. 'Yes, you can. You have to.'

'I have to get through today.' The words made her sneer.

'As trite as that sounds, yes. Detective . . . Olivia, nobody said this would be easy.'

Olivia looked at the elevator, watched people getting on. Knew if she got on with them, she'd go into full panic mode. She looked back at Donahue, whose eyes had softened with understanding.

'Let's take the stairs,' Donahue said. 'Fewer people can see my face like this.'

Grateful for the excuse, Olivia followed her. They'd climbed two flights when Olivia stopped. Donahue paused on the next stair and looked down, waiting.

'I'm afraid of crime scenes,' she heard herself admit. 'Afraid to look at the bodies.'

Donahue looked unsurprised. 'Was that so hard to say?'

Olivia swallowed hard. 'Yes. So was that the hard part?'

Donahue's mouth curved. 'Hell, no. The hard part's moving on, but at least now we can get to work. First, though, we have to get up these stairs.'

And past his desk. Olivia stared at the hat in her hand. And put it on her head.

'Nice,' Donahue murmured. 'Very Ingrid Bergman.'

Olivia pursed her lips, a new sob threatening to rip her

in two. She gripped the handrail until it passed. Until she could breathe again. Then she made her feet move.

The bull pen was eerily quiet. In front of her, Donahue moved like a soldier, eyes forward, feet almost marching. Olivia followed until she came to Kane's desk. She made herself look at it, made herself remember all that blood on the ground. Then squared her shoulders and went into Abbott's office where everyone was waiting.

'So what do we have?' Olivia asked briskly, taking the seat next to Noah. 'Has Austin Dent been transported down here yet?'

Noah hesitated. 'No. He's gone.'

Olivia slowly turned to stare at Noah's profile. 'He's what?'

'Gone,' Abbott said. 'State police got to his house last night and found he'd left through a back window. We've had an all-out hunt for this kid for the last four hours.'

A spurt of fury geysered inside her. 'And you didn't *tell* me?'

'My decision,' Noah said. 'You needed to sleep. Gut me later, but I'd do it again.'

'I backed him,' Abbott said quietly. 'There wasn't anything you could have done. We're sweeping fields, doing road stops. Every agency is searching.'

'Who is Austin Dent,' Donahue asked, 'and why did he run?'

Abbott quickly brought the doctor up to speed while Olivia's mind raced.

'The shooter has Kenny's phone,' she said. 'He used Val's phone to text me so I'd think she was okay. He could have lured Austin away. He could have him right now.' She looked over at Abbott. 'He takes their cell phones. Tomlinson, Val, and Kenny.'

Barlow looked up then. 'And Dorian Blunt's. We haven't found his phone yet.'

She looked around the table, saw this wasn't a new name to the rest of them and tried to stow her annoyance. 'Who?'

'He was found in the house that was the arson target last night,' Barlow said. 'At least we're pretty sure it's him. Ian's going to get dental records this morning.'

'Why do you think it's him?' Olivia asked. 'And who is he?'

'Because we found his wallet in his pants,' Barlow said. 'His license was buried in a stack of credit cards. The edges were all melted together, but when the lab separated them out, we could make out his name.'

'He's an accountant,' Noah said. 'His wife said he went out to meet with a client last night and never came back. She didn't know where the meeting was or who the client was. She said that he seemed desperate when he left, that their savings are drying up and they've got a lot of debt. She hadn't heard of Tomlinson, had no idea why her husband would have been in that house. So far we don't have a connection to Tomlinson or Rankin and Sons.'

'Lots of debt, just like Tomlinson,' Olivia said. 'Did they use gasoline?'

Barlow nodded. 'Outside, but not on him, just like Tomlinson. He was found sitting at a desk in a home office. He was face down.'

'Back of the head with a hollow-point?' Olivia asked, trying not to think of Kane.

'Yes,' Micki said. 'Slug is in ballistics.'

But it would be a match. Olivia had no doubt. 'He's been a busy bastard,' she said coldly. 'Three in one day, assuming he got to Val. Kenny would have made it four. What have we done to communicate with Austin?'

'His mother has sent him texts, telling him that he's not in trouble,' Noah said. 'We had Kenny send one, too, from a new account. We canceled Kenny's old account so that the "busy bastard" can't use it. I woke up the construction manager at Rankin and asked him to get me the names of all the carpenters who'd worked on the condo. We called until we found the one who'd employed Austin last summer. We had that guy send a text, too. We've tried to get everyone he might trust to tell him to contact the police, that he's in danger and not in trouble.'

'So, everything anyone could do,' she said quietly. 'Everything I would have done.'

'We even had Bruce record a personal message, and we sat a sign language interpreter next to him,' Noah said. 'Hopefully Austin's still alive to see it.'

'And Kenny?' she asked.

'His parents are here,' Abbott said. 'They've agreed to stay in a safe house until we can arrange for more long-term protection or until we catch the busy bastard.'

'Has anyone talked to him again? He was in the guy's van. Maybe just a minute, but maybe he saw something that could help us.'

'Not yet,' Noah said. 'We can do that today, you and I.'

'Okay.' She looked down at the table, tried to organize her thoughts. 'The hat you found at the scene last night. The one the shooter left behind. Anything?'

'Yes,' Micki said. 'A few hairs and face putty around the hat's brim.'

'He changed his face,' Olivia said. 'So even if we got a sketch artist with the dorm staffer or Kenny, it wouldn't be accurate. Joel Fischer was at the condo fire, but he was dead before the Tomlinson fire. Let's find out who he hung with. What did you find in his bedroom?'

'The glue on the shoes is definitely the carpet-padding adhesive used to start the condo fire,' Micki said. 'He was there, in the condo.'

'And he was hit on the head,' Olivia said. 'Just like Weems. I think they carried him away from the condo because he was unconscious.'

'Which would explain only one set of tracks at the fence,' Micki murmured.

'Different agendas,' Donahue said thoughtfully. 'Joel changed his mind.'

'Kane and I thought so,' Olivia said and the room went silent. She dropped her eyes for a moment, waited until her chest eased, then lifted her eyes and forged on. 'Kane found a note stuck in one of Joel's textbooks. It was from a girl and it was signed "M." He also had a friend named Eric Marsh. Maybe either this girl or Eric know who Joel might have fallen in with. What did you find on his cell phone and his laptop?'

Micki frowned. 'We didn't find a laptop in his room. Or a cell phone.'

'He would have had the cell phone with him when he died,' Noah said. 'The morgue didn't send one over with his clothes?'

Micki shook her head. 'No, I'm certain they didn't. No cell phone.'

'Let's go to Joel's classes,' Olivia said, 'see who he knew. He should be buried today. Maybe his friends will come to the service.'

'I had the cadaver dog at the fire scene last night,' Barlow said. 'The dog's handler is the daughter of the vet who took the guard dog from Tomlinson's. Brie said the dog's going to pull through.'

'One bonus,' Olivia said, her smile wan.

'Oh.' Micki searched through her folder. 'I got the lab results on the dog. He was given oxycodone. A lot of it.'

Olivia frowned. 'Really? That's what Ian found in Joel. Joel OD'd on oxy.'

'We didn't find any evidence of drugs in Joel's room,' Micki said. 'We vacuumed every surface and haven't gone through the dust yet, but there were no visible signs. There were no pill bottles in his car either.'

'Somebody else had the pills,' Olivia said, 'because they gave them to the dog Monday night. What if Joel didn't take them voluntarily either?'

'Sounds like we need to start with Ian,' Noah said. 'Find out if it's possible to know how he ingested the oxy that killed him.'

Olivia winced. 'The Fischers won't be happy if we further delay Joel's service, but if we can show he was drugged, it might ease their minds.'

'You two focus on Joel. I'll talk to Kenny,' Abbott said.

'What about Val?' Olivia asked. 'We need to find her. Her family deserves that.'

'I'll send Jack Phelps and Sam Wyatt,' Abbott said. 'Where should they start?'

'She said she always went to a sub shop, three blocks from the school. It makes sense that the man who . . . who shot Kane, also took Val. He was focused on finding out what we knew about Austin Dent.'

'We'll trace her last movements, but we may not find her till we find him,' Abbott said. 'So go find him.' He put up his hand when they all moved to go. 'Everybody wears vests. Everywhere you go. No arguments. Be careful.'

Outside Abbott's office, Noah placed his hat on his head and after a moment's hesitation Olivia did the same. 'Don't tell me it's very Ingrid Bergman,' she warned.

Noah's mouth curved sadly. 'I was going to say Kane would approve.'

Olivia gave him a hard nod. 'Let's get this done.'

Wednesday, September 22, 9:30 A.M.

David had cleared his maintenance duty list, cooked breakfast for the team, called the hospital once again to check on Jeff – no change – and cleaned the kitchen.

There were no more tasks keeping him from calling Dana's husband. With a sigh and an inward curse at his own issues, he pulled out the card Tom had given him and stepped out into the truck bay, half hoping for the station's call tone to peal.

Ethan Buchanan answered on the first ring, almost as if he'd been expecting the call. 'What can I do for you, David?' he asked.

'I guess I want to hire you,' David said, rubbing a tense muscle in his neck.

'Don't make me hurt you, Hunter. What do you need, for God's sake?'

That was better. Warm and fuzzy would have been way too awkward and former Marine Ethan Buchanan was one of the few who could have delivered on that threat.

'I had an intruder yesterday.' He explained the situation to Ethan who said nothing until he was finished. 'I want to know who helped this guy, because I don't want to worry about anyone coming back and hurting anyone in my building. The idea of insane zealots with guns being angry with me has me a little rattled.'

'I understand. I felt that way over in the Gulf,' Ethan said wryly, 'and I had bigger guns. How are the cops involved?'

'The cops have bigger problems. They don't have the resources to work this right now. Except that I know that one of the website visitors is on Olivia's radar – Joel Fischer. He died two days ago. Drove his car off the road and into a couple trees.'

'Why's he on Olivia's radar?'

'He was at the first fire.'

'Got it. So we'll be giving her what we turn up?'

'I don't know. Will we get arrested?'

'You wound me. We can make an anonymous contribution. Usually all we provide is a lead versus solid proof for a jury. E-mail me the phone numbers you couldn't trace. Give me a few hours. I'll call you.'

'Thanks, man.' The call siren squealed. 'I have to go, we have a call. I'll send the phone numbers when I get back. Thanks, Ethan.'

Wednesday, September 22, 9:45 A.M.

Austin nodded to a man coming out of the gas station convenience store as he went in. He was down to twenty bucks, which wouldn't buy much. Luckily his mom kept her tank filled. He had enough fuel to make it the rest of the way.

He grabbed a cola, trying to play it cool even as he wondered if anyone was saying anything behind him. If someone was calling the cops this minute. Then he lifted his eyes to the television mounted behind the register and froze.

My face. That's my face. The tiny screen was filled with last year's school picture, his hair bright red and curly. There was no captioning, so he had no idea if they wanted to arrest him or wanted to keep him safe. *Fuck.* He turned away, pretending to examine the selection of wiper blades. His face was on the fucking television. At least he had his hoodie on and it covered most of his hair. He rubbed his cheek, relieved at the stubble that scratched his fingertips. At least he didn't look like a high school kid.

I have to get rid of the hair. It's like a fucking neon sign.

He looked around the store, unwilling to draw attention to himself by buying scissors and not seeing any anyway. He settled on a cheap souvenir Swiss army knife and a three-pack of razors. On a whim he grabbed a roll of cough drops, hoping that would keep anyone from questioning why he didn't talk.

He dumped his purchases on the counter, keeping his eyes down and trying not to wince at the total. He had less than two dollars left. Faking a cough, he kept his hand over his mouth and pointed to the toilet key, hanging from an old license plate.

Bored, the guy behind the counter handed it to him. *So far so good.*

Wednesday, September 22, 9:45 A.M.

Olivia stopped the car at the Fischers' curb. 'I wish we could have told them that Joel was injected or something.'

'Me too,' Noah said, 'but you can't argue with stomach contents. Ian found the binders from the pills still in his lining. Joel swallowed the oxy.' He started to get out of the car but settled back when she didn't move. 'What?'

'I was wondering why I'm still on this case.' She'd been thinking about it since morning meeting was over. 'I would have thought Abbott would pull me off.'

'He did think about it,' Noah said. 'I told him I thought it would be the wrong thing. You have the background and all the data. And you held yourself together pretty well with Kenny. A lot of cops would have been tempted to tear his arm off.'

'I was.'

'But you didn't. That alone scored you the most points. So keep it together, Sutherland. You'll find this guy and the system will make him pay.'

'Okay. Let's go talk to the Fischers. Take your shoes off at the door.'

Mr Fischer greeted them at the door before they could knock. 'My son's burial is today,' he said harshly. 'Why are you here? And who is this man?'

'We need to talk to you about your son. This is Detective Webster. He'll be working this case with me from now on.'

'What happened to the other detective?'

She lifted her chin. 'Detective Kane was killed last night in the line of duty.'

Fischer looked as though he'd been slapped. 'Oh no. Come in. I didn't know,' he said when they'd deposited their shoes at the door and entered. 'I'm sorry.'

'Thank you,' Olivia said. 'Is Mrs Fischer available, too?'

'I'll get her. Please sit down.'

They did, Olivia scanning the room. Twelve hours ago, everything had been different for her, but not for this family. They'd been living with their grief for two days.

'They have a daughter, too,' Noah murmured, pointing to the kitchen door. A girl of about sixteen stood there, watching them, a mixture of caution and anger on her face.

'I didn't know that last night,' Olivia murmured back. 'We'll want to talk to her, too.'

The Fischers came to the living room, Mrs Fischer frowning slightly. 'Go back to your room, Sasha. I'll come get you when they're gone.'

Sasha obeyed and Mrs Fischer settled herself on the sofa next to her husband. 'We're sorry about your partner, Detective,' she said stiffly.

'Thank you. This won't be an easy conversation and I'm going to apologize in advance, but we need to talk to you about Joel's overdose.'

Mrs Fischer's lips thinned. 'I told you he was no druggie.'

'And I believe you,' Olivia said gently. 'But there were drugs found in Joel's system and we need to know where he got them.'

'We think he got them from someone else who was at the fire,' Noah said. 'The same drug was found elsewhere Monday night, after Joel was gone.'

'The drug was oxycodone, also called Percocet,' Olivia said. 'It's prescribed for pain. Sometimes it's bought off the street. Did Joel have friends who might have—'

'No,' Mrs Fischer exclaimed, starting to rise. 'Now get out.'

'Norma,' Mr Fischer said quietly, putting pressure on her thigh until she sat back down. 'No, Detective, we don't know anyone who would have those drugs.'

'All right,' Olivia said. 'We'll talk to his friends, then.

We also need to ask you about Joel's girlfriend. She wrote a note, signed it "M."'

'He didn't have a girlfriend,' Mrs Fischer insisted. 'He would have told us.'

'No, Mama.'

The adults whipped their gazes to the right, where Sasha stood in the hallway, clenching her hands together. 'Sasha, go to your room,' Mrs Fischer commanded.

'No, Mama.' Sasha came forward, her lips quivering, her eyes dark against a face drained of color. 'Joel had a girlfriend. I heard him talking to her on the phone.'

'When, honey?' Noah asked softly.

'Lots of times. I never met her.' The teen looked miserable. 'I'm sorry, Mama.'

'Why didn't he tell us, Sasha?' Mr Fischer asked, pain in his eyes.

Sasha hesitated. 'She wasn't Jewish.'

'What makes you think that?' Noah asked her.

'On the phone once, Joel was explaining why he couldn't meet her. He sounded like he was trying to calm her down. It was at Shavuot and he had to go to Temple.'

Noah glanced at Olivia. 'It's a holiday,' she murmured. 'Late spring.'

'So Joel knew her that long ago,' Noah said. 'When did you last hear them speak?'

'Last Thursday. I wasn't eavesdropping, but the wall is thin. I just . . . heard.'

'What exactly did you hear, Sasha?' Olivia asked, and the girl blushed a dark red.

'I can't. I can't say.' She darted a panicked look at her parents. 'Please.'

Olivia remembered the lipstick on the pillow and understood. 'It's all right, honey.'

'No, it's not,' Mrs Fischer cried. 'What's going on here?'

'Were you home on Thursday night, ma'am?' Olivia asked.

'No. Thursdays we play bridge.'

'We found evidence Joel had a girl in his room. We need to find this girl.'

Mrs Fischer closed her eyes. 'We don't know her. Please, just leave.'

'Ma'am,' Olivia said urgently, 'these arsonists set a fire last night that killed four more people. Innocent people. A firefighter was critically injured. Later last night a boy Sasha's age was almost kidnapped by one of them. My partner *died* saving that boy's life. We need to stop them and if this girlfriend can help us, then we need to find her.'

'What do you want us to do?' Mrs Fischer asked dully.

'We haven't recovered Joel's phone,' Noah said. 'Do you have it?'

Both Fischers shook their heads. 'But we can get you the records of who he called,' Mr Fischer said.

Again Sasha hesitated. 'He had another phone. One of the prepaid ones, so that he could have privacy. So that you couldn't see who he'd called.'

'How do you know this?' Noah asked.

She put her hand in her pocket and pulled out a flip phone. 'He gave me one on my birthday. Said I was sixteen, old enough for privacy. I'm sorry, Dad.'

'What is her name?' Olivia asked. 'And do you know where they'd meet?'

'He called her Mary. I'm sorry, I don't know a last name. Usually he'd tell her to meet him outside the library. Once he told her to meet him at the Deli. It's a sandwich place near the school, but she must've said no, because he said he'd go to her dorm.'

Olivia leaned forward. 'Do you remember which dorm Mary lives in?'

'No. He just said "the dorm." I'm sorry.'

'Don't be,' Olivia said. 'You were an amazing help and brave. Thank you.'

She waited until she and Noah were in the car. 'How many girls named Mary do you think live in the university dorms?' she asked glumly.

'I don't know, but I have a feeling we're about to find out.'

Olivia started the car. 'It may not be that difficult. If Joel visited her in the dorm, she had to sign him in. He'd be in the log.' She'd pulled to the end of the Fischers' street when Noah's cell phone rang.

'Change that plan,' he said when he hung up. 'Ian wants us back at the morgue. He's about to let the Fischer boy go, but needs us to see something first.'

Wednesday, September 22, 10:05 A.M.

Austin winced as he jerked the souvenir knife's dull blade over the last of his hair. It wasn't sharp enough to cut butter, but he'd made do. Now he dropped the last of his hair into the gas station's totally gross, outside toilet and flushed it down. No reason to leave handfuls of red hair in a trash can for everyone to see.

He pulled the first of the three disposable razor blades from the package and winced again as he prepared to shave his head. The sink only ran cold water, but beggars couldn't be choosers. Three very dull blades later, he ran his hand over his mostly bald head. Add to that three days' growth of his beard, and he looked nothing like the picture that was being flashed on the television.

Logic told him that he should believe the texts on his phone were really from the cops. Except that the ones from Kenny were playing with his mind. *They lie. Don't trust them.* He'd drive the rest of the way into town. Somewhere he'd find a television with closed-captioning and he'd see what was really happening.

Wednesday, September 22, 10:30 A.M.

'This is embarrassing,' David muttered, then flinched when a petite ER doctor pulled the suture on his chin a little too hard. 'Ow. That hurts. Aren't you done yet?'

She rolled her eyes. 'You big guys are the worst, you know. Whine, whine, whine.'

He felt the need to defend himself. 'Hey, it's fifteen stitches.'

Her lips tipped up as she pulled another suture. 'Only fourteen. You'll have a scar, though, so you can brag about it for years to come.'

'Oh, for God's sake.' Casey burst through the curtain, anger in his eyes that David knew was leftover panic. 'What the hell did you do to yourself, Hunter?'

'I was stupid, okay?' David said, now angry with himself. 'Ouch.'

'Hold still, cowboy,' she said. 'Could you please sit down, whoever you are?'

Casey pulled up a chair and dropped into it. 'I'm his captain. He'll live?'

'Oh, sure. He'll have a hell of a headache, but he'll

survive. Not so sure if he'll survive the ribbing he'll get later.'

'Thank you,' David said sarcastically. 'I tripped, okay? It was an easy fire. Lady had left a towel on the stove, husband accidentally turned it on, and the kitchen went up. We put the damn thing out in three minutes. Less, even.'

'So what did you trip on?' Casey asked.

'Her damn cat.' He clenched his teeth. 'I went down, hit my chin on some stupid metal modern-art sculpture . . . thing.'

'I have to say, I'm relieved you're not invincible. I was getting kinda spooked there.'

The doctor's brows lifted. 'What horrible fates have you barely escaped?'

'Falling four stories and getting pinned by a beam,' David said flatly. 'This week.'

Her eyes widened. 'You caught the ball? Well, I guess you were due a scratch. I'm almost done.'

'Good,' he said, 'then I can get back to work.'

Casey shook his head. 'No.'

'What do you mean? She's gonna stitch me up, send me back in the game. Right, Doc?'

She shook her head. 'He's the boss, big guy. I just do the needlepoint.'

Casey had his stubborn face on now. 'You can't work with stitches in your chin. It's against policy. And even if it wasn't, I'd still say no. You're distracted, and you have a right to be. But I'm not putting your team in danger because you can't concentrate.'

It was fair. He'd gone in, seen it was an easy fire and his mind had exploded three million different directions. Olivia, Kane, Zell, Lincoln Jefferson, that damn website and the boy who'd been at the fire . . . 'I'm sorry, Captain. I know we're shorthanded.'

'It's okay. I should have seen the signs and told you to take a day off. I was preoccupied with Zell, too. Is he done?'

'He is. Go home, let your girl fuss over you. You'll be back to work in a week.'

She left and David pushed himself to his feet. 'Let's get out of here.' His head hurt and he was feeling really surly. And a little nauseous, too. Wonderful.

'Who'll fuss over you?' Casey said. 'Your girl's a little busy right now.'

'I know. She was just here last night. This is where they brought Kane.'

'I know. That was my first thought when Carrie called and told me you were hurt and the medics were bringing you here. I'll take you back to the firehouse to get your stuff and get the paperwork done. Your stitches have to be healed before you can come back. You're officially on leave.'

Chapter Twenty-Three

Wednesday, September 22, 10:30 A.M.

Olivia had hoped not to come back to the morgue today. She'd already had enough gut-churning for one morning. Feet like lead, she followed Noah through the hallways that seemed to grow narrower with each step.

Earlier this morning they'd met Ian in one of the offices up front to talk about Joel. This time they were going back to the autopsy suite. Somewhere in there, lay Kane.

Her heart pounding, she stopped, trying to slow her breathing. 'Noah. Wait.'

He turned, surprised. 'What's wrong?'

It was humiliating, but somehow easier since she'd blurted it to Donahue that morning. 'I've been getting panic attacks. Since the pit.'

Understanding softened his features. 'What can I do?'

'Nothing. I just have to get through it on my own. But . . . this is harder than usual.'

'You know, you're really hard on yourself. Do you think you're the first cop this has happened to?'

'You?'

He nodded once. 'Long time ago. You okay to go in now?'

'I have to be. How do you handle it?' she murmured when they were walking side by side. 'When you get overwhelmed?'

'Therapeutic sex,' he said wryly. 'I'm serious,' he added when she snorted a surprised laugh. 'Sometimes you need to hold back reality for a little while.'

She thought about the amazing ride she'd taken with David that morning. Part of her had been feeling a little guilty for forgetting her grief for those few minutes. The other part of her knew it was silly and that Kane of all people would have told her that. But hearing it from Noah made it a little easier. 'Thanks. I needed to hear that.'

'Anytime.' Opening the door, he stuck his head in, then looked back. 'Just Joel.'

He'd understood that, too, her fear of seeing Kane here. Like this. She drew a breath and made her feet move. Ian stood waiting impatiently.

'I've got an angry undertaker pacing out front,' Ian said. 'We need to hurry.'

'What's so important?' Noah asked.

'This.' Ian lifted the sheet, exposing Joel's pelvis. 'Right here. A needle mark.'

Noah winced. 'He shot up in his groin? God. I hate when they do that.'

Olivia gritted her teeth and made herself look. 'That's usually a behavior for long-term IV drug users. Did you find track marks in other places?'

'No, I didn't and I doubt he injected himself,' Ian said. 'I found the binder from the pills in his stomach contents, like I told you earlier, but I started thinking after you left. The pills he swallowed to get that much binder in his stomach weren't consistent with the high level of narcotics in his system. I figure he swallowed the first two, then the rest was injected. Given no evidence of prior IV drug use, and a couple pills already in his system, I doubt he'd have been able to access the femoral vein with a steady hand.'

'So somebody did it for him.' Olivia felt relief for the Fischers.

'I wonder if Joel was about to tell on the others,' Noah said. 'They shut him up.'

'Something else,' Ian said. 'Injected, it would have been a fast high and not the slower action of swallowing the pills. I don't know how he managed to drive anywhere.'

Olivia frowned. 'What are you saying?'

'I don't think he drove his own car off the road,' Ian said.

'They would have had to put him behind the wheel, shove his foot on the gas, and put the car in gear from outside the car,' Noah said. 'It's been done.'

'Whoever did this had to be strong enough to put Joel in the driver's seat,' she said.

'Or they could have shoved him over the gearshift,' Ian said. 'When you know what you're looking for, you see things differently.' He pointed out a bruise on Joel's left hip. 'Could have been from being thrown from the car. Could have been from the shift.'

'I think this will give the Fischers some peace, but worsen their grief, too,' Olivia said. 'Someone murdered their son.'

Wednesday, September 22, 11:15 A.M.

Austin stood on a downtown Minneapolis sidewalk, at the large plate-glass window of a gym with televisions suspended from the ceiling. They had the closed-captioning

440

going for the exercisers, who sweated on treadmills.

His face was all over the news. The arsonists had struck again last night. Four dead. So many hurt. *This has to stop. I have to make this stop.* Then the next story started and his blood went cold. A bomb-threat scare. *At my school.* An unidentified student narrowly escaped kidnapping. Police detective killed. An interpreter missing.

That the bomb threat related back to him, he had no doubt. Were they trying to kill him to keep him from talking? Were they trying to keep Kenny from talking?

A man identified as Captain Bruce Abbott came on the screen, a sign language interpreter at his side. *Call us, Austin. You are in danger. We'll keep you safe.*

He dropped his eyes to the cell phone in his hand. Kenny had sent another text. *Don't trust the cops. Call me. I can hide you.*

Austin knew one way to separate the truth from the lies. He opened the latest from Kenny's new account. *Here in TC. Scared. Where can I meet u?*

He hit SEND before he could change his mind. Then started walking. He didn't want to stay in one place, didn't want to draw attention. *Keep walking.*

Wednesday, September 22, 11:15 A.M.

He'd had to exert a great deal of discipline this morning not to obsess over the silence of Austin Dent. Austin was still top of the news, so the police hadn't found him yet. He'd sent one more text from Kenny's 'new' account. He hadn't wanted to lay it on too thickly, but for God's sake, where was the damn kid?

There had been heavy traffic all morning due to

Detective Kane. Cops gathered here to soberly talk, to mourn. To wonder how it could have happened. Such a good cop. Such a nice guy. About ready to retire. Not fair.

Well, life isn't fair. So get over it. He'd taken the next order when the cell phone in his pocket buzzed.

Austin. Finally. 'Hey, Buster, I need to take a break. Can you handle things?'

'Sure,' Buster said, not looking up from the latte he was mixing.

The men's room was empty. He checked his cell phone and smiled. Austin was back, in the Twin Cities. Very good.

Need to meet U, he typed. *You're in danger*.

When? Where?

He was supposed to be Kenny, who was supposed to be at school, twenty minutes from downtown. *12:30*, he typed. *Will sneak away at lunch.*

McD's by school?

He frowned then. The McDonald's was across from the sub shop, where he'd grabbed the interpreter. *Too many cops looking for you. Library parking lot.*

Okay.

Hide till then. Cops looking for you. They lie. Don't trust them.

That should take care of Austin Dent until he could take care of him in person.

Wednesday, September 22, 11:20 A.M.

'Not home,' Olivia muttered, standing on Eric Marsh's welcome mat.

'We could try for a warrant,' Noah said and she shook her head.

'Brian Ramsey couldn't get me one last night for Joel and that was with proof he'd been in a fire. We're not getting a warrant. Not unless we find something else.'

The apartment door to the left opened and a grumpy-looking old man stared out. 'He's probably at school. Some kind of engineering major. Whaddya want with him?'

'We want to talk to him,' Olivia said. 'I'm Detective Sutherland and this is Detective . . . Webster.' She'd almost said Kane. 'And you are?'

'Jed Early.' Early glared. 'Comings and goings and goings-on. Give a kid that age an apartment and you're just asking for trouble.'

'Who's been coming and going?' Olivia asked.

'Kids. Mostly that Frenchie. *Albert*,' he sneered. 'I guess they're free to do what they want in their own place, but I should be free not to have to listen to it.'

'So Eric and Albert were . . .' Olivia said and Early nodded sourly.

'Every night. All night. God.' He shuddered. 'Made me wish I needed hearing aids.'

'You mentioned kids, more than one,' Noah said. 'Who else?'

'Another boy and a girl.'

Olivia's ears pricked. 'You get any names?'

He frowned. 'I don't snoop.'

'But you've got good hearing,' Olivia responded cagily and he grinned.

'I do indeed. Mary and Joel. No last names, though. I think they were studying together. Always had their laptops. Sometimes Joel brought big charts, rolled up.'

Of course you don't snoop, Olivia thought. 'When did you last see Eric?'

'Yesterday, carrying a box. I didn't see him after that. I had to go to the doctor.'

'When did you come back from the doctor?' Noah asked.

'I got back after two, and I haven't seen them since. But something was going on over there. They were all arguing early Monday morning. Woke me up.'

The hairs rose on the back of Olivia's neck. 'What time, sir?'

'About one, two. My eyes aren't so good and I couldn't see the clock. Sorry.'

'No, you've been very helpful,' Olivia said. 'Will you be around later?'

He nodded. 'They did something pretty bad, didn't they? I mean, I recognize you now. You worked the case of all those murders in that pit. You're a homicide cop.'

'I am. Right now, we don't know what they have or haven't done. But thank you.' She waited until they were back in Noah's car to talk. 'I think we can get a warrant now.'

'You call the ADA. I'm going to call the airports and make sure Eric doesn't slip away. The Fischers said he had money. He could be a flight risk.'

They each made their calls and Olivia was relaying all the details to ADA Brian Ramsey when Noah waved at her to wait.

'Tell him that Eric Marsh bought a ticket yesterday morning – one way to Paris. It took off at five-thirty yesterday afternoon, but he never showed.'

'I heard,' Brian said. 'I'll have the warrant in thirty.'

Olivia hung up. 'Let's do a halftime check. We've got Joel who was at the fire. Lovers with Mary and friends with Eric, who is lovers with Albert.'

'Maybe they all did it together. Didn't Micki say there were at least three?'

'She did. But how do Joel and pals connect to Tomlinson and this Dorian Blunt?'

'And which of them did Austin Dent see shoot Weems and then get in a boat at the dock on Sunday night?'

'And how does Tomlinson's wife factor in?' Olivia's eyes narrowed. 'Why lie to us?'

'And why the glass balls? Why only two? Why not leave one at last night's fire?'

'Something tells me that once we find Eric, Mary, and Albert, we'll get answers. Let's get a key from the super and wait by Eric's door. I don't want him slipping by us.'

Wednesday, September 22, 12:00 P.M.

Insisting he not drive, Glenn and his mother had met him at the firehouse. His mom had driven him back to the apartment, Glenn following behind in David's truck. His mother was making a pot of soup, which David knew would cure anything that ailed him. It always had. Or maybe it was just having her fuss over him. Both worked.

Now he and Glenn sat in the Gorski sisters' garden, David on the phone with Ethan while Glenn looked on, chomping at the bit.

'Well?' Glenn asked when David hung up the phone.

'That man is scarily efficient,' David said. 'Ethan says the domain registration for Lincoln's website was paid for by a Mary Francesca O'Reilly, aged twenty-three.'

'Did Mr Efficient get an address for Ms O'Reilly?'

'PO box on the card, but her social security number

brings up several addresses. Most recent is a dorm at the university.'

'Where that kid Joel Fischer went,' Glenn said thoughtfully.

'Where thousands of kids go. Doesn't mean she knew Joel. Doesn't mean she was at the fire. But it does mean she had some contact with Lincoln Jefferson. She couldn't just go in and pay his bill without his user name and password.'

'Unless she had somebody like Ethan helping her. Or she is somebody like Ethan.'

'Ethan's a white hat,' David murmured, then smiled when Glenn laughed. 'That's what they call them. Guys who use their hacking skills for good and not evil. I'm thinking Mary isn't a white hat. Plus, she paid with her own credit card. How covert is that?'

'You're probably right. Still, I'm thinking your pretty detective needs to know this.'

'I'm thinking the same thing. She's not gonna be happy about the way I found it.'

'After last night, do you think she'll really care? After last night, do you?'

David thought about Jeff. About Kane. 'No. And no. It could be that this Mary O'Reilly is just some Moss fan, like Lincoln. Maybe she's the one who helped Lincoln track me down yesterday and again I have to ask why?'

'More importantly, will she do it again? Better call your cop.'

David reached for his cell just as it rang, Ethan's number on the caller ID.

'I checked out Truman Jefferson,' Ethan said. 'Lincoln called him from his cell.'

'Lincoln's older brother,' David said. 'I found his name last night. What about him?'

'He's a Realtor. It would have been nothing for him to look up your friend's address.'

'So Truman helped him. Not Mary.'

'Truman is likely, Mary is unknown. The only other call Lincoln made was to a prepaid. The prepaids are traceable, but they take more coordination to do so. I'd need a lot more time and contact with the holder of the phone. You need anything more?'

'This brother, Truman. Any idea on his stability?'

'You're asking if he's crazy? That I don't know. Has he been in trouble? No. Hasn't even had a parking ticket. Lincoln on the other hand, had a long string of problems over the years. Mostly loitering, public disturbance, a couple shopliftings. On paper, Truman seems like a regular guy.'

'Thanks, Ethan.' David hung up his own cell and from his pocket pulled the prepaid phone he'd purchased the night before.

'What are you doing now?'

'I'm setting up an appointment with Truman Jefferson and I don't want him knowing it's me. I want to meet him, be sure that he's not nuts and that he understands what would happen if he helped Lincoln again. And then I'm calling Olivia to give her this info.'

Luckily Truman Jefferson had an afternoon free and, laboring under the misconception that his name was David Smith and that he was looking for real estate, his secretary gave him an appointment for one-thirty.

Olivia wasn't so available. He got her voice mail and left a message. 'It's me. I need to talk to you about a woman named Mary O'Reilly. Call me. It's important.'

'Now what?' Glenn said.

'I'm going upstairs to have some of Ma's soup before I meet Lincoln's brother.'

Glenn followed him out of the garden. 'Tripping over cats works up an appetite.'

'Smacking down smug old men works up a bigger one. You coming?'

Glenn's smile was sweet. 'Sure, I like your mom's cooking.'

Wednesday, September 22, 12:00 P.M.

The super opened Eric Marsh's door and he, Olivia, and Noah flinched in unison. The odor wasn't unbearable yet, but it was definitely getting there.

'Ah, damn,' the super muttered. 'I hate it when this happens.'

Me too, Olivia thought. Noah took her elbow surreptitiously and gave her a shove forward. It was what she needed to move. The body was in the bedroom, lying on the bed, sprawled on his back, nude, an empty plastic baggie on the nightstand.

'That's him,' the super said. 'Eric Marsh. Never thought he'd go this way.'

'How did you think he'd go?' Noah asked, giving Olivia a chance to settle down.

'Always thought that friend of his would do him in. Guy was a thug.'

Olivia didn't think anyone would describe Joel as a thug. 'You mean Albert?'

The super nodded grimly, still staring at the body. 'Yeah. Good old Al. Always thought his accent was a put-on, but it was good enough to get the ladies to swoon.'

Noah's brows lifted. 'We thought Albert and Eric were a couple.'

'They were. But Albert has a key and when Eric was away . . . Albert was a man who saw opportunity knocking. Maybe Eric found out Al was cheating on him.'

'Did he ever cheat with Mary?' Olivia asked and the super frowned.

'Don't know that name. But if she was pretty and had money, I wouldn't doubt it.'

'What does Albert look like?' Noah asked.

'Big guy. Hockey player at the university. Helluva checker, but no finesse with the stick.' He pointed to a photo in which Eric stood arm in arm with a tall, dark, good-looking guy with very broad shoulders. 'He looks exactly like that. That's him.'

Perfect, she thought with satisfaction. 'Sir, we're going to need to get the ME and crime lab up here. Can you wait for us outside? And please, don't talk to the press.'

'Nah. I got no patience for those people.' He backed away with a sigh. 'At least the rent was paid for next month. It'll take that long to get rid of the smell.'

Noah walked him out while Olivia called for the ME and CSU. Then she crouched next to the bed and, on a hunch, shone her flashlight on Eric's pelvic region.

'Everything still there?' Noah asked dryly when he came back in.

She looked up. 'Little knot of dried blood, right where Joel was injected.'

Noah's brows went up in surprise. 'Sonofabitch. Looking at the photo, Albert's big enough to haul Joel around and put him in the front seat of a car.'

'Ian said whoever hit Weems would have had to be at least six feet, based on the placement of the crack in Weems's skull. Albert is easily six feet.' Olivia looked around the room. 'No sign of struggle.'

'You seem okay now,' Noah noted.

'Once I get past the body, I'm usually all right. Thanks for the nudge before.'

'Anytime. Abbott called when I was walking the super out. He talked to Kenny in the safe house. Said the boy remembers seeing a police scanner in the shooter's van.'

'He's listening to us,' Olivia said.

'Yeah. Abbott wants to keep him in the dark on Austin's whereabouts, so we have a special frequency for any mention of the search. Also, somebody's been burning paper in the fireplace. Looked like blueprints.'

'Getting rid of evidence. Even if we find Albert's fingerprints in here, he can just say he lived here, so that's no good. We need a way to tie him to this.'

'Maybe he kept his kit. No sign of syringes or spoons anywhere.'

'And you have to heat the oxy to get it to dissolve in water so you can inject it,' Olivia said. 'Whoever hit these guys with a needle did it right.' She opened drawers, frowning. 'No cell, no laptop.'

'None in the other room either. Next stop, the university's registrar's office. They'll have Albert's address. Can't be too many Alberts on the hockey team.'

'We still need to find Mary, though. Grumpy Early next door said she and Joel came here together to study, with rolled-up paper – the blueprints. She's in on this.'

'And,' Noah said, 'if Albert's killing off his cohorts, she could be next.'

'I'm thinking she can give us the connection to Tomlinson and Dorian Blunt. Those fires still make no sense unless the first one was just a cover and they were planning something bigger all along.'

'Or like you and Dr Donahue said yesterday – different agendas. Somebody left glass balls at the first two fires, but not the third. An environmentalist agenda links fires one and two. But Tomlinson links fires two and three.'

Olivia bit at her lip. 'Joel was dead before fire two. Micki said there were three people. Albert was there, because he's the only one tall enough to whack Weems in the head. Joel was there because we've got smoke in his lungs and glue in his shoes.'

Noah opened Eric's closet. 'Whoa, this kid spent some serious money on clothes.' He crouched down and a moment later stood, a running shoe in his hand. 'Glue. They must not have known they tracked through it, or they'd have gotten rid of the shoes, too.'

'So Eric was also there. That's three. Kenny said Austin saw a guy getting into a boat off the dock. That's four. Was Albert the guy at the dock? He shot Weems?'

And Kane. A spurt of fury shot up inside her, but then Olivia frowned. Something wasn't right, didn't fit. 'One set of glue tracks at the fence where they got away, no glue on the dock side of the condo, so neither Eric nor Joel walked over there. Let's assume Joel wanted to change his mind and Albert whacked him, too. Could Eric have carried Joel away on his own, leaving none of Joel's tracks behind while Albert ran around the building to escape off the dock, shooting Weems on the way?'

Noah studied Eric's body. 'He's pretty skinny. He might have been able to haul Joel, especially if he was scared. But it makes more sense that Albert carried him out, especially since he whacked him.'

'Mary wasn't on the dock, because Austin saw a man. Maybe it was Albert on the dock and Mary helped Eric carry Joel away.'

'Maybe, maybe. Let's find Albert and Mary and get something solid.'

Wednesday, September 22, 12:30 P.M.

Austin hung back in the shadows in the alley beside the library. From here he could see any car coming in from the street and at his back was a chain-link fence, eight feet tall, so no one would sneak up from behind.

It was as safe as he was going to get under the circumstances.

He held his breath, although his gut told him what was about to happen. The library was almost a mile from the school. For Kenny to make it here by 12:30, he'd have to cut the last ten minutes of his third-period English class. And old lady McMann did not give bathroom passes. Ever. Chances that Kenny was coming? Close to nil.

A white van pulled into the parking lot and a man got out and walked by Austin's mom's car. Frozen where he stood, Austin's eyes fixed on the face of the man who'd shot that guard, who'd set the fire that killed Tracey. When he moved, his jacket shifted and Austin could see the glint of metal. He had a gun. The gun he'd used on the guard.

The man looked around again, his face red and furious, then started walking again.

This way. He's coming this way. Oh God. What do I do?

Run. But there was nowhere to go and he had only a dull souvenir knife in his pocket. *Don't move. Do not move.*

The man stopped abruptly, got back in his van and drove away.

Austin slumped against the brick wall, trembling. What made the man leave? He needed to find the cops. But he was afraid to move. Afraid to breathe. Afraid the man was waiting on the street for him to emerge from his hiding place.

Hands shaking, Austin opened his phone, found the text from Captain Bruce Abbott. *It's Austin*, he typed. *I need help*. He hit SEND.

In seconds he got a reply. *Where are you?*

He hesitated, then figured at least the cops wouldn't shoot him. *Library near school*.

I'll have an officer there in two minutes. Do not leave. Please.

Two minutes was too long. The man would be back, Austin knew. He'd park his van and come back on foot. He opened the text from the fake Kenny and typed a fake reply. *Cops came. Had to run. Hiding behind Swindoll's*. Swindoll's was an Italian ice shop, six blocks away in the other direction. *Please come fast. Scared*.

In a moment the man with the gun replied. *Okay. Stay there*.

Two men in dark suits ran by, one with a radio in his hand. Cops. They'd scared the man away. Legs like rubber, Austin walked into the sunlight.

'Help,' he cried, hoping they'd understand. The two suits wheeled around and ran back toward him. Austin fell to his knees behind a stranger's car, huddled over so that he was hidden from the road. 'He's coming,' he signed, trying to say the words clearly, but his heart was beating so hard and his tongue wouldn't work. 'He'll see me. He has a white van.'

One of the men ran off, the other giving him a nod before lifting his eyes to watch the road. They'd understood. A minute later a dark car drove up and he was bundled in the backseat where he cowered out of sight. Peeking over the backseat, he saw a cruiser pull up, lights flashing. The two men in suits were talking to the two cops.

'Hey,' Austin said and mimicked writing. One of the suits gave him paper and pen.

He was here, Austin wrote quickly. *He saw you and left. I txt him that I ran to Swindoll's.* He handed the paper back to the suit and pointed toward Swindoll's.

The suit motioned for Austin to stay down, then spoke to the other men before leaning against his car and writing a reply. He passed the paper back to Austin.

Why did you meet him here?

Austin sighed. *He said he was my friend Kenny*, he wrote. *Said you wanted to arrest me. Didn't know who to trust. I figured I'd bring him here, see if it was Kenny, but it wasn't. It was the man who shot the guard.* Wearily he passed the paper back.

The man in the suit made a call on his cell phone, then said something in his radio. He proceeded to write in the book for a long time, then handed it back.

I'm Detective Phelps. You're safe now. Keep your head down. We think this man has a police scanner in his van. Your friend Kenny saw it last night when the man grabbed him. We put out on the radio that we found your car but that you escaped. We want that white van to keep looking for you so we can find him. So stay down and don't use your phone again. When we get to the precinct, we'll get an interpreter.

Austin's pounding heart started to slow down. *What about my mom?* he wrote.

My captain will contact her and tell her you're safe. We'll bring her here.

Austin let himself relax a little. For now he was safe, but that man was still out there. *How will the cops know to look for him? And where is Kenny?* he wrote, then passed the book back.

We have a special radio frequency for this case. Kenny's in a safe house. I'll be back in a minute. Keep your head down. The detective gave him the notebook, then held out his hand to take it back when Austin had read what he'd written. Then he disappeared, leaving Austin to hope like hell he'd done the right thing.

He turned down his scanner. The cops had seen the kid's car, dammit, but the kid had given them the slip. The whole neighborhood was suddenly crawling with cops, who after last night would be looking for a white van.

'Now what?' he muttered aloud. The kid was on foot, he couldn't have gone far. He drove past the ice-cream shop slowly, courtesy of the drivers in front of him who were rubbernecking. No kid. He kept going, past the school, stopping in a grocery parking lot. There were so many vans parked here that his vehicle wouldn't stick out.

He'd started walking, looking for the kid, when another text came through. Different phone, other pocket. It was from the phone he'd given Eric, now controlled by Albert.

Fuck you, it read. There was an attachment. Opening it, he found himself staring at the picture on his small telephone screen. This day was not getting any better.

Chapter Twenty-Four

Wednesday, September 22, 1:00 P.M.

They shouldn't have wasted their time with the registrar, Olivia thought grimly. Albert's dorm hadn't been very hard to find at all. *It would be the one with all the police cars and the rescue squad in front.* 'I have a bad feeling about this,' she said.

'Let's hurry before they touch anything,' Noah said, already jogging.

A uniformed officer waited in the small sitting area of Albert's dorm suite. 'Body's in the back bedroom. Roommate found him.' The officer pointed to a young man who stood to one side, his face pale. 'He says he didn't touch anything.'

'We'd appreciate it if you could talk to us,' Noah said to the kid. 'Stay here, okay?'

'Dammit,' Olivia muttered when she stood in the doorway. A twin bed was situated against one wall and Albert's large body dominated it. He lay on his back, much as Eric had, nude. A paramedic was kneeling on the floor next to him, packing up his kit.

'He's dead, Detective,' the paramedic said. 'ME can tell you for sure, but at least for a few hours. Looks like he took too many.' He pointed to the nightstand, where there was a small plastic baggie with a few pills remaining inside. 'Percocet.'

Emotions churned inside her – frustration, but mostly impotent rage. Albert and Eric had hurt so many, but they'd never stand for their crimes.

Pushing the rage aside, she bent to study Albert's pelvis, earning her a stare from the medic. 'Right there,' she said. 'Same needle hole as the others. Sonofabitch.'

'There's a note on the desk,' the medic said. 'Next to the printer.'

'But no laptop or cell phone,' Noah observed. 'Big surprise. No signature on the note. It's in French. Starts with *Adieu*. Ends in *mon ami*. The rest I don't know.'

'My French is rusty,' the medic said, 'but it's basically "Good-bye cruel world. Soon I will be with you, my love." I guess you don't buy the whole love-gone-sour suicide?'

'No,' Olivia said flatly. 'We'll take it from here, thanks.'

'And then there was one,' Noah murmured when the medic was gone.

Olivia looked at Noah grimly. '*Mary* killed them all?'

'She's the only one left. Let's talk to Albert's roommate, but if he doesn't know Mary, we'll work the dorms to see who signed Joel in for visits.'

The roommate was visibly shaken, so Olivia gentled her voice. 'I'm Detective Sutherland and this is Detective Webster. What's your name?'

'B-Bill. Bill Westmoreland.'

'Did you know Albert well?' she asked him gently.

'No. He didn't stay here very often. He had a relationship with a guy named Eric. Engineering major. Eric's dad is loaded. He has his own place. Albert flopped there.'

'Did you ever see him with anyone else? Any girls?'

'Sure, sometimes. Not lately.'

'Were you here all morning?' Noah asked and Bill shook his head.

'I've got class at nine. He was here when I left. He's been here a lot the last few days. I think he and Eric had a fight.'

'What makes you say that?' Olivia asked.

'Albert normally ignored me, but the last few days he's been upset. I heard him Monday, no words, just his tone. He was angry. I stay out of his way when he's angry.'

'Was he violent?' Olivia asked and Bill shrugged.

'Never hit me, but there were a few times I thought he might.'

'Did he know anyone named Mary?' Noah asked and Bill shook his head.

'When did you get back from class today?' Olivia asked.

'About eleven-thirty. His bedroom door was wide open. At first I was like, dude, put on some clothes, and then I saw he wasn't breathing, so I called 911, then the RA.'

Olivia stood. 'Thanks for your help. Is there anywhere you can stay?'

'I have a friend with a place,' he said. 'I have an exam in two hours. This sucks.'

'I think maybe this'll get you a makeup,' Noah said. 'The officer will help you pack a bag. Not that we don't trust you, it's just procedure.'

Bill's eyes narrowed, understanding dawning for the first time and with it a flare of fear. 'He didn't kill himself. Oh my God. He was murdered. Here, in my room.'

'We're investigating,' Noah said calmly. 'For now, don't talk to the press. Please.'

Bill's eyes flickered again, this time with canny greed. 'Of course not.'

Out in the hallway, Olivia rolled her eyes. 'Let's find Mary before she reads her name on Yahoo! We need to update Abbott.'

Noah called Abbott while Olivia gave the first responder instructions. When they got in the elevator, Noah looked relieved. 'They found Austin. They're bringing him in.'

'Where's he been?'

'Abbott hasn't talked to him yet. He'll call us when he has more. Said they weren't going to announce he's been found just yet, so we should keep it quiet. Abbott also wanted to know if Tracey Mullen's mother ever got here from Florida.'

'I need to check my messages. I'll do it when we're outside. I got no bars in this elevator.' Which moved in slow-mo. The elevator finally reached the ground and they stopped at the receptionist's desk.

'Visitors have to sign in and I make a copy of their licenses,' the receptionist said. 'Students swipe their ID card. Here's everyone who's been through in the last week.'

It was a thick printout that made Olivia's eyes cross. 'Can you check for a name? Joel Fischer?'

The receptionist typed, then shook her head. 'Didn't come in here.'

They thanked her and went outside into the sun. 'I'll get a couple of sandwiches from the food truck,' Noah said. 'You check your messages.'

He jogged off to one of the silver food trucks and she listened to her messages. Paige. Paige again. Mia, three times. She'd heard about Kane and was coming to Minnesota. Olivia felt a tiny piece of her settle. Mia would understand. She'd lost a partner herself, years ago.

The last message was from David. Her eyes narrowed as she listened, saving his message just as Noah returned. She took one of the sandwiches he offered and made herself take a bite while turning back to Albert's dorm, walking fast. 'We got a last name on Mary. Mary O'Reilly. Let's see if that nice receptionist can locate her for us.'

Noah was frowning. 'Where did you get the last name?'

'From David, on my voice mail. And no, I don't know how he knew. I suspect we don't want to know. I'll call him back in a few minutes. Let's find Mary first.'

Noah sighed. 'Eve's got class all morning. She's not involved, as far as I know.'

'That Chicago group is so used to skulking online, they do it without breathing.' But she smiled sadly. 'Kane always thought that was so cool.'

''Cause it is,' Noah said with a wry grin. 'Always makes me hot to see Eve hack.'

She chuckled, and felt better for it. 'I'm sure David's story will be entertaining.'

They reentered Albert's dorm, the receptionist looking up in surprise. 'You're back.'

'We are indeed,' Olivia said. 'Can you find a student for us? Mary O'Reilly.'

'Mary Francesca O'Reilly,' the receptionist said after entering the name. 'She's a senior.' She produced a campus map. 'Her dorm is a four-minute walk from here.'

Olivia gave her a smile while Noah called for backup. 'Thanks.'

Wednesday, September 22, 1:30 P.M.

He pulled his van into his shop parking lot after driving around in circles to ensure he wasn't being followed. Wearily he climbed the outside stairs to the apartment he kept above the shop, locked his door, and fell into his easy chair. He'd searched for the kid, but no luck. Cops had swarmed and he'd retreated.

Austin had not replied since telling him he'd run to the ice-cream shop, behind which he had not been. He sent the kid another text, from 'Kenny's' account.

Where the hell r u? Looked everywhere. Town crawling w/ cops. Let me know u r ok.

There had been no reply, but so far the cops hadn't found him either. He'd just have to wait for the kid to text back when he felt safe. His eyes fell on the other text he'd received and he opened the photo attachment again. Albert was dead. Just like Eric.

Just like Joel. All supposed ODs. *Mary, Mary, Mary.* He hadn't thought she had it in her, but she was the only one left. If he released the tape now, the cops would be on her doorstep in five minutes. But her point last night was well taken. The video proved a fifth person at the scene – *me*. To think that the cops wouldn't link a fifth person at the scene with the shootings of the guard and Detective Kane was simply foolish.

The video was useful only as long as it frightened the College Four into doing his bidding. But the four were down to one, and the one left was a fucking psycho.

Although he'd love to see her rot in a jail cell forever, at this point it made more sense to silence her forever. But his hands were shaking from lack of sleep. A few hours' rest would be all he needed. Hopefully by then Austin would have contacted him.

And then he could finally give Mary the Bitch what she so richly deserved.

Wednesday, September 22, 1:30 P.M.

'She's not here.' An officer met Olivia and Noah at the door to Mary's dorm room. 'That's her roommate. Name's Helen Sanford.'

A young woman sat on a sofa, her clasped hands between her knees. Olivia sat next to her while Noah searched Mary's room. 'Do you know where she is, Helen?'

Helen shook her head. 'We aren't friends. We don't talk. Mary keeps to herself.'

'Any visitors?'

'Her boyfriend, mainly. She was really upset this week.'

'Upset? How so?'

'Cried for hours. I could hear her through the wall. Joel died Monday. Car wreck.'

'Does Mary have family in the area, anywhere she'd go?'

'She has a father and a brother who's some doctor. I think her mother died.'

'Detective Sutherland.' Noah was standing in the hall. 'You need to see this.'

'Wait here,' Olivia said to Helen, then went to Mary's room and looked inside the bureau drawer Noah had opened. 'Two glass balls,' she said, 'and baby diapers. That's where she got the gel she used to keep the glass ball from cracking in the fires.'

'And look at this.' Noah lifted the lid of a small box. 'Found it behind some books on the top shelf. It wasn't hidden well, almost like she'd tossed it up there.'

Olivia sighed. 'Her stash.' There was cotton and syringes and two worn metal spoons that bore the marks of being heated again and again. 'She's a user.'

'Let's get her permanent address and send out a unit. She might have gone there.'

'Mary was at the fire,' Olivia said. 'It was probably Albert on the dock and at the school. Which means Albert killed Kane.' Again she pushed aside the rage. 'But we still have no connection to Barney Tomlinson or Dorian Blunt. It makes no sense.'

'We need to talk to Tomlinson's wife. But first, let's see if we can figure out where Mary would go. How did David know about her?'

'I'll call David and find out.'

'And I'll call in the BOLO on Mary O'Reilly.' Noah started dialing. 'I'll make sure the airports are also notified in case she decides to buy her own ticket on Air France.'

Wednesday, September 22, 1:30 P.M.

'Thanks for seeing me,' David said, settling into a chair next to Truman Jefferson's big desk. He'd been shown in by a young woman who'd announced him as Mr Smith, then discreetly closed the door behind them. 'I know it was short notice.'

'Always a pleasure to meet new clients,' Truman said broadly, then winced when he saw David's chin. 'That's quite a shaving nick you got there. Must hurt like the devil.'

'That it does.' It still hurt like hell and he was still dizzy if he moved too quickly.

His mother had been very upset when he'd tried to leave the house, going as far as to take his keys. The only way he'd managed to get here at all was to allow her to drive. Of course Glenn had come and the two of them sat in the front seat of his mother's car, waiting for him to conclude his business with Lincoln's brother. Then they were going to the hospital to see Jeff, who was finally conscious and taking visitors.

'So, how can we help you, Mr Smith?'

David studied Truman's face, his eyes. The family pictures on his desk. If he was schizophrenic like Lincoln, he masked it well. 'Actually, my name isn't Smith. It's Hunter. David Hunter. I'm a firefighter. Yesterday your brother broke into my friend's house.'

Truman's brows snapped in a snarl. 'What's this about? If you're planning to sue—'

'I'm not.'

'Then why are you here?'

'Sir, your brother is not well.'

'Tell me something I don't know,' Truman said bitterly. 'They say he set fires with that terrorist Preston Moss. The FBI came to our house, upset my mother . . . Please leave my mother out of this. She's not well either.'

'I'm sorry to hear that,' David said. 'I'm not here to cause your family pain. I'm here because I need to know who helped Lincoln find me yesterday.'

Truman's eyes flickered in nervous fear. 'Who said anyone helped him?'

'I'm not going to sue,' David repeated. 'But I have a family, too. Lincoln came to my apartment house, asked a tenant where I lived. She told him I lived in a friend's cabin. The owner isn't listed in the phone book, but Lincoln managed to find the cabin quickly.'

'He's not stupid,' Truman protested.

'No, but he's mentally ill and at the moment, off his meds. I don't believe he found my friend's cabin alone. If you helped him, I need to know and I need to know why. If you didn't, I need to find who did. If there's another zealot out there who thinks I've besmirched the name of Preston Moss, I need to protect my family. If Lincoln had gone to my loft first, he would have found my mother, not me. He had a gun, Mr Jefferson.'

Truman's eyes fixed on David's face, then looked away. 'I want to say Lincoln would never hurt anyone. But obviously that's not true.'

David frowned, then understood. 'He didn't do this,' he said, pointing to his chin. 'This happened on the job.'

Truman sagged. 'Thank God. I've been afraid of this, but getting him to take his meds . . . I even gave him a job here so that I could watch over him, but it's hard. It's killing my mother. I made her agree to let the system handle Lincoln this time.'

'Did you help him, Mr Jefferson?' David asked. 'Please, I just need the truth.'

'Yesterday Lincoln called me. He needed to find a man named Glenn Redman. He said it was about the website, that he needed to pay. Lincoln does website work for me. I thought this was about a bill.' He shrugged helplessly. 'I was busy and told Mary to look it up. She gave me the address, I called Lincoln back, and the next thing I knew my mother was calling me crying because he'd been arrested.'

It took a second for the detail to sink in, but when it did David lurched to his feet. 'Your secretary is Mary? O'Reilly?' Truman stood as well, uncertainly.

'Why yes, of course. Mary Fran's been with me since last summer. Why?'

Without answering, David threw open the office door. 'Oh my God.' Glenn lay lifelessly on the floor, blood oozing from his head. Truman's secretary leaned over him, pushing at his body, but at the sound of the door opening she wheeled around, her face white. She held a gun in her hand.

David leapt at her but she scrambled back, and holding the gun in both hands, fired. The shot went wide and she ran from the office. David ran after her, then ducked behind a car when she fired a second time. The shot pinged off the car next to him, wide again.

'Stop!' he shouted and barreled forward, but she was fast.

Then sheer terror grabbed his throat when she wrenched open the passenger door of his mother's car and jumped inside. Mary looked straight at him as she put the gun to his mother's head. He saw her mouth move. A single word. 'Drive.'

His mother shrank back, but Mary shoved the gun harder and the car began to move. 'No. Mom, no!' he screamed and hurled himself at the back bumper.

And came up with a handful of air and a mouthful of gravel. He pushed himself to his feet and ran, but the car was screeching out of the parking lot.

He had no keys. He had no car. He spun around and ran back to Truman's office, where the man knelt next to Glenn, openmouthed and in shock.

'Your keys. Goddammit, give me your keys!'

Stunned, Truman handed them over and David ran outside, yelling, 'Call 911.' He started Truman's car and took off after them. Pulse hammering, he fumbled his phone as he punched the gas, fishtailing in the road.

He couldn't see her car. Goddammit, he could not see his mom's car. Hand shaking he dialed 911, driving faster and cursing himself for even allowing her to come.

'What is the nature of your emergency?'

'My mother has been kidnapped. She's in a green Ford Taurus, heading north towards 35W.' He pictured his mother's car in his mind and recited the license plate. 'Her name is Phoebe Hunter. She's been taken by Mary O'Reilly who has a gun.' His head was pounding but he managed to keep his voice level. 'We also need a rescue squad at Presidential Realty. Sixty-two-year-old man, head wound. He's unconscious.'

'Where are you, sir?'

'Chasing my mother's car,' he said, his voice cracking. 'Just hurry, and inform Captain Bruce Abbott and Detective Olivia Sutherland.' He came to an intersection and realized he had no idea which way they'd gone. 'I don't see them. Not anywhere.'

'Sir, please return to the scene. I have help on the way.'

David pulled into a gas station. He covered his mouth with his hand, unable to think. Unable to breathe. He stared at his phone, willing it to ring, jumping when it did. Olivia.

'Oh God,' he said weakly, staring at the intersection in front of him. 'She's gone.'

'Who's gone?' Olivia asked sharply. 'David? What's wrong?'

She didn't know. Dispatch wouldn't have had time to call her. 'My mother. She's been abducted.' His voice sounded thin, unreal. 'By Mary O'Reilly.'

'*What?* Where are you?'

'I don't know.' He looked around, saw the signs, drew a

breath and gave her the intersection. 'I have to go back. Glenn's hurt.'

'David. Stop and talk to me.'

But he was turning Truman's car around and heading back. 'Did you get my message before, about Mary O'Reilly?'

'Yes. We're looking for her. How did you find out about her?'

'Why are you looking for her?' he asked dully, blinking hard to focus on the cars.

'How did you learn about her?'

She hadn't answered his question and his blood went even colder. 'Lincoln is the webmaster for that Moss website I found. Mary O'Reilly paid his web expenses.'

She was quiet a moment. 'Okay. Where did you find Mary?'

'I went to visit Lincoln's brother, Truman. He helped Lincoln find Glenn's cabin yesterday. Mary is his secretary.' He'd arrived back at Truman's realty office, his body numb. 'Glenn's hurt. I don't know how bad. I have to go. I called 911.'

'All right,' she said calmly. 'Where are you?'

'Presidential Realty.' He stumbled through the door. Truman knelt next to Glenn, pressing a towel to his head. 'I have to go.' Blindly he set his phone aside and pressed his fingers to Glenn's neck where an unsteady pulse stuttered.

David rolled Glenn to his side. And saw what Mary had been trying to get.

'Her purse,' Truman murmured. 'Your friend grabbed her purse. Why?'

David shoved the purse aside. 'Tell me about Mary O'Reilly. Pull her personnel file so you can give it to the cops when they get here.'

Shaking, Truman did as he was told, opening a file cabinet, removing a folder. 'She applied for a job last summer. Our old receptionist died unexpectedly. One day Mary showed up to fill out an app. I was relieved. I didn't even have to place a want ad.'

David's blood ran cold. 'Your receptionist died? How?'

'She fell down some stairs. She was older. Lost her footing.' Truman's eyes grew more fearful. 'Why? Mary's always been a good worker and she's good with Lincoln.'

'How was she good with Lincoln?'

'She calmed him when he got agitated. Sometimes on a slow day, they'd talk.'

Keeping pressure on Glenn's head, David made himself think. 'What did they talk about?' Although he bet he could guess. Preston Moss.

'I don't know. I was just happy Lincoln was quiet so I could work.' Truman sat back on his heels, bewildered and afraid. 'This is about Lincoln. What's going on?'

David could hear sirens. 'That's what we all want to know,' he said grimly.

The medics rushed in. 'What happened?'

Truman pointed to the floor near Mary's desk. 'I think she hit him with that.' It was a trophy for sales performance. It had traces of blood on one side.

Giving the medics room to work, David searched the desk without touching anything. 'Glenn must have come inside. He can never sit still. He must have seen this.' It was a pay stub, with Mary's name clearly visible. 'He knew it was her.'

Truman was staring at the desk phone. 'She had the intercom on, listening to us. She knew you were asking about Lincoln. What the hell is going on here?'

David stared at the pay stub, terror stealing his breath. 'She's got my mom.'

Wednesday, September 22, 2:00 P.M.

Phoebe clenched the wheel and tried to stay calm. Difficult when a gun was pointing at her head. The woman was young, early twenties. She'd run out of the realty office only to realize she was parked in. Phoebe had been ready to move her car when the woman jumped in, pointed a gun, and told her to drive.

'Who are you?' she asked, her voice trembling.

'Shut up and drive,' the young woman snapped.

'Are you going to kill me?'

The young woman laughed bitterly. 'Do you want me to?'

'Not particularly. My friend was in there with my son. Did you hurt him?'

'I didn't kill him, but if you don't shut up, I will kill you. Up here, turn right.'

Phoebe obeyed, her eyes darting around for any way she could stop the car.

'I don't recommend you do that,' the woman said quietly. 'Really.'

Phoebe drew a breath. 'I'll give you the car and my phone. I won't call the police.'

'Too late. Your old man already tried. But I will take your phone.' Mary pawed through Phoebe's purse, found her phone, pulled out the battery, and threw it in the backseat. 'Now they can't track you.'

Phoebe thought of how many times her family had been in trouble over the years, how many times they'd nearly been killed. She'd always thought in some ways it had to be harder, to have to sit and wait for news. To pray. *I was wrong*. But her family had always kept their heads, had played it smart, buying time until help arrived. *So will I*.

She began to pray, silently mouthing the words that she'd said so often for others.

'What are you saying?' the woman snapped.

'I'm praying.'

'Well, stop. Nobody's going to hear your prayers anyway.'

'I'll know,' Phoebe murmured. 'That's enough.' They'd be looking for her, she knew. She wouldn't let herself fear. Instead she'd focus on landmarks so that when she got away, she could find her way back.

The woman turned on the radio, tuning it until she found the news.

'Two college students were found dead today,' the announcer reported soberly, 'one in his apartment, the other in his university dorm. Police are searching for Mary O'Reilly for questioning regarding these deaths. If you have any knowledge of the whereabouts of Mary Francesca O'Reilly, please call the police.'

Phoebe glanced at the woman. 'I'm assuming you're Mary.'

Mary's jaw was taut. 'Shut. Up. And. Drive.'

Wednesday, September 22, 2:15 P.M.

Olivia found David sitting on the floor of Jefferson's realty office, his face pale beneath his tan. A nasty row of stitches lined his jaw. There was blood on his shirt.

She crouched beside him. 'Are *you* all right?'

471

His eyes were blank. 'Glenn saw Mary's name on her pay stub and she hit him. I chased her and she shot at me. She's not a good shot.'

Olivia touched his wrist, felt his pulse racing wildly. 'David, are *you* all right?'

He closed his eyes. 'I chased them, but I wasn't fast enough. She took my mother.'

She slid her hand over his forearm. 'Is this your blood on your shirt, or Glenn's?'

'Glenn's.'

'I thought you were on duty today.'

His mouth quirked bitterly. 'If I had been, this wouldn't have happened. Damn cat.'

'You're not making any sense, David.'

'OTJ accident. Mom and Glenn picked me up at the firehouse. I was supposed to rest, but I didn't listen. I got information on Lincoln's website. He's had it for ten years under a dead professor's name.'

'You said Mary paid some of Lincoln's bills. You tracked her credit card?'

'Yes. And then I called you with the information. Hours ago.' His tone took a slightly accusing edge and he looked away. 'I'm sorry. I didn't mean that.'

'I know,' she said gently. 'How did you know about Lincoln's brother?'

'Lincoln called his cell yesterday.'

Oh. 'You checked Lincoln's cell log while you waited for us yesterday, didn't you?'

He nodded, unrepentant. 'Priorities. Yours was catching a killer. Mine was making sure there wasn't another Lincoln out there to come to my place, hurt my people.'

He would do that, protect his people. 'When did you find out Mary was the secretary?'

'Truman mentioned her name when we were meeting. I didn't know before. I would have called you. I wouldn't have put my mother and Glenn in danger.'

'I know. We've got the state police helicopter in the air, searching for her car.'

He pinned her with his gaze. 'Why were you looking for Mary? Tell me.'

Olivia sighed. 'We think she killed at least one of the arsonists, maybe all three.'

David closed his eyes, his throat working as he swallowed hard. 'With the gun?'

'No.'

'Didn't think so. She couldn't shoot worth a damn. That's the only thing that's keeping me going, knowing she's not comfortable with that gun. Maybe she won't . . .' He stopped, battling for control. 'Oh God. She's got my mother.'

'I know,' Olivia murmured. 'We'll find her.'

'Mary applied for the job here to get close to Lincoln. Truman says their last receptionist tumbled down some stairs.'

'Oh no.'

He opened his eyes, terrified but functioning. 'She talked to Lincoln. That must be how she found out about the glass balls, about the VE scratched in the pole.'

'How did she find him?'

'Through the website, I guess. Let's ask Lincoln.'

She nodded. 'I will.'

'I'm coming.' The look he flashed her was full of fury. 'Don't consider telling me no. You might need me again.' His mouth twisted bitterly. 'I'm the cat-saving fireman.'

'Olivia.' Noah was standing at Mary's desk, studying the contents of her purse. Noah was also pale. Phoebe Hunter was like Eve's mother. But Noah had proven himself under pressure. Olivia knew he'd keep it together. 'Phones. Lots of phones.' He held up an MP3 player in his gloved hand, turned it around. 'It says, "number one."'

'Play it,' David said tersely.

Noah did, while Olivia and David watched, huddled around the earpiece that was connected. A tinny rendition of the *Mission Impossible* theme could be faintly heard, then Olivia saw the first photo and understood.

'Oh my God,' she breathed. 'It's Tracey Mullen.' It was her face in the condo window, her mouth open on a silent scream as she pounded the glass.

'Somebody videotaped this,' David said, horror in his voice as Tracey slipped from view, her hands trailing down the glass. 'I saw the tracks of her hands on the window.'

The camera panned back to four figures, their faces clearly visible in the moonlight.

'Joel, Mary, Eric, and Albert,' Olivia said. 'Joel's fighting to get back inside. Eric and Albert hold him back, then Albert hits Joel in the head.'

'Then Albert and Eric drag Joel away,' Noah said. 'Just like we thought.'

Olivia watched Mary take a last look up at the window, then follow Albert and Eric to the fence where they shoved Joel through. 'Just like we thought,' she murmured.

'Someone videotaped this,' David repeated. 'They just watched while Tracey died.'

Noah blew out a breath. 'We have a fifth man.'

The video changed. 'Tomlinson's warehouse, before the fire,' David murmured.

'This is the connection,' Noah said. 'The fifth man was blackmailing them.'

The video stopped and the three of them stood for a

moment, silent. Then Olivia sorted through the phones until she found one that said '#2' on the back.

'Lots of texts. Attachments. Photos. Tomlinson's warehouse burning, Eric's body, just like we found it.' She opened the next attachment.

'Dorian Blunt's house,' David said. 'Before the neighborhood went up in flames.'

'And one of Albert, dead,' Olivia said. 'The text says "Fuck you." I guess Mary was tired of being pushed around. This is how they've been communicating with the blackmailer. We need to call Abbott.'

Noah did. 'Bruce, we have a fifth person involved . . .' He listened with a frown. 'How did *you* know?' He looked at Olivia. 'Austin Dent is in the precinct. Abbott showed him pictures of Joel, Eric, and Albert, and he said the man he saw wasn't any of them.'

Olivia gathered the contents of Mary's purse. 'Tell him we're coming in.' She looked up at David. 'Should I have someone drive you to the hospital to meet Glenn?'

'No, I need to talk to Lincoln. If I don't do something, I'll go insane.'

She nodded, hoping Abbott and Donahue would concur. 'Okay. Let's go.'

Chapter Twenty-Five

Wednesday, September 22, 2:25 P.M.

'Slow down,' Mary snapped and Phoebe flinched. They were the first words the young woman had uttered in almost half an hour. They'd kept to side roads and had passed only a few cars. 'Stop behind that car.' There was a black Lexus abandoned on the side of the road ahead.

Phoebe obeyed, hardly daring to breathe. 'I won't tell anyone when you're gone.'

Mary scoffed. 'No, you won't because you're coming with me.'

Phoebe closed her eyes. 'Why?'

'Because I may need you.' She shoved the gun against Phoebe's ribs. 'If you want to see that handsome son of yours again, you will do as I ask. Get out of the car.'

Phoebe obeyed, her legs like rubber. 'I can help you. You don't have to do this.'

Mary rolled her eyes. 'Walk.' Phoebe walked, Mary trailing about two feet behind. 'Now on your knees next to the driver's door and feel underneath. There will be one of those magnetic boxes with a key. Take the key out and throw it at my feet.'

Conscious of the gun pointed at her head, Phoebe knelt.

'Speed it up a little or you die here,' Mary said impatiently.

'I'm old,' Phoebe said curtly. 'I move slow.'

'Move faster or you'll get no older.'

Phoebe reached under the car, sending the small medallion she wore around her neck swinging on its chain. Hoping the police would find it and her, she gave it a yank, letting the chain fall in the dirt as she reached for the key. She thought of tossing the key away, but decided against it. Mary had killed two men. Phoebe had no doubt she'd kill her, too. *David, where are you?*

Phoebe struggled to her feet and held out the key. 'What would your mother say about you kidnapping an old woman, Mary?'

Mary flinched, then snatched the key. 'My mother is dead,' she snapped.

Phoebe drew a quick breath. 'I'm sorry.'

'Don't be. Maybe I killed her, too.' Mary unlocked the passenger car door. 'Get in. Then shut up and drive.'

Phoebe got in and scooted to the driver's side, Mary crawling in behind her, the gun still pointing . . . *at me.* Heart pounding, Phoebe took the key Mary thrust at her.

'I need to know. *Did* you kill your mother, Mary?'

Mary shook her head, but her voice trembled. 'No. It wasn't my fault. Now drive, or it won't be my fault again.'

Phoebe gave her a little nod, then started the car. *Dear God. Now what do I do?*

Wednesday, September 22, 3:30 P.M.

David sat in the chair at Olivia's desk, his eyes fixed on the window into Abbott's office. She was in there, with Noah, Abbott, Barlow, and Micki, rereading texts from the cell phones and reviewing the video they'd found in Mary's purse. Periodically she'd lift her eyes, meet his through the window, and shake her head. *No news*.

Noah dragged a white board into the office and David could see they'd developed a timeline. Each arson, each murder. But only one thing mattered anymore.

His gut was in constant churn. He tried not to think about the pictures he'd seen, the bodies of the two college students Mary had killed, but they filled his mind. Tracey Mullen's death had been an accident, but the others . . . Mary was a killer.

And she has my mom. It had been almost two hours. They could be anywhere. He'd filled her gas tank earlier, enough fuel to reach Canada before they had to stop.

Behind him, Tom paced frantically. David had called the boy from Olivia's car on the way from Truman's office and Tom had been waiting for him here, white-faced and terrified.

'I can't believe I took her with me,' David murmured. 'That I let this happen.'

Tom sighed heavily. 'Shut up, David. You didn't make this happen. You didn't make any of this happen. Bad shit happens around us and we make it stop.'

'I should have made her stay home.'

Tom dropped into Kane's chair. 'She wouldn't have listened. Did you check Truman Jefferson before you drove out there?'

'Ethan did. Truman's a solid businessman, never been in trouble.'

'Then you had no reason to think it would have been dangerous. It was a real estate office, for God's sake. I swear to God, sometimes I think you think you are.'

David met Tom's angry eyes with a frown. 'I think I'm what?'

'*God*.' Tom hit the desk with his fist. 'You can't always be the goddamned hero.'

David blinked at Tom's fury, unexpected and ... incorrect. 'I'm not.'

'What*ever*.' Tom drew a breath, let it out. 'I shouldn't have yelled. You couldn't tell Grandma what to do. Nobody can. Stop blaming yourself and start using your brain.'

David closed his eyes. The kid was right. 'What do we know about Mary O'Reilly?'

'Besides that she's a card-carrying whack job?' Tom patted his computer bag, his mouth flattening to a grim line. 'Let's get out of here and find out.'

'Let me tell Olivia,' he said. 'I'll be right back.' David tapped on Abbott's door and she came out, motioning him into an empty conference room, closing the door.

'Nothing new,' she said. 'Every available body is looking. IT's tracing texts from Mary's phone and e-mails from the laptop we found in her car outside the realty office.' She looked up, her blue eyes intense. 'We'll find your mom. Mary has nothing to gain by harming her.'

'What about the cell phone number?' he asked hoarsely. 'The one Lincoln called?'

'It was Mary's phone, in her purse. We've called your mom several times, but it goes to voice mail. We can't track a GPS signal, but we'll keep trying. We've got detectives talking to anyone who knew Mary in the dorm, anyone who sat next to her in class. Trying to find out where she might have gone.' She lifted her hand to his cheek. 'I'd tell you to go rest, but I know you won't.'

He turned his face into her hand. 'I can't think,' he admitted. 'I can't breathe.'

Her thumb caressed his lips, soothing, not sexual. 'Then let me think for you, for just a little while. Go see Glenn. I promise I'll call you as soon as I know anything.'

'What about Lincoln?'

'Dr Donahue's with him. They sedated him this morning. He overheard two guards talking about another arson and he lost it. She says when he's lucid, she'll arrange for me to talk to him. I'll call you, so you can be there.'

He pulled her to him, holding on tight, his voice breaking as the words tumbled out. 'I keep seeing her with that gun to her head.'

'I know,' she whispered. She held on a moment more, then pulled away. 'I've got to get back. I will call you the second I hear anything. We will find her, David.'

He knew she would do anything in her power to keep her word, but he couldn't sit idly. Steeling his spine, he returned to Tom. 'Let's go, kid. Show me what you can do.'

Wednesday, September 22, 3:45 P.M.

Olivia stood at Abbott's window, watching David and Tom walk to the elevator. 'I hate this,' she murmured. Two priorities. A man who shot bullets and a woman who shot drugs. Both were killers. But the woman had a hostage.

'We all do,' Abbott said. 'Sit down and let's get a plan.'

They'd reviewed the texts from all the students' phones,

piecing together the timeline. Replays of the video made it clear that the four students hadn't known Tracey Mullen was in the building.

'The first fire they did for a cause,' Noah said. 'Joel was the champion, but Mary, who is friends with Lincoln, left the glass ball as the tribute to Moss.'

'She was only eleven when Moss set that last fire,' Micki said.

'But he's a legend in radical circles.' Barlow shrugged. 'Somehow she heard of him. Maybe through a teacher, a parent, her own Internet wandering.'

Olivia reread Mary's personal information that they'd gotten from Truman Jefferson and the university. 'She's twenty-three, single. Parents deceased. She paid for her own tuition, no loans or financial aid. She has to have some alternate source of income. Her job at the real estate office didn't pay enough for room and board.'

'Emergency contacts are left blank,' Noah added. 'She was a loner.'

'With an IV drug addiction,' Olivia said. 'Her transcripts say she was majoring in philosophy and took Environmental Ethics last spring. That's where she met Joel.'

'The car she parked in front of Truman's office was paid for,' Noah said. 'Other than her laptop, we found nothing unusual. The car was registered to her dorm address.'

'Where does she live during the summer?' Micki asked.

Olivia tossed the paper to the table, frustrated. 'PO box. Dammit.'

'Okay,' Abbott said calmly. 'We've gone over Mary and we're stuck. Let's talk about the blackmailer, because somewhere they intersect.'

Olivia nodded. 'The night of the condo fire, the

blackmailer knew they'd be there, because he showed up with a camera. He also knew Tomlinson and Dorian Blunt. They tie somehow. On some plane, they *all* intersect. Where?'

'The blackmailer is the shooter,' Micki said. 'He went around to the dock side of the condo where Austin was hiding.'

'Austin said he ran when he smelled smoke,' Abbott said. 'He made it out the door on the dock side and realized Tracey wasn't there. He never saw the arsonists – they were on the other side of the building. Austin saw the shooter come around the building. Weems confronted him, the man fired, got in a boat, took off his ski mask and sped off.' He tossed a sketch on the table. 'Our shooter.'

'I've seen that face a thousand times, a thousand different places,' Olivia said.

'I know, but right now, it's the only face we've got.'

Noah studied the timeline. 'The blackmailer knew Eric had bought a ticket to Paris, because he texted Albert's cell with the flight time. How would he know that?'

'Same way he knew the interpreter was helping us,' Olivia said. 'He followed us.'

Noah shook his head. 'He didn't physically follow Eric. Eric paid for his plane ticket over the Internet, straight out of his bank account. He had access to Eric's computer.'

Olivia suddenly remembered the sight of David's cell phone next to hers on his nightstand. 'Or his cell phone,' she said slowly. 'That's why he took their phones.'

'But he didn't take Eric's phone,' Barlow said. 'Mary did.'

'Maybe because he didn't kill Eric,' Olivia replied, 'and Mary did. He needed Eric to have his own phone and the prepaid he provided. It's how he communicated with him.'

'But that doesn't explain how the blackmailer knew Eric had bought a plane ticket,' Noah said. 'Unless he was monitoring Eric's cell activity.' He turned to Micki, whose suddenly narrowed eyes told them she'd figured it out. 'So, how did he do it?'

'Sonofabitch. Somehow he got access to their passwords and user names. I'll bet he snuck in through an unsecured wireless connection.'

'In other words, airports, bookstores, coffee shops,' Abbott said and Micki nodded.

'People get the warning that any data they send can be seen by others, but don't realize that with the right software, it's not just data you send. It's any data on your device.'

'So if Eric saved his bank account information . . .' Noah said.

Micki took Eric's phone, hit some buttons, and made a satisfied sound. 'Eric's info is all right here. I'm in his bank account now. Somebody wiped him out yesterday, right about the time Albert received the text warning him Eric was going to flee the country.'

'Trace where the money went,' Abbott commanded crisply.

'It's not just bank info. Phones store e-mail server information and passwords. Once he got that, he could look at their e-mail from anywhere. Find out about all kinds of things.' Micki paged back through Eric's stored messages, then turned the phone to show them. 'Like saving the wetlands. It's all here. Eric and Joel's whole plan.'

'Or like affairs,' Barlow said. 'Tomlinson had photos of him with his mistress on his desk when he died. That was his blackmail.'

'Oh,' Olivia said, a piece of the puzzle connecting. 'The pictures of Tomlinson. The blackmailer found out about his affair and took those pictures a long time ago.'

Micki's smile was sharp. 'Last winter, when the mistress wore snow boots.'

Olivia nodded. 'Louise had the "before" pictures. I bet the blackmailer sent them to her because Tomlinson didn't pay. She then hired the private detective who took the "after" pictures. Louise mixed them all together to give to her divorce attorney. The hit was exactly what you said, Barlow. An execution. Payback.'

'So where did he cross paths with Eric, Tomlinson, and Blunt?' Abbott asked.

'I'll have another look at Tomlinson's financials,' Barlow said, 'cross-referencing them to Dorian's and Eric's. Maybe they spent money at, or visited, the same place.'

'That helps us with the blackmailer,' Olivia said. *Who killed Kane.* She wanted to focus on him, find him. Gut him like he deserved. But she could see the harrowed terror in David's eyes. 'What about Mary? If Phoebe's still alive, Mary's probably keeping her for leverage. But we're no closer to knowing where.'

Noah pulled Mary's personal data sheet close and went through it once again. 'There's one old address that came up on her background check, but the uniforms we sent to check it said no one knew her. She might have lived there years ago, but not recently and there was no sign of Phoebe's car in the neighborhood.'

Olivia frowned, belatedly realizing something didn't fit. 'Wait. Her father's not dead. Her roommate said she had a dad and a brother who's a doctor.'

'Go back and talk to the roommate again,' Abbott said.

Olivia gathered the Mary pages. 'What about Lincoln?

They're friends or have some relationship. Maybe Lincoln would know where she'd go.'

'Donahue said she'd call when he was interviewable,' Abbott said.

'I know,' Olivia said. 'But Truman said the Feds searched his house last night. I bet they have files, a laptop, something that tells us how Mary found Lincoln to begin with.'

Abbott's expression darkened. 'Lincoln's still ours on the B and E and assault.'

'Tell that to Special Agent Crawford,' Noah said, 'because that's who Truman claims did the search.'

Abbott's jaw cocked. 'I will. Micki, trace Eric's money. Barlow, check for places Eric, Tomlinson, and Blunt intersected. Keep me informed and nobody take off their vest.'

Wednesday, September 22, 4:05 P.M.

David put his tray on the table Tom had staked at the Deli. 'Busy today.'

Tom glanced up from his laptop. 'I know. Students are talking about the dead guy found in the dorm, the cops are talking about Kane, and the firefighters are either talking about your partner or . . . you.'

'Wonderful.' David sat and slid Tom's sandwich across the table. 'Eat.'

Tom frowned at the food, then at David's lack of it. 'Where's yours?'

'Can't.'

Tom pushed the plate to the middle of the table. 'Neither can I. Eat half.'

He managed to choke down a few bites, watching as

Tom plugged his wireless card into his laptop's slot. 'I'm still not sure I get the allure of this place,' David said. 'Food's only okay.'

'It's better than the dining hall. But most people come here to socialize.' He pointed at all the customers on their laptops. 'And because Kirby has free Wi-Fi.'

David looked up at the counter. 'Which one's Kirby?'

'The manager. Not up there right now. He's the one who chats and says "buh-bye."'

'Oh. Him.'

Tom looked up. 'Kirby bothers you?'

David fought the urge to squirm. 'He's just . . . intense.'

Tom shrugged. 'I think the flirtation is an act. He's not a bad guy. He helped Eve seven months ago when that so-called reporter was following her. Made sure she knew the reporter had been talking to that professor's secretary, stalking her and her friend.'

David remembered it. 'That information helped save Eve's life so I guess he can make eyes at me. Plus, he always sends coffee to the fire scenes if we've been there all night.' Still, there was something about the man that made him uncomfortable.

Tom nodded. 'There, I'm in.'

David eyed the card sticking out of Tom's laptop. 'If they have free wireless here, why use your card?'

Tom's eyes widened in dismay. 'Tell me you don't use free, unsecured Wi-Fi?'

David nodded warily. 'Yeah. Why?'

'Just askin' to be hacked,' Tom muttered. 'This card is secure. Nobody can touch my hard drive.' He slid his chair around the table so David could see the screen. 'I also put a coating over my screen so you have to be right in front of it to see anything.'

'Trusting soul, aren't you?' David asked.

'No.' Tom typed Mary's name and a screen full of links appeared. The first two pages were references to the two dead college students. There were three, David knew, but the police hadn't released the connection to Joel Fischer yet.

Tom kept paging and frowned. 'I get nothing on the name. What else you got?'

'Ethan gave me her social.' David turned the laptop toward him and typed it in from memory.

'I would have started with that,' Tom grumbled. 'Results – twenty-three, single. No dependents. No outstanding student loans. One savings, one checking account.'

'That's the other address Ethan gave me.' David pointed to the screen. 'The police checked already. She doesn't live there and the current residents don't know her. Can you check who were the previous residents?'

Tom entered the address into a property tax website. 'Current owners have been there for three years. The previous owner used this as a rental property. Previous owner is Mrs Annie Walsh, who is still alive and local.'

David was already on his feet. 'Let's go.'

Wednesday, September 22, 4:35 P.M.

Olivia and Noah got out of their car and approached the abandoned green Taurus. They'd been en route to the university to reinterview Mary's roommate when they'd gotten the call that Phoebe's car had been sighted on a remote road.

The officer who'd called it in pointed to a man who stood soberly watching them. 'He lives a half mile from here, heard about the victim on the radio.'

'We'll talk to him in a second, thanks.' Olivia walked around the car, afraid of what she'd see. 'No blood. Unlocked.' Her stomach clenched, she popped the trunk. Then sagged in relief when she saw it was empty. 'I had a bad picture in my mind.'

'So did I,' Noah said unsteadily.

Olivia walked the shoulder ahead of Phoebe's car, stopping when a flash of silver caught her eye. With a pen, she dug the chain from the dirt and held it up so the medallion swung. 'Noah. It's a St Jude medallion. Do you know if Phoebe wore one?'

'I think so. Eve has one just like it.'

She dropped it in a baggie and carefully tucked it in her pocket. For David. *Just in case.* But she wouldn't let herself think that way. For David.

'Tire treads,' Olivia noted. 'There was another car here.' They crossed the road and introduced themselves to the man who waited. 'When did you notice the green car?'

'About a half hour ago. I was coming back from an appointment in town. It wasn't here on my way in, but another car was. That was two hours ago.'

'Which car was there, sir?' Noah asked.

'A black Lexus.' He rattled off the license plate. 'I was going to give them a day to move it before I had it towed. I first noticed it today. It wasn't there as of ten last night.'

Olivia called in the plate number, then hung up, annoyed with herself. 'Thank you, sir. You've been a big help.' She hurried back to their car and got on the radio, Noah close behind. 'It's Eric's car,' she said. 'We never checked to see if he had one.'

'We were in a rush to find Albert,' he said after she'd put out a BOLO.

'I know.' But they couldn't worry about that now. 'All right. We know Phoebe was here and not bleeding. That's good. Let's check to see if Eric's Lexus has GPS.'

Wednesday, September 22, 5:05 P.M.

'Goddammit,' Olivia snarled as they pulled in front of Mary's dorm. 'Eric's road assist was disconnected four days ago. They tried contacting him and got no answer.'

'Then I hope the roommate has some new information for us.'

They found Mary's roommate, Helen, in the resident advisor's room, trying to study.

'Helen, earlier you said you met Mary's dad,' Olivia said. 'When was this?'

'After Christmas, last year. He brought her a present and she threw it in his face. Called him *Daddy.*' Helen mimicked a mocking tone. 'Like he was a douche.'

'What did he give her for the present?' Noah asked.

'Ten fifty-dollar bills.' She shrugged. 'I was eaves-dropping big-time. I've roomed with this group of girls for two years now. The others are okay, but Mary kept to herself. Everything was a big mystery. So when the man came up, I was surprised. So was she.'

'She didn't go down and get him?' Noah asked. 'I thought that was the rule.'

Helen shrugged again. 'I guess his badge got him through.'

Olivia got another very bad feeling. 'What kind of badge?'

'A cop, I think. You can check with security downstairs. They might have a record of it. It was after we came back from winter break. Mid-January. He said something about it being ten years and mending fences. Mary threw the money in his face, told him she never wanted anything from him, and ran to her room, crying.'

'What did Daddy do?' Olivia asked.

'Picked up the money. I was kind of hoping he'd leave it, but he didn't.'

'What about the doctor brother?' Noah asked.

'I saw her taking a sleeping pill once. Said she'd had trouble sleeping and her brother called it in. I asked if he could call me in a script and she said she'd ask. She never volunteered and I never brought it up again. Like I said, we weren't close.'

'Thanks,' Olivia said.

Downstairs, they asked the receptionist if she could track the cop's visit last year based on Mary's name and the approximate date.

'Of course. We can sort by the form of ID used,' the woman said. She did the search, then turned her screen. 'The visitors that week. Only one used a badge.'

Olivia stared, then looked up at Noah, stunned. 'This changes everything.'

Wednesday, September 22, 5:15 P.M.

'How can I help you?' Mrs Annie Walsh greeted them with a warm smile, instantly making David think of his mother. *Please*. His heart swelled to fill his throat, choking him. *Please don't let her be hurt. Please. I'll do anything*.

'Gentlemen?' Mrs Walsh stared at the two of them. 'Is something wrong?'

David cleared his throat harshly. 'We're looking for

information on a woman who lived in one of your rental properties. Her name is Mary O'Reilly. It would have been at least three years ago, maybe more.' He gave her the address.

'No, I never rented to any O'Reillys at that or any of my properties.' She started to close the door and David held up his hand, watching fear flicker over her face.

'Please, we're not criminals. My mother is missing. Her name is Phoebe Hunter.'

'My grandmother,' Tom added. 'It's been on the news today.'

Mrs Walsh's eyes widened. 'Oh my. I did hear about that. You poor boys. But I can't help you. I don't know any O'Reilly family.'

David pursed his lips, thinking. 'Her name was Mary Francesca. Maybe—'

'Mary Fran? Oh, of course, I remember her. Poor lamb. She'd lost her mother. That was before they came to live in my property, though.'

'How?' David asked and she hesitated, pity in her face. 'Please, ma'am.'

'It was a nightmare. Her father had left the house, to work. There was an intruder, and Mary Fran's mother was killed. Bludgeoned, I'm afraid. Mary's brother was badly injured. He lived, though. I think he was trying to protect their mother. Mary was found hiding in a closet, the phone in her hand. She'd heard the whole thing.'

'She called 911?' Tom asked.

'No, she didn't. That's the story I heard anyway. I never asked them if it was true.'

Panic was slowly chipping away at David's composure. 'When did this happen?'

'Lord, must've been ten years now. Maybe eleven. Mary

Fran was only twelve or thirteen, and Jonathan was sixteen or so.'

'Could we get the name of her father, of Mr O'Reilly?'

'I told you, there was no O'Reilly. Mary Fran's last name was Crawford.'

David's mouth fell open. He blinked, not believing he'd heard right. *Not a coincidence.* '*Crawford*?'

'Who's Crawford?' Tom demanded. 'David.'

'He's FBI. He chased Moss for years.'

Mrs Walsh nodded. 'Yes, that was his work. He left to investigate a case, and one of the criminals he'd put in jail was released and came back to harm his family.'

'Mrs Walsh, do you have an address or phone number for the brother, Jonathan?'

'I haven't heard from them since they moved. I wish I could help you. I'm sorry.'

'No, ma'am, you've helped us more than you know. Thank you.'

'Mr Hunter,' she called as they turned to go. 'I'll be praying for your mother.'

'Thank you,' David managed. As they were running to the car, David dialed Olivia, grimacing when he got her voice mail again. 'Olivia, it's David. Call me. Agent Crawford is Mary O'Reilly's father. She has a brother. *Call me.*'

They got in and Tom pulled into traffic. 'Where now?'

'We find Crawford. Go to the jail. I'm betting he's there, waiting to talk to Lincoln.'

'Why hasn't Crawford said anything?' Tom asked furiously. 'He has to have heard about Mary on the news. About Grandma. Why hasn't he said anything?'

'I don't know. But I'm sure as hell planning to ask. Drive faster, kid.'

Wednesday, September 22, 5:30 P.M.

He woke with a start, squinted at his alarm clock and groaned. He'd slept much longer than he'd planned. Rubbing his hands over his face, he grabbed his phone to check his texts. No word from Austin. Damn kid. Where the hell was he?

He aimed the remote at the television and the news filled the screen. Same old, same old. Fire, arson, dead cop, injured firefighter . . . He waited, then relaxed.

'Sixteen-year-old Austin Dent is still missing. Police ask anyone with any information . . .' *Excellent.* 'We continue to follow the story of the abduction of a woman by Mary O'Reilly.'

What the hell?

'Mrs Phoebe Hunter, of Chicago, was forced at gunpoint to become O'Reilly's getaway driver. O'Reilly was fleeing authorities who wish to question her in the deaths of two university students.'

He stood slowly, pushing his laptop to the bed. 'What the hell?' he whispered.

'O'Reilly is believed to be driving a black Lexus. She is armed and considered very dangerous. If you have information, please call MPD at the number on your screen.'

He tossed his phone to the bed and went to stand in front of the television, fists on his hips. 'What the fucking hell have you done now, you stupid bitch?'

He went still at the knock on his door. Quickly he logged out of his bank account, shut down his laptop, and pushed the bag of phones under his bed. Maybe it was Girl Scouts. Maybe they'd go away.

But they knocked again, harder. 'Open the door. I know you're in there.'

He gritted his teeth, recognizing the voice. *Thank you, Mary. So fucking much.* He pulled on a pair of pants and walked shirtless to the door. Through the peephole he could see the man he hadn't wanted to see in years.

The man still wore a tie and had his hair in that same 1960s flattop. He still wore a black suit, shiny shoes, and a gun at his hip. And he still carried a badge that he took way too seriously. One of these days it would be the death of him. *I hope.*

The knocking grew louder as did the man's voice. 'Open. This. Door. Now.'

So he did, standing with his head tilted to one side, his most flamboyant smile on his face. 'Hello, Dad. Long time no see.'

Chapter Twenty-Six

Wednesday, September 22, 5:45 P.M.

Crawford looked at him in disgust. 'Thank *God* I'm not your father. Are you alone?'

'Very. Come on in.' He aimed Crawford a seductive look, just for old times' sake.

It was all an act, of course. It had always been an act, conceived at first to piss Crawford off. Then later he'd realized that the macho cops in his shop didn't make eye contact when he flirted. It made him invisible. Just the way he liked it.

'Shut up. Look, all I want to know is, have you seen your sister?'

'No, but I saw the news. Naughty, naughty Mary. This is not gonna look good for you.' He tilted his head again, smiling. 'Maybe that was her plan all along.'

Crawford's jaw was clenched so tightly it was a wonder his teeth didn't shatter. 'Fine. That's all I wanted to know. Now we don't have to see each other, ever again.'

He shrugged lightly. 'I'm surprised you knew where to find me, quite frankly.'

'I've always known. This is my town. You don't sneeze without me knowing.'

He wanted to tell Crawford what he didn't know. 'Oh. Because *you* carry a badge.'

'You,' Crawford ground out, 'will never amount to anything.'

His eyes narrowed, anger long denied now bubbling up. 'You're right. Good thing you have one perfect son. But wait. He doesn't speak to you, either, and weren't you kind of demoted? This isn't *your town* anymore. Too bad you can't find Mary. At least you'd have one decent arrest before they put you out to pasture. Fresh triple homicide's gotta be worth more than a twelve-year-old single. See y'later. Buh-bye.'

Through his curtains he could see Crawford march to his car. But then the man stopped and looked up with a frown before getting in his car and driving away.

His gut clenched. He knew that look. Knew it was Crawford's I-just-discovered-a-truth look. *What did I say?* He wasn't sure.

And then he knew. 'Oh, shit,' he breathed. 'Oh, shit.' He grabbed a shirt, shoes, and his laptop. And his gun. Mary had only been linked to Albert and Eric in the news. Not Joel. *I shouldn't have known it was a triple homicide.*

The police were watching for the white van, so he jumped into his car, going the direction Crawford had gone. Maybe Crawford would think he'd meant that Phoebe Hunter was the third of Mary's homicides. Maybe. But he couldn't take that chance.

He caught up with Crawford and slowed his pace, staying far enough back that he couldn't be seen. He'd wait till Crawford stopped, then he'd take the bastard out.

He'd always wanted to, ever since his mother brought Crawford home. He'd been nine and had hated him then. His hate had grown considerably since. He hadn't realized how much until he'd seen Crawford's face again. He wondered what had set Mary off. She'd gone to a lot of trouble to leave the glass balls at each fire. She'd known what the discovery of the glass balls would mean. Exactly who it would bring.

Mary had always been a manipulative little bitch. She was improving with age.

Putting a bullet in Crawford's head would be almost as good as putting one in Mary's, which would be his next step. Because he had a pretty good idea of where she'd go.

Wednesday, September 22, 6:00 P.M.

'Pull over and let me out,' David said urgently, pointing to the police department. He'd been calling Olivia, Noah, and Abbott for twenty-five minutes with no success.

Tom pulled over. 'I'll find a place to park and come up.'

David had one foot on the pavement when his body went rigid. *Crawford.* 'There he is.' Fury exploded and he ran at Crawford, who had only a second to register alarm before David had him off the ground by the lapels of his black suit. 'Where is she?' He shoved Crawford up against the brick wall. *'Where the fuck is Mary?'*

'David!' Tom was behind him, pulling him away. 'Let him go.'

Crawford's face was crimson. 'Get your hands off me. This is assault on a—'

David shook Crawford hard, his vision going red at the edges. 'The next words out of your fucking mouth better be where we can find Mary. Because she has my mother.'

'*David!*' Olivia ran from the parking garage, Noah at her side. Dodging oncoming cars, she crossed the street and grabbed his arm. 'Not like this. Let him go.'

David lowered Crawford to the ground, slowly releasing his lapels. His fists dropped to his sides, but he didn't retreat an inch. 'Tell them, Crawford. Tell them about Mary.'

'David. We know about Mary and her brother. Take a breath.' She took his fist in her hands, held it, calming him. 'We'll get what we want to know. Trust me.'

'Arrest him,' Crawford sputtered. 'That was assault on a fed—'

Olivia turned, eyes flashing. 'If you say *federal agent*, I will walk away and let him take you apart, I swear to God. You sonofabitch. You had to have known what she did.'

Crawford's eyes flickered. 'I don't know where she is. I talked to her brother and he doesn't know either. Leave me alone.'

'She's your *daughter*,' Tom cried, his voice shaking. 'She has my grandmother.'

'She's not my daughter,' Crawford said coldly. 'I can't help you with your relative.'

David heard popping inside his brain. 'Your daughter has killed three men and has injured my friend. Her arsons killed five people, wiped out a neighborhood, and may have put my partner in a wheelchair. So you'd better find a way to help us.'

'You'd better consider your answer carefully, Agent Crawford,' Noah said, his face like stone. 'Your family appears to mean little to you, but it means a lot to us.'

'She is not my daughter. I married her mother, got her two psycho brats,' he spat.

'Because their mother was murdered,' David said.

498

'What case were you chasing the night an ex-con broke into your house and bludgeoned your wife to death?'

Crawford stepped back, hitting the brick wall. 'Preston Moss.'

'Barlow said you were a man obsessed,' Olivia murmured.

'No, I was doing my job. I was chasing a man who'd set fires, who'd killed.'

'You are going to stop chasing Moss,' Olivia said quietly, 'and start chasing Mary.'

'I don't know where she is.' His eyes gleamed, slyly, David thought and felt a shiver of repulsion skitter across his skin. 'But I can give you something else.'

'What?' Olivia demanded.

'My sources say that you've identified Mary and her three cohorts,' Crawford said, 'but there's someone else involved. Someone who knew she killed the Fischer kid. I'll tell you if you give me Lincoln Jefferson.'

She looked up at Crawford in disbelief. 'You want Moss that badly? You have no idea how much I want to turn away and let David kill you with his bare hands. I'm done with your games, your need-to-know, and your *quid pro quo*. You're sick. You don't deserve your badge.' She pulled out her cell, walked a few paces. 'I'm calling my captain.'

'Wait.' Crawford followed, closing his hand over hers. 'Don't call him. I'll tell—'

David flinched at the sound that cracked the air and threw himself forward, knocking Olivia and Crawford to the ground. People were screaming and from the corner of his eye he saw Tom throw himself over two women who'd crept close to overhear.

Noah sprinted across the street and David heard the squeal of tires and two more shots fired in rapid succession.

He hunkered over Crawford and Olivia as the doors of the police department flew open and six officers ran into the street, guns drawn.

Shaking, David pushed to his knees. 'Olivia. *Olivia*.' He pushed Crawford off her and his heart stopped. She was covered in blood and she wasn't moving. '*Olivia*.' He pressed his fingertips to her throat. And breathed. 'She's got a strong pulse,' he told the officer who'd knelt beside him. 'I can handle this. Go see to the others.'

The officer rushed off. David checked Crawford's pulse, but the man was dead, his blood pooling on the sidewalk from the huge hole in his chest. The bullet had blasted straight through him. Straight into Olivia. Probably hit her shoulder.

David swiftly unbuttoned her blouse to check for the bullet's entry, breathing a sigh of relief at the sight of the Kevlar vest she wore.

'What the hell is going on here?' Abbott fell to his knees beside them.

'She's unconscious. She hit her head on the concrete. I think all this blood is Crawford's.' Gingerly David pulled the Kevlar away, exposing her shoulder and he calmed a little more. Already forming was what would be a nasty bruise, but there was no blood, no gaping hole. Just beautiful skin. 'The bullet hit the vest.'

'Thank God.' Abbott looked paler than Olivia. 'I couldn't handle another one.'

She stirred, moaning a little, lifting her hand to her head. 'Ow.'

David pulled her hand away gently, his hand shaking now that he could see she was all right. Her fedora was half off her head and he set it aside, checking her head. 'You'll have a goose egg, but there's no open wound.'

'Good,' she murmured. 'You have enough stitches for both of us.'

He'd forgotten. Tentatively he ran his fingers over his jaw, relieved none of the sutures had burst. 'Can you sit up?'

She nodded and he helped her, giving in to the need to hold her for a moment. He pulled her close and felt her shudder. Or maybe it was his. 'Crawford?' she asked.

'He's dead,' David said, feeling only regret that they hadn't made him talk first.

Noah crouched beside them, breathing hard. 'Bullet came from a brown late-model Explorer. I chased, but he got away. I got the plate and called it in.'

'What the hell happened?' Abbott demanded.

'Crawford was Mary's stepfather,' Olivia said. 'I called to tell you, but you were in a meeting with the commander, closed door. Crawford said he didn't know where she was, but was about to tell us who else was involved when somebody shot him.'

Abbott frowned. 'He knew who the blackmailer is and didn't tell us right away?'

'Tried to bargain for custody of Lincoln,' Noah said.

'Sonofabitch,' Abbott said, looking down at Crawford's body with disgust.

David's mind was spinning. 'He said he'd talked to Mary's brother, who didn't know where she was. But what if the brother was lying? What if Jonathan's involved?'

Olivia looked at Noah, then back up at David, confused. 'Who's Jonathan?'

'Mary's brother,' David said.

Olivia struggled to her feet. 'No, Mary's brother is a doctor. Andy Crawford.'

David frowned. 'She's got two brothers then. One is

named Jonathan.' He told them what he and Tom had learned.

'Jonathan's who Crawford meant,' Olivia said. 'He couldn't have talked to Andy, because I was talking to him on my way back here. Andy's coming from Wisconsin, to try to help us find Mary.'

'Then let's find Jonathan,' David said grimly.

Wednesday, September 22, 6:20 P.M.

He would have preferred to have shot Crawford in the head, but he'd been forced to choose a wider target as he'd shot from a moving car. He thought Crawford would never duck around those tall men. He'd been arguing with Sutherland. *If he'd told them about me, they would have run for their cars.* So he thought he was safe, for now.

He pulled over, taking his gun and laptop. Webster had made out his plate, which didn't matter as the plate was stolen. Still, it was too dangerous to keep driving this car around with a million cops searching for him. He'd steal one, then go find Mary.

Then it was time to go. He'd had a good run here, developed some skills. He'd get the fake ID he kept stashed in his safe-deposit box and start over somewhere cool. As long as he had his offshore bank numbers, the world was his damn oyster.

Wednesday, September 22, 6:30 P.M.

Olivia looked up when the conference room door opened and immediately wished she hadn't. The room careened

502

around her, taking her stomach with it. David closed the door behind him, in his eyes the abject terror that had been there since Mary drove off with his mother.

'You need to get x-rayed.' He dropped the handful of items he carried on the table. 'Tylenol, ice packs, a clean T-shirt from Micki, and a clean vest from Abbott.'

She shrugged out of the shirt, happy not to be wearing Crawford's blood and guts anymore. But she couldn't manage the button at her wrist, and David took up the task.

His gaze fixed on the hole in the fabric. He stared a few seconds, his face stark.

Her mind replayed the moment, as she knew his was. The shot, the impact of the bullet, the sudden warmth of blood, the three of them, falling. 'I'm sorry, David. I should have gotten what Crawford knew. If I hadn't been so angry . . .' She closed her eyes, miserable. 'We'd know who the blackmailer is. We might know where Mary is.'

He was quiet as he peeled the bloody vest away and taped an ice pack to her shoulder. 'You need to keep that ice pack on for at least twenty minutes, then you can put the vest back on. You're going to have some loss of rotation in your shoulder.'

He hadn't responded to her apology and it stung. But what did she expect him to say? That it was all right? It wasn't. She'd been outraged, acted impulsively, and now Crawford was dead, taking his knowledge with him. If they didn't get to Phoebe in time . . . *David won't forgive me. I won't forgive myself.*

'It's my left arm. I can still shoot.' She popped a Tylenol and pressed the second ice pack to her head. 'I need to get back. Thanks for the first aid.'

He helped her to her feet, holding her when she would

have bolted. 'Olivia, wait. Look at me.' She did and saw no accusation in his eyes. Just raw fear. 'You didn't know Crawford would be killed. Do I wish we knew what he knew? Hell, yes. But in your place, I would have done the same thing. Lincoln did a terrible thing twelve years ago and he should pay for his crime, but Crawford . . . he was somehow worse.'

She shuddered out a breath and leaned into him. 'We'll find Mary a different way.'

His arms came around her and they clung, taking comfort and strength. 'Don't leave without the new vest,' he whispered fiercely. 'Promise me.'

She kissed him softly. 'I won't take chances. I have to get back now.'

She stepped out of the conference room and blinked. Louise Tomlinson was coming out of the elevator. 'Mrs Tomlinson?'

Louise hesitated, then squared her shoulders. 'Detective Sutherland. I need to talk to you. It's important. I heard about Detective Kane on the news. I'm sorry.'

Olivia forced herself to meet the woman's gaze, rather than looking at Kane's empty desk. 'Thank you. I'm working with Detective Webster on your husband's murder. Please come with me.'

She led Louise into Abbott's office where Noah sat at the round table with Barlow and Micki. 'Abbott's with the Feds, dealing with Crawford's shooting,' he said without looking up. He was studying a printout with narrowed eyes. 'I got cell LUDs on both Blunt and Tomlinson. Barlow and Micki have their credit card statements.'

Olivia cleared her throat. 'This is Mrs Tomlinson. This is Detective Webster and Sergeants Barlow and Ridgewell.'

The three of them abruptly lifted their eyes, then Noah

stood. 'Mrs Tomlinson, please sit down. We're all very sorry for your loss.'

Louise took the chair he held out for her. 'Thank you. I had a visitor at my house this morning. He said he was a reporter, asked me a lot of questions about my husband, his finances. He started asking very personal questions about the nature of my divorce and I asked him to leave. Thankfully my son was with me. The young man was large and intimidating. The visit upset me and my son insisted I take one of the sleeping pills my doctor prescribed. When I woke up hours later, I watched the news and saw the young man who'd come to my house.'

'What did he look like?' Olivia asked, trying to keep her excitement contained.

'Like this.' Louise drew a folded paper from her purse. 'I got it from the Internet. I had to look it up to be sure it was the same man.'

Olivia unfolded it and swallowed her sigh. 'Albert.'

Louise nodded. 'I didn't know he was dead until an hour ago. I didn't know Detective Kane was dead either. My son's been trying to keep me from becoming too upset. When I realized what had happened, I knew I needed to talk to you. From the questions he asked, I think this Albert person knew my husband had been blackmailed.'

She said it as though the blackmail came as no surprise to her. *The sex pictures*, Olivia thought. Tomlinson's blackmail. 'How did you know your husband was having an affair, ma'am?'

'He was getting undressed one night and his underwear were on inside out. I've folded and put them in his drawer for thirty years. I knew they were right when he put them on. I kept watching, found more signs. Finally I had lunch with a friend and got the name of her PI. A week later the

PI brought me pictures. The next day, I got another envelope of pictures in the mail. I was in shock, seeing Barney with that whore . . .' She swallowed hard. 'The pictures that came in the mail weren't labeled. I guess I assumed they'd come from the PI, too. Now, after that young man visited . . . I'm not sure.'

'They were taken at different times,' Micki said. 'The PI's photos and the others.'

Louise frowned. 'I didn't notice. I didn't look at them too closely. I couldn't.'

'You combined all the pictures and gave them to your attorney?' Olivia asked.

'Yes. If I'd thought about it two nights ago, I would have told you.' Louise's eyes filled. 'I heard about last night's fire, the firefighter, your partner. I'm so sorry.'

Olivia squeezed her hand. 'You didn't know. You're here now. You told your friend and the PI about your suspicions about your husband. Did anyone else know?'

'No. I knew Barney would put up a fight if he knew I knew. Maybe even take our money. I had to think of our son, his future. I kept my mouth shut until my lawyer filed the divorce papers.'

'Where did you meet your friend?' Noah asked.

'This sandwich place near the hospital, where I volunteer. It's called the Deli.'

Barlow's eyes lit up and Olivia's pulse picked up pace. 'That's the connection? The Deli?' she asked excitedly and Barlow nodded.

'It's gotta be. I have Deli charges on both Tomlinson's and Blunt's credit cards.'

'And we found a cup from the Deli in the trash at Eric's,' Micki said. 'Somebody could have been sitting next to all of them and intercepted their data. Let's get the store video, match these dates with the day Mrs Tomlinson and her friend met and see who pops.' She started to get up, but Noah shook his head.

'The Deli only has a camera on the cash register. Remember, we asked for that seven months ago, when we were looking for Pit-Guy's victims.'

Micki slumped back in her chair. 'You're right. Well, dammit.'

'I don't think I noticed who was sitting around me,' Louise said. 'I'm sorry. If you want to hypnotize me or something, I'd be good with that.'

Olivia frowned, a thought forming in her mind. *No, it couldn't be. But what if it was?*

'Mrs Tomlinson, thank you for coming in. I need to ask you to wait outside, please.' She motioned to Abbott's clerk, who quickly hurried over. 'Faye, can you get Mrs Tomlinson a coffee? Thanks.'

When Louise was gone, Olivia grabbed the sketch of the man Austin had seen. *It could be.* She held it up. '"Thanks for coming. Buh-bye,"' she said and Micki's eyes widened.

'No freaking way,' Micki said. '*Kirby*?'

'No.' Noah shook his head. 'Not possible. He helped Eve last year.' Then his eyes closed. 'Because of a conversation he overheard. Hell.'

Micki sat back, stunned. 'He has free Wi-Fi. I've even used it. Oh my God.'

'That could have been him in the brown Explorer,' Noah said. 'Right body type.'

'We need units to the Deli,' Olivia said. 'If he goes back, we need to be ready.'

Barlow grabbed the phone on Abbott's desk. 'I'll do it.'

Olivia stared at the sketch. 'Austin. We never announced that we picked him up.'

'He may think Austin's still missing,' Micki said.

'And he wanted him enough to kill Kane.' Olivia closed her eyes, trying to focus but the back of her head throbbed like a bitch. 'What if we sent a message from Austin's phone, asking to meet "Kenny"?'

'We could be waiting, catch him,' Noah said.

'Or let him get away again,' Olivia countered evenly. 'He might go to Mary.'

'He might go to France,' Micki said flatly. 'I don't want to lose him.'

'You think I do?' Olivia snapped. 'He murdered Kane. I want to gut him and watch him bleed and beg for mercy. But Phoebe's still out there. If you have a better idea, let's have it.'

'He's killed five people,' Noah said. 'I don't want Phoebe to be number six. Let's run it by Abbott. He has to approve it.'

Barlow hung up Abbott's phone. 'No Kirby at the Deli and no brown Explorer. But there is a white van parked around the back.'

Micki's smile was sharp. 'I'll get a warrant for the van and property. You set the Austin trap. We'll find a way to track him.'

Olivia pushed herself to her feet. She could see David and Tom standing near her desk, David bandaging Tom's hand. She could feel his fear from here. Would feel his heartache if she failed. 'We can't lose him. We have to find Mary.'

'Are you going to tell them?' Noah asked, pointing to the two men.

'About Kirby, but not about trying to lure him. I don't want to get their hopes up.'

Noah patted the shoulder that wasn't iced down. 'I'm going to find Abbott, get this moving. Sit down and rest for a few minutes. I'll be back.'

'No, we'll need a positive ID from Austin to get a warrant. I'll get a six-pack photo array together and get Kirby's license photo to drop in. I'll meet you back here.'

Wednesday, September 22, 6:30 P.M.

Mary pointed to a side road. 'Stop the car and get out.'

Her bones creaking, Phoebe obeyed. She let out a quiet groan as she tried to straighten her back, then grimaced as she drew a breath. The air was heavy with the stale odor of burned wood. Phoebe couldn't see the burned condo, but she knew it couldn't be far. They'd taken so many turns, she had no idea where she was exactly. They were on a lake, but they'd passed a lot of those. *Minnesota*, she thought, *land of ten thousand lakes*. She'd thought the brochures had been exaggerating.

'Why are we here?' *I'll never find my way out of here, even if I get away.*

Mary shoved the barrel of the gun into her back. 'Move.'

They'd parked the car on a side road that appeared not to have been used for some time. The trees were so thick that they hadn't walked fifty feet before the car was completely hidden. Phoebe's feet were numb from sitting so long in the car and she had rather pressing needs elsewhere. 'Is it far?'

'No,' Mary said tightly. Her hands were shaking. The woman had become increasingly tense as the hours had passed.

'Mary, I need to know. They said you killed those men. Is it true?'

Mary's chin lifted as she walked. 'Yes.'

Phoebe's blood chilled. 'Okay. Why?'

'Eric was going to run away. He was going to leave me and Albert holding the bag. He *used* me to save his own hide. He thought he knew everything, but in the end he was just a damn coward. Running away to France. Nobody uses me.'

'How did you know?'

'I went to his place because we were supposed to go to Joel's funeral together. He wasn't home, but Joel had a key, so I went in.'

'Joel is dead, too?'

Her face twisted. 'Yes. It was a car accident.'

Phoebe frowned, trying to remember. 'Oh. Joel. I heard about that on the news.' And now pieces she'd overheard David and Glenn muttering about became clearer. 'You cared for Joel?'

'Yes. Joel had a thing for causes,' she said bitterly. She was running her free hand up and down her arm in jagged little movements as she walked, a twitch in each step.

'Causes are usually good things.'

'I was his cause. And now he's dead.'

Her tone made Phoebe's blood chill a little more. 'Did you kill him, too?' Mary said nothing and Phoebe had her answer. 'I see. What about the other one?'

Her eyes narrowed. 'Albert. That sonofabitch. Said he'd break my neck if I didn't do what he said. Nobody says that to me. Nobody. Uses. Me.'

'I'll keep that in mind,' Phoebe said dryly. 'What about Lincoln? Did he use you?'

'No.' Her voice abruptly softened. 'Lincoln loved me.'

Phoebe thought of the man her son had described as pathetic and tortured. 'Did you love him?'

'Not like that. But he thought I did, when he was on his meds.'

'My son said Lincoln is mentally ill.'

'Yes.'

'David said the FBI was interested in Lincoln for an old arson.'

'They couldn't find him with all their guns and bugs and spycams, but I did,' she boasted. 'Yes, I used him. But I won't let him kill him,' she added.

'What? Him, who?'

Mary blinked, as if surprised she'd said the last thing. 'Just . . . shut up and walk. That's where we're going, that cabin.'

Wednesday, September 22, 6:50 P.M.

'It's just a scrape,' Tom said between clenched teeth. He'd shaved a layer of skin diving to protect two bystanders when the shot that killed Crawford was fired. 'Don't fuss.'

'I have to. It's keeping me sane.' David finished bandaging Tom's hand and looked to the window where Olivia stood, watching them. A new shaft of fear pierced him.

'It's like when there's turbulence and the flight attendants are scared,' Tom murmured, his eyes on Olivia as well.

David sank into Olivia's chair, closing his eyes to focus. 'Being terrified won't bring Mom home. What do we know about Mary?'

'She was pissed at her stepfather,' Tom said.

'Because she holds him responsible for her mother's death. She loved her mother.'

'So she might not hurt Grandma.' Tom's voice took a hopeful note.

'Right.' It might not be true, but, like tending others, the notion helped him stay sane. 'What else?'

'We know Mary and Joel met in an environmental ethics class,' Olivia said behind him. He started to get up, but she perched on her desk. 'And that killing Joel upset her.'

'She believed,' Tom murmured. 'She believed in Preston Moss.'

'Or she knew re-creating Moss's fires was the best way to get back at Crawford,' David said. 'Somehow she sought out Lincoln through that website, earned his confidence. He told her information that nobody else had. I wonder who first brought up the idea of the condo arson. Mary or Joel?'

'I'm betting Mary,' Olivia said, 'and that Joel thought it was his idea.' She hesitated. 'We also think we know who Jonathan is. Or at least who the blackmailer is.'

Both David and Tom stared. 'Who?' David demanded.

'I know it sounds crazy, but Kirby. From the Deli. All the blackmail victims went there. He has access to their e-mail. And he resembles the man Austin saw.'

Tom's eyes narrowed. 'I told you about that free Wi-Fi. You said I was paranoid.'

David's mind was reeling. 'You are, but that's okay.'

'Why aren't we going to the Deli to get him?' Tom demanded.

'He's not there,' Olivia said patiently. 'We're going for a warrant and I've got some work to do to help with that. You guys should go get some food or coffee or something. Just not at the Deli. Promise me. I don't want him scared off.'

She met David's eyes, hers a little too intense. 'Don't lose faith.'

His eyes narrowed. 'Something's about to happen.'

'We may have another trick up our sleeve.' She laid her finger across his lips. 'Don't ask. I wasn't going to tell you that much. I don't want you to be hurt.'

If it doesn't work. 'Why did you tell me then?' he murmured against her finger.

Pain filled her eyes. 'I need you to know I'm doing everything I can.'

Covering her hand with his, he pressed it hard to his lips. 'I know you are.'

'Go get something to eat,' she whispered. 'Let us do our jobs.'

He watched her walk away, then hauled his body out of the chair, feeling a million years old. 'We haven't checked on Glenn.'

'I did, when you were bandaging up Olivia,' Tom said. 'He's physically fine. They'll let him go tomorrow. He told me to tell you to keep looking for Grandma, not to visit him.'

'Then let's go.'

'To do which? Look for Grandma or get something to eat?'

'Both,' David said grimly.

They went down the elevator and out the door, and David couldn't hold back the shudder at the blood-stains on the sidewalk. The area was barricaded off with yellow tape and passersby stared. *Olivia's okay*, he told himself. *She wasn't shot*. But she could have been. If not today, then next week. Next month. Any time in the future.

'Part of me wants to keep her out of the path of bullets.'

He blinked, unaware he'd said it out loud until he heard it.

'She probably wants to keep you out of the path of fiery, falling beams,' Tom replied soberly. 'And I'd agree with her. But she won't ask and neither will I.'

'It's who I am. It's who she is, too.'

'She's careful,' Tom said. 'Dana never was.'

That's how Olivia's different. She had the same need to protect without the drama Dana had always had swirling around her. Olivia got the job done. Efficiently and quietly. She'd do what needed to be done, the right way. A ringing phone startled him from his thoughts and David realized it was coming from his own pocket. He pulled out the prepaid cell he'd forgotten he still had. 'Hello?'

'David? This is Truman Jefferson. I'm sorry to bother you.'

'Not at all. What's wrong?'

'After you left, the police shut me down for the afternoon, to process the scene. I went home, tried to get some work done, and I found some pictures that Lincoln took. One of his jobs was taking photos of new listings to put on our website, but these pictures show a property that isn't one of my listings. I don't recognize the location, but it's a cabin near some kind of a park. Some of the pictures show a lake, which I know isn't helpful. But I wanted to tell you because some of the pictures have Mary in them. I guess they went there together. I thought you needed to know.'

David's mind started racing and then his feet were, too. Tom pulled ahead, leading him to where he'd parked the car. 'Can you describe the park?' David asked urgently.

'It's old. Just an old-fashioned park, like when I was a

kid. A sandbox, a metal swing set, a merry-go-round – you know, the ones that look like a flat spaceship.'

'Yeah, I know.' He did. He'd seen that little park, Monday morning when he'd taken Olivia up in the bucket. She'd taken pictures. She'd have the layout. 'Any specific features on this cabin?' He got in the passenger side of the car, and Tom was pulling into traffic before he'd shut his door. 'The condo,' he told Tom.

'It has a green awning on the back,' Truman said, 'but no house number. I'm sorry.'

'No, this is amazing. This is good.'

'Mary may not be there, but it's a place she and Lincoln must have liked.'

'Have you seen Lincoln?'

'They let me visit him this afternoon, but he was too doped up to talk. The psychiatrist told me you were kind to him. I wanted to thank you.'

'It's okay. If you find anything else out, please call me.'

'Wait,' Tom said. 'Ask if he can scan those pictures in and send them to my e-mail.'

'Yes,' Truman said after David gave him Tom's e-mail address. 'I'll do that right now. Good luck. God bless.'

'Thank you.' David closed his phone and closed his eyes, visualizing the scene. 'It's one of those cabins at the lake near the condo. I took Olivia up in the bucket to see the layout and I saw the park. From the bucket, it was at eleven o'clock. We won't be able to see the awning from the road. We'll have to come in from the back.'

'Do you have any weapons?' Tom asked.

'No. Hopefully Mary hasn't improved her marksmanship in the last five hours.' He dialed Olivia and swore softly when he got her voice mail, again. 'It's David. I may know where they are. Check the photos you took from the bucket at the condo. It's a cabin with a green awning. Call me.' He called the police department's main number and gave them the same information, then he buckled his seat belt. 'Drive faster, kid.'

Wednesday, September 22, 7:10 P.M.

The sun was setting and for the first time Phoebe wondered if David would be too late. Mary was growing more agitated, hugging herself as she paced the floor. Phoebe had seen the track marks on her arms and knew she was starting to withdraw. Mary had been unpredictable. She still held the gun, but carelessly by the barrel, not by the handle.

Mary had made her stop the car about a half mile from the cabin in which they now hid. She'd obviously been here before, going straight to an unlocked window and forcing Phoebe through. She'd then tied her to a chair with, ironically, the pull cords from the window blinds. *If I ever get out of here, David and Glenn will laugh at that.*

Mary was pacing, tapping the gun against her palm. *Calm her down, if you can.* 'If you'll untie me, I'll make you some hot tea,' Phoebe said. 'I see a kettle on the stove.'

Mary threw her a glare. 'You're crazy. I tie you up and you want to be nice to me?'

'Frankly, if I had that gun I would shoot you. I wouldn't kill you, but I'd make it so you couldn't chase me. But I don't have the gun and you look like you need some tea.'

'You're a strange woman, Phoebe.' Her mouth trembled. 'I don't want to hurt you.'

'I don't want you to hurt me either. Mary, what are you planning to do with me? You haven't made any calls, made any demands.'

Her laugh was brittle. 'In the movies, they ask for passage to Mexico.'

'But you'd always be looking over your shoulder. No way to live.'

'Prison is no way to live either.'

'Then you've got a hard choice to make. But you need to make it, because I don't like being forced around at gunpoint. You can't hide here forever.'

Mary looked around the room longingly. 'I wanted to. Live here forever, I mean.'

'When was this?' Phoebe asked gently.

'When I was little. My mom and dad – my real dad – would come up here and we'd have a normal family vacation.'

'How old were you?'

'Four. I was five when he died.' Her jaw tightened. 'And then she married *him*.'

'Who, honey?'

'Crawford. He had a kid already. Andy was nice, but Crawford . . . We had to be perfect. Make the beds. Up at sunrise. Straight As. I hated Crawford the day I met him.'

'Your mother must have loved him.'

'My mother had no family and no job. When my real dad died, we were so poor. Food stamps. Government cheese. My mother couldn't feed us. She needed a man.'

'My husband died when my youngest was still in school. It was hard.'

Mary was pacing again, gun in her hand. 'How did he die?'

'Car accident. One of my sons was with him. He was paralyzed for a while.'

Mary's face shadowed. 'Like the firefighter will be. I didn't mean for that to happen. I didn't want to set the other two fires. Eric and Albert made me.'

She sounded like a wounded child, and Phoebe suspected that, deep down, she was. But the wounded child had killed so many and right now held a gun. The wounded child needed to be stopped, however possible. Phoebe had spoken the truth. If she had to, she would use the gun to stop Mary. *If I have to, I'll kill her.*

For now, all Phoebe had was her quiet voice and her instinct that was screaming that this girl craved a mother. 'I know, honey. But you did. There are consequences to your actions. The condo fire you set killed two people.'

Mary shook her head. 'No. No. We didn't know the girl was there. And somebody else killed the guard. That wasn't me.'

'My son almost died that night. He almost fell four stories. David would have died.'

'He caught the ball,' she murmured. 'I didn't mean for him to get hurt.'

'What did you think would happen when you set the fire, Mary? Did you think it would burn nicely and stop all by itself? You set fires, firefighters come. It's what they do. You lit a match and put a dozen men and women in mortal danger.'

'Nothing happened to them.'

'Not Sunday night. What about last night? David almost died again, and his partner may never walk again. And don't tell me you didn't mean for that to happen, Mary,' she ordered sharply and saw the girl flinch. Satisfied she'd delivered her point, she softened her tone. 'You have to run or turn yourself in. Those are the only choices I see here.'

'Eric was going to France. I should have kept him alive so he could take me, too.'

Phoebe didn't think her blood could go much colder,

but she was wrong. There was no remorse for the murder, only Mary's regret that she hadn't been more forward-thinking.

'Well, you didn't. So, coming full circle, what do you plan to do with me?'

Mary tensed, then slapped the gun on the counter. 'I'm going to shut you up.'

Phoebe watched, breath held, as Mary rummaged in the kitchen drawers. She came out of the kitchen with a pair of scissors and a large roll of duct tape. 'Lincoln brought this with him the last time we came. He fixed the swing outside for me.' She slapped a piece of tape over Phoebe's mouth, dragged the chair around the back of the sofa, and shoved it over on its side. 'Now I don't have to look at you or listen to you.'

Phoebe tried to ignore the pain jolting through her stiff joints. She'd pushed the girl as far as she dared. It was clear Mary didn't want to hurt her now, but if the girl became more desperate, that could change.

There was a chill at her back. The sliding glass door was a few feet away. If Mary went to sleep, and if she could scoot close enough, and if she could manage to get the door open . . . It was damn frustrating to have an escape so close and so far away.

Okay, David, I'm ready for you to come get me now.

Chapter Twenty-Seven

Wednesday, September 22, 7:15 P.M.

'That's done.' Olivia glued Kirby's photo into the array. Austin was on his way in with his mother, so hopefully the ID and the subsequent warrant wouldn't take long.

'I sent the text from Austin's phone to the fake Kenny account,' Noah said. 'We've got SWAT and snipers surrounding the meet. We picked an area that'll be deserted this time of night. I'll stake it out. You go home, rest your head.'

'I'll go, too, as soon as Austin ID's Kirby.' Too nervous to sit, she checked her messages. Deleting the ones from reporters, she stopped dead in her tracks as she listened to David's voice, then pulled her camera from her desk drawer before the message was over. 'Noah, David knows where Mary went. Up at the lake, near the condo.'

'David and Tom went up alone?' he demanded and she flashed him a look.

'What do you think?'

They started to run, then stopped at Abbott's command. 'What going on?'

'David found Mary,' Olivia said. 'We have to move.'

'Where's your vest?'

She slapped at her shoulder, realized she still wore the ice pack. 'In the conference room. Go get the car,' she said to Noah. 'I'll suit up and meet you downstairs.'

Wednesday, September 22, 7:25 P.M.

'That's it.' David pointed to a green awning, about a hundred yards away. They'd parked as close as they dared and now crept through the heavy trees lining the lakeshore. 'I wish I had binoculars.'

'I wish I had a gun,' Tom muttered. 'What's our plan?'

'I don't know,' David whispered back. 'Yet. Just hurry.' They ran as noiselessly as possible. And then David's heart stopped. *No. Please, no.*

They were at the edge of the cabin's backyard. There was a sliding glass patio door in the rear wall. A few feet from the glass door was the back of a sofa. And behind that sofa lay his mother on her side, tied to a chair.

He heard the swift intake of Tom's breath. 'Is she moving?'

'I can't see. Stay here, I'll get closer. If anything happens, you run.'

'Where are the police?' Tom hissed, grabbing his arm.

'I don't know. Maybe they're coming without sirens. Trust me.'

He came up on the house from the side, his feet light. Crouching low, he moved along the back of the cabin, peering in the glass door, and relief hit him like an iron fist.

His mother was shifting her feet. She was bound at the ankles, her arms wrapped around the chair and tied at the wrists. There was no blood. No injuries he could see. He could cut her free in under ten seconds.

Except that Mary was in the kitchen, stirring a pot on the stove. The gun was on the counter next to her. Mary might be a lousy shot, but if she saw the glass door slide open, she might shoot, get lucky, and actually hit one of them.

He motioned to Tom who followed the path he'd taken, hunkering down next to him. 'She's okay,' David whispered. 'Mary still has a gun. We need a diversion.'

'We need a damn gun,' Tom muttered.

'Well, we don't have one,' David snapped quietly. 'I want you to go to the front and find the biggest whatever you can find. Rock, tree branch, anything you can heft. Throw it through that kitchen window and run like hell. If you hit Mary, great. If not, she'll be startled enough by the glass breaking that I can get through that door and get Mom out.'

'And if she's not startled, or goes after you?'

'I'll get Mom out.'

'And get shot.'

'Not if you hit Mary with the damn rock. You're the hoops star. Pretend like it's a throw from the three-point line.'

'It's a stupid plan. You're going to get yourself killed.'

David twisted to stare him down. 'You got a better one?'

Tom gritted his teeth. 'No.' He started to move, then David grabbed his arm.

'Wait. Someone's coming.'

Tom's sigh was relieved. 'The cops. With guns.' He started to move again.

'Wait. It's not a cop car.' The engine sound was wrong. 'It's got a bad plug.'

'What?'

'It's got a bad spark plug,' David said between his teeth. 'Wait.'

'We need to get her out of there,' Tom insisted.

'You move now, you might get her killed. Wait. Trust me.' He didn't breathe, just stood there waiting, dreading what would come next. His instincts were right.

He could hear the cabin's front door burst open, a shrill scream, and the voice that had often asked him how many creams for his coffee.

'Hey, sis,' Kirby said. 'Miss me?'

Next to him, Tom's eyes narrowed angrily. 'Now what?' he mouthed.

He stood there grinning at Mary's slack-jawed shock at seeing him, especially the gun in his hand. Her eyes flicked to the puny gun on the counter and he chuckled. 'Don't even think about it.'

'How . . . ?' Mary stared. 'How did you know?'

'What, that you were here? Mary Fran. I figured you hadn't picked the condo at random.' He looked around. 'The place hasn't changed much since Mom and Dad brought us here. I bet you had Joel thinking it was all his idea. Savin' the wetlands.'

Realization dawned in her eyes. '*You*. You were there. You videotaped us. You made us do the other fires. You *blackmailed* us.'

'I did.' He nodded smugly. 'I totally did. I have to admit I wondered what game you were playing – until I heard about the glass ball. Nice touch. Brought the old man down out of reservation lands. Got his hopes up for the big kill. Kudos.'

Her chin lifted. 'I wanted him to think he'd finally gotten his great white whale.'

'For thirty seconds he might have, but the balls were different. Even Crawford was smart enough to see a copycat.'

She shook her head. 'No. I had details nobody else knew. Crawford thinks it's Moss's people. He thinks he has someone who can lead him to Moss, but he can't.'

'Really?' He had to admit he was now intrigued. 'How did you find these details?'

'I e-mailed the webmaster of Moss's website. Flattered him, told him that I loved Moss, too. We met in person and he trusted me. Told me things I used to set Crawford up, to bring him to me. I wanted to make Crawford think his dream was in reach.'

E-mail . . . She merely updated her old tricks with new technology. 'And then?'

Her eyes narrowed. 'I know where Moss is. I would have made him beg, like Mom begged. Then I would have killed him.'

'Well, you can die knowing that I did it for you.' He aimed his gun, watched the remaining color drain from her face. 'You set me up ten years ago. Today you pay.'

She took a step back. 'I didn't mean to, Jonathan. I never meant it to happen.'

'I'm sure you didn't. Because you never think past the end of your goddamn nose. Where's the old lady? The hostage you took. Hunter, right? I bet she's related to that pretty firefighter who caught your glass ball. Where did you stash her? In the *closet*?'

She shook her head. 'I killed her already. Left her body in her car.'

'That was stupid. She could have been your ticket to France.' He laughed at that. 'Eric was an idiot. Did you kill him, or was it Albert?'

'No,' she said faintly, her eyes on the gun in his hand. 'I killed them all.'

'Even Joel? I'd given that one to Albert.'

She closed her eyes, her throat working as she swallowed hard. 'Joel was losing it. He was going to tell. I gave him the first pill, just to calm him down.'

'But when he woke up, he'd still be hysterical. He couldn't live with that girl's face in the window. So you decided to make it easier for everyone. Or for yourself. I have to give it you. You've never changed.'

'I didn't mean for that to happen,' she said desperately. 'I was only thirteen. I froze.'

'In the closet, with the cordless phone in your hand. If I'd known you were going to play that game, I would have called 911 myself. But I gave you the phone . . .' His jaw tightened as the memory came back, as clear as if it had happened this morning instead of ten years ago. 'And I tried to fight an ex-con with a big grudge and a bigger bat.' He stepped closer to her. 'An ex-con *you* brought there.'

She shook her head. 'No. He wanted revenge against Crawford. It was supposed to have been Crawford who died. Not Mom. Never Mom.'

'But Crawford wasn't home, 'cuz he was off chasin' Moss, and the mean ex-con wasn't choosy, was he?' he asked bitterly. 'I got to watch him beat Mom's head in and then I enjoyed a little of his revenge. Put me in the hospital for a month.'

'I know,' she gritted from behind clenched teeth.

'Ah, because you were *there*. Listening. In the *closet*. Did you hear him call for you? I did. He called your name again and again. He knew your name.' He leaned forward, eyes narrowed. 'Did you really think no one would find out, Mary Fran?'

She took an unsteady step back. 'You knew?'

'Oh yeah. I knew. After I got out of the hospital, they told me they'd caught the bad ex-con. That they'd thrown away the key and he'd never get out of prison. But I kept remembering how he'd called your name. I thought I'd dreamed it but knew I hadn't. So I visited him and I asked him how he knew you. Why he called for you.'

'He told you about the letters,' she murmured.

'He did. What did you *think* would *happen* when you wrote letters to men in prison saying how you hated your stepdaddy as much as they did and if they ever wanted your help to kill him, you'd be happy to oblige? Why did you do it?'

'Because I was thirteen and I thought they'd never get out!' she cried. She sank to the floor, sobbing. 'I thought they'd never get out of jail, and if they did, they'd come after Crawford. He was the one who put them there. Not me. It wasn't my fault.'

'No, it never is, is it? It's never your fault.'

David watched, horrified, as Kirby rounded the kitchen counter, his gun aimed at Mary's head. Thought about how coolly Kirby had shot Crawford in front of a police station. There was no doubt that Mary would be next. He glanced at his mother, still tied to the chair. Kirby didn't yet know she was there, but they couldn't take the chance that he'd find out. Once the gun was pointed at his mother's head, it would be too late.

Kirby wouldn't let any witnesses live.

He looked at his empty hands, wishing like hell he had a weapon. Any weapon. But all he had was a stupid penknife. *I need a gun. Why the hell didn't I get a gun?*

But he didn't have one and he couldn't change that

now. He made himself shut out the fear and focus on a way to get his mother free. He could hear Kirby's car out front, still running, and a plan formed in his mind. He leaned over to whisper in his nephew's ear. 'Tom, this is what I want you to do. Don't argue, just trust me. Can you do that?'

Tom nodded shakily. 'Yes.'

He looked down at his sister in disgust. 'What set you off? After all these years, what made you want to draw Crawford out?'

She looked up, her eyes wild like an animal's. 'He came to visit me. On the tenth anniversary. He gave me money. He said he wanted to make amends. *Amends*. There were no amends for what he did. If he'd been there, he could have saved her.'

He had to blink at her. 'You're really fucking nuts, aren't you? You brought a dangerous criminal to the house and you blamed Crawford? Almost makes me feel sorry for the prick. Except that he didn't believe me when I tried to tell him about you.'

Her eyes widened. 'You told him?'

'Oh yeah. But he didn't listen. You were so distraught. How could I make up such lies? And you looked like Mom. He couldn't believe you'd be so . . . bad.'

'You told him?' she repeated, stunned.

'Are you deaf on top of crazy? Yes. I told him, but he called me a liar. He couldn't look at me because I did what he should have been there to do. I tried to save her while you cowered in the closet.' He aimed at her head. 'If you'd just left well enough alone, nothing needed to change. But you had to leave that damn ball. Buh-bye, Mary Fran.'

*

'David's still not answering,' Olivia said, her cell phone clenched in her hand as she watched the lake cabins flash by. Not much farther . . .

'They're playing cowboy,' Noah muttered.

'She's his mother. When Eve was in danger, you were quite the cowboy, too.'

'That was different. I had a gun. David and Tom don't.'

A fact of which she was very aware. 'David can handle himself,' she said and prayed it was true. She studied the screen of her camera, trying to match the aerial image of the lake she'd taken from the bucket with the actual layout on the ground. They were close. There was a cabin another few minutes away that could be the one.

She saw the cabin up ahead, her eyes widening as a shirtless figure crept around the side of the cabin to the front. 'That's Tom.' He was getting in a sedan idling in the driveway. 'What the hell is he doing?' she demanded and Noah's jaw clenched.

'Don't know.' Then a shot split the air and Noah punched the gas, their car going momentarily airborne.

With Tom behind the wheel, the old sedan screeched in reverse, then, driver's door wide open, he gunned the engine, aiming for the house. The car lurched forward and Tom leapt free, rolling on the lawn, coming to his feet as lithely as a dancer. He took off running around the back as Noah brought their car to a blistering stop.

Olivia jumped out and followed Tom to the back, her gun drawn.

David stared in horror as Kirby pulled the trigger and Mary went down. And then, a second later, the house shook on its foundation. *Move.* Heart pounding, penknife clutched in his fist and Tom's shirt over his head, David crashed through the glass door shoulder-first. Landing in a shower of glass, he threw Tom's shirt to the side as his mother stared up at him, stunned.

'Are you okay?' he whispered fiercely, his heart settling a fraction when she nodded. She closed her eyes, tears seeping from her eyelids as he sliced through her bonds, picked her up and shoved her through the shattered back door.

To where Tom waited to carry her away. *Good boy*. Tom had followed his instruction to the last detail. *Get out*. David sprung toward the hole in the glass, when a body hurled over the back of the sofa and a hand grabbed his collar, yanking him back, the two of them falling in the broken glass.

'*Sonofabitch*.' The epithet was thundered in a rage, followed by the cold bite of steel against the back of his head. 'Get up, Hunter. Hands where I can see them. You want me, now you've got me. Toss your gun.'

David rose, conscious of each passing second. His mother and Tom had slipped away, unseen. *Don't stop running until you're safe*. 'I don't have a gun.'

Kirby's arm came around his neck, his forearm threatening to crush his throat, bending him backward as he awkwardly patted David down. 'You really don't. What the hell kind of hero are you anyway, charging me without a gun?'

David reached for Kirby's arm, but Kirby jabbed the gun barrel against his head, hard. 'I said keep your hands where I can see them.'

David couldn't breathe. 'The cops are coming,' he rasped and Kirby laughed.

'Nice try. They're not coming because they're all waiting

for me downtown. They think I'm stupid. They think I can't smell a setup.'

'What the fuck are you talking about?' David grated out. He leaned back an inch, freeing his windpipe enough to draw a decent breath. Kirby was taller than he'd seemed standing behind the counter. Stronger too. *I underestimated him. Never looked at him. He made me uncomfortable, so I never really looked at him.*

'Their little ruse, their text from Austin. "Help. I'm scared. Meet me," ' Kirby mocked.

The trick Olivia had up her sleeve. It obviously had not worked as planned. 'How do you know it's a ruse? Last I heard, they hadn't caught the kid. He's wily.'

'Because they got my place surrounded. Fucking cops everywhere.'

'There are always cops in your place. You sell coffee and doughnuts.'

'Funny guy. You won't be laughing in a min— *Fuck*.' Kirby viciously kicked at the overturned chair. 'What the fucking hell is this?'

David didn't move. Didn't say a word. Kirby hadn't known his mother was there. For some reason that God only knew, Mary had lied, told Kirby she'd killed his mother already. By now Tom should have his mother halfway to the car. He'd made the boy promise to keep moving. *Even if I don't follow.* He needed to buy his family more time.

'Goddammit,' Kirby hissed. 'She lied, the bitch. She didn't kill the old lady. Where is she?' He shoved the gun harder into David's skull. 'Where the hell is she?'

David tried to stay calm. Tried to buy another few minutes to give Tom time to get his mother to safety. 'I don't know what you mean.'

'Goddammit, there's rope on the floor. Walk, Hunter.' He shoved David forward, over the threshold of the shattered glass door, onto the patio. 'Old lady Hunter!' he bellowed. 'Come back or your son dies. I will shoot him. I have nothing to lose. You do.'

No, Ma. Don't do it. David prayed Tom had her out of earshot. Fat chance, not with his mother's hearing. She'd come. Tom would follow and then all three of them would die. *Dammit, Olivia, where the hell are you?* He held his breath, listening for any sign that his mother was coming back, but there was nothing. *Thank you.*

'Fine,' Kirby muttered. 'They can't have gotten far. You're done, Hunter.'

He's going to shoot me. Then he'd go after them, the people he loved. *Not while I still breathe. I'll take him with me.* David's stomach roiled. He wasn't nearly as zen with the prospect as he'd always expected he'd be. *I walk into fire, ready to die every day.* But this was different. There was no rush. No adrenaline. Just fear and dread, heavy in his gut. It wouldn't, however, change the outcome.

Now. Take him down now. He shifted to the balls of his feet, then shoved backward as hard as he could, twisting to the side, grabbing Kirby's wrist as they fell. David's head hit the patio hard, and the world spun, but he had Kirby's wrist in a lock and the gun pointed away from them.

With a howl of rage, Kirby grabbed his collar with his free hand and slammed David's head onto the concrete again. Pain crashed through his skull, but he held Kirby's wrist. They rolled, fighting for the gun. David pinned him to the concrete, but Kirby's finger was curled around the trigger and it was all David could do to keep the barrel pointed away.

Sucking in a breath, David's head cleared and so did his

view of Kirby's face. Fury exploded and he ploughed his fist into Kirby's face with all the force he could summon, but Kirby countered, twisting his collar until his knuckles dug into David's throat.

Can't breathe. He twisted, but Kirby tightened his hold. *Can't breathe.* White lights twinkled before his eyes as, one-handed, he yanked at the knuckles cutting off his air, but Kirby held. Both hands. He needed both hands. *He'll shoot. I'll die. No. Not today. Relax the throat.* It worked, allowing him a shallow breath through his nose.

And he smelled her. *Honeysuckle. She's here.* In his mind he could see her, ready, aiming, unable to get a clear shot as they fought. *Let go of the gun. Move.* Abruptly he released Kirby's wrist, throwing himself to the side. Kirby rolled with him, his fist still twisted in his collar and from the corner of his eye he could see the gun arc around . . . *pointing at me.* He stared at the barrel, every muscle clenched.

The shot made David flinch and made Kirby jerk as his body dropped away, dead before David drew a full breath. Stunned, David hung there, staring at the neat new hole in Kirby's temple. Then, with a hoarse cough, he pulled Kirby's lifeless hand from his collar and rolled to his back, his chest heaving as he struggled to fill his lungs. When he forced his eyes open, Olivia still held her gun in both hands, still pointed at Kirby's head, her face an expression-less mask. Slowly she lowered the gun, reholstering it.

Pushing himself to his knees, David pressed his fingers to Kirby's neck, then looked up at Olivia with grim satisfaction. 'That's all, folks,' he murmured.

She choked out a sound that was neither laugh nor sob, then fell to her knees next to David, her fingertips lightly grazing his face. 'Oh God, look at you.' Sitting on his heels, he winced when she touched the back of his head, then frowned at the blood on her fingers. 'You're bleeding,' she said.

David blinked hard. Now that it was over the adrenaline was fading, pain seeping in to take its place. 'Hit my head,' he said fractiously, then ran his fingers over his jaw, his frown deepening. 'And busted a few stitches. Hurts like a bitch.'

'I guess so.' She brushed her lips over his temple. 'I couldn't get the shot without risking you. How did you know what to do?'

He breathed her scent and it calmed him. 'I smelled honeysuckle. I knew you were there. I knew you'd do the right thing.'

She rested her brow against his. 'I was afraid he'd take you, too,' she whispered.

His arms closed around her, absorbing her shudder. 'He didn't. You didn't let him.'

'Liv?' Noah stood in the ruined glass doorway, reholstering his gun. Olivia pulled away, glancing at Kirby's body before lifting her eyes to Noah's.

'Kirby's dead.'

'I know. I saw it all.' He nodded once, hard. 'Very nice shot. You okay, David?'

Olivia stood up. 'He needs an ambulance,' she answered for him.

'No, I don't,' David said, rising as well, riding out the wave of dizziness and nausea. 'Where's my mother and Tom?'

'I called the EMTs,' Noah said, as if David hadn't spoken. 'They're five minutes out. Your mother is in our car with Tom. She's fine.'

David let out a relieved breath. 'Kirby called to her. I thought for sure she'd come back and that Kirby would shoot her, too.'

'We were here already,' Noah said. 'We heard Kirby yell. Phoebe almost did run back here. I convinced her to trust us. To let Olivia and me do our jobs.'

David closed his eyes. Between the relief and the pain in his head, he was feeling sick. 'Thank you.'

'What about Mary?' Olivia asked. 'Where is she?'

'In the kitchen,' Noah said. 'She's dead.'

David grimaced, remembering how her head had exploded. 'Kirby shot her.'

Olivia sighed. 'Now we'll never get answers.'

'We have a few,' David said, and told them what he'd overheard.

'Mary issued the ex-con attacker an engraved invitation,' Noah said. 'I guess I can't blame Kirby for being a little annoyed at that. But the rest . . .'

'He was a sociopath,' Olivia said flatly. 'He killed without blinking an eye.'

So had she. But that was entirely different. He thought of her cold focus in spite of everything she'd been through and was proud of her. He brushed at the glass sticking to his shirt, his ears pricking at the sound of a siren. The police. Finally.

'What took the cops so long?' he demanded.

'They didn't have the aerial view that we did,' Olivia said. 'Lots of cabins have green awnings. They've been searching from the ground while we waited for the state's helicopter. I called in the address right before Tom crashed his car into the cabin.'

'Why *did* Tom crash the car into the house?' Noah asked.

'It was the only diversion I could think of big enough to keep Kirby busy while I got my mom out. He'd just shot his sister and he didn't believe Mary when she said she'd already killed my mom. I knew he'd go looking for Mom next. I had to do something.'

Olivia blinked. 'Mary told him she'd killed your mom already? She lied?'

'Yeah. Kirby came in, pointing his gun and asked where her hostage was. He'd guessed she was my mother. Asked if she'd stashed her in the closet. But Mary lied.'

'Because she didn't want to hurt me.'

David spun around. His mother stood on the patio, Tom at her side. She was pale but otherwise unharmed. 'Mom.' Heart in his throat, he met her halfway, intending to keep his hug light but tightening his arms when she started to cry. 'Are you hurt?'

'No.' She shook her head. 'I'm fine. I just . . . I could hear him. He shot his own sister. I thought he was going to kill you.'

'I thought he was, too,' David murmured. 'But I'm fine. You're fine. We're fine.'

'We are.' She pulled back to search his face, wincing at the cuts and bruises, her eyes haunted. 'I waited in the car as long as I could. Oh, honey, your face.'

'Just a few cuts and bruises. I'll heal. Are you sure that you're all right?'

'She was moving pretty fast,' Tom said wryly. 'I could barely keep up with her when Noah gave us the all-clear signal after the gunshot.'

Unconvinced, David looked her over. 'We'll get a doctor's opinion.'

'I do not need—' his mother began, but David cut her off with a look.

'For me. Please.'

She lifted her chin. 'I will if you will.'

David had to smile. 'You did that once, when I was six.'

'When you fell out of that tree and I thought you'd broken your arm. It worked then, it'll work today.' She turned to Olivia, her heart in her eyes. 'Thank you.'

'Thank you for trusting us just now. I know waiting and listening was hard to do.'

His mother lifted a visibly trembling hand to Olivia's face, cupping her jaw. 'You saved my son's life.'

Olivia's eyes closed briefly, as if absorbing the contact. 'It was my pleasure.' Her eyes flickered down to Kirby. 'On many levels.' She lifted her gaze to David. 'Let's get you sewn up again.'

He touched the knot on the back of her head. She tried to hide her flinch and failed terribly. 'I will if you will,' he said. 'You could have a concussion.'

'I can't go now,' she protested. 'I killed Kirby. I have reports to write.'

His mother frowned. 'Those reports can wait a few hours, can't they, Noah?'

'Absolutely,' Noah said. 'Go, Olivia. I can handle things here.'

David slid his arm around Olivia's waist. 'Come,' he murmured in her ear. 'Let go now. It's all over. Let me take care of you.'

She leaned into him, and it felt right. 'We'll take care of each other.'

Chapter Twenty-Eight

Thursday, September 23, 2:00 P.M.

'Excuse me. I'm looking for Detective Sutherland.'

David looked away from the window into Abbott's office where the team had been debriefing for nearly an hour. A small woman in a dark dress was walking across the bull pen and David came to his feet. Her eyes were red, her face weary, and in her hands she held a large box. Instinctively, he knew who she was. If so, he could guess what was in the box.

'Detective Sutherland is in a debriefing,' David said.

Abbott had called Olivia while they'd been about to sit down to lunch with his family, asking her to come in, that they had some ends to tie off as the investigation wound down. David had insisted on accompanying her, aware that he'd be sitting, waiting until the cops were done. But her eyes still showed signs of strain and he was afraid that after the meeting, she'd lose herself in paperwork, even though she'd taken the day off. He could make sure that didn't happen. 'I'm just waiting for her, but one of the other detectives can help you.'

'No, that's all right. You're the firefighter. The one who caught the ball.'

'Yes, ma'am. I'm David Hunter.'

'I'm Jennie Kane.'

'I thought so. I'm sorry.'

She nodded once. 'Thank you.' She said it determinedly, as if getting used to the taste of the words in her mouth. 'I didn't really come to talk to the detectives. I'm not sure I can right now.' She lifted her chin. 'You're Olivia's young man?'

'Yes, ma'am. I am.'

Her lips whisked up in a ghost of a smile. 'And your mother? She's well?'

'She is.' David wanted to ask her to sit down, but he sensed Jennie Kane wanted to get out as soon as she possibly could. 'Can I help you with something?'

She nodded again, relieved. 'I want Olivia to have this. Tell her it was Kane's favorite. Tell her . . .' Her voice trembled and she drew a breath. 'Tell her she was, too. Of all the rookie detectives he trained, she was his favorite.' She held out the box and David took it, respectfully. She drew another breath, her hands fluttering at her sides. 'He worried about her. So did I. But you'll take good care of her.'

It wasn't really a question. 'Yes, ma'am. I promise.'

'Good. Thank you.' Then she rushed away before anyone saw her.

A few minutes later, the door to Abbott's office opened and the team filed out, quietly going about their business. Noah went to his desk, a thick folder in his hand.

'Micki's group got into the files on Kirby's laptop,' Noah said. 'These were his blackmail victims.'

'All those?' David asked. 'Are you going to tell them?'

'We have to,' Noah said. 'Most of these people are still paying him. You should have seen the operation this guy had. Microphones all over the Deli, recorders in the apartment above. It's going to take us weeks to go through everything we found.'

David moved from Olivia's chair to the edge of her desk, sliding the box behind him for the moment. Wearily she sank into her chair. 'They found this little gizmo in his pocket. It let him tune in to any conversation that he wanted. I've been racking my brain trying to think of what I said to Kane standing in that line, waiting for coffee over the years. We met Val the interpreter there. That had to be where he found out about her.'

'Any idea of where he may have taken her?' David asked her and she closed her eyes. Once the dust had settled last night, finding the interpreter had been uppermost in her mind.

'Yes. Micki found blood in his van, Val's blood type. Then she realized Kirby had a GPS unit. They worked all night to trace where he'd gone and found he'd taken a drive to the country.' She opened her eyes and he saw sadness and more than a little guilt. 'Micki and Bruce had Brie and GusGus go over the area. Didn't take them long to find Val's body.'

'Olivia.'

She swallowed hard. 'He tortured her.'

'Not your fault, baby.'

'I know. But still . . .' She sighed heavily. 'Dammit. Bruce had to tell her kids.'

David cleared his throat, not wanting to picture that scene but unable to keep himself from doing so. 'What did Andy Crawford have to say?' he asked, changing the subject. The FBI agent's son had been in Abbott's office when Olivia arrived and had left after a half hour, grim-faced and silent, not saying a word to David as he hurried out.

'When we told him Mary had been an IV drug user, he couldn't believe it. He said he knew she'd had Percocet once when she started college because she'd had dental surgery. He hadn't seen her in a long time. Didn't know she was an addict. But he funded it. He paid all her bills, gave her spending money and never asked questions. He felt guilty that his father had spent the family savings on him, leaving Jonathan and Mary with nothing. But Mary made him uncomfortable, too. So he kept his distance.'

'Why didn't he mention Jonathan when you talked to him yesterday?'

'Andy said he hadn't heard from Jonathan since the day he left home. Andy was in medical school by then, too busy with his own life to worry about Jonathan. And he said he was happy that was the case. Andy didn't like his father too well either. We asked him where Mary could be. We didn't think to ask about another brother and Andy didn't think that's where she'd go. Jonathan and Mary hated each other.'

'Yeah, I got that,' David murmured, thinking about what he'd heard. And seen.

'I know,' she said. 'I'm glad you and your mother heard them. Otherwise, we might never have known why.'

'And the blackmailing?' David asked. 'When did he start?'

'From his business records, it looks like Jonathan started working part-time at the Deli when he started college, then dropped out of school to work full-time.'

Noah patted the thick folder he was working through. 'Which corresponds to the time he started blackmailing.'

'He could make more money that way,' David said. 'Immoral, but sensible.'

'He was very sensible,' Noah said coldly. 'He knew

540

when not to blackmail, when to stay the hell away.' He held up a DVD. 'We found this in his nightstand drawer. It's the first victim I found hanging in her apartment last February. We knew she'd met her killer at a coffee shop. Our lead suspect at the time went to the Deli every day, so we asked Kirby for his tapes. He said he had cameras only on the register, but he obviously lied. He saw the victim here that night. Saw the killer follow her. He knew.'

'And said nothing.' Then David frowned. 'But he warned Eve that she was being stalked by that guy posing as a reporter. That helped save her life.'

'I don't know why,' Noah admitted. 'Maybe we'll figure him out through his files.'

'I know enough.' Olivia's jaw was clenched. 'He killed Kane. Killed Weems and Val. Killed Tomlinson and Blunt. Crawford and Mary. And he would have killed you.'

David shuddered, the memory of Kirby's gun in his face all too clear. 'But he didn't.'

'No.' She looked at her hands, then back up to meet his eyes. 'Abbott had the parents of Tracey Mullen in yesterday, while we were searching for your mother. He showed them the autopsy report – the abuse. The parents pointed fingers at each other, but finally her mother confessed. She'd been angry with Tracey for refusing to use her cochlear implant. Tracey had been purposely leaving it in a drawer. The mother's new husband was annoyed that he'd spent money on the surgery and that Tracey "wasn't even trying" to learn to use it. Mom got mad and twisted her arm, told Tracey that if she couldn't sign, she'd have to try harder with the implant. Mom's been living with the guilt.'

'Will she be charged?' David asked.

'Oh yes. She's being handed over to the Florida authorities.'

'So Tracey ran away, to Austin Dent,' David said. 'Why not tell her father?'

'Because she was sixteen and scared. And thought she was in love with Austin. Austin told the same story, that Tracey was running from her mother, afraid her father would do something foolish if she told him the truth. I keep wondering what Kirby would have done if Tracey hadn't been there that night. If he'd have pushed Mary and the others to set more fires. He wouldn't have been searching for Kenny at the school had Tracey and Austin not been involved. Val would still be alive. And so would Kane.'

'You can't think like that, Olivia,' David said gently. 'You can't lay what happened to Kane on Tracey's mother's shoulders. The incidents are linked, but so many other factors came into play.'

'I know. But it's hard not to.'

'I know. You, uh, had a visitor while you were in the meeting. Jennie was here.'

She sat up straighter in her chair. 'Why didn't you tell me?'

'Because she really didn't want to talk. She brought you this.' He put the box in front of her and watched as she stared at it, recognition in her eyes.

'I can't take it,' she whispered.

'Olivia. She wanted you to have it.'

Her hands trembled as she lifted the hat from the box. 'This was his favorite.'

'Jennie said you were, too.'

Her eyes filled. 'What do I do with it?'

David took her fedora from the head of the goddess bust on her desk. 'Wear yours and keep his there.'

Her mouth opened, then closed before she found her voice. 'And look at it every day?'

He said nothing, letting her make the decision.

It didn't take her long. She carefully put Kane's hat on the goddess head. 'Where we can all see it every day. It's good.' She met David's eyes. 'Thank you.'

'You're welcome. Your hat needs to be cleaned. It's got blood on the brim.'

'It's Crawford's.' She put her hat in the box. 'Kane presented this fedora when I cleared my first homicide. Said "Nice job." ' She smiled at the memory. 'From Kane that was high praise.'

Noah cleared his throat. 'His burial is Saturday. Full honors, brass in dress, bagpipes – Kane'll get the works.'

Olivia looked at Kane's hat, her expression sadly fond. 'He'd like that. Especially the brass in their dress uniforms and tight shoes. He'd be happy that their feet hurt. Come on. Dr Donahue called while we were in meeting. Lincoln is awake and asking to talk to you.' Olivia patted Noah's shoulder as she passed by. 'Tomorrow, partner.'

'It's official?' David asked. Noah would be a good partner. He'd watch her back. And Olivia would watch his. 'That means both Evie and I will sleep better at night.' Noah lifted his brows and David chuckled. 'In our respective places. You knew that.'

Noah smiled. 'I knew. How's your partner? Zell?'

'He's got a little feeling in his toes, so that's good news. Nobody's sure how much better it'll get. However it ends up, he'll be on disability for a long time. Which means I'll get a new partner after these damn stitches come out. Hey, my mother's planning a big dinner at my loft tonight, since the family's here. You're coming?'

'Wouldn't miss it,' Noah said. 'Your mom's a good cook. I guess she taught you.'

'Everything I know. All the good things anyway.' He

put his arm around Olivia's shoulders. 'Let's see Lincoln, then I want to get back and see my brothers and sisters.'

Thursday, September 23, 3:15 P.M.

David had to blink as he sat down across the table from Lincoln Jefferson. Lucid and cleaned up, he looked like a different man. In one corner of the interview room stood Special Agent John Temple, who seemed rational. Always a good thing. David knew that on the other side of the glass a small army watched – FBI agents, Lincoln's psychiatrist, Truman, and Olivia. Sitting next to Lincoln was his attorney.

'Hi, Lincoln. How are you?'

For a moment, Lincoln said nothing. He simply sat and studied David, his eyes sharp. Piercing, even. 'I'm fine,' he said finally. 'How are you?'

'A bit banged up, but I'll live.'

'I'm glad. I asked to see you. I wanted to thank you. I broke into your place and threatened you, but you were kind to me. Kinder than you should have been.'

'It's okay.'

Emotion flickered in Lincoln's eyes. 'They told me Mary is dead.'

'Her brother killed her. I'm sorry. Your brother told me that you two were friends.'

'I loved her. I stayed on my meds for her. But I found out she had someone else.'

'Joel.'

'Yeah. I saw them together, at the university, two weeks ago. She didn't know I was there. I got depressed, went off my meds. When I heard a glass ball had been found at those fires, where people had been shot to death . . . I lost it and I don't even remember doing it.'

'You don't remember my friend's cabin?'

'No. I read the police report. Read how you'd been kind. Read what I said.'

'Always there,' David murmured and Lincoln briefly closed his eyes.

'I lived with that guilt for so long. I'd go off my meds so I couldn't see her face, but it never helped. She was always there. I've given a full confession about that night we set the fire twelve years ago. It's time to face what I did. I can't make amends, though.'

David thought about how hollowed out he'd felt after telling Olivia his own secret. There had been peace, but also the knowledge that the clock could never be turned back. 'I understand. How did you meet Mary?'

'She sent e-mails to me through the webmaster address on my site. She seemed so sincere. She was a believer, or so I thought. Now I hear she was only using me to get back at her stepfather, and Truman says the police are reopening the case of his old receptionist as a possible homicide. I never saw that side of her. But she killed people. On purpose.'

'If it helps, she told my mother she wouldn't have let Crawford kill you. "I won't let him kill him," she said. She'd planned to kill Crawford herself.'

'That helps. Thank you. I fell for her, like a rock. I'd never told a soul about Moss, but I told her.'

'You trusted her.'

'I was a fool.'

'No, Lincoln. You weren't a fool to trust. She deceived you.'

Lincoln shrugged. 'Regardless, I told her everything.

All the details. That's how she knew to leave the ball at the fires.'

'And to scratch *VE* into the North Pole, for authenticity. Lincoln, right before she died, she told her brother that she knew where Preston Moss was.'

Lincoln smiled. 'And believe me, this nice FBI man really wants to know where he is. That's why you're here. I wouldn't give them that until I'd had a chance to meet you.' He pointed to his attorney's notebook and pen. 'May I?'

David watched as Lincoln drew a detailed map, finishing with an X to mark a spot.

'The day after that fire twelve years ago, I went to see Moss. He had a place where we'd meet, a place nobody knew about but us. His most devoted followers. We'd sit there and listen to him talk, like disciples. He was . . . mesmerizing. Anyway, the next day I went there, so upset. We'd all scattered after setting the timer on the device, like we always did. But I heard on the radio that there was a fatality. I couldn't believe it. I rushed back in time to see the body and I just fell apart.'

'I can imagine,' David said steadily. 'That's the kind of thing that haunts you.'

Lincoln nodded. 'Forever. I got there, found Moss. He'd taken a bottleful of pills. He was dead.' He let out a breath. 'It was horrible. I couldn't think. I just reacted. I took his body, put it in my car, and buried him.' He tapped the map. 'Here. I go there often. The grave is undisturbed. You should find him there.'

'And the place where you met?'

'Burned it to the ground. Fitting, I thought.'

'And then?'

Lincoln shrugged. 'Time passed and reality slipped

away. I knew it and was terrified. I thought I was losing my mind because God was taking it, to punish me.'

I understand that, too. 'Thank you, Lincoln, for telling me.'

Lincoln regarded him evenly. 'I don't remember going to your place. But I remember your voice. I remember . . . compassion. And I felt safe.'

'I'm glad. Good luck. I mean that.'

Lincoln's smile was sad. 'I know.'

David shook his hand and watched as they took him away. Special Agent Temple took the map Lincoln had drawn. 'Thank you, Mr Hunter,' he said.

'I didn't do anything. Not really. Will you release a statement when you confirm the remains are Moss's? I know a lot of firefighters who need the closure.'

'Of course. I know a lot of agents who need the closure, too. And now I understand you have a celebration to attend. I'm glad it ended well for you and your mother.'

'Me too.' David found Olivia in the observation area, on her cell phone.

'I have to go,' she said. 'I love you, too.' She hung up, her eyes a little too bright. 'That was Mia. We've been playing phone tag for days. She said she worked all night to tie up some loose ends so she could come out for the weekend. I told her she and Reed and their kids could use my place. I assume we can still stay at the cabin?'

David smiled at her. 'You bet. It'll be good to see her again.'

Olivia's lips twitched. 'You might change your mind. She says she wants to talk to you. She didn't realize we'd had a "biblical thing." Where the hell did she get that?'

'From Paige to me, overheard by my mother and Glenn.'

'Ah, well, then that explains everything.'

'So she's going to talk to me? Just talk, right?'

'Hey, you fought off Lincoln and Kirby. You're the cat-saving fireman. Surely you can hold your own against Mia.'

'I don't know. She's a sister. They fight dirty.'

Olivia chuckled. 'Don't worry. I'll protect you.'

Friday, September 24, 2:55 A.M.

Olivia heard the cabin door open, then close. Sitting on the edge of the dock, she wiped at her wet cheeks with her sleeves. The dock rumbled as David came closer.

He lowered himself to the edge of the dock, then slid his arm around her shoulders. She leaned into him, burrowing closer, feeling safer than she had in a very long time. It had been an evening full of joy and laughter with every member of David's considerable family. Brothers, sisters, nieces, and nephews. The Hunter clan had unnerved her at Mia's wedding with their boisterous ways. *But now . . . I belong.*

Phoebe Hunter, an arm around her shoulders, had proudly introduced her as the woman who 'saved David's life.' And somehow Olivia had known Phoebe hadn't meant just from Kirby.

Mia had arrived an hour after the party started and had immediately taken David aside with a stern expression. But she must have approved of what he said because he still lived. Her sister was a tigress with a marshmallow center and Olivia was so glad to have her. Mia promised to stay through Kane's funeral. *I'll need her.* Because despite the laughter and love around her, Olivia was continually, painfully conscious of who was absent.

'I didn't mean to wake you,' she murmured, and David kissed the top of her head.

'You didn't,' he said. 'Painkillers wore off and I woke up. But you weren't there.'

'I had a bad dream,' she confessed. 'Kirby killed you and you were lying on the ground. And then you were Kane. So I've been sitting here, thinking of him. Missing him. Trying to think of what I could have done differently. If only I'd been a little faster.'

'Olivia, missing Kane is natural. Trying to think of what you might have done differently will eat you up inside.'

One side of her mouth lifted. 'Pot calling the kettle?'

'Yes, but you'd say the same thing to me and you know it. You did everything you could have done. Everything you should have done. You're a good cop.'

He made her believe it was so. 'Thank you.'

'You're too hard on yourself, you know.'

She considered. 'Yeah, I am. So are you.'

'Well, we both need to stop. We do only what we can and that has to be enough.'

'Because it can never be enough,' she whispered, then drew a breath. 'I talked to the shrink. Dr Donahue. I've been having panic attacks at crime scenes. Since the pit.'

'I'd be shocked if you didn't,' he said in a matter-of-fact way that made her shame seem silly. 'What did she say?'

'That the hard part's just starting.'

'She's right. Still, I'm proud of you. It's not easy to open up.'

She hesitated. 'I think it was harder to tell you just now.'

'Why?' he asked softly.

'Because your opinion means more. I didn't want you

to think I was' – she hesitated, then shrugged, looking away. 'Less.'

'Less than what? Less than who? You are not less than anyone.' He frowned when she said nothing. 'Come with me. I have something to show you.'

He rose and pulled her to her feet, up into the house, and back to the bedroom where he quickly searched his duffel bag. 'Look at this.'

It was a letter from the Minneapolis Fire Department. '"Dear Mr Hunter, We've received your application for employment. We will inform you should any openings become available."' She looked up at him, confused. 'Why did you give me this?'

He didn't answer and her eyes dropped back to the page. And then she saw the date. Her eyes shot back to his. 'You applied a month after Mia's wedding.'

'Actually the week after. They didn't get back to me for a few weeks.'

Her mind was racing. 'You were willing to leave your job for me? Way back then?'

'Yes. I'd been looking for you for a long time, but I didn't know it until I saw you. I thought if I ever had the courage to approach you after that night, I should be prepared for whatever followed. I always hoped it would be this. You and me, together after a long day. Just like this. Except I hope that our future days aren't quite so long.'

'David . . .' Her words failed her.

'You asked if I'd go back to Dana if she were free. I thought about telling you this then, but after what I'd said that night, I didn't think you'd believe me. I still don't have the right to expect you to believe me, but once I'd met you, I knew what I wanted. Who I wanted. If I'd known how you felt I never would have let so much time slip away. I'm sorry, Olivia. If I could get the time back, I would.'

She stared up into the face she'd never been able to forget. His face was bruised and battered from his battle with Jonathan Crawford, but he was still the most beautiful man she'd ever seen. Inside and out. 'Then let's not waste another minute looking back.' Sliding her arms around his neck, she kissed him, intending to keep it gentle, but he pulled her closer and the kiss became deeper. Just . . . more.

He walked her backward to the bed and followed her down. 'What do you want?' he asked huskily.

Everything. I want everything. 'You. I want you.'

The earlier times they'd loved, it had been urgent. Explosive. This time it was slow and deliberate. Their eyes stayed open as they moved together, watching every flicker, every nuance. Her climax came as a huge swell, lifting her up, enveloping her so that there was nothing in the world but him. When he came, it was her name he groaned, his head thrown back, body bowed.

In the moments after, they held each other in the quiet. This was comfort, solace. Refuge. This they could give each other, again and again.

Now you can buy any of these other bestselling
Headline books from your bookshop
or *direct from the publisher*.

FREE P&P AND UK DELIVERY
(Overseas and Ireland £3.50 per book)

Count to Ten	Karen Rose	£6.99
I'm Watching You	Karen Rose	£6.99
Nothing to Fear	Karen Rose	£6.99
Die For Me	Karen Rose	£6.99
Scream For Me	Karen Rose	£6.99
Kill For Me	Karen Rose	£6.99
I Can See You	Karen Rose	£6.99
Point of No Return	Scott Frost	£6.99
Run The Risk	Scott Frost	£6.99
Never Fear	Scott Frost	£6.99
Smoked	Patrick Quinlan	£6.99
The Takedown	Patrick Quinlan	£6.99
Stripped	Brian Freeman	£6.99
Stalked	Brian Freeman	£6.99
Double Homicide	Faye & Jonathan Kellerman	£6.99
Capital Crimes	Faye & Jonathan Kellerman	£6.99

TO ORDER SIMPLY CALL THIS NUMBER

01235 400 414

or visit our website: www.headline.co.uk

Prices and availability subject to change without notice.